Praise for *LOTE*

Winner of the James Tait Black Prize 2021
Winner of the Republic of Consciousness Prize 2021

"*LOTE* is a decadent celebration of portraiture, queer history and Blackness, and a bitingly funny work of fiction. In this book, von Reinhold provides us with a mischievous new work of aesthetic theory, as well as a glorious and gorgeously imagined fictional world. Ingenious; irresistible; a dazzling first novel."—NAOMI BOOTH, author of *Sealed* and *The Lost Art of Sinking*

"*LOTE* is one of the most compelling works in trans fiction I've read in a long time."—MCKENZIE WARK, author of *Philosophy for Spiders: On the Low Theory of Kathy Acker*

"Shola von Reinhold's *LOTE* recruits literary innovation into the project of examining social marginalisation, queerness, class, Black Modernisms and archival absences. A critically important and hugely original debut."—ISABEL WAIDNER, author of *We Are Made of Diamond Stuff* and *Gaudy Bauble*

"Von Reinhold's rich and glorious writing... reads as though—to put it in their own description of a room draped in candlelight—everything has been smeared with gold oil.... It's more than just the bliss of representation: history here is *feeling*, not just narrative."—SKYE ARUNDHATI THOMAS, *Frieze Magazine*

"Set amid an artist residency, this arresting debut effortlessly explores infatuation, reinvention, the erasure of black figures from history and gender identities in what marks von Reinhold as a unique new voice in literary fiction."—LAYLA HAIDRANI, *AnOther Magazine*

"An inspirational, cutting, exquisitely written, multilevel excavation of forgotten Black lives and an Afro-queer celebration of art, aesthetics, literature, and society."—PAUL MENDEZ, author of *Rainbow Milk*, speaking to *The Strategist*

"In choosing to conjure Black voices through historical revisionism, rather than, say, Afrofuturism or pure fiction, the novel produces a new archive—a radical reference tool populated by real and imagined historical figures, Anons who have been festooned, fleshed-out, and freed from the rude imposition of marginality, anonymity and defacement."—IZABELLA SCOTT, *White Review*

"As a celebration of eccentric esprit, *LOTE* practises what it preaches by being stubbornly its own thing."—HOUMAN BAREKAT, *The Guardian*

"The contemporary moment for Black life in the United States needs this decadent Black and queer meditation on beauty and aesthetics."—MARQUIS BEY, author of *Black Trans Feminism*

"*LOTE* is a rapturous first novel, a queer black fantasy with angels leaping off every page."—MOLARA WOOD, *Irish Times*

LOTE

shola von reinhold

LOTE

DUKE UNIVERSITY PRESS Durham & London 2022

Copyright © Shola von Reinhold 2020
First US edition published by Duke University Press, 2022
All rights reserved
Printed in the United States of America on acid-free paper ∞
Cover designed by Rodney Dive

Library of Congress Cataloging-in-Publication Data
Names: Reinhold, Shola von, [date] author.
Title: Lote / Shola von Reinhold.
Description: First US edition published by Duke University
Press, 2022. | Durham : Duke University Press, 2022.
Identifiers: LCCN 2021053296
ISBN 9781478018728 (paperback)
Subjects: LCSH: Sexual minority culture—Fiction. | Art—
Fiction. | Europe—Fiction. | LCGFT: Historical fiction. |
Detective and mystery fiction. | Novels.
Classification: LCC PR6118.E59552 L67 2022 | DDC 823/.92—
dc23/eng/20220112
LC record available at https://lccn.loc.gov/2021053296

COVER ART: (*Foreground*) Joerg Breu the Elder
(ca. 1475/80–1537), *Splendor Solis—Venus and Her
Children (Heat reveals the spirit hidden inside the earth)*
(detail). From "Splendor Solis—7 Traktate vom Stein
der Weisen" ("Splendor Solis—7 treatises of the Stone of
Wisdom"), 1531–1532. Southern Germany. Gouache on
parchment, 33.1 × 22.8 cm. Inv. 78 D 3, fol. 28 recto.
Photo by Jörg P. Anders. Courtesy of bpk Bildagentur /
Jörg P. Anders / Art Resource, NY. (*Background*) Mauro
Cateb, *Abalone nacre,* 2011. Licensed under CC BY 3.0.
SOURCE: Wikimedia Commons.

olidarity to all those resisting universal tedium, for all those struggling against fascism, racism, capitalism, or just sheer drabness.

PART ONE

Miniature from the illuminated manuscript *Splendor Solis*, 1532–1535, representing "the peacock stage" of alchemy when the oily black contents of the alembic flare iridescent

Miniature from the illuminated manuscript *Universal P. & Augment*, by Adolphus Ignatius de Mussy

Miniature from the illuminated manuscript *Aurora Consurgens*, 1420s

I

An incensed blond twink said, "Excuse me, miss! Where do you think you're going? This is a members-only club."
Knowing:

i. People rarely allow for Blackness and caprice (be it in dress or deportment) to coexist without the designation of Madness.
ii. People like to presume Madness over style whenever they have the chance.

I gathered that my eBay lab diamonds, silver leatherette and lead velvets had been mentally catalogued as a few of the traditional accoutrements of the Maniacal Black Person, who possesses no taste, only variations of a madness which comes down on her from on high.

He occupied a large built-in table of the kind at which a receptionist or concierge would customarily be stationed.

"I thought this was the new archive site? I'm volunteering."

He was more annoyed than embarrassed at being caught out.

"Oh," he said, smiling at a sheet of paper. "I've only been informed of two volunteers. You don't seem to be down?"

"Mathilda Adaramola."

"I see: '*Mathilda.*' Well, I wasn't given surnames, I was just told 'Agnes and Mathilda.' You're downstairs," he looked at the name and then at my face as if I'd performed a conjuration.

On the first step down I paused,

"Why were you just pretending to be on the reception of a members' club?"

He ignored me.

Downstairs, I saw the new site had at least once been a kind of Learned Society or specialist members' library, still replete with its blackish wood panelling and Lincrusta. The actual library was situated in the basement but there were no books lingering on the shelves to indicate specialism.

"Hate it," was the first thing Elizabeth/Joan said to me. And when I asked her what it had been specifically: "Oh, I don't know. Horrid Old Gents' Club, or something. Who cares. Anyway, it's all ours for the next couple of weeks until the rest of the department move over."

"Who was that on the door?"

"*God* yes, James."

I told her about his bizarre little roleplay.

"Probably his undying power fantasy to be front of house at a members-only club—people nurse all sorts of passions and they'll live them out whenever they have the chance."

I had befriended Elizabeth/Joan a month ago. I'd been going almost daily to the National Portrait Gallery Archive for some time to look at photographs of Stephen Tennant and some of my other Transfixions. My interactions with her up until then had been minimal. She was rude in an absent-minded sort of way and irritated me in her ostensible membership of a subset of a type I had once become familiar with. All week I would notice, upon looking up mid-reverie from my desk, that someone was watching me from across the room. It was the kind of shameless gaze that suggests the gazer has forgotten you can see them back. One day near the end of that week, as I was leaving, she asked me what I was researching. Her eyes glazed instantaneously when I started speaking and I saw she was, of course, seeking an opportunity to talk about herself so I indulged her by asking what it was like working at the archive. Here she launched into a monologue: she was extremely bored here, she was experiencing some kind of malaise, in fact. Hated the actual cataloguing side so had asked to be put on the readers' room welcome desk with the hope of some kind of interaction. "But everyone that comes here…" and her eyes fell on the only other reader, an admittedly tedious looking man. "Nobody ever speaks to me; it's actually kind of cruel if you think about it." She looked at me once more as if really taking me in and asked again what I was researching, then where I lived, where I had studied, and so on. I fed her a mixture of facts and lies which sated her enough for her to launch into gossip about every member of staff in the archives, none of whom I knew, and then what gossip she had gleaned from some of the regular visitors. "Churchill…" she sighed a sigh of true exasperation, nodding towards the man across who was definitely eavesdropping by this point.

Then she moved onto personal life, proving my estimation not far off: private day school, "then undergrad at Edinburgh. New Sloane rather than Sloane or Old Sloane because parents are old-old middle class but new to London. Neo Art Sloane, I suppose. Nobody uses the term 'Sloane' anymore, but I do, because that's what I am."

She was the perfect candidate for a new Escape. Would provide a new microcosm to slip into. My brain was already working out how best to go about it, but as she went on, I detected a weird grain in the mix: it was an act, an excellent one. She was not of that class or type; this excited me.

Sadly, a few days into our acquaintance, I realised she was not acting at all. The grain was something else. Something that would not properly surface, I predicted, until another couple of decades, at which point she would undergo an epiphany like an E. M. Forster character abroad, and revolt against the faintly alternative, ultimately conventional existence in which she'd entangled herself. (An event symbolised by the languid but vengeful flinging out the window onto the rocks below of a white clay bowl full of dandelion salad from a villa in wherever it was in two decades from now that had become the inevitable zone for mildly artistic wealthy English people. The bowl would not be dashed, however, but caught by the incoming tide, before being swallowed.)

I was sure she'd told me her name during her monologue, but I did not take it in. Later I looked up the staff. There were three cataloguing assistants. A James, whom she'd just identified as the evil blond man upstairs, an Elizabeth, and a Joan. I had never been able to ascertain whether she was Elizabeth or Joan and it had now been too long to ask.

It was Elizabeth/Joan who phoned me one day at about two in the morning—"We've just received a tonne of photos, or something." I only took a moment to realise who it was. "Full of stuff you're interested in. Who was that one? Yes, Stephen Tennant and all that lot, stuff from the '20s–'30s-etcetera. I mean an actual tonne in weight of photos, or something. Desperately need people to help sort through it. Especially if they can recognise any of the sitters. Unseen images. Good for your biography. I'll text you the details." And then a pause: the unfamiliar process of awaiting a reply.

She must have looked me up on the database and taken my number down for later use. I wasn't sure how authorised she was to appoint unofficial volunteers for the archive at two in the morning. I was also acutely aware of the fact that I would be doing the bulk of her assigned job for her without pay. She did, however, arrange for travel and lunch expenses which came to about fifty pounds a week, a significant amount for someone recently sanctioned.

The photographs were an unsolicited donation.

"Some shitbag's always leaving behind paintings and photos in their will, so we've got a constant flow coming in all the time. They think they're doing us a favour and they also imagine it's going to be hung in the main gallery next to Queen Elizabeth the First. Actually, we've got a strict donations and acquisitions policy. We can't accept ninety-five percent of the dross we get; don't know how that explains the dross we keep. Has to be significant to portraiture in some way. Someone famous or influential or, even rarer, 'something significant to the history of portraiture itself.' Not just some old shitbag's memory box we didn't ask for." So I was informed by Elizabeth/Joan on the first morning of volunteering.

In this case, a relative had carried out instructions on behalf of their shitbag great uncle or aunt and sent everything at once in cardboard boxes. Fortunately, following instructions of the deceased, a list of some of the figures of significance was also sent, even if none of the thick fabric-bound albums or loose photographs were named and dated. I soon discovered that they had not "just received" this donation, which had come about ten years prior, but rather had just gotten around to looking at it.

There were generally no more than three of us to sort through the images at a time. Usually two since Elizabeth/Joan hated nothing more. The other volunteer was a woman in her early 80s called Agnes, who wore pink pearls and tartan every day, and got as much pleasure from the whole thing as I did. She had been some kind of historian and it was not lost on me that we were the only two

Black people working for the archives, and that we were working for free. I wasn't sure where Elizabeth/Joan had poached her from—perhaps she was another archive user like me, wrangled into free labour, or perhaps one of the official volunteers pilfered from the database. Every so often Agnes, otherwise hardnosed, would hold out a photo and operatically exclaim,

"Now *look* at this, you've *got* to see this, you have *really* got to see this," and I would have to stop and come around to look. They were always intriguing pictures. Twice some quite scandalous ones that I would have been too embarrassed to show her. The group shot of skiers laughing in the snow would bring about the same delighted arpeggio as the lakeside tableau of erect Pans: a Beardsley drawing corporealised.

As Agnes and I sat at a table sifting through images, taking notes, suggesting dates, Elizabeth/Joan would float in and out of the room if there was nobody senior in the vicinity, which there generally wasn't because at the main site everyone else worked on the other side of the building. Sometimes she sat at her desk muttering to herself, sighing in irritation, calling me over to talk when she was bored or annoyed.

She also occasionally marched around the room's periphery, working herself up into silent rages, speaking under her breath about God knows what and making frantic hand gestures. When I first saw her rankled like this, I genuinely believed she was rehearsing for a play, but later realised she was tremendously coked-up.

Today she was in such a mood.

"Told you he's a little drip," she picked up the subject of James two hours later as if there had been no break in our conversation. She was pacing the new room. "Thank fuck he's gone. You know he wasn't even supposed to be here till next week. Wanted to 'see the space,' and then said he had work to do. I don't see why he couldn't do whatever it is he has to do back where he usually does it."

Agnes, who had been particularly engrossed in a batch of photos, never appeared to notice Elizabeth/Joan's rages anyway. During this current outpour she stood up, probably to go for lunch, when Elizabeth/Joan spun to face her and snapped, "Oh sit back down you stupid fool," rather aggressively, at which point I found myself telling Elizabeth/Joan to sit down herself. She pivoted to face me, and I thought for a moment she was going to hit me, and she probably was, but then all the fury in her eyes died out. She went back to her desk. Agnes, having ignored all this, had gone to switch on the kettle and returned to her work as it boiled.

"I think I need to go for lunch," Elizabeth/Joan said, which I knew to be an apology. She went out for her second lunch that day.

Perhaps twenty minutes after she was gone, James the catalogue assistant, who had supposedly left hours ago, surprised us when he came down into the room with his eyebrows raised in the fashion of a particular brand of self-assured heterosexual.

"Where's Eliza?" he said.

"She just went out to get some paper," Agnes said.

"How long has she been gone?" he was clearly annoyed.

"Not long, Mr. Collins," Agnes said; she could be very strict. "Would you like us to leave a message?"

"No need."

"Well I'll be sure to tell her you were looking for her, Mr. Collins," Agnes said. James went back out, visibly red—rose red. Or actually, I thought, carnational.

About five minutes after this Agnes put down her pencil, got up and went out the room. I sat in silence, thinking about carnations and still processing the unexpected knowledge of Elizabeth/Joan's name. I tried to insert the unfamiliar *Eliza* into my head but clearly *Elizabeth/Joan* had situated itself forever.

"Mathilda," called Agnes from upstairs. "Come up."

She was waiting for me halfway up the ground floor staircase. "He's gone, thank heavens. Come and have a look at this please."

I had not been upstairs yet but was aware the first and second floors were going to be converted into office space for the photographic archive. She led me into a room which was named smugly in brass, *The Old Smoking Room*. Agnes was already behind the bar, which still had various remaining bottles of alcohol. She poured us both an expensive-looking clear brown liquid.

"It's all going to be discarded anyway," she said. "Health and safety." She lit a cigarette with a defiant flourish and offered me one which I took. "I thought to myself: why not let's Mathilda and I appreciate it, hmm?"

After a moment,

"She's not a bad girl, I'm sure you can see that. Unfortunately, that other one: Mr. Collins. Smarmy creature. *Jobsworth*. James the Jobsworth!" She gave a little laugh. "Now I don't know what you're here for exactly, Mathilda, but I do know you enjoy the setup. That I can see. It would be wise to make sure he doesn't get her into trouble. On my part, I have very important work to do and I *hope* you do too. Oh yes. You ought to." I didn't know what to make of this but felt it prudent not to stand there looking out of the loop.

Behind the bar, in a garish gilt frame was a large mirror. It was more suited to the Folies Bergère than an old English members' club. We sipped our drinks and smoked our cigarettes as we wandered around the room—disdainful but loving it—looking through some of the residual objects ready to be thrown away, mostly plaques and newspapers.

The huge bow windows were like an observation deck and a climactic grey light came through them.

We had been staring under lamps in the basement all day and the contrast made the natural light pleasantly melodramatic. I began to feel the specific ghost of loveliness which transposes the body by means of unexpected expensive brandy and sudden daylight and thought about how once when waiting for a bus to school I had overheard something from the radio of a parked car. An artist was being interviewed and the conversation was uninteresting, but it had eventually caught my attention because the artist was not listening properly:

"How much does lithography matter in contemporary culture?"

"Oh absolutely! Lithography is everything to me." His responses did not quite match the questions, as if, rather than hearing interrogative phrases like, *how much*, or *why* he simply heard, *Lithography?* or *Childhood?*

In response to a question about prizes he told a story about getting some good news one day,

"Yes, that day I was working in the study and got the phone call and was in such a shock that I went to the living room and opened a bottle of cognac and watched trash all day! Daytime television and that sort of thing—this was the '90s you know . . ."

First, I thought there was something infinitely mesmerising about the idea of escaping from a day's work in the '90s. Then I thought that if I were ever in the position of the man on the radio, I would be drinking cognac all day and watching television. But then I wouldn't ever be able to feel the pleasure of escaping from a day's work. The dilemma caused me undue distress. I came down with a literal fever the next day and was sick for two weeks. I was diagnosed with the flu. I disagreed: on the one hand it was thinking about labour, about leisure, that rendered my body weak and feverous, even though the sense of unvarnished doom had seemed totally unwarranted, without cause at the time, separate from the dilemma of whether the pleasure of escaping work was greater than that of never having to. Even though I had realised how I never truly wanted to work in the future, realised the weight of how horrific work is.

On the other hand, it was the '90s. Not the period specifically, but the thought of being as I was—the same age and person—in the '90s, instead of then. A gear was sent spinning in my brain.

After a few minutes, the rigidity of the black and white photos would, if not depart, then liquify. A day's immersion left the same mental after-dazzle as a sun-glanced afternoon, lakeside.

These non-existent beams, hurled up from non-existent tree-fringed and flickering bodies of water, were the perfectly normal sensational offshoots of gazing at photos all day. They were access to, glimpses of, Arcadia: The Grand Ahistorical Mythical Paradise which is the ultimate project of all Arcadian Personality Types who crave a paradise knit out of visions of the past much like their more illustrious cousins, Utopians, do with the future. (It—paradise—is ultimately to be a collaboration.)

Utopian Personality Types, as a rule, find old things redolent of decay, and can just about put up with new things which are still not the future.

The classic counterpart traits of the Arcadian, like a fondness for old objects and buildings, and an inclination towards historicised figments, were, as far as I was concerned, much easier to inhabit for white people, who continued to cast and curate all the readymade, ready-to-hand visions. Being born in a body that's apparently historically impermissible, however, only meant I was not as prone to those traps that lie in wait for Arcadians—the various and insidious forms of history-worship and past-lust. I would not get thrown off track: I could rove over the past and seek out that lost detail to contribute to the great constitution: exhume a dead beautiful feeling, discover a wisp of radical attitude pickled since antiquity, revive revolutionary but lustrous sensibilities long perished.

Not prone but certainly not impervious.

The photographs we had been sorting through had thus far consisted mainly of holiday shots. Some quite spectacular. Europe in the '20s and '30s. Old *pensiones* and hotels. Scenes of a modernist Alpine Queerdom.

The photographer, I thought, must have been the short dark-haired man who occasionally came in and out of shot, but it was hard to say, as there was also a gloriously imperious woman that might have been his wife (which did not seem to stop either of them partaking in the Alpine Queerdom).

These photos had so far yielded two images of Stephen Tennant. One was a mountain scene in Bavaria, the other on a bright, empty beach, hand in hand with a doting Siegfried Sassoon. I had to lie down on the floor. Neither Elizabeth/Joan nor Agnes commented, for which I was grateful.

Today we had finished taking notes and ordering the first box of many, now ready for the next department where it would be sorted through all over again to verify our identified sitters and dates whilst looking for any others. This would happen twice more before they were all digitised.

There was a definite elation slicing open the next box, which Agnes did ceremoniously, putting on tweed gloves and using her mother-of-pearl nail scissors since, along with most of the equipment, the Stanley knife hadn't arrived.

This series struck upon a different channel. Less bucolic sight-seeing and more cosmopolitan. Pictures of Parisian nightclubs, many where the photographer had obviously been intoxicated. Elbows and blurred faces of interwar bohemia. One of what must have been the Revue Nègre where, though it was impossible to see who was on stage, Agnes immediately identified Josephine Baker by a visible scrap of dress. Many showed the London club scene of the '20s. Places like the original Café de Paris, the Gargoyle Club, Café Royal, the Blue Lantern. It was amongst these we began finding photographs of a particular party.

The party was at a country house I recognised at once as Garsington, home of patron and hostess Ottoline Morrell. It was a particularly animated looking soirée. Different to the usual pictures of Garsington parties I'd seen with members of the Bloomsbury Group lying about sedately in deck chairs chatting, bitching, smoking. Some of those figures were there—I screamed at Agnes when I pulled a picture of Vanessa Bell out of a pile, and then screamed again at one with half of Virginia Woolf in conversation with a whole Duncan Grant.

There was a comparatively loucher crowd at this party than the Bloomsberries; swathes of apparently uninvited guests. Ottoline Morrell herself was in one snapshot, towering above the rest, a tall woman who accentuated her height with heel extensions, looking not only unfazed but delighted by what were probably party crashers; laughing amidst dark, frayed young creatures. Some of the guests were in costume and half-costume and it looked as if they had come to Garsington directly from at least three different parties: a mixture of artists and students and various denominations of the Bright Young People.

My eyes picked out amongst the piles some blue-edged pictures which I knew immediately to be photographs taken by Ottoline Morrell; she'd always had these mounted on grainy blue cards and

I'd seen many of her thousands of photographs held at the archives, but those before me had probably not been seen for decades.

They were pictures of the same party. Unlike the photographs we had been going through, Ottoline annotated all of hers with names on the paper border. In one was the dark-headed, wicked elf of a man with the marvellously arrogant woman and some other people. It was the first where I had seen the man and woman in the same shot. Written below was,

Hugh and Florence St. Clair,

and on the back,

To Florence, You said you should like a photograph, please send me one of your own. Ottoline.

Which meant they could have been married, but looking at them it was obvious they were siblings. I was about to call out to Agnes that I had found the name of the photographer but there was another blue-lined image. Also at Garsington. A room panelled much like the one I was in. A young man and two women in elaborate costume as Late Renaissance angels. Arched wings impressively constructed of wax and what must have been peacock feathers. All three posed in a befittingly exaggerated Mannerist style, as if each occupied the panel of a triptych. The two on either side flaunted heraldic robes, whilst the central woman wore emblazoned pieces of armour over a fine mesh of chainmail. She had on a coronet, around which her hair was brushed into a commanding nimbus.

Beyond photographs taken for colonial documentation, I wasn't sure if I'd ever seen a photograph of a Black person from this era, with hair this texture, that hadn't been ironed or lye-straightened. Certainly never in such a setting. An excruciation of coil and kink, for it made me ache with jealousy and bliss. In a chain-mailed hand she clutched a champagne coupe like a holy grail. The other palm was angled just a bit away from the lens, fingers arranged in an obscure saintly message, but at the same time holding a cigarette. I was about to call out to Agnes again, but instead found my hand with the photo in it slipping under the table towards my coat pocket.

There was a second picture of the same trio. They'd changed position, all looking less mannerist but giving an excellent profile.

When I finally called Agnes over,

"Oh, that's your Mr. Tennant is it not?"

And yes, it was. I hadn't even noticed. The young man to the left was Rex Whistler, which I had already vaguely registered, but the other angel on the right, the second young woman, was of course Stephen Tennant.

"But who's the young lady in the middle, a singer?"

"No."

Even for Agnes it was the obvious suggestion: a Black woman at a bohemian party in England in the '20s was not unlikely a singer like Florence Mills, or Josephine Baker, who were sometimes invited to such events as entertainment and also sometimes as guests. But I thought not, without knowing why.

"What does the name say?"

Another thing I hadn't noticed.

Steenie, Hermia and Rex

Steenie was a nickname for Stephen. But on reading the name *Hermia,* another rose up in response: "Druitt." I was absolutely sure of it. Hermia Druitt. My mouth ached to say the name aloud.

"Hermia Druitt."

"I haven't heard of her. Should I have, Mathilda?"

Because Elizabeth/Joan did not come back, which was to be expected, and because of the weather, which was unexpected, we decided to have another brandy upstairs before leaving. The room held an odd fascination for us and we clearly loved to stand about in it, two awed but smug trespassers. Whenever I glanced at Agnes she had a sort of shining, triumphant light in her eyes and I thought I understood something of it—of being in this room, of having this space to ourselves. But eventually a cruelness I also understood came into her face and she buttoned up her coat and said,

"Make sure you pull the bottom door shut properly behind you; are you listening? Right, see you tomorrow."

I watched as she passed below. Rain fizzed white on the ledge like soda water. Then the rain fell differently, glossing the streets and rooftops into a state of divine lamination.

I took a slim bottle of something green from behind the bar and ventured outside into a loch of granite and bobbing umbrellas. All the trains had stopped, and I would have to take three or four buses.

I limited myself to a maximum of three inspections of the photograph per bus. I felt it might dissolve in my possession, outside of the archive, but instead it became more substantial, if anything materialising not dissolving—sucking in atoms, becoming more of an object, more vivid. I became fearful that commuters would notice I had stolen something almost a century old, that it was glowing with the undeniable aura of valuable old things, of masterpieces and antiquities. But, of course, no one did notice. It was not valuable.

What was beyond doubt by the time I got back was that a new Transfixion had arrived in the form of Hermia Druitt, the woman in this photograph. This was confirmed by the sensations: flashes from Arcadia. Moonlight, of a kind, sighed up and down the tube of my spine, but above all, that indescribable note which accompanied all my Transfixions was present: humming beneath the high fine rush—probably not dissimilar to holy rapture—was an almost violent familiarity. The feeling of not only recognising, but of having been recognised.

A new Transfixion.

In the month prior to my discovery of Hermia Druitt, I often found myself 'recording' my other Transfixions, working backwards to the first, who came to me at about fourteen, though I suspected they were happening before this in a more abstract manner. These records took the following form:

On silver card written in shell-coloured ink (barely legible)

Front:

Stephen Napier Tennant

(Image—photograph of Tennant in costume as Prince Charming, lying like the effigy on a tomb, hands in prayer and with a glossy silk cape spread out around him, by Cecil Beaton.)

SPAN: 21 April 1906—28 February 1987

MEMORABILIA: Queer English socialite most prominent during interwar era. Is frequently quoted as responding, when asked by his father what he wanted to be when he grew up, "...a Great Beauty, Sir!," which became the case.

A human orchid who said he heard the flowers, his siblings, chant his name whilst walking on the Salisbury Plains as a boy.

"You needn't wave and dye it like that, because you don't need to at all... You know, a man doesn't want to look pretty," said Tallulah Bankhead when he met her in New York in 1931.

"Well, some men, I think, do want to look pretty. And nicer still, beautiful!" he replied.

Marcelled not only his hair but daily existence, by which is meant he induced the decorative wave in all things.

Is said to have lived in bed. This is not quite true. Certainly spent later life in comparative seclusion but by no means a total recluse. Friends included Virginia Woolf, E. M. Forster, Gertrude Stein, Elizabeth Bowen, Jean Cocteau and Willa Cather. Ended his four-year relationship with Siegfried Sassoon after Sassoon, turning up unannounced, found him without makeup on. Spent most of his life working on his novel *Lascar: A Story You Must Forget*, producing over 500,000 words but never completing it. Rarely mentioned is the unpublished novel he did complete, *The Second Chance*.

"What in life could be more ecstatic an occupation than putting orchids in an ice-box and then taking them out again?"

Back:

SENSATIONS: Silver wafer into lead-white paste, soundless string instruments involving beeswax in their production.

FURTHER NOTES: Was an aesthete in the purest sense—a lover of beauty; but not a dandy, which traditionally entails a certain adherence to masculinity.

Other Transfixions included Jeanne Duval, Roberte Horth, Luisa Casati, Josephine Baker, Nancy Cunard, Richard Bruce Nugent, Ludwig II Bavaria and Bel-Shalti Nannar, Babylonian High Priestess of the moon god, Sin.

I hadn't planned for cards at all but something visually more complex, involving star charts and tabulations, looking mystical and mathematical. Something diagnostic that would capture the essence of each figure, establishing intricate patterns between them, before at last identifying in a serious manner the source of my fixations.

The result displayed none of the hoped-for rigour, resembling a teenager's overly embellished revision flashcards. But they soon took on a devotional function, like prayer cards. Miniature icons.

I caught myself shuffling them, trying to intuit hidden meanings, and it was because of this I threw them in a high-street bin one day. It was clear that the making of these cards was atavistic, a basically perilous regression. There were other figures who fascinated me but did not produce these feelings, who transfixed but did not Transfix, and in answer to this I was given to constructing explanatory theories. Initially it was to do with reincarnation. All at once I had been Lola Montez, Ludwig II Bavaria, Jeanne Duval and so on, with a tangential theory to justify so many overlapping lives and just one soul. When this at last became insupportable (and unbearable—the shock of realisation was like nothing else, I was locked out of Arcadia) another gleaming narrative was constructed. In this one I belonged to some divine clan of being, a sort of celestial siblinghood to whom I was irrevocably connected (I imagined a network of silver cords) and so, when I heard the music of Ardizzoni and felt like I was suddenly 'home,' it was because through his music echoed the undeniable timbre of my kinsfolk (the twitching of numinous cables). This was also too flimsy a reverie to surf, and the resulting comedown was such that it became necessary to put a stop to these self-induced delusions.

I was grateful to Grace, whom I'd never met, for letting me flatsit, and in my gratitude wanted desperately to like her, but so much made this difficult including the fact that she had chosen to live in this particular location.

I always watched from the window before leaving because I was aware that every morning a couple called Christian and Tom, and their flatmate, Eleanor, performed morbid calisthenics on the grounds of the complex.

They were there today, running around in huge incandescent green jackets. The jackets—which inflated like life-jackets depending on your temperature and were part of a new fitness regime—made them look weightless as they wove around the overabundance of zinc-clad concrete that gave shape and shell to the complex.

Every so often they would stop running and do their aerobics, a warning semaphore from the land of the hale and vigorous. I had to remind myself that they did not actually know I was staying here. As far as I was aware, they didn't even know Grace, but it was still extremely unfortunate.

I had been to one of Christian & Tom + Eleanor's dinners just a month ago. The sole charming thing about them had been their insoluble trinity, but this swiftly became part of the unique drudgery of knowing them. They lived, if I remembered correctly, in the tallest building opposite. The flat was even larger than Grace's; a pale, vast and chairless cocoon. The lack of chairs may well have been part of the same fitness regime as the jackets, or it could have been a matter of style, which was really the same: the taste for frugality that year had reached new heights. It was the Summer of Self-Deprivation. A period of dramatically bland food and sham guilt. Endless exercise. Some began sporting actual sackcloth shirts, as if practicing mortification of the flesh.

At Christian & Tom + Eleanor's upright supper, we all stood around, plates in hand, no one daring to comment on the chairlessness or the food because, in this group, Christian & Tom + Eleanor were really quite fundamental and radical people. Then I dropped a half-moon plate of something lime-coloured onto their carpet. Harmony: it had tasted like apple sauce, but also carpet (already).

I had never known Christian & Tom + Eleanor particularly well, but any number of former friends and escaped-from associates might come to visit them and in doing so catch sight of me, which would prove disastrous.

From the foyer, I spied through the glass doors. They were out of sight and must have just started a new circuit. I'd counted from above using the stopwatch on my phone. By the time they came back round the building I would be gone so I stepped out onto the plaza.

Palm trees, or something like them, had recently been inserted throughout, serving only to punctuate the industrial unearthliness with a vegetal equivalent. The Wreath Complex was a large ring of flats marooned on the farthest transport zone which, after almost a decade in abeyance, had been bought over and rebranded "The Wreath" in an attempt to counteract its out-and-out ghostliness. This luxury rebirth had proven moderately successful, appealing to the likes of Grace, not to mention Tom & Christian + Eleanor.

There was, of course, nothing novel about industrial luxury or the people who flocked to it, but this was pushing it as far as I was concerned. Surely the brainchild of bullfaced psychogeographers. You sometimes saw such men on weekends, aspiring urban prophets and arbiters of grit, pacing about with pads, practically genuflecting every time they met the dull gleam of The Wreath. They walked for hours to see it or stumbled upon it and thought it was the kind of social housing that it had been intended for, prior to redevelopment.

I had no love for Industriana, prefab, Brutalism, faux Gropiusstadts, or anything conspicuously utilitarian because I still coughed up grit particles in my sleep and concrete fragments worked their way out my system by night. I was allergic, in a word, to the architecture of my youth, which perpetually resurfaced, haunting me in ever more unnerving forms like this.

(I had, after all, only just begun casting off the sly aesthetic fascism that barred me from seeing any romance in the conditions of my birth before I was forced to see those conditions through their eyes.)

It took under a week for the place to leave long-lasting effects on me. I noticed since living there all personal adornment become exaggerated, possibly because, at least passing through, I could catch sight of myself in the zinc and steel: a spectre, over-bedecked. I discovered, in that site of anti-ornament, the depths of my craving for the decorative. I was insatiable, panging for the kind of adornment anathema to Christian & Tom + Eleanor, too reminiscent of the trappings of their parents, though really nothing to do with them. They shivered at the prospect of a cornice, gazed longingly at me, jealously even: born absolved of unshakeable bourgeoise signifiers, why on earth would she want to dabble with that shit, shit that looked like that shit, whether it was inherently bourgeoise or not?

The mouth of a pedestrian tunnel perpetually sighed into the midst of the usually empty plaza. Just as I approached, I heard voices behind me.

"Saaaaad-ie!"

"Saaadie!"

"Sadie!"

Bright green reflected in the steel of a baluster. Somewhere behind me were Tom & Christian + Eleanor. I tried to maintain a natural pace until I cleared the steps of the tunnel and was sure I was out of sight; I had to stop myself vaulting over the barriers when I saw the train was already on the platform.

Even as the doors shut, I sat down and the train started pulling away, I had an image of all three buffeting into the station, arms linked, swelling jackets lending them levitational force as they jumped on top of the train, swung down and broke through the glass.

"Sadie!" they would say. "Sadie! Sadie! Sadie! Sadie!"

And I would revert. From Mathilda to Morgana, Morgana to Mona, Mona to Temi, Temi to Sadie—but then I'd keep on unfurling, all the way to she who came first:

Brief Chronology of Unfurling

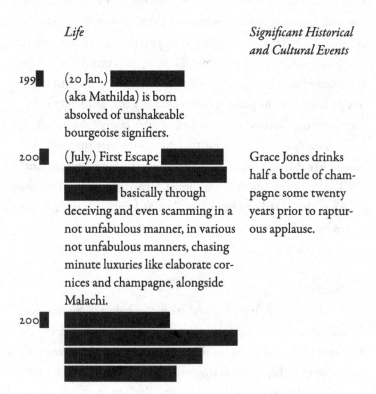

	Life	*Significant Historical and Cultural Events*
199█	(20 Jan.) ██████████ (aka Mathilda) is born absolved of unshakeable bourgeoise signifiers.	
200█	(July.) First Escape ████████ ██████████████████ ████████ basically through deceiving and even scamming in a not unfabulous manner, in various not unfabulous manners, chasing minute luxuries like elaborate cornices and champagne, alongside Malachi.	Grace Jones drinks half a bottle of champagne some twenty years prior to rapturous applause.
200█	████████████ █████████████████ ████████████ █████████████	

200█ Escapes and becomes Sadie   Summer of
Escapes and becomes Temi   Self-Deprivation
Escapes and becomes Mona
Escapes and becomes Morgana
(June 3, 2:30)
Becomes Gillian
Featherstonehaugh
(June 3, 3:30)
Becomes Sarah Montmorency
(June 4) Escapes and
becomes Mathilda
(15 July, 13:13:03) Reverts to
Sarah Montmorency
Reverts to Gillian
Featherstonehaugh
Reverts to Morgana
(13:13:05) Reverts to Mona,
(13:13:06) Reverts to Temi,
(13:13:07) Reverts to Sadie
(13:13:11) Reverts to ███
(13:13:12) Reverts to ███
(13:13:13) Reverts to
She Who Came First

20█ Full autobiographical collapse on
the train, darling.

—Or something to this extent, I imagined.

*

Whenever we finished a pile of photos it was customary for us to switch. I hoped to find more pictures of Hermia in Agnes' pile the following morning but did not. I'd been up late going through my own notes, all the scrawlings I'd ever made with regards to my Transfixions, in the hope of finding out where I had come across a mention of Hermia Druitt, but there was nothing. There was nothing on the internet either. It seemed obvious, then, to follow the source of the photographs and I asked Elizabeth/Joan, when she came in from a long lunch, where exactly they had come from.

"How the hell should I know?" she said, looking accosted. "I've got enough on my plate." And then finally after a pause, "The Mac-Someone family."

"Do you think we could get in touch with them?"

"Jesus Christ," she said, looking up from her computer. "Don't know, why?"

"I was hoping to find out something about one of the photographs."

"Right, well it doesn't really matter as long as we get a few identified and put the rest in order. It's all going to be done over again by someone else, and then again, and then—"

"But I want to know."

"Want to know?"

"I really don't think anyone else will care enough to find out. I have a personal interest." I hoped this personalisation of the matter might draw her in.

"Right, well..." she picked her phone up and became distracted, so I sat back down. After about five minutes she wandered off, which I took to mean she really wasn't going to help. I'd already returned to the new batch of photographs, annoyed. Furthermore, this ream of pictures was all family holidays from the 1990s.

"Let's get going, Mattie, I'm bored to death in here." Elizabeth/Joan was standing in the doorway, bag in hand. "Agnes, you're in charge for the rest of the day."

By the time I'd searched through our neatly organised piles, found the other photograph of Hermia, the one I hadn't stolen, and made it upstairs, I couldn't see Elizabeth/Joan anywhere. I was about to go back down when I spotted her waiting in a taxi across the street, face illuminated by her phone.

"The St. Clairs," she said to me when I got in, which I took to mean the aforementioned MacSomeones.

The taxi took us west into Chelsea. We were soon sitting in the living room of Emma St. Clair, great grandniece of the people who had donated the photographs. A shadow of acknowledgement passed between Emma and Elizabeth/Joan, some Old Girls' cross-generational code; as if they were sizing each other up without really noticing they were doing it.

"I haven't been to the Portrait Gallery for years you know. Studied art history too." This was to Elizabeth/Joan, who hadn't mentioned her education to Emma St. Clair (and Emma was not wrong). "I have a gallery nearby, just down the road on Linton Street..."

I noticed that Elizabeth/Joan was visibly bristling. It was a look I knew from when she worked on the welcome desk and had urgent gossip that couldn't be repeated in front of the readers. It was always succulent gossip.

"Now you said there was something I might help with?"

Emma St. Clair didn't take the photograph from me, but instead stood inspecting it as I held it out. She didn't speak until my arm was aching.

"Mm. Yes, from what I understand, my father's uncle and aunt were both very keen amateur photographers. Actually, this must have been donated about twenty years ago. I don't blame you; *we* didn't manage to send these off until about a decade after they died. They were I suppose what you would call bohemian. This was their house. They encountered a few notables of the period. No one *really* significant in my opinion. A few writers. But mostly what they called the Bright Young People," she smiled and looked above my head. "That was what they called the smart set in those days, what you might call the fashio—"

"Yes, Mathilda's working on a book on the period."

"Oh, are you?" she said. "Who for?"

"Just a small independent press."

Again, I saw Elizabeth/Joan become excited as if she couldn't wait to get out and talk.

"Well, there are a few papers and things. Much had to be disposed of in the end. Countless diaries. Only kept a couple. If I can find them I'll be in touch. It's a shame really, but we just didn't have the space," and she gestured to the room as if to suggest this were really, after all, only a poky old place. She paused in a way that made me look up. Yes, she was staring at me. And as if deducing my thoughts she said,

"Did you know Chelsea used to be considered awfully disreputable?"

"Yes I did, actually."

"Oh?"

In the taxi on the way back to the archive, Elizabeth/Joan was unusually quiet, by which is meant she wasn't even looking at her phone, for her a silent, purer form of chatter. She had her face inclined towards the window but clearly wasn't looking out of it. I couldn't imagine any morsel of gossip about Helen St. Clair that would put her into such a state.

At last at bursting point, she turned to me and practically shouted,

"So you're not *actually* working on a biography are you?"

"What?"

"I mean you're not *actually* doing research for a biography are you?"

Even the driver looked at me via the mirror in anticipation.

"Well, I suppose it's not technically a biography, no."

"But you're not working on anything. Fuck all! You told *me* you were doing a biography for a university press; you just told *her* it was for an independent one. And that's not the only thing you've made up."

I was surprised she'd listened to anything I'd told her. And though I could have easily smoothed out this apparent contradiction, could have said it was an independent university-affiliated press and thus the same thing, I saw from a look in her that it would ultimately be useless and she in turn caught my resignation.

"I knew it!"

"But I *am* doing research of a—"

"—because you're the same as Agnes," she was saying volubly, and when I did not reply, still trying to figure out what she meant (hoping the answer was not, "Black!"), she said, "one of the Necrophiles! They like to come in and stare and stare. We're a magnet for them. Not working on books, not researching anything in particular. And I always wondered what exactly it was they get out of it because the idea of voluntarily staring at pictures of dead people you don't know all day . . . So I call them the Necrophiles, which if you think about it can also mean love of the dead, or dead things, in a non-sexual way. It's an addiction, like social media addiction but it hasn't been pathologised. Of course, they're usually older, and whiter, than you. I think they're usually quite lonely people too. Anyway, it's actually one of the reasons I got you and Agnes to volunteer."

But I knew exactly the type she meant. Arcadians gone awry. It was alarming hearing myself lumped in with the kind of nostalgic, heritage-loving nationalist who liked to gaze at old images of Old England and ache about how it was all so much better. I did not lust away for ages gone by; in that way. I said so.

"I don't get the impression Agnes does either."

"Yes, I know, but you're both a different category of Necrophile."

Elizabeth/Joan had already decided she would take the rest of the day off but dropped me back at the archive on her way to a friend.

Agnes' things were still there but she must have gone to lunch, so after returning the photo to its pile, I did the same. On returning, instead of Agnes, I was met by the sight of James, sitting at our desk, going through a pile of photographs we had completed.

"Some of these dates are way out," he said without looking up.

"We've gone through them all properly, at least twice."

"This one for example," he said, and it was the picture of Hermia, the one I'd just put back. "Yes, look: one of you has put 'circa 1920' on the sheet but it's obviously no more than 30 years old. Black and white, maybe even an old camera, but contemporary. Eliza should have been clear that you're not to put down dates unless you're absolutely certain."

"But we were all absolutely certain."

Obviously, they were all in costume, and Rex Whistler and Tennant, the two figures of recognised significance, were somewhat less identifiable, but I was sure it was them. Not to mention that I'd seen several hundred other Ottoline Morrell photographs.

"Doesn't matter, they would have been corrected anyway, but it makes more work. I'm back to the main site so I may as well take this pile with me."

*

Black card with copper ink

Ardizzoni

(Image is from a small enamel of an unknown sitter on the back of an 18th-century silver hairbrush. First seen on a postcard from an Italian village museum. (Postcard found in London.) A figure in green velvet with gold threading, powdered grey hair. I suspect it to be Ardizzoni.)

SPAN: mid-18th-century

MEMORABILIA: Minor castrato singer and composer. Minor at least in that there is little information on him. Was called 'the Moor,' perhaps because of African descent, though this has been disputed (even though he obviously was) as there are cases of this appellation being given to white Europeans with dark complexions, or in at least one case for successfully playing Othello.

Wrote an unsuccessful opera based on the life of Saint Christina the Astonishing, the 12th-century saint who awoke during her funeral and flew up into the rafters because the stench of sin became too unbearable. Spent much of her saintly life living in trees and throwing herself into fires, which had no effect on her.

Beyond this, next to nothing is known of Ardizzoni.

SENSATIONS: Nocturnal gilding coats the bones.

*

I couldn't remember where some of my really obscure Transfixions came from. They appeared following obsessive, whirlwind nights. I would emerge with a name or a face or even a full Transfixion card and would not always be able to find the source later. A book I could never relocate, a web page looked at on a library computer, search history gone the next day. I'd try and follow the thought chain that got me there. With some I even questioned if they were cusp-of-sleep confections, dredged up the next morning as truth. Were my Transfixions not, at least in part, vessels for something else? Did it matter if they had been real people?

My recognising Hermia's name was because I'd come across it in one of these forgotten whirlwinds.

I'd found it at last—a note, rather cryptic; almost like a message to myself from the future, though it was over a year old. I had texted it to my own number whilst researching one of my other Transfixions without paper to hand, even then feeling Hermia might be a figure of interest.

Hermia druitt p 147 drawing the circ parker

It was at the British Library, so I went that afternoon wearing Grace's clothes in case I was recognised by any of the Escaped-from (in particular the group who knew me as Mona, an aspiring academic).

Drawing the Circle, History of the Modernist Clique by Edna Parker was, as the title suggested, a work tracing various overlapping British cultural circles such as the Bloomsbury Group, the Mayfair Set, the Bright Young People, the Corrupt Coterie, the

Neopagans, the Souls and so on. The section I had taken note of was a quote from a woman attending a garden party in London. The guest had no particular connection to any of the other literary attendees, but was taken aback by the appearance of one:

> [...] a woman—"the Negress of Dun" called Hermia Druitt. And how should I describe her parasol? An arboreal affair— a delicate branch, still with the green shooting out of it, and yet the handle, if it can be called that, the bough, then, carved to smooth delicacy—as if she'd lopped it from the tip of a pine or something equally coniferous that morning... The light shot through it and dappled her commendably [...]

The author of *Drawing the Circle* had selected this passage because of its use in illustrating some of the party antics that went on during this time, but also to illustrate the wide range of people that one might encounter (in other words, not all white). Parker noted that she had not had the opportunity to view the original source of this account, a letter, but had found it by way of another book. It was called *Black Modernisms* by a Professor Helena Morgan.

Nothing on the internet. When I entered the title into the search catalogue, however, it was there. Some hours later I was told they couldn't find it. "Perhaps it never actually made its way to us. It's quite rare but not unheard-of." They suggested I try the Bodleian, but after checking various major and minor library catalogues it was obvious nowhere held a copy. I proceeded to track down Professor Morgan. Dead. I had ignored the obituary that came up whenever I searched her name, presuming it was one of the other Helena Morgans that kept waylaying my searches. I sent out two dozen emails to possible associates, including the publisher. I then turned my attention back to Hermia and tried searching for the "Negress of Dun," and then "Dun," which was apparently a small town somewhere in Europe. The top search results were monopolised by commercial links. The first, a corporate retreat, the next, Gray & Dun Solicitors. Both obviously scams.

From Marseille to Untergrainau (Garmisch)

For "a Jewess and a Negress," we did very well indeed.

An American gentleman and his wife objected to H.'s pres-ence on the train (always these Americans abusing her!) and there was nothing we could do but leave. And we left with-out reimbursing our tickets. Consequently found ourselves stranded in a Swiss town with our mountain of cases and pecuniary abyss. We had no right in coming in the first place, but came anyway since Stephen had offered, insisted, to pay for our journey home and everything when there, if only we just hurry, for the excitement was too much. But we regretted it then because it was clear we would not make it.

Left the luggage at the station and made our way to the town to find a Poste or hotel where we might wire somebody or avail ourselves of a telephone.

Then it began. Children, running towards her, shout-ing, "Josephine! Josephine!" which I could only take to mean they had somehow confused H. with Josephine Baker. Soon half the town had gathered, asking for autographs. And as for Hermia, she of course—as usual dressed for the opera, Paris, 1889—just smiled imperiously at everyone until we were invited into the hotel by a gentleman—the local rake—and had no trouble entering (by the front entrance, which, H. tells me, is not always afforded to even the real Josephine). He fed us Swiss wine and cheese and white cakes and spoke at great length and with great pride about the town and his position in it (very wealthy, but practically a schoolboy, he could not have been more than twenty) all without discern-ing—though they hardly look anything alike—who H. was not. Perhaps he did not care. But before we knew it, he had a gramophone brought down to the lounge from his rooms and played Josephine Baker! Of course then H. had to sing. It was obvious what she would do—act the petulant songstress, become insulted and he would let off. But no. She began to sing! She sang opera, Donizetti—the rake positively had tears in his eyes and I thought was about to propose but the hotel manager came through and, when we relayed our troubles, we were given rooms for the night and escorted the next day to the station by the little rake and the manager and an entire party from the town, some handing us flowers. The station master was then 'gotten on to,' who in turn got onto the conductor. We were seated first class and in such a manner went on our merry way to Haus Hirth with no trouble at all. Dizzying how it can fall with H.—the reception: either mirth or calamity dependent on something fickle, infinitesimal—the way the light hits her, and she in turn reacts, means princess or criminal, Josephine Baker or servant. We had less worry about staying here at Haus Hirth, for Stephen told us there was another guest already there, "a young German lady with Tahitian blood" who is treated very well.

H. sleeps now.

Stephen—who has met Josephine Baker—was mesmerised by this tale and made us recite it to the hostess here, a woman they call Tante Johanna, and her husband, who have turned their house into a sort of hotel, and who, to their credit, clapped and cheered all the way through like children and also put on a Josephine Baker record.

I fear Stephen will not pay our return so that we might make more stories of this kind for his amusement. I imagine he thinks it all easy and cannot envisage the harm in it. Tomorrow, however, we make a trip to Munich where he will spend a small fortune on us from the sound of things.

So you see, we are doing very well indeed, all things considering.

HAUS HIRTH, *Untergrainau,* Jan 1928

Grace came home early. She was there when I got back from the library. Transfixion papers, books, makeup, clothes and fake diamonds were strewn throughout the flat from the previous few days. She was chopping a green pepper and came close to throwing the knife on sight of me letting myself in, but quickly realised who I was.

She said I could stay until next month if I needed, since that was what had been agreed and she wouldn't be home much. But I saw instantly that it would be hellish living with her.

As if to consolidate this there was a tap at the kitchen window and Christian & Tom + Eleanor came in holding tubs for dinner.

"Sadie! What are you doing here?" they said, as if they didn't already know I had been staying here.

"Sadie?" Grace said. "Oh, sorry for some reason I thought you were a Mathilda. Of all the names! Where did I get that from? What am I like."

I felt the involuntary metamorphosis begin—the reversion. It was exactly the sort of thing I most dreaded, the sort of occurrence that suspends you forever in a momentary guise. A guise selected itself for a previous Escape. I had to vanish.

"Anyway, yes, an old friend of mine was supposed to housesit. Dropped out last minute and suggested Sadie. I didn't really have the time to read the emails properly."

"Who was the friend?" Christian said to me, unable to filter out the suspicious tenor in his voice.

"Oh, Jack..." I said. "Winsome. Only an acquaintance really."

"Brave, Grace, letting people you don't know stay!" said Eleanor.

"Is it brave?" said Grace. "Better that than burgled. Anyway, how do you all know Sadie?"

After we finished Christian & Tom + Eleanor's meal:

"Actually, Sadie, here's an idea, why not let Grace get settled back in and stay with us for a couple of days? You could bring your stuff over and meet us there in half an hour. As a matter of fact, this is ideal: Alex and everyone will be round tomorrow. You haven't seen them for aeons, have you?"

*

I'd forgotten to leave the spare keys but could not go back.

Once packed, instead of heading to Christian & Tom + Eleanor's, I veered left, towards one of the pedestrian walkways that led to the river, where, if I walked far enough along for an hour, or an hour and a half with the suitcase, I would come to another complex. Unlike the complex I'd just left, this scheme had remained officially uninhabited for fifteen years. I thought about it daily since first coming to stay at The Wreath, though I'd tried not to dwell on its relative proximity.

It was there that Malachi, and various other young men, lived 'rent free' with permission from the owner. A private agreement that would possibly make the news if exposed. Malachi had initially only described the setup to me in the vaguest of terms, but I was able to infer that the owner made money through the 'non-paying residents' by means of an app. The app was a highly secure invite-only app on which customers of presumably significant wealth were able to book Malachi and the occupants, the isolated location making the whole thing highly convenient for all. The occupants received payment for their work straight to their accounts, the bulk of it going to the owner who'd replicated this arrangement and variants of it internationally. It was apparently ideal for hoarding empty properties before selling them.

They had been admonished by the owner after throwing a couple of parties in the early days.

"He turned up in person, with security. Not what you would imagine. Not much older than us, looking like a Silicon Valley hack; bit dated, but still. Anyway, said we're 'property guardians first, sex workers second.' Those words exactly."

Malachi told me this the first time I'd been here, two years ago.

This second visit was solely down to the fact that Christian & Tom + Eleanor's invitation to stay with them for a couple of days meant, of course, that I would be unable to take Grace up on her offer to stay on.

Even if I had been able to stay I would not. It was clear to me Grace's surprise about my name was staged; the four of them had discussed me as soon as Grace got back, and Christian & Tom + Eleanor had gone home to observe my return. Which meant an undesirable collision was in motion: the collision of two Escapes.

It was with Malachi I engineered my first Escape. We had come to the concept intuitively. With each Escape, as I saw it, I was brought closer to my Transfixions, each vanishing act pulling me towards the unknown source of an ache first felt years ago—that made me writhe around one day on the black-barred balcony of a grey tower, white towels draped over for privacy, sky copper green and seeming to reflect somewhere else. Somewhere Arcadian; perhaps a garden with charming people. Though it was, of course, only that sly old aesthetic fascism preventing this sky from belonging to the view from that tower, to that particular flat even, where it would still be possible to find blood dried on walls after the years, perhaps a few fresh smudges since departure. We did not want to become people hollowed out by generations of too much bad labour into leaving other people's blood on the walls.

Generation after generation of unused froth and frivolity would be finally uncorked in us! The classic impetus of working-class queer kidz fleeing the conformity and violence of a literal or metaphorical 'small town,' seeking queer and glittering new horizons, was turned into something else. Our escapes sent into overdrive.

The idea was that by disappearing from the inessential elements of one's own life, whatever they might be, you would inevitably be brought closer to the essential: a sublime self-subtraction. Thus, we spent years together self-constructing in private. Burnishing jewels that were already there and transplanting ones that seemingly had no place. This was crucial to our Escape, we decided, and was a betrayal only of our immediate circumstance, of incidentals, and not in any way a denial of who we were. The palace-bred insolence we cultivated came so naturally it could hardly be called cultivation.

Our notion of what we might launch into was hazy and we constructed ourselves mostly from books and period dramas (my influence). Like Europeans in a Henry James, we would be creatures of genteel penury, full of education, artifice, a little vampiric, duping all the dull rich people around us. Except we were Black, except were poor, except we were basically self-taught (by their standards), except we were infinitely more subtle and fabulous, as far as we were concerned.

Once set, we conducted in tandem the self-extraction from our given lives. Our first and only joint Escape. And almost magically, it worked. We had been lucky. Spindle-limbed, ganache-skinned, very young, we had been palatable enough at that moment to scale the heights of a group so far removed from where we had just come from that we became dizzy.

One of the first things Malachi and I learnt was that, as miserly as they are, rich people will happily prop up their own kind for years. If they, however, discover they are suspending someone not of their own kind, unwittingly dangling them by a thread, they will start to feel charitable, which is one of their most violent and short-lived states; giddy with benevolence, they soon feel indebted beyond all possible recompense—but it is not this that does it. They finally become obsessed with the knowledge of this dangling, not truly convinced anyone they know could actually have no safety net, and so they cut the thread.

It was after such a cutting, our first fall, we 'realised' (with the fatalism of two tragedians) that we would eventually have to Escape one another in order to really achieve the psychological break needed to live anew. Therefore, we decided (with the same fatalism) that we could only see each other three more times or the Grand Escape would be ineffective.

One problem with this way of living was that money could become suddenly difficult. Malachi was much better at this than I. Better at orchestrating new contacts, new groups to launch into whilst disappearing from the old ones. But also able to do things like forging all the necessary documents to get, say, housing benefits without a tenancy agreement (or accompanying 'house'), or a student loan without a degree.

Before I approached Malachi's building, I saw a young man in a long white coat strutting along a canal boat with blue lights flashing on it and music faintly audible over the water. He didn't seem to notice me, but I guessed he was from Malachi's complex. I shouted to him and he shouted back but we couldn't hear one another.

I stood at the centre of the pale cement courtyard around which the bulk of flats were arranged, trying to remember which one Malachi's was. Though built a year or two before, this complex was not at all like The Wreath. It was one of the loveliest places I'd ever seen.

I thought I saw a light go off as I looked around, and then another. It might be the case that they had left; it had, after all, been two years.

Then a light went on and someone leaned over the balcony.

"Morgana?" he said, tentatively.

"Mathilda," I said.

Malachi appreciated the significance of my problem with an immediacy I hadn't known for two years. We had both discussed this sort of complication during our last meeting (of which we'd one each, and a third for whoever needed it first).

Generally, most groups will let you slip away, and out of memory. They will forget you, largely. This does not apply to certain relationships, of course, but concerns those friendships conducted en masse; groups socialised with jointly. Every so often, however, there are individuals who will prevent this easy passage. Not because they remotely like you, or even dislike you, but because they experience a dissonance in the occurrence of an Escape, and, whether consciously or not, wish to stop it. It was a phenomenon both Malachi and I had observed separately.

I thought about it in terms of grand archetypes: that going back for centuries, millennia, there were untold Tom & Christian + Eleanors, there to put an end to movement of the kind we pursued. Immemorial gaolers.

Malachi spoke about it differently: things that rose up in systems automatically when trying to leave those systems, in the form of people's subconscious acts: "Unwitting antibodies of the Totality." At first it all sounded like rehashed Foucault. Ersatz deconstruction. But as he expanded, rambled, I felt the sleek and slightly distressing fin of authenticity glide and cut beneath us.

45

That said, I'd noted how conspiratorial he had become during our last meeting and put it down to his admittedly astonishing living arrangement. Now he even looked the part in shades of black and slate, dreads the colour of hummingbirds and oxidised metal. There was something faintly militaristic about his appearance, Panther-ish—not in imitation, but a material kiss blown back through history. It soon became evident he also lived the part—Queer Black liberation fighter from distant cybertopia—with three imposing monitors and two laptops on his desk, not to mention his coming and going from the houses of actual oligarchs and politicians, whenever they didn't visit him here.

We enjoyed and often played up our central difference: I was the Arcadian, he the Utopian. I the fantasist, he the futurist.

"Afrofuturist," he said.

He was never truly partial to drugs, but on rare occasions, such as our previous two meetings, brought out a light blue powder.

After we had some that night we went to the canal boat and danced with the person in the long coat I had shouted at who turned out to be Malachi's boyfriend, Sirhan. He played music and we strutted up and down the boat and I was delighted that Malachi knew such a light and shimmering person as this. The sky swelled and was slightly violet; the river glowed and heaved dull pearl slabs.

Later, waking in his room, I looked out the window where a car the colour of black atrium glass rolled along, before Malachi got in the back and it drove away.

I used one of his laptops to search for Hermia. There again was the business retreat which appeared whenever I typed in "Dun." But I had stopped typing in Dun altogether by this point when it came up. I couldn't later remember what it was I had searched for, what combination of words. Something containing "Hermia Druitt."

When I opened the page, I was met by the bright yellow screen.

**Please complete the questions below and press
submit for application to the Dun Residency.**

It looked more like some kind of conceptual artists' residency than a business retreat. In fact, I wasn't sure what had ever made me think of that. There was not much information, as if they expected you to know about the whole thing from elsewhere, but there was a mention of a stipend in Euros and free accommodation, so I applied. I had once, through an old friend, attended a weeklong artists' residency in Bognor Regis with free meals. The only problem had been passing as an artist, but as it happened, the general research my Transfixions required made it look like I was working on a project.

What do you think about the rising prominence of Dotage
Conduct and how would you best make use of it, if selected?

Still feeling the purr of Malachi's blue powder, I typed a five-page answer, discussing Dotage Conduct, whatever it was. I wrote about the limits of Dotage and how my own personal lack of it would buffer me from a true lack of Dotage which inevitably arises from a prominence of the stuff, then pressed *submit*.

Thank you for applying to the Dun Residence 2009.

It was several years old. I almost threw the laptop across the room until I remembered it was Malachi's, so I carefully slammed it shut and fell back asleep.

I awoke to my phone ringing; a private number.

It was Malachi. He had arranged somewhere for me to stay.

"It's only three weeks, sorry..." he said, "...but a taxi will come and get you in about an hour, so keep a lookout; it's been paid for already."

It was, I knew, the best he could do, short of having me stay with him, which would prove disastrous for him as well as me if he got caught.

And we both knew that it would be a concession to failure; an admission that we were ultimately doomed to no Escape at all, assigned to the drabness that underlies everything.

The taxi stopped outside.

As children we would frequently pass The Southwark Lodge, a disreputable local bed and breakfast that, on account of it being in a large Victorian building and a 'hotel,' we invested with untold Old-World glamour. It became a site of great interest for us though we had never been inside, until we turned nine or ten and spent weeks saving up money, acquiring our outfits, in order to visit The Lodge café in the guise of the children of West African dignitaries taking tea.

Inside was no different to any commercial chain of cheap hotel.

"So this is what they call a 'Palm Court' then is it, darling?"

We sat imperiously drinking our tea in the café cum reception area from small steel pots, which we thought were pure silver, babbling loudly about our fictional embassy parents:

"Oh, I can't *think* where mother is, darling, can you?"

"I cannot think myself, darling, but then you know she always takes so long putting on all that fur and all those diamond brooches!"

"Yes, that must be it, the brooches!"

"By the way, have you heard of the illustrious *chocolatier*, Elizabeth Shaw?"

"I cannot say that I have, but you know I've always preferred the consumption of caviar to the eating of chocolates."

"Oh, me too, me too, I cannot lie!"

*

On mottled cream card with green ink

Lola Montez aka **Eliza Gilbert,**
aka **the Countess of Landsfeld**

(Image—daguerreotype of Montez holding a thin tapering whip, wearing a cloak and a sort of tricorn hat; arm resting against a fake column looking generally formidable, by Antoine Samuel Adam-Saloman)

SPAN: 17 February 1821—17 January 1861

MEMORABILIA: After a childhood spent terrorising school teachers, churches and all other aspects of her respectable upbringing, Eliza Gilbert became Mrs. James when she eloped to India with a lieutenant whom she in turn fled to establish herself as a dancer under the name Lola Montez. Travelling across Europe, she whipped a Prussian officer from atop her horse in Berlin, produced a gun when the chief of police in Warsaw tried to detain her (instigating an immediate riot), whilst in Paris she became a luminary in artistic circles, adored by George Sands and Liszt, before moving on to Munich, where she met King Ludwig I Bavaria and not long after was made the Countess of Landsfeld and Baroness Rosenthal. Montez's political influence became such that right-wing mobs rioted against her and in answer a group of students formed under the name of Alemannia to defend her. Presiding over this group, the Countess was seen whipping back crowds of detractors before taking refuge in the church of the Theatines. Following this, she was exiled, eventually travelling to America where she became a lecturer and the first woman pictured smoking. Lectured on various topics such as 'Heroines of History' and the Romans. Later plotted part-time to become the Empress of California whilst helping destitute women.

After her death, a member of the Hermetic Order of the Golden Dawn, the occult society based in London, used a letter to authenticate the Order. The letter purported to be from Anna Sprengel, a Rosicrucianist and supposed daughter of Montez (by King Ludwig), living in Germany. Later, a woman appeared in London claiming to be Anna Sprengel. The head of the order believed her, but she was eventually arrested for fraud.

Back:

SENSATION: Thick pane of bevelled ruby through which is viewed a landscape, possibly the landscape is painted; euphoria in twinges as if experienced through moving slits.

*

Elizabeth/Joan was fired from the archives. She took me to dinner to celebrate, at somewhere of my choice. I chose a restaurant in Soho knowing this had once been the Gargoyle Club owned by Stephen Tennant's brother.

Apparently, our trip to Chelsea had set in motion various disasters. After leaving Helen St. Clair's house, "the conniving fucker was straight on the phone to the National Portrait Gallery."

"They put old Helen through to the archives; eventually to the Chief Archivist who was told that two members of staff had come around uninvited, and she was made to feel 'seriously uncomfortable,' and that there had been 'a degree of unprofessionalism.'"

She told me James the Jobsworth had been in the office at the time of the call and was very happy to answer all the Chief Archivist's questions, such as, "Who on earth could the other member of staff have been?" This led to the exposure of Elizabeth/Joan's many examples of self-initiative, including sending expense sheets to the finance team for Agnes and me.

"Maybe the whole thing would have resulted in a smack on the wrist, but James made it clear that something should be done, and the Chief Archivist couldn't be seen *not* following the rules.

"There was a big meeting, it was hilarious. Human Resources were there and the Gallery Director was there. All for me. They were all lovely, actually, and one of them was even good friends with Toby-Dog," by which she meant her mother, Faustina. "But there was nothing they could do, and they had to let me go. And, of course, it goes without saying that both you and Agnes are banned forever—they probably can't stop you going to the exhibitions etcetera, but you know, from the archives."

She took the whole thing with a kind of good humour. That it was through helping me she had been caught out did not enter into her logic of accountability (she was in a good mood)—Big Consequences brought her to life, whether they were hers or someone else's. I was angry, not because Elizabeth/Joan had lost her job, or even because of this ban, but because of the end of my and Agnes' expenses. I had no income for the foreseeable future, unable to access benefits—even Malachi couldn't have assisted with this had I been able to contact him. I was also being pursued by a credit company with a ghoulish Latin-sounding name; something like *Indictus*.

I wondered what would happen if I threw myself at the mercy of Elizabeth/Joan, or perhaps Agnes, since they were the only remaining contacts I had. I wondered how Elizabeth/Joan would react and remembered that in her own strange world she had probably made herself feel benevolent in making us work for her. Patron Saint of Necrophiles.

Certainly, at one moment during the lunch, I was sure I felt something pass between us, some vital bridge appear—appear and then fade, and I knew my opportunity to continue any friendship had come to an end. Already now I could see myself becoming history. Her glare adjusted to the future. She had a new job already.

"Where?"

"Oh, that's the really funny thing; I'm going to be working at Helen St. Clair's gallery."

"What the fuck, Eliza?"

"Well, after all that uproar it turns out old Toby-Dog helped out Helen once, with some kind of art inheritance scandal—I knew from the moment we walked in. So when Helen St. Clair realised she knew my mother she couldn't apologise enough and asked if I needed a job because she was looking for a gallery manager. I'll be running the gallery day to day, putting on exhibitions, scouting artists—much more suited to me than the archives actually. I went back today to get my things and thought, good riddance!

"Mathilda, when I was leaving some friends of yours were outside asking after you. I think an Ellie and a Christian and someone else? Except they called you Sadie and when I said I didn't know anyone called that, they described you. They said they were worried," she looked away as if distracted.

"Sadie?"

Now she was watching me like on that first day—as if I could not see her back, except now she looked mildly impressed.

*

About a week later as I was checking my emails on The Lodge guest computer, there was one from *Elizabeth@stclairsgallery.co.uk* entitled *JEEZ LOUISE*. It contained no message but a link to an article, the headline of which was, *Jamaican Pensioner Questioned for Threatening Major British Galleries,* and followed,

> *Jamaican pensioner Agnes Pantal was detained yesterday morning after a major public cultural institute contacted the police. The gallery claims to have received a number of threatening letters from the eighty-two-year-old dating back over twenty years, and after further investigation other galleries, including the Tate Britain and the National Gallery, have also had similar correspondences. Miss Pantal has reportedly accused these galleries of "withholding significant works by black artists pertaining to the historical presence of 'the African diaspora in Europe.'" Miss Pantal visited the gallery headquarters in person after not receiving a response and the gallery expressed concern for Miss Pantal's health: "We have to take all threats, implicit or otherwise, seriously, and sadly had no choice but to contact the police."*

It went on to say that Agnes (who was of Haitian descent, not Jamaican), had been released with a warning.

*

All I can recall of the week at The Lodge following the email from Elizabeth/Joan is being in a kind of Hermia-trance. I would read over the passage about her that I'd copied out. I would recite it in my mint-hued box room, the television murmuring along. I would look at the photograph for hours, a certain detail (the rings over the chain-mail gloves) would send me careering, only for my eyes to refocus, be taken by another aspect (Stephen's necklace) and cloud over again. I would go down to the lobby and search the internet for any reference to Hermia Druitt until another guest needed to use the computer.

Really, the full severity of my situation never dawned. Only once did I wake up feeling pure dread: the realisation that I would have nowhere to sleep in a matter of days. I had managed this for just under a week, primarily by sleeping on buses and the tube, before being able to pick up the keys to housesit for Grace. One day on the underground, I woke to a man about to sit next to me even though the whole carriage was empty. I flashed an antique dagger I'd been carrying just for this purpose. He turned and got off.

More immediate than any of this, however, was the realisation my Escape was over and that it was time to return to the world that had been so painstakingly constructed for me.

That this dread came only once and in the middle of sleep was fortuitous. I would have been rendered insensate by it. Other than this episode I was too Transfixion-addled to care.

It was on the Monday of the third week that my phone started ringing. I wasn't fully awake when I answered.

"Hello? Miss Adaramola? Hi! We received your application for the Dun Residency," said a soft-spoken German man. I remembered the yellow screen: *Thank you for applying for the Dun Residency 2009.*

"Very last minute of you, but we are conscious of the reality that some potential applicants were only recently made aware of the deadline and I have to give everybody a fair chance. It was an enticing application though not without some alarm bells. I'll be clear with you, someone has been unable to take up their place and I'm contacting shortlisted candidates. Can you give any indication of *why* the programme appeals to you?"

I cannot remember what I said. Something I imagined sounded suitably diffuse for a conceptual art programme. The man thanked me and was gone. Had that been the end of it, I might have thought the whole thing a dream, but within the hour my phone bleated, and the man was telling me I had been accepted, and that I should book transport within the next week.

"I'm afraid I don't have the funds."

"We may be able to reimburse you by making a small increase to your stipend."

"Oh that's wonderful, but I don't think I'll actually be able to get the money for flights on time."

"A flight here from London should only be in the region of two hundred pounds."

"Yes, that's what I feared."

"I see. Just a moment Miss Adaramola," I heard him talking to someone in the background.

"Hello? Okay Miss Adaramola, I've just spoken to the administrative team and it will be possible to advance you a portion of your stipend; we'll just need your account details."

It was presumably a scam. But then, they couldn't possibly scam me, I had no money they could get a hold of. If the money actually came through, I'd get a free flight.

When the money came into my account that evening, I thought it would be wiser to take it out and keep it. But then, surely this meant it was legitimate?

I remember leaving The Lodge for the first time in days and withdrawing ten pounds just to see if it was real. And then, before I changed my mind, I went to book a ticket.

*

Marbled card with gold ink

Richard Bruce Nugent

(Studio photograph of Nugent in a three-piece suit looking towards camera with a bust of Antinous above him and a stiff satin back-drop, by Carl Van Vechten.)

SPAN: July 2, 1906—May 27, 1987

MEMORABILIA: Writer and painter of the Harlem Renaissance. Became the first openly queer Black writer in the West (we know of) upon the publication of his experimental prose composition *Smoke, Lilies and Jade* in 1926, three decades before Baldwin's *Giovanni's Room*. Also wrote homoerotic biblical stories. Moved to New York as a teenager where he was introduced to avant-garde circles in Greenwich Village. At 18 he announced his artistic intentions, foremost that he no longer wanted to work. As a result, he was sent back to Washington to live with his grandmother. When he got off the train, however, he decided to try passing as South American under the name Ricardo Nugenti de Dosceta and walked miles towards the Wardman Park and Hotel, getting a taxi the final mile. When the bellboys came to let him out the taxi, he thought they would immediately catch him out on seeing his cardboard suitcase tied in rope and so didn't give them time to stop him, bounding into the hotel and up the stairs, where, as it happened, he bumped into an acquaintance he had made in New York, Princess Matchabelli. She was with "a very haaaandsome gentleman" from the Spanish legation who arranged accommodation for him at the embassy. Richard returned to his Grandmother's after four days, however, as having to pass was so stressful. On returning later to New York he was offered accommodation for next to nothing by the Harlem philanthropist and businesswoman Iolanthe Sydney, which he and his friends famously dubbed Nigeratti Manor, and Nugent decorated the walls with florid painted phalli and presided over what quickly became a queer party instituion where Harlem and Greenwich Village bohemia converged.

SENSATION: Internal fumes / pale blue ethanol vapours.

*

"Will you hurry the fuck up, Mattie. Aggy's got an entire gourmet banquet on the go or something."

Agnes' flat was not too far from The Lodge. Elizabeth/Joan was already there. She had called a few hours ago suggesting we visit Agnes, sounding displaced on the phone. In the sense that she had little interest in present situations—at least the ones I'd encountered—she was always displaced, but never from herself. On the phone, there had been an uncharacteristic doubt in her voice.

I still decided to be late. I knew Elizabeth/Joan had probably kept Agnes' address from the archive database and suspected that, in her mind, visiting Agnes did not entail warning or invitation. At least she could take the brunt of any shock or fury if she arrived first. But perhaps just turning up to say hello was something Agnes understood.

"I don't understand why you don't get a taxi." She was definitely more coked-up than usual.

"Because I don't have any money, and I'm almost outside, I can see it."

"I don't care, get a fucking taxi now."

Agnes resided in the kind of council flat that borders on twee with its blond-brown bricks and mere four storeys, and certainly one day, when the estate is no longer council-owned, will be considered quaint and iconic by all the wrong people. Or maybe this was already the case. This estate was tucked casually between two huge Georgian streets.

Agnes lived on the ground floor. It was Elizabeth/Joan who let me in.

"Jesus Christ," she said. "At fucking last," but looked more relieved than annoyed. I followed her into the kitchen where Agnes had made, amongst several other things, grilled lobster. It was almost impossible to move without knocking something off the table. I had only eaten free hotel breakfasts (continental) since Elizabeth/Joan took me out to dinner and almost cried. Elizabeth/Joan didn't eat. She simply drank and smoked and watched me. Agnes, in her everlasting pearls and plaid, didn't eat much either. I became drunk from the food before I even began to drink whatever it was Elizabeth/Joan had poured out for me.

Agnes didn't look surprised or put out by our presence. Or for that matter especially happy, except possibly in some disinterested way I couldn't pin down. Between this and Elizabeth/Joan's loose grip on empathy, I was surprised it wasn't unbearable. I was still unable to figure out what had compelled Elizabeth/Joan to come. She probably didn't know herself. She was often guided by some inconsistent inner éclat which would extinguish without warning.

"Here we are again," said Agnes.

"Yes," said Elizabeth/Joan profoundly.

"I've just been telling Eliza what a stupid girl she is." Agnes looked at me sharply whilst Elizabeth/Joan's back faintly straightened like she'd just been complimented. "A true dunderhead." Elizabeth/Joan looked delighted.

"She thinks I wasted that job at the archives, but I've told her I've got a new job."

"What does she want to be working for a lowbrow commercial gallery like that for?" Agnes said, looking genuinely bemused. The spirit of Miss Jean Brodie lived on, I thought, albeit politically realigned.

"It isn't lowbrow. What the bloody hell is lowbrow anyway? And at least *I've* got a job…" even Elizabeth/Joan seemed to realise what she was about to say was bordering on jobsworthish, and as if aware of this Agnes said,

"Well at least you're not stuck with that Mr. Collins anymore."

When Agnes left the kitchen to get a bottle of crème de menthe to make coffee liqueurs, Elizabeth/Joan crumbled a pill of some kind into my cup.

"Bring the coffee through," Agnes called. "My programme is on."

I must have already been quite inebriated and very soon whatever it was in my coffee, besides the crème de menthe, made me want to lie on the tartan carpet. There was a sweet smell in the living room air which I recognised. Elizabeth/Joan must have had one of the pills as well because she too was lying on the carpet staring at the lit-up fake coals of an electric heater.

"This is bloody glorious!" she said too volubly. "What the hell is it?" Agnes didn't seem to mind or notice. Great striped swells moved over the floor. She ignored us as we rolled around the thick tartan ocean, laughing.

"Literally lolling," I said to Elizabeth/Joan.

"Lollygagging," Elizabeth/Joan said to me.

"Yes, lolling on the tartan carpet."

Agnes' programme was about the history of Iran.

There was a large corner-bar in the room and I realised Agnes had amassed all the leftover bottles from *The Old Smoking Room*. Quite right. I was standing up to look at it when I noticed the other display cabinets. One held three cameos which might have been Roman, featuring profiles of mythical queens and goddesses long neglected, with physiognomies that would be considered distinctly unclassical. There were various sketches, photographs and papers in these cabinets too. An aquatint of Alessandro de' Medici, a daguerreotype of the Pre-Raphaelite model, Fanny Matilda Eaton, dressed as Medea. An original illuminated tarot card, La Papesse, sporting her three-tiered papal crown and sceptre, coiled golden hair, brown skin; identified as belonging to a Visconti-Sforza deck. An Elizabethan cabinet miniature of a young Black courtier.

The sweetness in the air was the smell of old paints and wood.

I opened the glass door to remove an old bound book from a polythene bag. It was handwritten in Old French. Someone had inserted modern translations on long strips of brown paper between the pages which said it was the diary of a "Moorish" courtier of James IV. I read a little. November 1589. Several other "blackamoors" had attended the Scottish king's wedding in Norway. Some as guests, like the diarist, and some as musicians and dancers. At the king's wish a few had danced in the snow, almost naked, because he thought the sight of their bodies against the white would look splendid. They all perished of pneumonia. The next night the King, who had already commended the diarist's legs, visited his bed and revisited the praise.

There was another bundle of papers. A manuscript from 1919. A lost modernist masterpiece. Someone had been looking into the writer, or as it happened writers, and managed to find a photograph of the pair, a brother and sister. Also on top of the large manuscript was a rejection letter from the Duckworth Press. An accompanying note mentioned they were London-based Dutch Caribbean twins from St. Maarten who had penned one large experimental novel, but never managed to secure publication and died in obscurity.

"Agnes," I said. "What is all this?"

"Hmm?" she looked up, "Evidence, Mathilda; *shh*, I'm watching this."

There was a circular painting on the wall, with a black and gold wooden frame. Renaissance surely, but very weird. Not any Renaissance theme I had ever seen.

It was a roofscape. A small town lined by a sheet of mist. Occasional jutting through of turret or spire, the silhouette of a large dome further back, and here and there through patches in the mist, hints of a busy medieval town. At the centre a rooftop garden emerged. Potted fruit trees; flowering vines. Most noticeably, on top of the roof was a statue in black marble, or onyx perhaps. The curls of its hair were delicately carved and gilded so that, though only taking up a couple of inches, this black and gold figure was brought out by the black and gold frame. The surface was studded in places with tiny jewels like a Carlo Crivelli painting, which it was in style, including the peacock which roamed the roof garden. But my eyes kept on coming unfocused. I was swaying looking at it. Elizabeth/Joan came and stood beside me, also swaying. She was trying to speak under her breath, but her voice projected.

"I know, some of this is really fucking valuable. Some of it's fake, I think, too, or forged, or something. But a lot of it must be stolen, as in, over the years. You're aware she's worked at other archives? I looked in her bedroom and there's more there."

"But wouldn't they notice if she'd stolen something like this?" I said.

"No." She started laughing which made me laugh.

"At the archives," she eventually said, "there was tonnes of this kind of shit which hasn't been looked at for a century, plenty which could easily just go missing. Actually, plenty has gone missing over the years. Things get lost and rediscovered all the time, not just there but everywhere. All the major galleries and museums. Anyway," she said looking at the painting in front of us, "I still don't get it." It was the most attentive I'd seen her.

Agnes' programme had finished. She was saying something to us.

"Yes, recovered cultural artefacts. And a little propaganda too, to ease the way."

"Oh Jesus Christ," Elizabeth/Joan said. The spark finally died, and she said, "Not this conspiracy stuff again. I'm getting bloody claustro in here; I've got to go anyway, the taxi's been waiting outside for ages. We'll meet tomorrow or something. Agnes, I'm off, thanks for dinner!"

I'd planned on speaking to her about the Dun Residency.

"Evidence for our sublimity, documentation of our monarchic blood. They would kill us all if they knew about this evidence . . ."

I looked at her. Lucid, a little drunk perhaps, but the most lucid person in the vicinity.

Elizabeth/Joan shut the front door behind her. I sat down and spoke with Agnes. She told me about her programme, and about how she had been associated with the British Black Panthers, about her friend Genevieve with whom she was going on holiday and shared a communal purse, and about being told you are a conspiracy theorist half your life. We both fell asleep watching the twenty-four-hour news channel. I woke up and turned it off. Before leaving, I went to look at the cabinet again, at the diary, and, with the same guileless abandon of a white teenager who on first seeing Millais' *Ophelia* fantasises about drowning, I fantasised that I was one of those dancers, perishing of pneumonia.

*

I didn't hear from Elizabeth/Joan the next day, though I didn't expect to. I used The Lodge telephone to call her mobile but couldn't get through, so I tried her at work.

"Hello, St. Clair's Gallery; Helen St. Clair."

"Hello, I was hoping to speak to Elizabeth/Joan."

"What?"

"I said I was hoping to speak to Eliza."

"Who is this?"

"I'm a friend of Eliza's."

"I'm afraid she's on holiday for the month—South of France—try her mobile; sorry but whom am I speaking to? What is your name?"

"Okay, thanks Helen, bye now."

*

Stamped onto tissue paper in black ink

Roberte Horth

(No photograph found)

SPAN: 1916—1932

NOTES: Parisian writer from French Guyana. Studied at the Sorbonne. Early figure of the Négritude movement. The transition to Paris as a Black woman is documented in languorous, acidic prose in her 1931 story *Histoire sans Importance,* published in the second issue of *La Revue du Monde Noir.* Léa, a young Black woman, travels "beyond the seas," to an institute where she develops a "bent for clear and precise logic" and "long and arduous research." She excels "amid the thousands of minds who have come here to seek advancement." Achieving intellectual satisfaction, she then enters society and the world of pleasure where she "shows a taste for dressing." "She is looked at like a beautiful weapon, a cabinet-curiosity to show to the inquisitive." Léa learns that although she is much in demand because of her brilliant mind, wit and style, she will never be fully accepted, never more than a fashionable accessory, because of her "mixed blood."

The story anticipates feminist Négritude writing and influenced the Nardal sisters. Horth was set to become a leading light but died of pneumonia at 26. She was at the time of her death working on an article about contemporary English women writers which would have provided a fascinating glimpse into English Modernism from a contemporary Black feminist perspective.

SENSATION: aerated waters on powdered eyelids

*

As I was printing off the boarding pass on the day of my flight, I checked my inbox anticipating a message from the Dun Residency cancelling everything and requesting their money back. I found instead a reply to one of the several emails I had sent out regarding *Black Modernisms,* which I was still chasing. I'd since been forwarded to the biographer's sister because she might have a copy. She had asked for my address and promised to send it; nothing ever arrived.

But now, here she was emailing me to say that she'd sent the book a few days ago and it should have arrived yesterday. Unfortunately, I'd given her my address at the time, which was of course, The Wreath.

I still had Grace's spare key and decided to make the rather extreme detour before my flight.

Grace wasn't home, or at least no one came to the door when I knocked, so I let myself in. The book was nowhere to be seen. It was only as I began looking for a convenient place to put the key in the hope my return would go unnoticed that I registered the card by the entrance, saying that a delivery had been left with a neighbour.

"Oh-ho!" the neighbour said and went in to get the package, which he had clearly opened. "Is this it? No: 'Mathilda...' Ah yes: 'Adaramola.'"

The palms quivered on the grounds of the complex. The concrete ground was, for the first time, composed of something like baked and compacted moonlight. It was dark and looking up towards Christian & Tom + Eleanor's building I saw yellow light gush through the panoramic windows second from the top. Subpenthouse. There was a silhouette, unmoving, like a stage villain. And then it was joined by another outline and soon there were four figures watching me. Then six. I waved archly, triumphantly, and not inelegantly, issuing an agitated ripple throughout the silhouettes.

**

Hermia
The Black Princess

IV

A coloured girl at the Slade dropped her handkerchief. On purpose I should say—when I picked it up, she had disappeared. I look to see if it was monogrammed and saw that it had embroidered on it, "HRH, The Black Princess."

—A fellow student at the Slade to his mother—1923

At the peak of her notoriety, Hermia Druitt was frequently referred to as "The Black Princess." This appellation may be due to one or more of the following:

I. She was, as has been suggested, the direct descendant of one of the various royal families extant in colonial Nigeria.

II. She was the illegitimate descendant of a minor European royal family.

III. It was a sobriquet given to her by a friend.

IV. She fabricated the title by taking liberty with detail or by pure invention. (With regards to the former, if she were the daughter of a Yoruba Oloye, for example, she may have felt inclined to use the designation of princess by interpreting Oloye as a kind of non-dynastic princedom, even though this would be closer to 'Lord' or even 'Honourable.')

That there is reason to believe it was in the nature of an anti-imperialist like Hermia to adopt a self-styled title, we shall also see later. Regardless, we can think now very easily of the immediate benefits, one such being that she anticipated the reception it would establish in the kind of circles in which she would become immersed. Her social status as a mixed-race woman would have been more than sufficient to force her to resort to such an invention.

Invention or not, Hermia deftly rode the wave of interwar-era romanticism to her advantage. This romanticism can be likened to Victorian Orientalism and most certainly overlaps the Paris based Négrophilie of the time. It permeated, in particular, avant-garde circles and the 'upper-class bohemia.' Foreign, brown-skinned royalty was bound to charm the likes of Nancy Cunard, Edward Burra, Edith Sitwell and Ottoline Morrell. Likewise, many of the Bright Young People were soon to be entranced with this young Black princess, most notably the homosexual aristocrat and aesthete Stephen Tennant. That she was an experimental poet to boot only intrigued them the more.

On the subject of her poetry, the minuscule run of the long work she was to print via Nancy Cunard's Hours Press, under the title *The Fainting Youth*, has proven impossible to recover. Possibly, a volume or two lies in an archive or attic somewhere in Europe, but we are now at a period in history where obscure and lost works from the early modernist period, especially literary works (being on rapidly deteriorating paper), are daily becoming irretrievable. The Hours Press closed in 1931, but Cunard continued to own and visit the physical site in Normandy. It may be that any holograph or proofs of the poem were still being stored there and were destroyed when the village was requisitioned during German occupation. The sole fragment of her poem which survives only does so through peculiar circumstances.

As we know from a letter, Hermia was passionate about Sappho and the prospect of her own work surviving solely in fragment may well have delighted her. It was transcribed by an audience member of the "café recital" she gave, and the annotations may be presumed to be an attempt at recording more unconventional aspects of the poem or alternatively indicate a stylised form of intoning, as was popular amongst other modernist poets.

By all accounts, *The Fainting Youth* was a long, formally innovative work concerned with androgyny and was much influenced by what it would not be too anachronistic to describe as the "queer femme society" in which she often found herself. It appears to feature, like its near-contemporary, *Orlando*, a transfiguration, though this is from woman to man to both to neither. It also supposedly contains what have been called "conventional turns," and "prosaic-ish interludes," in which the poem congeals into novelistic prose for several pages before melting back into poetry.

The existence and subsequent neglect of such a poem to the point of potential irretrievability is unsurprising when the likes of Hope Mirrlees' long poem *Paris*, an influence on *The Wasteland*, only properly came to critical attention in 2006, while Nancy Cunard's *Parallax* has gone largely unacknowledged.

Like Hermia's poetry, there is scant record of her life. Indeed, no definite birth record can be traced, most likely because Hermia Druitt was not her birth name. There is the striking possibility that Hermia was in fact Hestia Drummond, the daughter of a Glasgow solicitor, whose birthdate of 1899 would correspond. Indeed, Hermia's voice, which many struggled to place geographically, was on more than one occasion likened to the Scottish accent. Margot Asquith, having briefly observed the "mulatto daughter of an African dignitary" at her nephew Stephen Tennant's house in Wiltshire, someone who we can only presume is Hermia, is professed to have remarked on her tones as being "reminiscent of one of those purring Edinburgh hoteliers," whilst Brian Howard once commented after returning from a trip to Glasgow, where his lover Edward F. James was a painter at the art school, that it struck him Druitt's voice was similar to "those strains which are in fashion amongst certain cultured ladies of Scotland."

The story of Hestia Drummond, even if unconnected to Hermia, sheds some light, in and of itself, upon certain aspects of her life and more generally the many unspoken-of births resulting from mixed parentage that occurred all through colonial Britain and onwards.

The father, Mr. David Drummond, is known to have returned to Bearsden in 1899 following a prolonged business stint in West Africa, bringing, to his family's horror, his new daughter with him. Her mother is unaccounted for and it is not known if Hestia ever met her in later life.

Following what was a considerable local scandal, Hestia Drummond soon became a familiar and even accepted sight in the genteel outskirts of Glasgow (a city which was to experience the likes of the 1919 race riot) and is mentioned on several occasions in a local clergyman's diary:

[. . .] fears for the young Miss Drummond which had been entirely allayed are all at once alive again. Having just visited my good friend [David Drummond] I am as crestfallen

as he to note certain incontestable qualities in the girl and have encouraged him, once again, that a life devoted [to God] might well yield the best possible earthly future for her. That she is his only child leads me to believe the poor man still possesses hopes of her marrying. This, I anticipate, will be difficult for obvious reasons [...]

If Hestia is indeed Hermia, one might wonder why she would opt for such a similar surname and given name if she wished to conceal her origins. We do know that at some point the young Miss Drummond travelled, against her father's wishes, to study at the Académie Julian school in Paris. Perhaps this is where she was reborn as Hermia Druitt?

If it is important not to overstate the quality of life for Black Parisians at the time, it is certainly true that Hermia would have found in Paris a society unlike anything she had experienced in Britain. Already in the early '20s, a decade before the Négritude movement reached its height, there was a comparatively flourishing, culturally respected, Black artistic community. A Paris where the singer, actress and activist Josephine Baker, having lived through the intense racism prevalent in America, was to become the highest paid performer in Europe.

Here we might also think of the singer Evelyn Dove, a British-born, mixed-race, middle-class woman of West African descent, just like Hermia, and almost an exact

II

[. . .] contemporary. Though now much forgotten, Dove was once
held up as Britain's answer to Josephine Baker and gained world-
wide success. She became not only the first Black woman recorded
by the BBC *but [. . .]*

"Mathilda?"
I was still reading. The bus had apparently termi-
nated and must have been stationary for some time. It had stopped
once already to change driver and I presumed it was doing the same,
but the driver was smoking outside under a street lamp, talking
to a tall ponytailed woman whilst a man was leaning through the
door: "Mathilda? Hi!" I recognised his voice from the phone
interview. I apologised, pulled my luggage from under my seat
and stepped off—manoeuvres which took considerable effort as,
though my flight had been short, I hadn't slept for thirty or so
hours beforehand.

"Welcome to the Dun Residency, Mathilda," said the Man from
the Phone as the driver got back on the bus. The Man from the
Phone had eyes which buzzed as if they were computerised and a

smooth, clean face. "I'm Jonatan, the residency coordinator, and this is Lind, the deputy coordinator." The woman with the ponytail smiled and wished me welcome in an accent that might have been Dutch. Meanwhile, Jonatan stood there as if distracted and then said, "The nomenclature seems to have settled upon 'coordinator' or 'convenor,' but our technical, and preferred title is 'conveyor,' which as you can imagine is much more suitable."

"We're afraid," said Lind the Deputy Conveyor, "your accommodation arrangement was a bit last-minute. As has been the case for the past couple of years, a few late applicants always have to be lodged in private rooms in the town. But it's not far from here," she signalled down the street. Then she said: "No, *really*," as if I had protested.

I could barely see, now we had left the halo of the bus stop. I was overly conscious of how loudly my case rattled on the cobbles and how unpeopled the streets were. Adding to this, the Conveyors fell into silence as we walked, as if waiting for something from me, so I extemporised about how excited I was to be here which I knew would be true if I weren't exhausted.

As my eyes adjusted from the last few hours of synthetic light, I was met by a freakish whirl of exteriors. Pink-ice stucco by night and dull quilted bronze; intimations of baroque towers.

Then I was hauling my case up a shiny wooden staircase, letting it bang on each step. The Conveyors opened a door on the third floor and led me in. They spoke about the flat. I wanted them to go away and felt they were talking for an excessively long time about white goods, like estate agents, as if trying to make up for something, and I became worried that I would end up collapsing in front of them if they went on as they were so obviously prone to. They told me about the nearest shop for food and kept on saying "amenities." They simply would not stop talking: "... and as you know we aren't timetabled until..."..."... and as you know there are various facilities provided at the Residency Centre..." And as I didn't know any of this I wondered if I'd missed an email. They handed me a piece of paper, a printed-out map. "Come to the Residency Centre anytime. Even though we haven't officially started yet, our doors are open. Otherwise we'll leave you to get settled in... As you'll see on the map... Course of it... retorts... And as you'll see... amenities..."

"Mathilda? Okay, we're just leaving, the key is over here."

I had in fact fallen asleep sitting up on the bed. I heard the door shut and fell asleep, mortified that I had fallen asleep.

*

The room was almost entirely tiled with polished blue squares that insinuated marine grottoes and oceanic vaults. I spent a good hour burnishing them on my second day, resuscitating the blueness beneath the dust, imagining I was the royal aquarist of some obscure dynasty, scouring algae.

These tiles were bordered at the top by an elaborate floral scheme and even more elaborate arching cornices. There was also a tiny kitchen and a small bathroom, also tiled, but in green, with a copper-looking bath. The bedroom contained a positively antique coin metre, long out of use, and a writing desk affixed to the window with a plastic white telephone on it. Except for the patinated green crown of a clock tower, any view of the city was obscured by the back of the adjoining tenements which formed a square around some gardens.

It was a veritable pleasure-palace as far as I was concerned. My Escape was complete, with a setting to match, and in that first week I stared and stared at the tiled walls, the ceiling, out the window down into the gardens. Eventually, I realised I was trying to devour it all, upload it, secrete a ghostly imprint onto my subconscious for later use.

Otherwise I read. *Black Modernisms,* a large black tome printed by a university-affiliated micropress of the kind I had once pretended to be writing for, was an expansive and interlacing biographical account of race and the arts in Britain from 1880 to 1939. Hermia Druitt wove in and out alongside various other personas, like the singer Evelyn Dove and the Marxist writer C. L. R. James. Some of these figures Hermia had encountered. For example, in 1913 the Jamaican-born physician and activist Harold Moody moved to Peckham, where he set up his practice as a G.P. He eventually opened his house to all people of colour in London unable to find rooms or somewhere to eat and also founded the League of Coloured People, in effect the first Black activist group in Britain. Dr Moody was a figure of such magnitude and popularity that it was said his name was known by every person of colour in Britain at the time. *Black Modernisms* related how Hermia at some point befriended his brother, Ronald Moody, who, after qualifying from King's as a dentist and being unable to find a post due to his race, retrained as a sculptor. It was whilst researching Ronald Moody that the biographer accidentally came across a Hermia Druitt registered living on the same street in 1931. Visiting England from Dun for a few months, Hermia had apparently been struggling to find accommodation. It was presumed that she must have stayed with the Moodys for a period and through them found temporary lodgings nearby. The biographer had also discovered record of a H. Druitt enrolled on a course in costume design at the nearby Camberwell School of Arts and Crafts and then also a Miss H. Druitt, a painters' model, on the archived account books.

I had discovered, therefore, that the woman in my stolen photograph, which I now kept in the book, had been a minor artistic figure in Europe. Sometimes all I was able to do was lie back with my eyes shut, glutted with this knowledge, nerves intoxicated, and fall asleep.

I would doze at regular intervals.

These sleeps, Transfixion-sleeps, were quite frankly the equivalent of sunlit opiate-baths. Enveloping morphine-soaks in which I dreamt of all my Transfixions. They were the apotheosis of the sensations I experienced.

I was aware from night-time glimpses through the kitchen window—which was behind the fridge so you had to lean and couldn't see much—that the town was exquisite. But I didn't dare even think about setting foot outside. I honestly believed my substance and soundness would be blown apart, atomized by so much beauty all at once.

Come daylight, I slept a more solid, normal sleep and thus, including the Transfixion-dozes, I was getting about sixteen hours a day. I was used to sleeping during the day and had long ago trained myself to get up, part the curtains and take scalding sips of daylight, having once read something macabre about vitamin D deficiency.

Eventually I did leave the flat. This was on my second night. A ravenous, delirious stroll to the shop on my street where I bought bread, cheese and tomatoes—the only perishable foods they had left. I made a special effort to take in my building on the way back: a long gaunt tenement, art nouveau, and a rather fabulous place to live.

Two weeks must have passed in this triumphal haze. It was during those weeks that I became immune to the knocking. The building ferried sound about in a way that could give the impression someone was tapping at the door. This architectural ventriloquism was especially effective in my sleep, when it sounded as if people were pacing the room, naturally Hermia and Stephen. All my Transfixions would visit me in fluttering apparitions.

But on this occasion, I was awake, and I must have, in the back of my mind, registered the knocking, dismissed it as someone rattling about above or below. It was not—

"Hello? Mathilda?"

Silence, then: "Fuck's sake!" The voice was touched by, if not laughter itself, then a suggestion of laughter. Someone had come into the flat and was standing over my bed. An extremely handsome person. A Byronic, rakish sort of person. She glared down at me.

"I was expecting a dead body. They sent me back with the spare key," she said, "since you didn't answer. Wanted someone to check on you . . . Thought you might be sick. You honestly didn't hear me knocking?" I couldn't tell if she was amused, she mostly seemed angry. Disbelief perhaps, at seeing me lying in bed during the day, as if there was nothing more preposterous in all the world. "You'd better come to the induction. It's the final one. Get up."

And then she went out, after which I got up, bolted the door and lay back down for half an hour.

I knew perfectly well that I had woken one day with the realisation that the residency had started. But with that sleight-of-mind particular to such sleep, my brain had managed to conveniently tuck away this knowledge alongside anything else that might interrupt my pleasure.

Unsteadily, I moved myself out of bed, finally roused by the fear that if I didn't attend, I would be asked to leave the residency, would have my stipend cut off, and face a forcible eviction from this flat. I saw myself barricading the doors and throwing ice water from the kitchen window onto potential intruders below, at Lind and Jonatan and the scary young woman who had just come in.

Finally outside, I was so stunned by the force of light that I wandered around lost, trying to read the map, which was really quite simple. Flashes through side streets over-whelmed me; I had to avert my eyes.

The Residency Centre, when I came to it, was in a satisfying deco building. A tall-ish hexagonal structure, smooth and white, with about three floors in one consolidated mass, then three tiered floors on top like a cake, the last capped with a neat slate roof. I could hear shouting from somewhere within. Through the main entrance, a vast hallway encircled the building and directly ahead some double doors led to a large, searingly white studio space.

At the centre of this room was a ring of sullen people.

A yellow sponge ball spun through the air and a feverish looking merman caught it.

"THE FIRST DOCUMENTED GROUP FACILITATION EXERCISE OR 'ICEBREAKER' WAS IN 1929," bellowed the merman, who was really a human with seaweed hair. He fired the ball towards someone in yellow, who boomed,

"HOWEVER, THERE IS REASON TO BELIEVE THE ICE-BREAKER WAS IN USE AS EARLY AS 1905," the ball was hurled and caught again,

"IT WAS NOT UNTIL THE 1950S THAT THE ICEBREAKER BECAME A STANDARDISED PRACTICE IN BUSINESSES AND INSTITUTIONS AS WE WOULD RECOGNISE TODAY."

It went on like this: hurl and boom, pelt and holler. Only twice was there any kind of lag, once when someone dropped the ball and once when someone momentarily forgot the next line. On this occasion the whole group then shouted the line in unison.

"Very good, I think that's enough," said the Conveyor with the Buzzing Eyes, who was standing just outside the ring. "Yes, very good. Now that we are complete—" And from amidst the collage of half-smiles and full-blown scowls that turned my way, I couldn't help but catch eyes with the glowering individual who'd come into my room. She looked disgusted.

"—I think we can begin! Okay, so let's have Jenny D and Max, Deborah and Felix," people paired up, dispersing into a wider circle, "Giuli and Mathilda," at which the Conveyor pointed at me and the merman leant down, picked up a fat, lurid-yellow textbook he must have put down for the ball game, and came over. I was quite lucky in being paired with him, I supposed, because he resembled a type I recognised socially, whilst I could not yet gauge the others.

"This particular exercise is a simple example of those we discussed earlier. Simply exchange your names, where you're from and what you hope to gain from the Residency. Five minutes each and then those of you on the inside of the circle move along clockwise to the next person."

We finished well before our allotted five minutes. His name was Giuliano, he was from Rome and he hoped to gain a wider and deeper understanding of the works of Garreaux, he said, waving his yellow textbook.

I told him that I wanted to "improve my practice" and this was received without suspicion.

He was unreceptive to conversation. He turned out, in fact, to be so dour that I shifted my attention to the rest of our cohort. They did not strike me at all as artists. There was something decidedly business-like about them, and business was a thing which even the most avaricious artist liked to conceal (unless making a point of it). Bankers on their day off, pictorially speaking. But not quite this, no, they were too austere for that.

Most them also wore expensive-looking white or pale blue shirts, like a financier might wear. Top button undone. Their wearing this kind of shirt pissed me off immeasurably. The boys at least, because if they really were artists they were likely pretending their all dressing like this was something other than a kind of hyper-conformity, which would be a lie: every time a white straight man chose to step out in such generic trappings he was upholding—creating—the conditions for every time a visibly queer Queer stepped out and got attacked. Fine, if he was doing something else about it. Fine, even, if he was aware of it. Not fine if he thought it was some kind of capitalist drag. This was not Executive Realness.

And turning reluctantly back to Giuliano, who wore the same kind of shirt, but beneath a grey hoodie and with white trainers instead of formal shoes, I realised my social estimation of him had been entirely mistaken. The hair was misleading. He shared the same decidedly humdrum markers, broadcast the same forbidding greyness as the rest of them. Except it was not really grey, it was white and cubic.

Remembering my original impression, I panicked at the prospect of having landed on some kind of business programme, and looking about I saw something really *was* off with the idea that this was a studio. It was not that the white plaster walls were pristine, as I knew conceptual artists adored working on their computers in spotless studios. It wasn't even the ribbed grey carpet, which was undeniably officey. Maybe then, it was the lighting, which consisted of the kind of in-the-ceiling spotlights found in certain living rooms.

"And you got here when?" the merman was saying as if at last aware of the silence between us.

"Just over a week."

"And you were unwell?" he looked very concerned. "I only ask as you were missing from the last few days' inductions. I'm sorry to hear it."

"On no. I actually just got the days mixed up."

"How do you mean?"

"Well, I suppose I just forgot."

"Did you not write down the day? Make a note of it?"

"No, I'm afraid not," and then feeling scrutinised, "I suppose I was unwell." He fell silent again but I could tell he was about to resume his line of inquiry so elected to change the subject. "How many induction days have there been? It seems a bit excessive—one is gruelling enough, wouldn't you say?"

Before he could reply, the Conveyor announced for us to switch. But there was no need for an answer: the merman was not amused.

My fellow whatevers-in-residence were predominantly from Europe or America, all white, and many with international accents. They were vaguely young, about my own age. Many mentioned Garreaux and also held the same yellow textbook that Giuli had. No one mentioned art so perhaps it simply wasn't anything to do with it. But then, no one mentioned anything else, or, when I thought about it, gave away anything personal. Almost all conversation was kept to the subject of the Residency, or the town or the city. Some spoke about where they came from, negative or positive, but not what they did, except two who mentioned PhDs on the subject of Garreaux. When I ventured asking someone what her practice was, since my having a practice was swallowed unquestioned by everyone, all she said was, "mostly Soundbites, that sort of thing." When I asked what she meant exactly by Soundbites she looked stand-offish, as if I were making fun of her.

Beyond all of this, there was something else I couldn't settle. Familiar waves that broke upon me, that made me think of a certain period around my first Escape. Not really anything in relation to me, but the period itself. They even smelled like that year, I thought.

"Of course," enjoined Theo from Wisconsin, "there's very little to do here, in town, that's relevant. The whole thing should be relocated to the city, but the building was donated to the University years ago for the specific purpose of this residency and the funds are all tied up with that, from what I'm aware." He was very white. Teeth bleached. Hair and brows an accidental dot of ochre mixed into buckets of lead white. So white as to almost seem like an arch remark on my darkness. An affront upon me. But he could not help that. Not right now.

I recognised in Theo the universal spirit of the gossipchatterbox that also inhabited Elizabeth/Joan, but suspected it found a rather unworthy receptacle in him, clearly lacking as he did the carnivorous spark that made Elizabeth/Joan interesting no matter how dull her subject-matter.

Next was a particularly puritanical entity in Easter yellow: "Jenny D; Bath; Siphoning." She did not look at me even as she spoke. "I think we're supposed to stick to the guidelines?" she said when I made to say something beyond my three details. After reigning over an arid silence for the remaining minutes, before everyone switched partners, she looked at me straight in the eyes and I saw the face of a Witchfinder General, looking back at me across the aeons through her face.

"I understand the general principles, I just need to get a solid grounding," said a caustic young man called Hector whose top lip was abbreviated into a perpetual snarl. They were crimson lips that startled the whiteness of the walls as he spoke, and at times looked set to bleed over altogether, flood the room from floor to ceiling. And then his top lip assumed a more pronounced snarl, and then both lips were pursed, as if he were trying to dam them up or, failing that, drown them in themselves; and then he was looking at me blandly. I hadn't been listening to him.

After Hector came my rude awakener—Griselda—whom I had been dreading, and I saw straight away from the expression on her face that I would have to try not to be intimidated by her. I decided not to stick to the guidelines.

"Griselda," she said. "Connecticut via England—I grew up between both which is why I have this accent," for it was, I supposed, transatlantic rather than international. "And obviously, I hope to put into practice the Lesser Concepts of Garreaux," she spoke with something of the same hubris as Hector who had come before her. They both had the same narrow face.

"I'm not familiar with Garreaux," I said, and she grimaced.

"Well of course you're not fucking familiar. Don't think anyone here, at our level, can be said to be 'familiar' with Garreaux. Not even the Conveyors. Lind maybe."

"No, I mean I haven't read *any*. I'm presuming he's a theorist?" And she didn't say anything, she just stared at me. Not the scandalised or patronising looks that a couple of her peers had given over the course of this frankly horrid exercise, but a downright volcanic glare, an unbearable contemplation. She finally looked away— towards Hector. I could not see her face properly as we switched partners, but I thought she was smiling.

"Now that we've completed this exercise and you are considerably more familiar with your colleagues, I'll be giving you the final introductory talk about the programme after lunch, which will be upstairs," said Jonatan the Conveyor half an hour later. We went through double doors on the other side of the studio which led to a flight of stairs.

On the first floor was a hall not dissimilar to the one we had just left, but with tables and chairs and a line of trestle tables with cheese sandwiches, scarlet soup, plastic cups, two coffee urns and caterers standing to attention. There was also a conveyor-belt toaster with a long queue in front of it. People dropped their bread on and took away toast, unbuttered, to their tables.

Once I had selected a sandwich, I found to my horror that I was sitting next to Griselda and Hector. They ignored me, muttering quietly between themselves.

Horrified though I was, I couldn't deny that of all the people here, they were the most interesting. They were simultaneously angular and robust—like a couple of Gothic arches made flesh. The same dimensions used to calculate their limbs and faces. I felt the old pull to infiltrate and remembered I didn't need to. I had already Escaped.

Jonatan the Conveyor was moving around from table to table like a host at a wedding, talking to each group.

"Ah, I'm so glad to see you finally made it, Mathilda," he said. "And I'm so glad to see you've found Griselda and Hector—all three very interesting applications. Mathilda was a late applicant as she may have already informed you—but very interesting." As he wandered off I felt their eyes land on me. At this point Lind the Deputy Conveyor came through the doors and Jonatan joined her at the front. He addressed the room.

People were nodding along vigorously but I didn't understand a word he was saying. Initially, I didn't realise this lack of comprehension. I knew most of the words separately. But as he spoke, I found myself increasingly indignant.

It was the same language I had detected over the course of the day, the same phrasings I had encountered on the website application. But here, at length, it was intolerable. Seeming for moments to make sense—but then came the buzzwords, the catchphrases; he spoke in opposites and odd couplings: the cold and tinny argot of Pyramid Schemes came out his mouth coiled around something borderline Churchy. Then what sounded like Self Help suddenly hardened, grew spikes and became Continental Theory. It could have been any of these as far as I was concerned. I remembered how Malachi had once told me about a fashionable organisation dedicated to reconciling Deleuze and Jesus, and so I toyed with the idea that it was less business retreat and more cult, the residency being not only here, in this town, but another one to come, in the lap of God; the Conveyors here to convey us to the afterlife. As I searched my neighbours for clues, for crucifixes or anything religious, Griselda must have felt my eyes because she was looking at me, and to my horror mouthed, "What?" so that I had to shake my head as if I'd been absentmindedly staring into space, *not* at her and Hector. After a while I looked more discreetly about me and saw nothing truly suspect except perhaps a fleece sported by one of the Conveyors, in a style that might be considered vaguely culty. But no, it was probably not a cult. Furthermore, I was tired; I was delirious, actually, having been disturbed on the verge of sleep that morning. I'd also missed the first few days when something crucial was obviously explained.

"As you will remember from yesterday's induction, Garreaux's attitude, his response as it were (and as it were not), to insolvency in the city is ultimately one of 'Nepotism.' Does anyone remember the precise quote...?"

Here Hector put his hand up.

"'If Nepotism is the sweet insolvency, then why not Incest the brave and noble nouveau-bankruptcy?'"

A few people made sounds of approval at which Hector sneered.

I desperately wanted to go to bed and read about Hermia. Whatever this residency was, I had to be honest with myself, the people were undeniably a medley of the most woebegone drips I had ever encountered, and the prospect of several months with them already had me plotting how I might best keep my stipend and accommodation without having to interact or participate from that moment onwards.

Eventually Lind the Deputy Conveyor began speaking in terms that were partially understandable: she was going to take us on a tour of the town, thus completing induction week. I was excited by this because not only was this town, from all my glimpses, an excruciatingly beautiful place to live, but Hermia Druitt had chosen to live here.

Lind led us downstairs and out onto the streets at what seemed an ever-increasing speed. We were marshalled to a bus stop and told the main times.

"The Dotage levels in this particular area are naturally of little to no use. We expect the large majority of your locus to come from the city proper," Lind said, before power-walking us to a pharmacy then the other residency building, which was primarily for administration, before taking us back towards the bus stop. We were to go off on a "markation" around the "city proper," a project we were permitted to do "in groups or individually."

On the way to the bus stop we cut through a very charming square. Lind paused as we were about to file down a narrow street.

"So remember, the next bus departs in ten minutes, the one after that in an hour if you need to collect anything," she called out, then dived down the passageway.

I was contemplating how I was going to approach doing a project I knew nothing about when some of the group started making a noise that turned out to be laughter. I looked around to see what the source was. At the centre of the square was an obelisk or pillar. Someone was kneeling before this obelisk-thing, looking up to the top of it and wearing a particularly beatific expression.

I quaked. For a moment I thought it was a vision of Hermia Druitt, brown-skinned, berouged cheeks. Perhaps I was even more exhausted, less lucid, than I imagined. This kneeling apparition wore a powdered peruke, something like Louis XIV or a more moderate version of an Antoinette pouf, except this was dark and dusted with a fine pearlescent substance. Thighs were also prominent, a delicacy begot by the tapering costume of whatever era. That it was this person's attire and not fancy-dress was evident in the lack of discernible era: part Renaissance page, part high-priestess, resembling some gentle and glittering courtier from a court that never existed and an epoch that never happened. High-ornament-on-the-move.

Artifice-in-motion.

This person must have heard the laughter because they looked toward our crowd and, with a flash of visible panic, turned on their rococo heels and gently glid away in the opposite direction, down the nearest side street, up some steps and out of sight. I was sure their eyes had fallen on my face momentarily, which, being the only face other than theirs that wasn't white, surely stood out.

This was my first glimpse of Erskine-Lily.

Griselda came up from behind and started asking me something but I didn't hear. She was possibly curious as to why I'd stopped.

"Do you know who that was? Are they also on the residency?" Even as I asked I knew this wasn't possible.

"Not on the residency, no."

Griselda looked at me then started off after the group.

It was that "no" at the end.

We were to meet back in Dun at 6 p.m. to present our "thought markations." I went home to get *Black Modernisms*, stopping at a café for something to eat, and by the time I got to the bus stop there were only a few people waiting, including Theo the Wisconsinite. Griselda and the others must have left straight away. I stood as far apart as possible without it seeming like I was making a point, hoping to eavesdrop, to find out anything more about the residency. Then Hector came around the corner and joined the silent group. He didn't notice me. Or having caught sight of me, feigned ignorance, as I was doing.

The daylight, of which I'd had so little, was now becoming obscene and dabbed a blond wet fog into my eyes. I stood scandalised by such an abundance of light and began to consume a white floss from a paper packet. I had eyed this confection in the café-bar-shop. It was sprinkled with some sort of dried sugared petal, rose perhaps, and nut fragments. Something between candyfloss and nougat. It barely tasted of anything but I could not stop eating it and almost risked venturing off to buy another packet when the bus came.

A pale single-decker conveyed us out of the town and passed through a pallid seizure of suburban leafiness: diffuse green which disintegrated within minutes, then semi-industrial warehouses, then houses, then more insipid green, all of which I'd missed on my night-time inbound journey.

People trickled off the bus ("in groups or individually"). Eventually it was empty, except for Hector, who sat a few seats in front of me, and Theo the Wisconsinite at the front. I was right at the back, and, if either had ever been conscious of my presence, they weren't any longer.

We reached the city centre. I was bound for the west side, whipped up into a state of purpose by that vision of the Hermia-like figure on the street. I'd decided that, since I didn't have a clue about the project we were supposed to do, I would make the most of the journey. The mottled light had left my eyes. I took out the book and found the relevant passage:

[. . .] It would be quite a difficult task for anyone to take stock of the images still extant of Hermia. As noted, she mesmerised many an artist she came into contact with, and if she attended one of the art schools in Paris and later both the Camberwell School of Arts and Crafts and the Slade in London, it seems inevitable she would have sat for other students, particularly if in need of money. As discussed in chapter three, recent scholarship has revealed the population of African and Asian students in interwar London to have been much greater than once believed or even considered, with art establishments a particular site of neglect. In the Slade, for example, students of colour were frequently sought out by peers as models and we find various models of colour from outside the college on the books.

Though almost a century prior, one might also think back to the Victorian model Fanny Eaton, who sat for the Pre-Raphaelites. Lizzie Siddal aside, most other minor Pre-Raphaelite muses have received their unstinting praise, and (much-needed) feminist reappraisal, whilst Eaton has been left on the brink of obscurity. It is only by dint of recent attention that such portraits, labelled by galleries as "Head of a Mulatto Woman," have been identified as portraits of Eaton and relabelled accordingly.

Located in the neighbouring city to the small town of Dun, in which Druitt was to spend the greatest known portion of her life, the National Museum contains a particularly fascinating study by Augustus John which is similarly titled "Portrait of a Mulattress." The sitter is irrefutably Hermia. Whether or not a figure as obscure as Druitt will ever warrant a revision of title by the museum is uncertain, but the portrait is worth a look and occupies the left-hand corner in gallery LXVIII (F) [. . .]

When I looked up, Hector was gone. The bus was wedged in traffic in the city centre. I shut the book. No, he was not gone. He had moved and now was sitting next to the Wisconsinite at the front, speaking quietly to him without looking at his face. The bus pulled out of the traffic. They got off, and then as the bus drove away, the Wisconsinite elbowed Hector and said something. Hector's face changed. He turned around, eyes roving over the departing vehicle, and caught mine through the glass. His face changed again, into a kind of expressionless mask, then they were out of sight.

The bus finally stopped outside the museum. A stolid, huge neoclassical building that, like much of the other architecture in the city, shared little in common with Dun.

The gallery was labyrinthine. I asked at the information desk where room LXVIII (F) was and was given a gallery map and directions. I did not stop to look at the Old Masters, and practically ran through a large exhibition concerning the City Through the Ages. I slowed when I found myself in the LXVIIIs: LXVIII (G), LXVIII (E), LXVIII (F).

I gasped a little bit, involuntarily, upon entering. Then the air audibly went out of my lungs. These aerial utterances were loud enough for a passing gallery attendant, dressed in gallery-attendants'-royal-blue, to look over her shoulder before she left the room and tut. I didn't care. Where the portrait had apparently been, was supposed to be—a humongous pastoral scene of the dullest order. Well-varnished cows wading through a limitless jadeite gruel.

And so I marched out of gallery LXVIII (F), bursting through heavy swing-door after heavy swing-door, back to the main desk to ask them where they had relocated the portrait.

They couldn't recall such a portrait. But there were of course so many. It was one of the largest art collections in Europe after all. I gave them the name and they checked the listed floor plan for me. It was not there. They tried searching the database but it was not there either. Could be the wrong museum? There's another—

I showed them the book.

"Ah ... well this book was probably from a few years or so ago, no? It could have been on loan for an exhibition. Otherwise the painting will probably be in our archives. I'm afraid we don't allow public access to our archives. Although looking now we do have another portrait by Augustus John on display if you'd like to see that."

It was well after five when I got back, and I had no intention of going to the Thought Markation presentation, having no idea what it was.

Instead, I took a tour of Dun, a real tour, also hoping to catch sight of the person whom I had taken for an apparition of Hermia.

There were three towers. One was of blueish granular stone and I walked around it trying to find a way in for a while before continuing down the street. Some of the residents—the actual inhabitants of the town—were out on evening walks. To my surprise, no-one gawked. It was a largely older population. I had expected curiosity in a small, cloistered sort of town like this with few to no tourists, and possibly downright bigotry of the kind I'd encountered in small towns in England. Perhaps it was bigoted, but I received fewer glances than I was accustomed to. Indeed, even in London I was used to at least one or two vicious heckles but had received no such thing here. I thought again of that figure, far more outlandish than I, kneeling before the obelisk. Were they a local after all?

Every so often I would pass a café, of which there were many. Most were small, some so small that they only had standing room.

A few had one or two customers, though that word hardly felt appropriate as I had the impression most of these places were glorified sitting rooms for friends and family. Many were empty and, stopping to look through the glass of one, it may well have been undisturbed for decades, frozen in the '80s. I tried to make out the cover of a dusty magazine.

At this time of day, when the light suspended everything in various coloured gels, certain features of the town protruded more than others. For example, I noted a lot of moss on stone. It practically swelled out. I also noticed how on various buildings, in high-up crevices, wildflowers had rooted themselves. Many of these buildings must have been entirely unoccupied. They would be perfect for squatting, and for some minutes, as I walked around, I entertained a fantasy in which Malachi and Sirhan and all their friends came and stayed here and we lived in ecstatic harmony, which was of course impossible.

But still, I thought, looking around, Hermia had lived here.

Helena Morgan said in *Black Modernisms* that Hermia had most likely first visited in 1926 when the town had enjoyed a very brief period as a fashionable summer resort, popular with various members of the artistic bohemia. The poet Edith Sitwell had stayed somewhere relatively near, in an old castle or villa, and one of her brothers, Sacheverell perhaps, claimed to have 'discovered' the town when he got lost on a drive. Then Aldous Huxley visited. The Bright Young People had come. Virginia and Leonard Woolf had even come. Stephen had come. Hermia. Almost all within the same two summers. Unlike other places on the continent popular amongst these artists, such as Ravello (also visited by Woolf), Dun was practically unheard-of by any of them and thus all the more appealing.

Now I had come, precariously, through Hermia.

Despite, or perhaps because of, my Transfixions I'd always been wary of artistic, biographical pilgrimages. Doomed for anti-climax but also fraudulent to the true lover of any personae. Much like expecting the living descendants of a poet you admire to exhibit a glimmer of the work, reduction to place or anything else material was cheapening, I thought. But I had just that morning read that, in 1909, after Edith Sitwell's grandmother piously incinerated the young poet's cherished *Collected Swinburne*, Edith arose vengefully at dawn, stole out of the house and boarded the paddle steamer from Bournemouth to the Isle of Wight where in the mist she presented a jug of milk, wreath of bay and comb of honey to the poet's tomb. I was immediately converted and it hit me standing there in Hermia's town. My head swam as I met and held the gaze of a malevolent face niched in limestone. It had the most succulent moss-lined eyes. The whole thing was very Merchant and Ivory, and I imagined the scene from a lost reel of an aborted film of Hermia's life: the Black Princess arriving in Dun, 1926, chorus from an Italian opera playing, the shock of white faces as she passes through the town dressed like an 18th-century Macaroni. Her attire is inspired by Julius Soubise, the Black British regency beau, born in 1754 and known as "the fop among fops."

I was hungry and thought about how, as soon as the first stipend payment was through, I would sit in one of these café places, upon which I realised that it must have come through days ago.

After finding the only cash machine in the town, which was artfully built into an ornamental stone wall, bordered by a chiselled grotesque of winged and antlered things, I was soon sitting in a minuscule establishment with chequered black-and-white floors and a curved wooden bar that might have once been part of a cruise liner and took up most of the space. The owner was a woman of about forty through whom the spirit of cynicism lived on—the place was decorated with little plaques saying once cynical now trite things in various languages like, "*I drink to make other people more interesting" (Ernest Hemingway)*. She brought me a menu.

I was inclined to find the notion of a multi-coloured cocktail tacky, but found myself ordering one because I saw something called a *Pousse Café Royale* on the list and happened to know that the *Pousse-café* was a popular drink in the early Twentieth Century, came served in a tulip glass, and consisted of a rainbow of alcohols floating on top of one another and never mixing, including yellow chartreuse and maraschino liqueur, and that, according to Helena Morgan, Hermia Druitt and Stephen had been quite a fan of these, declaring that with each incremental sip (preferably taken through a glass or silver straw), one receives an electric thrill that whisks you closer to paradise. Thus, although the idea of them remained tacky, it was in a glamorous, irresistible sort of way.

But even I was surprised when, at some point after ordering, the lights went out, and a sparkler started up and floated towards me as she brought the cocktail over. I had to sit looking polite in the dark—in case she could see me by the light of the sparkler—until it burnt out and she turned the light back on and promptly occupied herself with cleaning the counter of the bar. All of which, presumably, including the blue sugar gracing the rim of the glass, constituted the *Royale* element. A passing man stopped to see what all the commotion was, sticking his head in to chat with the owner, signalling at me a lot, but I couldn't understand. He may have been asking if I was celebrating my birthday, alone.

I finished my drink so quickly and without thinking that I didn't at all savour it and so when the man left, I ordered another one. The owner looked up at the ceiling in an exaggerated, long-suffering sort of way and I pounced upon this tiniest hint of bonhomie to ask her if she'd ever heard of a Hermia Druitt who had once lived here. When she brought the drink over, without turning the lights off or the sparkler this time, I showed her the photo, at which she shook her head, so I asked her about the obelisk.

"The Needle of St. Christine, in English. The oldest monument in the town. When St. Christine was flying through the air and stitching at the same time, as she liked to do, she dropped her needle, and the pillar rose up. Not the best story, I know," and she rolled her eyes, shaking her head, because she was, after all, cynical.

When I stepped out under the seven-layered enchantment of the *Pousse Café Royale* I decided at once that I too would go and kneel before the Needle of St. Christine, certain that St. Christine was the same Christina the Astonishing whom Ardizzoni had written an opera about.

"Mathilda!"

It was a bark designed to prize me from bewitchment. Griselda was standing in a side street across from me in another café. I wondered if she'd watched me receive my sparkling drink through the window. She didn't come over and seemed to expect me to. I walked as slowly as possible.

"Missed the presentation," she said.

"Yes?"

"You should probably know it's the first White Book Submission tomorrow morning at nine. We're celebrating first hand in."

"What submission?"

"The White Book Submission," she looked through the open doors into the bar for a minute where a couple of other residency members were sitting. She looked back at me and said in a low voice, "What the fuck are you doing here?"

"On the residency?" I asked, stunned.

"On the residency," she said. She was already moving back to her seat inside with the others.

I had to travel all the way to the city again in order to look for a white sketchbook.

I was livid, on returning to the flat some three hours later, that my evening and following morning were to be consumed by an ultimately arbitrary task. I had been looking forward to hurtling back into Hermiadom, and to sleep (which was almost the same thing given my dreams). I was already fatigued, having been so abruptly disturbed that morning by Griselda, just on the point of sleep. Now she had given me reason to prolong my fatigue. I supposed I should have been grateful for her even telling me, but I also didn't get the impression she particularly cared. Possibly, she wanted to see me flustered. In fact, it was this probable ruthlessness that stopped me asking what exactly the White Book Project entailed. I did not believe it prudent to further broadcast my ignorance about the residency: missing inductions and a presentation was one thing, but not actually knowing what any of it was about, applying on a whim and coming because of the money—the knowledge of such facts would most certainly spur any one of that puritanical assemblage into reporting me.

My plan, therefore, was to submit something as ambiguous as possible. I had, after all, made it here that way.

Unfortunately, the large art shop in the city centre didn't have white sketchbooks. They were all black, so I bought one of those, as slender as I thought I would get away with, some white acrylic, and a paintbrush. Spray paint would have been more efficient, but I didn't think of this until I was sitting in my room trying to add a smooth layer of paint. When this dried the black was still visible from beneath so I added a thicker coat and during the process the paint all clumped together on the top right-hand corner but there was nothing I could do.

Eventually, I began writing. Hoping to strike the balance between technical and vague, trying to remember my application and using all terminology I had gleaned: *Markations. Siphoning. Dotage.* Semblance, was it? No, *Semblage.*

> *The Markations gathered and thus inevitably ungathered cannot be engaged in.*
> *The semblance of Semblage is unrelated to the City Proper, thereby generating the asphyxiation (and resuscitation) of the joint sub-liminality of Dotage.*

I tried out Divinity: *Absolution, Anabaptism. Diaphaneity*— was that religious? It would do. Then business jargon. *Bankruptcy, Integers, Insolvency, Stakeholders*, and so on.

After two hours of this gibberish, having only managed to fill a quarter of the book, adrenaline kicked in. I became reckless and started interspersing my text with geometrical shapes and patterns that went on for pages, with little arrows pointing at random to lines, annotated with things like *Insolvency vs. Dotage?* Then, feeling like a veritable daredevil, I went through my case, which I had still not properly unpacked, looking for anything I could use, and found a disposable camera which I had for no reason carried about for a couple of years unused.

It was entirely dark outside and so I had little idea of what I was photographing. The flash only worked for every other photo.

I swayed a little and looked around. The blackness, though black, made scenes of brightness and sunlight burn in my head. I took all thirty-six photos then went back in.

I could not have told you afterwards what any of the latter third of the book contained. But I continued all night, wondering if the whole White Book Project were a cruel prank on Griselda's part. Then I heard the tower bell. I had fallen asleep. There was about an hour before the submission. I ran along the street, remembering the pharmacy. The town was still empty, but it was open. The pharmacist nodded: Yes, of course we develop photos. Express takes half an hour.

I didn't dare go back to my room, though it was so close, because I would fall asleep again. Instead I went to the square to wait, the one where St. Christine's Needle was. I sat with my back to it and read about Hermia until I heard the bell again, then stood in the pharmacy gluing the photos to the book wherever I'd left a space. The photos, as I expected, were too obscure to make out when they were not entirely dark. The pharmacist watched for a moment as I frantically smeared glue and slapped in pictures and daydreamed involuntarily of people wrapped in black fabrics eating translucent red and green fruits beneath clouds like enamel.

★

there would be case for the parure. I never saw it. Then we mustn't forget the doldrums which he so very much liked to induce. 'And to mine the mental solarium.'"

"Enamoured enamel!"

"Gilt guilt."

Earlier in her room—

The sky was all marmalade billows and craquelure cloud. Beyond this, further back: a rink of unregistered silver. It was an old sky, an antique sky, that glowered above Southwark that morning, and the Black Princess looked away from it and down onto the street, at the motion and commotion, the supple and serious navigation of secretary and clerk, until she could not bear this state of spectatorship any longer and reinstated herself at the dressing glass. She picked up the hairbrush. Silver and turquoise. Though it was a large implement it hardly sufficed the coil, kink and whorl of her hair (for it had all three), which she refused to iron when receiving guests indoors. She had plans to keep the handle, remove the head, and add prongs of the kind her Parisian friends had used.

"Negro ladies and gentlemen," she murmured to herself mindlessly. The phrase had this morning achieved a rhythm of its own, a tattoo which she beat out in sopranistic measures, only later realising she could be heard throughout the house: "*Miss Moncreiff's fuuurnished lodgings for negro ladies* and *gent-le-men!*" She had seen the notice in yesterday's paper, quite accidentally, for it was through her connection with Mr Moody the sculptor that she had found the rooms. They were certainly adequate, though she could not help but feel that her first season back in London—for what was it? Three years?—lacked a certain *charisma*. But supposedly nobody spoke about "seasons" anymore and it was certainly better than the old bed-sitting room on Maddox Street where luminous yellow mould carpeted the stairs and purple weeds flowered up through the sink. It was not a boarding house, on this Miss Moncreiff had been very clear. The Scotswoman, "a Moncrieff of the accented but by no means impoverished branch," was a spinster who might have resigned herself to a solitary life but instead had inherited and established her current existence on advice from Mr. Moody's brother Dr Moody. Though in essence charitable, her sisters found the nature of it shameful.

"Negro ladies," and another house for gentle-men across the road. The Black Princess was not certain what sufficed as lady or gentleman in Miss Moncrieff's mind, but she had passed a woman on the stairs who, Miss Moncrieff whispered, was the daughter of an English Duke; illegitimate, of course.

They exchanged the Glint telegraphically on the stairs. The Black Princess wished she had engaged Miss Howard in any kind of talk. She had never lived with another of her own 'combination.' She suspected this fellow lodger was not the daughter of an English Duke, illegitimate or otherwise, and she wanted her to know she would not give her away. She remembered hearing that Miss Howard had found work as a secretary and this made the Black Princess feel unaccountably pleased; she could not say why.

Downstairs presently—

"Enamoured enamel!"

Something of the boreal glitter, the arctic crunch and chime always about her.

And he—so full of rain and pearlescent nimbi. Even when dry: hair dripping! A rake deliquescent.

"It's true, but what was the term—'ultra-wicked'?" she said.

"We think it's so-so, but it will do," he said.

Everything was marvellous in the parlour, or the salon, as Miss Moncrieff called it.

"She could be the Scottish Recamier!"

The St. Clair siblings. Ultra-disgraceful. Charming. Both photographers. He a wicked elf, feet up at the fender. She...

Furthermore, they were acquainted with Adeline and Lester Fox, the painters, whom she had not met. She had designs and they were this: an introduction to the Foxes. Chiefly Mrs. Fox, whose work she admired, though even now the prospect of such an interview issued a whirr throughout the body. She was gravely, unusually, intimidated. The fact was . . . The fact was they might not wish to meet a negro lady.

Upstairs prior—

She put down her hairbrush . . . silver and turquoise . . . no, not the easiest implement to wield!

A knock at the door, then she was being told that Mr and Miss St. Clair were outside. The Black Princess descended.

Downstairs presently—

They were away, the St. Clair siblings, sucked almost by some incalculable force. Up through Westminster Bridge. Then along the river, West! West! Boreas was it? Zephyrus was it?

Upstairs that night—

How the phrases ran through her head: "Enamoured enamel!" Who had said that? "Gilt guilt." What had that been about? It was too often this way with the siblings. The rush of meeting so intense that she forgot the details. Came away sometimes with only an impression.

* * * * *

* * *

*

*

"You see, maybe your being here…"

I sat across from the Conveyor and Deputy Conveyor.

"…is also your not being… *hear*…?" the Conveyor continued, and pointed to his ear, as if all meaning would be revealed by this gesture; all that was cryptic not just with regard to whatever he was going on about, but about Life in general, would fall away.

"Hear your being," said Lind the Conveyor, and they both laughed. I laughed too, almost for a solid minute. I thought I wouldn't be able to stop.

"But no," she continued. "Back to a more serious note, I think what Jonatan said is something you should take into consideration. Do you want to be *here*, Mathilda?"

"Of course," I said.

"Then *please* do remember that the Dun Residency isn't here for your amusement," Jonatan said. "This is not, Mathilda, a pick 'n' mix residency, if you will: you cannot just consume the bits you like and ignore the bits you don't. Nonetheless…"

"We're impressed…" said his second in command. And as she spoke, Jonatan passed his hand over my sketchbook, which was on the table between us. It was a funny movement, as if he were a psychic predicting shapes beneath the cards. As if he were refreshing his memory by holding his hand over the book. Perhaps, if it was a cult, or something else charlatanic, he pretended to have such a gift. Maybe this was how he assessed suitability. The book could have gone entirely unread.

Behind them were piled several white sketchbooks and I couldn't help feel some relief in my decision. The White Book Project was, after all, a project involving a white book. But I also noticed a powdery flake of white paint crack and break off the corner when they placed my book on the table.

"It's lacking, but we're . . . impressed," he continued, turning this last word on his tongue as if he were amused by it, but not quite satisfied with his colleague's usage.

"Yes, extremely lacking," said the Deputy Conveyor, at which I thought I saw Jonatan flinch, as if again finding fault in her choice of words.

"Thank goodness it was just a practice round. This is what we normally expect," he said waving his hand to the floor on his left at the other sketchbooks. "This is a joint project, but we would still usually expect at least around half of this level of documentation." He waved his hand again. "But we are, as Lind says, impressed. The quality was there."

Lind smiled wanly.

"As you did not attend the majority of our inductions, a couple of which included tasters, you will have to select your elective blind, as it were. Though the general subject areas are self-explanatory." They passed me a sheet of paper.

Markating the Mark—Dotage in the City and why we deny it	□
Still Here—Entrepreneurial Bowdowns	□
Heavenly Hermeneutics aka Hosting the Host (A)/(B)	□
Siphoning with Garreaux	□
Praising Correct Health Cultures (physical elements)	□

Avoiding the last, I ticked a box at random and handed it back to them.

"Yes . . . we suspected you might be a Garreauxvian," Lind said, and Jonatan laughed.

*

I only managed to acquire the Garreaux textbook on the morning of the elective. They sold them in the administrative building, where they also, to my annoyance, sold white sketchbooks.

It turned out to be the same yellow book I had noticed people carrying around without ever observing one closely before. The cover was so bright it literally hurt the eyes. A shade of fluoro or neon. I was in retinal hell and wondered what kind of chemical they had used for the coating. The eyes rejected it.

I attempted to read the first paragraph, to no avail. As I suspected, it was impenetrable, the language highly unpleasant. A condensed version of the already opaque residency-speak. I did not like the way my brain passed through a sentence and came out the other side bereft and slightly anaesthetised; as if still numb from an operation, unsure what had been removed. The unpleasantness was all part of it, I imagined. My exposure to theory had been second-hand, through Malachi, but I was familiar enough with the idea of selecting language that was dissonant in order to expose and subvert the dissonance and tyranny of everyday communication systems and so on. But here, I felt something else at play. And this kind of language was clearly *not* unpleasant to many. It was coffee, it was bitters, it was cigars. Consumed like a rarefied commodity.

Seven people were in this seminar, which turned out to be so popular they had to schedule multiples. I barely remembered anyone from induction. The majority of the Residents were interchangeable in both appearance and personality. I did recognise the Merman and the one whose face I was convinced was a tunnel through history to the face of a wicked Inquisitor, and her friend, Max, whose face was the same. There was a palpable excitement as everyone stood outside clasping their book. People even exchanged knowing jokes about the hideous colour of the cover and the datedness of the design, which really didn't seem funny to me. It was too unnerving for irony. Griselda and Hector were there looking more serious than ever. Everyone fell quiet when they passed a comment.

Then came Lind along the corridor like a Prime Minister, and I found myself standing a bit more keenly to make it known to her that I was not only here, but early.

What proceeded was initially no worse than anticipated. At moments I thought I caught the sense of this or that sentence, or at least the sensibility, the tone of something that was said, but then it fell away. Finally, I became so worked up and convinced that everyone was just pretending to understand that when Lind asked—

"And if Bankruptcy is a matter of course, if we invest in the Domains, then we must all begin to unhinge?"

I answered—

"Surely not, Lind?" And everyone turned to look at me.

"I suggest you elaborate Mathilda, please."

"Well, simply that we can take *nothing* as a matter of course."

Everyone kept silent, heads pulling away from me to look back at Lind, baying for blood.

"Well," said Griselda. "There is another convexity in Garreaux that would permit a grounded Bankruptcy."

Lind smiled and nodded. Everyone looked to Griselda and then to me then back to Lind before Hector suddenly launched into a long talk about something else. As he spoke he made reference to pages and people flicked through, opening and closing their books. It was at this point my head began aching because of the covers. They seemed practically to glow. It was the strip lighting in the room. Everyone else flourished under it. Looked radiant. But, finally, the lesson was over.

I fried and ate an oblong of rainbow trout in the hope I would feel better, and I did. Much better. Enough even to try and read some more Garreaux. If I attacked it from another direction, when it was least expected, maybe I would be able to take it in. And something about it had really seemed like it could make sense at one point. Perhaps I was approaching it as more difficult than it was, or just missing one or two key points.

But as I read I noticed how even the pages were a secret shade of yellow and appeared to bleed out the brightness of the cover. The rectangle of text looked off-centre, the margins tapering at an irritating angle but in such a way I could never be sure. I became obsessed with how the font from one letter to the next seemed to ever so subtly change, but on trying to determine any actual difference, I was unable. I snapped it shut, turned off the light, and went to bed.

Even after several minutes it was still looming, leeching the blackness from the corner of my eye. In fact, this was worse; it appeared to glow from across the room. Even with my eyes shut it was now glowing, so I sat back up to look at it and noticed that though it was night, and the room was dark, the book really did manage to catch every bit of light. It was practically radiating; 'glow' was the wrong word. A crooked vibrancy. It pulsed, brightened. Then dimmed, then even brighter. Became rayed, like a plastic star. A hideous, hideous yellow, so unbearable that without thinking I sprang up, threw the window open and hurled it out into the night where it plunged; extinguished. I slammed the window shut again.

Immediately soothed, I went back to bed until I worried the book could have hit someone, at which I rose and stared out through the glass. I could not see the book and risked opening the window again to lean out a little more. It was not visible. I turned away but, just as I did, I became aware of something below. It was a slow sort of movement.

A regal, lunar procession through the gardens.

The person paused and leaned down, picked something up from the basin of the dry, worn fountain at the centre of the gardens. And just as I realised what it was, they gave, almost at the same time as I did, a start. A near indiscernible flinch. They dropped the book as if singed. It fell onto the grass. The figure rose to full height again and then looked up, directly at my window. Or perhaps not. They could have been looking at the stars. For they had now resumed their gentle, their fey, their hypnagogic stroll out of the gardens.

I slept on and off for two days: a passionate, drunken sleep.

Upon waking, I almost didn't dare look. But it was with more relief than anxiety when at about lunchtime I stuck my head out of the window and could not spot the yellow book; and it was with unstinted pleasure half a minute later that I returned to the world of Hermia Druitt.

Almost as soon as I began to read, the sensations started, as if they had been waiting impatiently. I was desperate to look back over a particular section:

[. . .] a family acquaintance wrote to the poet and eccentric Edith Sitwell who was holidaying in the countryside with her brothers, Sacheverell and Osbert. They were not far away from the town in which Hermia had established herself that summer:

> [. . .] and is it true there is some kind of celebrated negress there? And further: is it true they call her a priestess? Or is it a princess? Sounds a lot of bosh. And further again: I hear that the Hon. Stephen Tennant has taken her up as a sort of amusement. I really can't see why you would consort with that boy, if you can call him

*that—Siegfried I'll allow. Then there is news of even more
deranged types than Stephen: Miss [Nancy] Cunard visited the negress? She is the most abominable consorter
with negroes and a great friend of yours is she not? At
least you were not present at that point. Did you not hear
poor Maud's [Maud Emerald Cunard, Nancy's mother]
lament?*

The reply is not accounted for, though we cannot imagine the
ferocious Edith ("a dangerous Bolshevik, terror of the colo-
nels, horror of the golf clubs and causing panic amongst dog
lovers everywhere") taking kindly to such a letter (particularly
one full of inaccuracies—Sitwell was not an especially great
friend of Cunard's nor a particular fan of Tennant).

Edith was hardly lacking in controversy of her own. It is
therefore all the more telling that a distant family associ-
ate would see fit to write regarding a possible association
with Hermia. Sitwell's correspondent is very much invoking
the prospect of social exile by way of the poet, publisher
and activist Nancy Cunard, who was then in a relationship
with the African American musician and co-publisher Henry
Crowder and was consequently disowned, disinherited (she
had been the heiress to the Cunard shipping line fortune),
and ostracised even by members of her mother's set who
were considered socially liberal such as George Moore ("I do
not think I should get on with a black man or a brown man.")
All this, following threats and attempts by Cunard's well-
connected mother to have Crowder arrested and deported.
These attempts failed, but Cunard was investigated by the
British intelligence services for the rest of her life. For Cunard,
shame and embarrassment weren't really on the table (though

abuse and hatred did not go unfelt, leading to more than one breakdown), and this may have also been the case for Sitwell, but it is interesting to see that the mere connection with Hermia might be considered damaging in such a way that those barely acquainted with her may have been routinely forced to reconsider their friendships and proximity. We must also add to this that where men of colour like Mulk Raj Anand and C. L. R. James may well have been friends with the Woolfs and E. M. Forster, a Black woman was another matter, further challenging orthodox social relations. It is almost impossible to imagine, then, how Druitt experienced all this alongside the frequent exoticisation from those that were supposedly close to her. Certainly, the wild swings from feared to celebrated arose from her status as a mixed-race woman of African descent who was schooled in the mores of the middle and upper classes. This was something people didn't quite know how to engage with. Historically speaking, Hermia's experiences challenge perceptions about race in Britain during this period, as do those of other figures in this book such as the opera singer Luranah Aldridge, her sister the popular composer Amanda Aldridge, known as "Montague Ring," and the performer Evelyn Dove.

We also get an impression from this letter, albeit a highly filtered, third-hand impression, of Hermia's early days in Dun, as the town was commonly referred to by Anglophone speakers. Perhaps most curiously we find the designation of "priestess." This may have arisen in confusion. It was whilst in Dun that Hermia and Stephen began an informal society called the "Lote-Os" and it is likely, hearing about this, that the correspondent confused it for the kind of occult society that had been in circulation since the mid-19th-century. The actual purpose of the Lote-Os, however, is unclear. This is probably because it lacked any real focus, being something of a whim on the founders' part. In one letter Tennant cryptically mentions a "society" dedicated to "The Luxuries," and so we can probably assume the short-lived group was in some way for the revival of 1890s aestheticism and its more hedonistic associations. Beyond the personal interests of those concerned, this is further indicated by the name "Lote-Os," which probably refers to the mythical *Lotophagi*, or Lotus Eaters.

Though the group was informal, members may have been wary of broadcasting its interests. Whilst Tennant and Druitt and other "Lote-Os" had exhibited an interest in aestheticism individually, the Wilde trials were still very much in the air, with "decadence" and "aestheticism" effectively operating as bywords for homosexuality. Some of the members may not have been too keen to flaunt their association. Hermia's involvement may have been further cause for [...]

This was contradicted that afternoon on visiting the National Library and typing "Lote-Os" into their search catalogue. I found a reference book with the following entry:

Enochian Order of the Luxuries, also: Order of the Lotus Eaters, The Lote-Os, the New Lotophagi, the Yellow Heralds, LOTE *(est. London/Dun. circa 1926–1928)*: Short-lived society bearing faint superficial similarities to the Hermetic Order of the Golden Dawn (pp. 337–360) which was known for its members, who included literary and artistic figures.

Associated members: Hon. Stephen Tennant, Marchesa Luisa Casti, Richard Bruce Nugent, Nancy Cunard, Arke Drumm.

It was a tiny entry, as I had expected. The book was the humongous two volume *Survey of Mystical and Occult Societies in Europe 1889–1989*, featuring known, unconfirmed and fictional societies.

Arke was Hermia. Had to be. Carrier of a caduceus, winged herald of the gods, Iris was something of a counterpart to Hermes (of which the name Hermia was a derivation). Golden-winged Iris had a twin, Arke, who rebelled and went to serve the Titans. In punishment, Zeus tore off her rainbow wings.

But the thrill of coming across Hermia in this way was for once outstripped. They had *all* been part of this group, my Transfixions. Had all been in the Lote-Os. I was sure of it. Even the ones who had been long dead before the group was founded.

So sated and certain was I that I put it from my mind for the time being: I had also sent for a selection of newspapers on microfiche to be brought up, and to celebrate my discovery I spent the next two hours devouring, through the screen of the viewer, all the old society columns, the gossip and antics of my Transfixions.

*

When I got back to town I realised that the Garreaux seminar would be starting, and the very thought made my eyes burn. I decided to take myself for dinner.

There was an establishment unlike the other cafés. It was on the obelisk square. A sand-coloured rotunda which I'd taken for an old theatre or music hall or possibly a town hall. I ascended the portico steps to the entrance, then descended carpeted stairs to a territory beyond view.

On entering, I saw it was a restaurant, with studded leather booths forming an outer ring around the central dining area, and shadowy stone balconies above them. There was a stage, the curtains drawn open. The painted backdrop showed a purple mountainous terrain.

The restaurant was empty. I sat down at a table in the centre and looked up at the ceiling where there was a small blue glass dome which, it still being bright outside, exerted a therapeutic wizardry over the room. It powdered the lascivious frescoes on the walls and the dilapidated friezework that ran all the way up to the glass.

A man came out through a door and spotted me. I must have looked odd sitting there and half expected him to tell me to get out, but he brought a menu over. I was wearing a grey silk and lace hat with a huge brim projecting out like a planetary ring. I decided instead that he thought I looked spectacular and when he later asked me what I wanted, I told him, "An actress," because I thought he asked me what I did, and it was the sort of hackneyed lie I'd always wanted to dabble in. When he asked again in English, I chose from the menu at random but with theatrical languor.

Consequently, I dined on oysters, chips and Cointreau— a very strange combination, but not at all awful. I sat there amazed, looking about myself at this near-deserted place, wondering how it managed to stay in business. The other establishments in town probably cost nothing to keep afloat, but this was a grander operation. After dinner the man wheeled in a trolley of once-vogueish desserts and I ordered three including something akin to Cherries Jubilee and a creamless but dynamic-looking chocolate gâteau.

The blue light, which had been all powder before, changed, refracted, became the ultra-filtered light in sea caves.

Just as I was thinking how I would love garish sunglasses made out of that terribly fey blue glass (with gold rims, or tortoise shell— no—mother of pearl!), I noticed how one of the faces in the frieze, up there at the base of the glass cupola, looked like Stephen Tennant, and another opposite could have been Hermia Druitt, gazing obliquely upon me where I sat. It was hard to tell down here. Really, it would not be implausible. They could easily have dined here. Perhaps the designer had modelled it on them or perhaps they had designed it themselves. I tried asking the waiter-chef-owner about them, but my grasp of the language was too poor and the Cointreau swam in my brain and mingled with the lingering delirium that had been brought about by a day immersed in my Transfixions.

I was ready, however, to think about the implications of my other discovery. The Lote-Os. Like the existence of these faces, it was actually not remarkable. In and of itself wonderful, but the *process* of discovery entirely run-of-the-mill. It was often whilst researching one of my Transfixions that I came across another. Many of them had crossed paths. So much about them overlapped—queerness, a penchant for excess—that it made perfect sense they were connected in a more formal manner than I'd previously imagined.

I paid and sauntered home, a little dejected at the realisation that I had not alighted on a divine secret.

I was still curious as to what the Lote-Os had specifically been about. A sort of mystical society: but how had they operated? What had they believed, if anything? Either way, I was delighted to know that Hermia had belonged to this group, that she could very well have been its high-priestess.

The town was quiet. During the first couple of weeks of the residency the Residents were to be found sitting and sulking in the cafés, forever clutching their yellow books, ignoring the towers and various architectural follies, ignoring the general splendour. Now if they didn't have a seminar and weren't working in the Residency

Centre, they went to the city, where they felt more at home. The locals were all indoors. I had the place to myself and basked in its empty, gutted air.

I was finally about to turn into the passageway of my building and up the staircase when I saw Griselda walking straight towards me. My first instinct was to duck quickly in, but it would be obvious I had seen her. I was annoyed; she would have something to say about the fact I'd missed today's Garreaux seminar and probably had news of some other absurd and consuming project I had to do.

I saw that she might not have noticed me at all. I couldn't be sure, but she was staring into space, an air of oblivion thick about her. I also realised, as she neared, that she should be at the Garreaux seminar herself. They must have sent her to find me. Or it had been cancelled. Either way I was still disturbed by her last remark, her *"What the fuck are you doing here?"* and I decided to dive into the building, but now she had definitely spotted me.

Her eyes fell over me for a moment on her approach before she said, "Off for a drink?" and continued marching up the street. At least I took it to be a question. The fact is she didn't stop and could have been telling me, in passing, she was off for a drink, or asking me if I was heading off for a drink, not inviting me. Nevertheless, I found myself accompanying her.

She paused for a few seconds to roll a cigarette and as she rolled, I noticed her knuckles were speckled with tiny garnet beads that must have been blood.

She strode as if pacing across a country field; a brisk walk over the moors. Absentmindedly she made a swishing movement with her non-injured hand which put me in mind of someone thrashing back brambles with a walking stick and was hilarious. It was that very first impression: that Romantic poet. Positively Byronic.

Or more like Swinburne, or Chatterton. Or not. More like just an idea of one. Highly disconcerting. Nothing in anything she had ever said or even in her appearance could have propagated such a vision and I was sure she would find the description repugnant. I wasn't sure I didn't myself—but then it didn't quite capture the impression.

We passed through an alley and up some steps into a small courtyard where there was yet another tiny café, with only sitting space on the outside. It was presided over by a woman with red hair who watched a small television that glowed from the back. It looked like the lottery. Griselda ordered two drinks and the woman apparently ignored us, but once we had sat down the last number was announced, and she let out a scream of anger before calling to Griselda to ask what we had ordered.

What the fuck was I doing here?—Had she actually asked me that? There was no way of her knowing for certain that I wasn't here for the same reasons as the other Residents. I wondered if she was going to interrogate me. I thought not. Her manner was different. It put me at ease. Even as we sat there and the distance in her eyes came to a focus—like she was taking me in properly for the first time—there was no animosity.

The proprietor placed our drinks down and started speaking rapidly with Griselda (who I later discovered spoke about seven languages fluently). I couldn't understand any more than when I first arrived. The Residency Centre did not offer language classes.

The two tumblers contained small amounts of transparent red liquid with what appeared to be herbal sediment at the bottom. I tried some: it was appalling. Extremely bitter, but not the bitterness of Campari I had expected. For all its herbal residue it tasted entirely chemical and I had to stop myself from spitting it out.

"A disgusting concoction," I said when the owner went back to her television.

"Don't like it?" Griselda said, distant again. She looked at her phone for a moment, then called for another drink and poured the contents of my glass into her own. The owner came back and deftly dropped a small bottle in front of me with a cordial glass.

I poured some out. It was also red, but more on the pink side. I wondered how long we would have to go through this process of Griselda ordering and my not liking, but in fact it was exquisite.

Griselda looked with mild disdain at the bottle. "They're both made from the same plant. In the heather family. Supposedly you either like one or the other," she paused as if deliberating whether to go on. She took a last puff of her cigarette, stubbed it out, then launched into a history of the two drinks, becoming increasingly animated. Each drink was invented by nuns in the fourteen-hundreds, soon becoming so part of the culture that they had governing spirits ascribed to them, basically translated as The Red Entity and The Pink Entity. Thus, if you liked the red you were said to be an extrovert, money loving and warmongering whereas pink you were said to be an introvert, cold and indecisive, "or something along those lines, I forget positive attributes. Hector says he likes them both but he's lying, he hates both."

She must have registered something in my face because her brow twitched and she said, "Oh, don't worry, nobody likes Hector, he's as conceited and priggish as he looks."

"How do you know him?"

"He's my cousin."

She ordered more drinks and we were soon very drunk. The light was fading rapidly in the courtyard as she told me about growing up in Connecticut with Hector. They had both been extremely antisocial children, their parents antisocial academics, so that when Griselda' parents both moved to take up professorships in England, Griselda had to visit Connecticut, and Hector Sussex, at regular intervals because neither could bear other children.

I mostly asked questions, too wary to add anything to the conversation myself. But it was pleasant sitting there with her. It was not that she was more accommodating in manner or tone. That obdurateness she'd displayed previously, that volcanic filament running through her, was clearly a permanent aspect. It was rather that her extreme hubris was accompanied by a kind of humour. Relief unexpectedly suffused me. Perhaps I'd been bereft of human—living—company after all. The social part of my brain was evidently delighted with these scraps of cordial exchange.

All the way through her talk, the disconcerting impression would revisit me. It would settle upon her like dust and flies: that roguish poet, that country swain; and as if sensing it her eyes would return to hot black coals and she would be her astringent self again, brushing it off, consciously or not.

"You should probably know it's the White Book Submission at the end of the week."

"But we just finished that?" I was unable to keep the alarm out of my voice.

"It's an ongoing project."

I was furious. Another book. At least I knew now where to purchase the sketchbooks, but the mere thought of filling one or more was almost as bad as having to read Garreaux.

"Have you been to the Residency Archive yet?" she was asking, looking at me with that horrible intense stare of hers.

"No, I haven't. In fact, I didn't even know there was one."

She nodded and ordered another Red.

I asked her why she hadn't attended today's seminar.

"But I did," and again that pause: deliberation. "There was an incident," she said, clenching her grazed fist: a bygone gangsterish pose that was as close to silly as I had witnessed anyone behave since arriving. "No, but actually," she went on, "there was a fight."

"During the seminar?"

"Yes. Hector was disputing one of the principles of Garreaux with Giuli. Got quite heated and one of them threw a book at the other, then it kicked off and they were lunging at each other over the desks. A table got knocked over and they weren't going to stop so I gave each a quick smack in the face and they came to their senses and apologised to everyone."

This was all so incredibly impossible to picture, except perhaps Griselda's part in it, that I had to turn away to conceal my amusement, but she caught it.

"Yes, it was quite comical," she continued. "Especially on account of the fact that it was really you that started it."

She was watching me yet again.

"When you spoke at the first seminar. About a grounded Bankruptcy in Garreaux. Well that led, in later seminars, to an ongoing argument. But yes, as I say, quite comical. In the sense that you didn't really know what you were talking about, did you?"

I didn't say anything. Then her voice was menacing, like she'd been that day outside the café.

"*The Residency Archive?*"

It had been a trap. She knew. Why on earth had I joined her here?

"There isn't one? I wouldn't know to be perfectly honest—"

"Of course there's an Archive. That's the whole point. That's the whole fucking point of the Residency. The entire project of Thought Art."

I was quite drunk by now. Even the sky that seeped into the courtyard had an inebriated dynamic—clotted turquoise clasping at silver too vaporous to hold; the light made mackerel scales out of the cobblestones. I was aware that I should probably be engaging in some kind of parry, but I couldn't think of anything.

"Thought Art?"

"You haven't even heard of Thought Art?" Not mock, but genuine incredulity.

"No."

"Jesus, Mathilda," she said.

Despite her moral outrage, and her assurance that she was not about to explain something as basic as Thought Art—a term she despised but was using because she presumed it was the one I was most familiar with—she clearly couldn't resist but explain, in alternate tones of derision and disbelief. I suspected she was enjoying herself.

I did not understand everything she said but kept quiet so as not to further rile her. Her explanation was interrupted with variations of, "You seriously don't know?" and "You must be fucking kidding me?" so frequently I came close to getting up and leaving.

What I gleaned was this: the Dun Residency was, after all, an artists' residency. It was established in the mid-'70s for the practice of a branch of performance art known informally as "Thought Art," which was founded on the principles of the theorist John Garreaux. The term, she stressed, was disliked and viewed as reductive by most practitioners, including her, but was the only available term to explain it to me, if I honestly didn't know anything about it and wasn't just taking the piss.

Thought Art was a movement that viewed the production of art that negated the Self as efficiently negating Capitalism. It held surface similarities with Auto-Destructive Art, but the comparison was a superficial one, she said. For example, in 1966 the Auto-Destructive artist John Latham famously led a group of Central St Martins art students to shred and masticate a library book before puréeing and finally distilling the essence which was returned to the library in a phial upon receiving an overdue notice. The performance serves as a well-known example of destructive art. It was also in 1966 that John Garreaux, who was a young lecturer at the nearby Institute of Art—now formally affiliated with the Dun Residency—convinced almost half an art class prior to their final submission to incinerate their projects in a rented laboratory. The fumes were siphoned into glass phials which were sealed and labelled with the name of each student and submitted for the project; all the students were failed.

"So clearly worlds apart," she said.

"Yes..."

Around a decade later, Thought Art developed into something more specific with the Dun Residency. The Residency ("—don't tell me you don't know *this*—") was in one sense an ongoing collective Thought Art performance piece to which each successive year of Residents contributed. This took the form of the White Book Project. The White Book Project culminated in the production of a work of considerable psychological and intellectual effort guided by the principles of Garreauxvian theory including "Dotage" and "Markation"—ways of engaging with the world as a Thought Artist.

The Conveyors were participants in this ongoing performance. Through the initial White Book Submissions they were the only ones to ever look at the work. This was to make sure the artist was "siphoning" (exerting themselves) as much as possible, otherwise the Negation would not be satisfied, as well as to guide and push the artist in correspondence with Garreaux's Lesser and Greater Principles.

"People have been pulled off the Residency because they simply weren't cutting it."

As work which would never have an audience, the final White Book submission was seen as an almost-perfect negation of the Self. On the day of final submission, each resident was given a time during which they would go to the Archives and place their work on the allotted shelf. This was to avoid passing any of the other Residents on the way. This project was not seen by the Conveyors.

Some Garreauxvians never participated in the Dun Residency, whilst some Dun Residents never fully grappled with the theory beyond the basics—merely practiced it. But around Thought Art and the Residency and Garreaux's theory had crystallised the various tropes, practices and fashions that one might expect with any art movement—though they did not consider themselves an art movement. These were considered Garreaux-lite but generally regarded as more conducive to the project of Thought Art than the alternatives. The anti-aesthetic dimension found in Garreaux's theory structured their relation to cultural pursuits of all kinds, including a dislike of the decorative, of overt form, and which trickled into things like dress. (I couldn't help but notice a slight gesture toward me on the last point.)

"Sounds utterly tedious," I said, now hoping to irk her after enduring this protracted condescension.

"That settles it then." She stood up and paid. I felt the whole courtyard do a revolution. Murky pink clouds swooped below my head. I was upside down then upright and trembling, suddenly aware: I had mindlessly given her everything she needed to report me to the Conveyors. I knew with perfect sense that it was inevitable that I had been brought to Dun only so that I could feel more viciously my return to the drabness that owned me before my first Escape.

"Settles what?" I said when she came back.

"The Residency Archive—you'll come and see it?"

"Why?"

"Surely that doesn't matter to you—you didn't even know what it was half an hour ago."

"Then why would I want to go and see it?"

She looked at me—openly hostile.

"Why do *you* want to go to the Archive?" I said.

It was a look that said she no longer even cared to conceal that she was setting me up. But then the look went away.

"Hector and I have been talking for a long time about the idea that through the very process designed to Negate—the repeated performance of the White Book Submission which is supposed to constitute an ever expanding, self-regulating mass of abnegation— the whole project has become fraudulent. Even though the work doesn't get directly consumed, we're participating in a joint performance, with an awareness that's making the art valuable again— lending it social cachet.

"I've been discussing with Hector the possibility of going into the Archive and looking at some of the submissions. By giving it an audience we would render the whole practice impotent, therefore making it pointless, therefore validating the practice again. A Garreauxvian dialectic. I'm obviously simplifying here. For Hector, of course, this is all speculative. Not something he would actually imagine doing until he's fully immersed in the book, which even the Conveyors aren't. It would require, by Garreauxvian logic, more than one subject for a True Audience. So, do you see, Mathilda?"

Hermia
& Napier

V

The Black Princess is coming!!! I'm quite sure it would be nothing short of negligent if we did not arrange some sort of escapade. Would you like to visit & take our portraits?
—*Stephen Napier Tennant to Cecil Beaton, August 1923*

Although she initially began training in Paris at the Académie Julian, Hermia, on relocating to London in 1923, enrolled, at least for a time, at the Slade. There she was to make one of her most personally significant friendships. It was also arguably one of her most advantageous, ultimately drawing her into the orbit of various social sets, introducing her directly or indirectly to luminaries such as Langston Hughes, Nancy Cunard and Jessie Redmon Fauset; brushing her up against her own literary idol Virginia Woolf. This friend was the homosexual artist, writer and "England's last professional beauty," Stephen Tennant—or Napier, as Hermia always knew him.

As we now know, institutions in Britain at this period were possessed of a far larger demographic of students of colour than has previously been allowed for. Growing focus has been on the Universities of Oxford, Cambridge, Edinburgh and Glasgow, but Art and Design institutes such as the Slade, the Royal Academy of Arts, the Regent Street Polytechnic and the Harrow School of Art were also attended by students from Egypt, India and Nigeria, as documented by school records, self-portraits and class photographs. It is also the case that these art schools were likewise attended, to a greater degree than has been recognised, by British students of colour. Black and mixed-raced British students, for example, cannot as frequently be identified by surname. Many Black Britons have escaped notice because historians have relied on clear references to race in documents as various as legal records, diary entries and business accounts, but we now know that race often goes unmentioned in all these sources. For example, Church annals pertaining to Sydney Black, a priest living in Oxfordshire in the 18th-century, detail his character and mention his wife, his children, his congregation. It was only through further records that we learn he was Black. From the Elizabethan period, all the way up to the 1950s, there are similar cases of the diaspora, indistinguishable on paper from the white Europeans they lived and worked amongst (at almost every level of society), being overlooked.

There is little direct reference to Hermia's time at the

Slade. One account, however, gives an intriguing snapshot. Both Hermia and Stephen make references to "the white bouquet incident" without proper explication. We find the anecdote given in Laurence Whistler's biography of his brother, the artist Rex Whistler, who attended the Slade with Tennant. One day, Rex and Stephen burst into the Life Room, in which they were not allowed (it was then segregated by gender), and "to the delight of the class," presented a bouquet of white roses to a "mulatto lady." This was done with "such winning grace that she too was enchanted." This public spectacle, of two white, socially prominent men, one an aristocrat, effectively declaring their love to a mixed-race woman, was designed to raise eyebrows. The event was obviously staged, with Hermia as arch-collaborator.

Admission to the Slade by the dreaded principal, Henry Tonks, required a high standard of draughtsmanship. Once there, Tonks was a harsh, even vicious taskmaster, prone to humiliating pupils with a runaway remark, or in some cases, diatribe. His insistence on technical rigour famously entailed a purgatory in the Antique Room copying statues to the point of excruciation before being allowed to progress to Life Class, with not all students making it. But it is in the Life Class that we first encounter Hermia. All of which is to say, she must have been exceptionally talented.

In spite of many students of colour passing through its halls, we should not jump to the conclusion that life at the Slade was some kind of proto-multicultural haven. As a Black British woman this simply would not have been the case. Entry to such an institution likely had extra hoops to jump through for Black and brown students, not to speak of the hurdles of London life: finding accommodation, entry into establishments, daily racism on the streets.

But Hermia had already learnt a lot in Paris about white bohemianism and its unsatisfactory, but sometimes useful, reception of 'the other.' She soon became a sought-after model amongst her peers, attended many a London party where she was often referred to as "the mulatto paintress." At the same time, she was struggling to find places to regularly lunch outside the confines of the Slade, as well as proper long-term rooms, having to fall upon the services of International Student House, visited a decade later in 1932 by C. L. R. James. These wild discrepancies in reception could not have been lost on her.

Like James, Hermia was enthusiastically inducted into a version of what has been referred to as "Low Bloomsbury." Accompanied by Stephen, however, life gained an altogether more elevated note. They appeared at galleries together, met world famous artists; Hermia was treated to lavish meals at London hotels, visited his apartment where the walls and ceilings were plastered in silver foil and polar bear rugs lined the floors. Anywhere she went with Stephen she was sure to go by herself the next day—a tactic she was to use for the rest of her life—procuring favour by extension, by association. Sometimes it worked and sometimes it didn't. It is also around this time we see the first reference to her as the Black Princess. Perhaps seeing what a title could do, Hermia wanted to try out one for herself; claw back some of the privileges she was born bereft of. Stephen, on his side, loved being able to speak of "my friend, the mulatto princess." Beyond all this, the two genuinely relished one another's company, with overlapping interests in fashion, art and literature underpinned by their shared queer existences. At the same time, they were conscious of their affiliation and it was not long before they became careful about being seen together too frequently. It was as if each had a sense of how fragile their friendship was, how if gossip went the wrong way it could be socially disastrous for them both. After the Slade they tended to conduct their friendship primarily abroad, almost like an illicit romance, with Hermia appearing at the beginning or end of Stephen's holidays, or Stephen stealing away to nearby towns and villages to meet Hermia.

The peak of their friendship, as we shall see in the succeeding chapter, was not until a few summers later when they worked on an opera together in Dun. If it was the peak, it was also the end of an era. After Stephen left Dun, and Hermia stayed on to live there, they inexplicably drifted apart.

The Residency Centre was open on a twenty-four-hour basis so that Residents had constant access to the studio and computer room. In the vibrating plaster-whiteness our intoxication became lewd; we could hear our breathing as we went upstairs, passed through the lunchroom, then upstairs again, two or possibly three more flights until we pushed through some double doors and were met by a white large wall, less than a metre away, which ran the length of this part of the building. I almost walked into it. We must have been in one of the upper tiers. It was so bright that it seemed an integral faculty of vision had been displaced or ripped out.

There was a metal door in the wall, like a fire escape except it had a keyhole, no "Push bar to open." It was locked but Griselda had the keys.

The heavy door shut behind us. For a moment, vaporous jellyfish careered through the dark, the afterglow of all that white. There was a double-click as Griselda tugged a light string and the room illuminated. White again. But red also. Apart from this colour scheme, it was no different to many '70s-built libraries. The rows of metal shelves were painted red. They were compacted together in groups, with spoked wheels on the side to part them. They could slide along metal tramtrack-like rails on the floor. Several of the rows we could see were empty—but as we went further, on either side were shelves containing identical white bound sketchbooks which must have numbered at least a thousand.

Griselda looked as if she'd just exhumed a tomb; I supposed she had. We wandered down until we came to a narrow passageway which led to a smaller room, also full of identical stacks. When we reached the back of this room Griselda spun the handle to release one of the long shelves from its cohort, making an aisle between them. I watched as she passed down the newly made corridor, examining the ripple of blank white spines. When I followed, I noticed she was actually looking at the labels under each row. Each one had a year, and we stopped at 1976.

"The first batch of submissions," she said.

I noted, on drawing one out, that the books were only finely dusted. They were more like an extremely pale yellow than white.

"Put that back down." A low cruel voice carried along the row.

"What?"

"Did you fucking hear me? Put it back," Griselda said, so I did, but by the time I had she was marching out through to the main room.

When I made it back through the passage, the lights in the main archive were off so that the doorway had a paradisiacal glow. Abundant white light.

I half-expected she was going to slam the door shut and get the Conveyors. Or leave me locked in there.

It was dark when we stepped out of the Residency Centre after returning the key in silence.

"What happened?"

"I was lying," she said.

"About?"

"About my theory. Not that we haven't discussed it before, but I wouldn't look at a submission any more than Hector, or anyone else on the Residency."

It really was incredibly dark in the town. I wanted to leap into it and away from Griselda. She had entrapped me again.

"I thought I'd catch you out. But you *really* don't know a thing. I didn't think you'd go anywhere near the Archive. Certainly didn't think you'd try to look at a submission."

"What?"

"Right," she said curtly. "I suppose that wouldn't even make sense to you. To put it simply—even more simply—"

"Oh shut up," I said.

"—I honestly thought you were feigning ignorance, pretending not to know anything about the Residency or Garreaux or the White Book Submission. It was Hector's idea actually—that it was a pretence to render your final submission a truer Negation. The knowledge that your peers believe you to be ignorant in all things Garreaux subtracts any social value from the work."

"And you tried to sabotage me?"

"Well, as I said it was Hector's idea that you were feigning ignorance to successfully conduct your project. I believed you were only trying to make us think you were. So you'd gain the tacit validation. Oh that happens all the time believe me, everyone's always trying to hint that their submission is grandiose or somehow a greater carrying out of the Principles, but this particularly pissed me off. To be perfectly honest, I'm still not completely sure you aren't still at it. You're still here on the Residency after the first submission—genuinely committed people have been kicked out sooner. And you didn't actually look at the book. I'm not sure how you got onto the Residency but if the Conveyors knew, you'd be straight off the programme."

"I imagine, in the process, they'd discover you broke into the Archive, wouldn't they?"

She smiled, malevolently. Then her face became expressionless—reminding me of Hector's that day, glimpsed from the bus.

"Goodnight, Mathilda," she said, and after a few steps was invisible.

I also smiled malevolently walking home. It must have been two in the morning.

I read about Hermia until it was light. As soon as it was open, I went to the administrative centre, bought one of the regulation white sketchbooks and returned to my room.

I slept for several hours and when I woke it was the same time we had left the Archives last night.

I walked to the Residency Centre, found the same keys in Jonatan's office which Griselda had stolen and ascended to the Archive.

I located the shelf we had previously come to and took out one of the sketchbooks, replacing it with my own empty one. Before I left, I wound the handle, sliding the bookshelf back to its previous position, something we'd forgotten about last night.

III

Griselda asked me to meet at hers.

"Oh, we both fucking loathe it," Hector looked up briefly at the cornices. "I mean—" and he made a dismissive, agitated movement at the room before returning to his book, which was of course the heinous yellow book, only occasionally shifting his frown to the laptop to look something up. Whenever he did this the screen made his grey eyes—the tint of office foyer glass—disintegrate and glitter. He never once looked at you, or at objects, only occasionally pointed these eyes in the general direction of person or thing. They appeared to perceive nothing, except when reading. Looking, for him, was almost an undesirable function.

The bulk of the Residents were accommodated in a tenement near the Residency Centre. It was similar but, in my opinion, inferior to my own half-empty building. Griselda and Hector had not been lodged in the Residency accommodation either. They'd requested a shared apartment since they would be working jointly. Joint submissions were rare, because in so many ways they contradicted the terms of the White Book Project, but in certain cases where the combined output would be a greater self-abnegation than two separate submissions, allowances were made. They'd had to make a case in their application as to why their joint project would be superior to individual submissions and explaining how they were not serving as one another's audience.

Griselda and Hector had been put in an old grey stone edifice located north of the town and about as far out as you could get, though this meant not very far. It was a large flat on the top floor with an actual turret, and like my building seemed to be mostly devoid of other occupants.

The pair had done their best to make it as spartan as possible. For example, various lamps about the place were missing shades, and I once discovered, on looking for the toilet, a cupboard full of glass lampshades that had been hidden away alongside some brocade curtains, a lacquered occasional table and a large item of furniture, dismembered and in pieces—the constituent limbs and base of a four-poster bed (or so I realised on looking into Griselda's room and seeing a camp bed).

There was a Gothic Revival staircase that led up to a small wooden gallery from where it was possible to look through the turret window. On the end of the banister was a ragged tea towel. I pulled it off to reveal an ornately carved finial. The tea towel looked as if it had been thrown there casually and forgotten about, but I knew immediately it had been put there on purpose, because such elements of interior artifice were especially repulsive to them. This placing of the tea towel was reminiscent of shrouds placed over mirrors during wakes. It was also reminiscent of that person hacking the phallus off the monument on Wilde's grave. But neither Griselda nor Hector could have been accused of prudery. Priggish, in relation to their work and the Residency, but not prudish. They sometimes exercised a kind of lewd and brutal way of talking, though generally in form more than content.

"Henry James reads like lacerated dick," Hector said when I picked *The Bostonians* off the floor and started reading it.

When I responded that this didn't make sense he laughed churlishly—the only time I'd ever seen him laugh.

He proceeded to make it clear that the book belonged to neither of them and had come with the flat. Having never read any James before they had deigned to sample it for the first time this morning. This was why it was on the floor.

I wanted to ask him if Thought Artists were supposed to read novels at all, but I wasn't sure how much Griselda had informed him about my ignorance.

Scrolls of toffee lay in a pile on the bathroom floor in front of a mirror. On closer examination, they were hair clippings. Hector had recently had a haircut.

His appearance overflowed, it seemed, to his annoyance. Effloresced uncontrollably. Just as measures had been taken with the apartment, so too had he employed measures against his form. He had cropped and buzzed away his ornamental head of curls, and I suspected he had even trimmed his lashes since I'd last seen him. But what could he do about those lips, that permanent and scarlet stain? It was evident all the Residents were trying to pare themselves into a state of scraped (traditionally) masc flatness and stay that way, to ward off Beauty and Romance and all attendant horrors. (Beauty and Romance, not beauty and romance: so many of them were symmetrical of face and fucking one another. Even from afar the incestuous intricacies of Residency relations terrified me.)

Sensing all this, I sat down with a rococo flourish. I started speaking about gauche, unResidency-ish things. I spoke about

Beauty. He frowned and began to fidget. I pretended not to notice his irritation:

"... don't you think it very beautiful? Don't you think it just *really* monumentally beautiful, Hector!" Whatever I was talking about by this point, his discomfort was palpable. He was about, I thought, to snap back with an abrasive retort when Griselda came in. She had been at a meeting with Lind and Jonatan.

"So you're awake then?"

"I've been waiting here for half an hour," I said.

"Yes, I said twelve because I knew you'd be late,"

"Well, I wasn't."

"If you've only been waiting half an hour you were twenty minutes later than I said to come, weren't you?"

"Hector and I have been talking about the joys of Beauty and the miracle of Henry James," I said.

This turned his knuckles to snowdrops.

A week after my visit to the Residency Archive with Griselda, the phone rang. I almost screamed because it had not gone off once and I'd forgotten its existence. Even when the Conveyors had been apparently worried enough to send Griselda around with the spare key that morning, they hadn't telephoned. Who could have my number? *I* didn't have my number. I was filled with trepidation that it might be bailiffs, or whatever they were: the vengeful knights of *Indictus* tracking me down across countries. Or most heinous of all—one of the Escaped-from.

I picked it up.

Griselda.

"How did you get this number?"

"What? Oh easy—all the places round here are still fitted with landlines and the numbers are listed by address."

She was phoning, she said, to invite me to an art opening.

I had been in a state of anxiety since the night of our odd escapade. Her discovery about me had been a source of constant disquiet—I was sure she was going to report me to the Conveyors; it was only a matter of how they would mete out justice. Visions came to me of Lind and Jonatan bursting into my room aided by Residents and armed with batons. Was I guilty, legally, of fraud by taking money from them after my fabricated application?

Much fuelling this state was the fact that I had stolen an Archive submission and passed it off as my own. After handing the book into the submissions office, I'd had to spend the day inebriated to evade the first waves of dread. Even my Transfixions did not completely keep this unease at bay. Either Griselda would report me, or the Conveyors would realise what my submission was of their own accord.

But instead, here she was phoning and inviting me to an exhibition. We went the same evening to a viewing at the National Art Institute.

I was surprised, on entering, because I recognised the work. I adored the work. It was by an English artist called Anton Amo (self-named after the 18th-century Ghanaian-born Nzema philosopher based in Germany after being unofficially 'adopted' by a prince) whose paintings Malachi had introduced me to. He primarily worked in oils on a grand scale. Huge portraits with intricately depicted interiors or landscapes. The paints were see-through by virtue of a new gel medium he had invented; transparent swathes built up in portions of impasto. The surfaces could be up to half a foot thick so that passages of sapphire could be glimpsed loitering behind inches of opal white. Spotlights were arranged around the paintings—Amo was adamant they were paintings and not installations or sculpture—so that the entire surface of each was lit up. At close quarters they resembled interlinking varnish accretions, and from a distance, quartz formations. These large paintings bordered on the holographic, and from the correct position, each revealed a delicate portrait. A matter of perspective but not technically anamorphic. Brass discs on the Institute floor designated the ideal viewpoint.

It was their accomplishment as portraits, however, which made them so impressive. The realisation of the figures, and the rendering of the background landscape or interior, somehow managed to unify the flurry of techniques; justified the grandness by making it grander. The subject matter would often be historical, sometimes contemporary; the sitters were usually always Black: Pushkin's great-grandfather strutting down a velvet avenue of Peterhof Palace, Eartha Kitt reading James Baldwin in a palazzo garden in Capri, James Baldwin walking just outside his cabin in Switzerland, Isadora Sway, the English disco singer, at a rally of the British Black Panthers.

Amo became infamous two years ago after responding to a critic's review of his first solo show. The critic had said the work was just technical grandstanding, all form and no substance, finally concluding that whilst Amo showed talent, the exhibition confirmed that painting has been, if not actually dead, then at Death's door for some decades and unable to generate anything really worthwhile—"It's no wonder the more interesting content of this artist's work seems to writhe away from being painting. Unfortunately, he insists on being a painter with a painter's redundant painterly qualms. This ultimately shows in all his work. Perhaps the artist might turn his talents to another field?"

Amo responded with an article entitled, *White People Shouldn't Paint (or Write Novels, or Study Ancient Greek).* The title sparked outrage and Amo was pulled from a group show at a Paris institute.

The premise of his article had been that countless white art critics and artists in the West have pronounced the death of painting, or some other variation thereof. In doing so, they deem it unworthy of exhibition. Such pronouncements, made after the luxury of several centuries' unhampered access to the form, wilfully ignore the fact that many have simply not had this access. Until the Black diaspora, amongst various other groups, has come close to that length of commodious interaction with the form (he could not speak, he said, for those beyond the West and the Global North, who have been engaging for millennia with painting and whose work has been ignored, destroyed or demoted), then perhaps these pronouncements should be rephrased from "painting is dead," to "white people shouldn't paint." This did not mean eliminating the medium from personal pursuits. The article admitted in the final paragraph to hoping to aggravate, to challenge assertions. It was clear that it was not really a true call for the end of white people making art. The argument could be reapplied to fiction, literary studies, classical studies and so on. Indeed, anything that has been claimed dead before *others* have been able to glut themselves upon it, and in doing so, provide new insights.

After being dropped, I hadn't heard a thing about Amo. This was possibly his first exhibition since.

Hector was at the Institute, as were others from the Residency: the Merman, the Wisconsinite.

All of them indignant. I saw that Max and Jenny D, in full inquisitor mode, had literally cornered the artist and were grilling him with relish.

The rest resigned themselves to muttering complaints about the work. Not in relation to the Anton Amo controversy, which they did not seem to be aware of, but because, apart from finding all forms of exhibition execrable and, as I overheard Hector say, ultimately a participation in a "prolonged act of barbarism," painting for Thought Artists as a medium was particularly high up on the scale of barbarity due to its "ripe opticality" and "ophthalmic-enshrining core."

As a matter of self-preservation I had long ago learnt to sneak my tastes into social circles. By tastes I do not mean my Transfixions, which were something else, but rather fashions, books, artists. Within reason. It was usually just a matter of showing them casually at the right angle: a subtle hand mirror snuck out to contravene the floodlight, glancing and diverting a few beams in the necessary direction, as per the group's strain of taste.

As I stood looking up at these paintings which I loved, and which loved me, I became overwhelmed by the prospect of convincing Griselda it was really she and the Residents who were vulgar and who had missed out something that meant that even by their own standards of judgement, the painting of Amo was glorious.

I waited for Griselda to give her peremptory disapproval like all the other Residents. She did.

"Sounds a little uninformed," I said afterwards. She perked up immediately. Ready for war, but clearly fascinated by the idea that she might be uninformed about anything.

I told her about the history of Anton Amo. About his unfair treatment.

"Oh," she said.

She looked blankly at a painting titled *Sylvester on Stage at the Vienna State Opera, Dressed as the Egyptian Goddess Hathor, Singing an Aria.*

"I don't really buy that kind of positioning—and not from the usual standpoint of not buying it," she said.

Thought Art, I soon discovered, also frowned on art that sought to express *identity*, believing it served the Self in seductive ways that appeared to do more than merely serve the Self. That it was an especially insidious form of art because some of it appeared to be aligned with some of the more basic fundamentals of Thought Art.

I wasn't quite sure how this—identity as beguilement—was different from other 'positionings,' but she assured me it was.

"And besides," she said looking at the nearest painting, the same kind of anti-gaze as Hector on her face (it undid me, seeing these paintings being *unlooked* at), "you don't mean to say you truthfully like it . . . stylistically speaking? If I went in for that sort of thing— painting, visual and material culture, I would most certainly not like *this sort of thing*. And if I weren't speaking from a Garreauxvian standpoint, I would also argue that the artist is upholding the white western traditions he's supposedly challenging."

She went to say hello to someone.

Though I did not care in theory what any of them liked, I exited the Institute mortified. The keen humiliation of childhood—of someone saying, when you're in the middle of eating something and passionately enjoying it, that it's disgusting. The unique sense of tragedy and desolation when peers—however much I loathed them, they were at that point my only social peers—en masse, lambast a beloved object on the grounds of taste. I left feeling for the first time in some years that I had been deemed provincial.

But the following day I had another call from Griselda inviting me to a different art opening. I went. Here the work really was awful. Annoyingly, in Griselda's eyes, it was better than Amo, but still barbaric. We agreed that it was terrible, argued why, but this time there was no sting.

The same night we went to a performance. It was Digital-Pastoral Month on level three of the National Art Institute and an art-duo clanged giant cymbals and gave ponderous, booming monologues which made me jump every time they began. A goat hopped about in a pen; the dissonance of its hooves against the concrete converted my teeth to metal.

This show we evidently agreed about: unable to smother our laughter, we were shushed and had to leave.

Over the course of a fortnight I joined the Residency gatherings. Mostly exhibitions and openings, but also sometimes the cafés in the city, which made up the backdrop to social life on the Residency. (As such, the Residents constituted a sort of unglamorous café society for the new millennium.)

It was all taking on a solidity, particularly because I now knew that it really was an artists' residency. I even attended a Garreaux seminar believing my newfound knowledge would prove enlightening. It did not, but gone was that vicious edge that had caused me such distress before. The textbooks no longer threatened me. Just difficult, not sinister. I could no longer trace that initial source of pain, beyond the difficulty, separate from it, that had put me off.

"Why do you go to so many exhibitions if you detest them so much? Aren't you supporting the whole format of the exhibition?"

"We're artists of a kind; we are expected to observe other artists. The notion that going or not going to exhibitions makes any change to anything would be no different to labouring under the delusion of ethical consumption being effective anti-capitalism.

"And besides, we're not necessarily opposed to bitching and gossip you know."

I was glad to hear it, but their so-called gossip was grim and lifeless, merely an extension of their technical conversation. I craved Elizabeth/Joan's afternoon tidbits about people I didn't know. The fact remained, most of the Residents made for agonizing company. I did not care for any of it. Almost all conversations led to Garreaux. The atmosphere they cultivated was oppressive.

I did enjoy the occasional evening at the lottery bar with Griselda where we sipped Pink and Red and argued so much we may well have been possessed by the antipodal spirits. Sometimes Hector was there and sometimes he was not. I wasn't sure how much she had informed him about my presence here. I had the impression they needed someone else there, the pair of them. Why I had been chosen I did not know. Possibly my distance from Residency life.

The two could speak about Garreaux with relentless vigour. I rarely listened, slipping unnoticed into thoughts about Hermia and my Transfixions, which I could keep up with a languor to match their vigour. When they did not speak about Garreaux, they spoke furtively about others on the residency, ranking them. I couldn't imagine where I sat upon this scale.

Something I had suspected about the pair from my first day amongst the Residents appeared now to be true. It was why I had marked them out then as being more appealing than all the others even if they had both irked me more—Hector with his dry monotony, Griselda and her astringent condescension—they exerted a kind of pull. The magnetism of the elite. I discovered myself to be irredeemably basic—drawn to status even now I didn't need it. Now that I had Escaped already.

It was quite possible their new association with me helped maintain their rank—I was almost totally detached from the social interplay of the others, did not figure into Residency politics, and so in choosing me nothing was upset. The allegiance was clean and free of unexpected requirements. And the choice, I thought, also cast dust in the eyes of everyone else. Confused them immensely.

I suspected Griselda was still wary that I was duping them all, at work at some kind of meta-project which would dislodge her and Hector from their grey sovereignty. But only at times, because it was clear that, when she was not suspicious, she was fascinated. On each occasion I failed to know or understand an aspect of Thought Art, this fascination, mingled with horror, dilated. It was not just my knowledge of things, but my actions. Without even thinking, I shocked and appalled. I saw that now she realised I did not dress as part of some elaborate stunt to throw them off, my choosing to do so for *style* was cause for amazement. All my tastes were a kind of daily revelation. My choice of cigarette, café, restaurant, gallery, ordering of food and alcohol might well have been designed as a personal assault on the dictums of Thought Art.

On my part, I'd never encountered a person so wholly dedicated to anything as Griselda was to Thought Art. The conviction captivated me—this was not at all like my Transfixions, but an interest borne of something completely opposite.

Today, after we finished arguing about my being late, we set out for yet another exhibition. Hector was coming too.

We took the bus into the city centre and then an overground train, getting off a stop before the airport, where we took a shuttle bus to a hotel. The journey seemed circuitous to me. Griselda and Hector spoke enthusiastically all the way there about transport systems. I could not tell if this was a personal interest of theirs or a tedious Residency equivalent of psychogeography—Markation perhaps.

Only business people got off the shuttle bus with us. We walked the rest of the way to a large motorway-side hotel. Upscale in the world of such hotels. The tallest glass building. We were the only people not in suits.

The three of us followed a crowd of business people into a large conference room with blue upholstered conference chairs and a large projector screen. "Masterclass Series" appeared in English, followed by "Foreign Exchange Trading" and "Social Media."

When the room was full, the doors shut. A man got on stage and introduced another man to the stage. The second man took to the stage and everyone applauded then went quiet.

Griselda and Hector took out note pads.

After the man stopped talking, everyone applauded again. Griselda and Hector rushed to the front to speak to the man and then we left.

By the time we were on the shuttle bus back to the station, I had a very disturbing thought that was undoubtedly bred out of the atmosphere of shuttle buses, innovation strategies and horrible blue chairs. It was about the way they had sat there, assiduously taking notes on tips for a successful morning business routine, looking up with expressions that were uncritical, unironic, totally absorbed, like they were having a moment at the symphony. No one else from the Residency had been there.

On the shuttle bus back to the city centre, they read through pamphlets in silence. At one point Hector passed Griselda a pamphlet and pointed to something on the page. They both smiled cruelly. When the bus stopped, Hector left the pamphlet on his chair and I picked it up as they got off. I hadn't been able to see what he had pointed out but had noticed something green on the page from the corner of my eye. I walked behind them towards the next station flicking through the pages. There was only one containing anything green. It was the last page. A green page, but otherwise totally blank.

On the train back to the city centre I began to suspect that they were testing me, or making fun of me, and, annoyed, resolved never to speak to them again.

I fell asleep and awoke to Griselda shaking my shoulder. I drowsily followed them to a café. Griselda ordered something boring and Hector ordered nothing. They began talking Garreaux again. It was an endurance test even listening to Residency discussion, but I espied downright masochism in Griselda and Hector's relentless cerebral grinding. An innate puritanical streak.

But my ability to fade out of these talks had become a pleasure in itself—I would call up reveries about Hermia and Stephen or simply go over the facts of their life, as Griselda and Hector jabbed at the air and jabbered away, like people behind glass. People on a television in another room. The knowledge that I could slip out like this was exhilarating. Here I was experiencing almost the full range of sensation as when I was alone. It was teleportation. I currently liked to revisit a particular passage of *Black Modernisms*. One I now knew by memory.

It concerned Hermia's visit to New York, where she stayed with friends of Richard Bruce Nugent in Harlem. The friends were the celebrated actress Edna Thomas and Edna's girlfriend Olivia Wyndam, who, as it happened was Stephen Tennant's cousin. Although they were already fond of one another, Richard and Hermia's friendship was consolidated by the trip:

> *Black, decadent, queer, Hermia had much in common with Richard Bruce Nugent. The two shared a taste for the lavish and profane. She must have been at ease with Nugent in a way that she could never be with white friends and the verbal bombs they could drop, unwittingly or not, at any minute. Here was someone that knew exactly what it was like to have to hustle and had . . .*

But I soon had the distinct sense of being called forth. Of being dragged out of my glazed state by something urgent.

"I think it's only ostensibly about Bankruptcy. That it relays other messages."

"A pivot?"

"Yes, but not in the usual sense. I'm really not sure of the possible valances here, of the bit in Greek: lamda omicron tau eta. Is it to be read as a single word or an acronym?"

. . . Nugent showed Hermia his Harlem. Though in some senses an outsider, Hermia found for the first time she could move through a crowd without notice, except for her attire, but at any rate, Harlem had its fair share of idiosyncratic dressers . . .

"If we look at where he uses Cyrillic or other alphabets it tends not to be so equivocal and almost always acronymic. So here it would be L.O.T.E. if transliterated rather than translated."

"Yes of course, that's what I was originally saying, but I'm not sure."

. . . but Nancy Cunard was having trouble in Harlem, once again hounded by the white press who had gotten wind of the English reportage of her relationship with Crowder and were additionally scandalised by the fact she was staying in a Black-owned hotel. Footage of her appeared on newsreels in cinemas and Nancy soon had to leave New York.

Before she left, Cunard visited a hair salon and came up against her own privilege on finding the hairdressers initially confused and not without reservations about having a white woman in their establishment. Meanwhile, Hermia, for the first time, found herself spoilt for choice when it came to getting her hair . . .

We were in the city in a large 'café' full of chrome and computers. Though still unreal, still behind glass, the place shocked me after my Transfixion and I snapped at them, quite vehemently,

"What were you just talking about?"

And they looked genuinely surprised, as if they really thought I'd been following their every word.

"Just now, what were you saying?"

They both stared and then repeated their dilemma.

"We were discussing the section on Dotage denominations," Hector said, pointing to the book on the table before us.

I snatched it to look, thinking I was now totally immune to its venomous hue, but I felt a little sick on touching its bible-thin paper and seeing its font. I must have been staring vacantly at it for a while because Griselda' finger appeared before me and was pointing to the section.

> *Dotage is invariably denominated by the despots and tyrants,*
> *ΛOTE is the peak syn and counteracts the project. Glaxo*
> *Kline . . .*

"LOTE?" I said.

"Yes," she said.

"Or L.O.T.E.," said Hector.

"What does LOTE have to do with any of this?"

They both shared a glance at my derisive "any of this" as I dropped the book back on the table.

"Well? What is it saying? Why is he talking about LOTE?"

"It's not 'saying' anything," Hector said. "But it's discussing LOTE, or L.O.T.E. in relation to Dotage." And then his voice strained itself into politeness, ". . . And you are familiar with LOTE as a concept? Do you think you might be able to posit another valency?"

"I know what it is, yes."

Hector looked at Griselda.

"I thought—"

"She doesn't," Griselda said, still watching me.

The magic glass caved in, something whooshed through. I was not scared exactly, but there was a definite cunningness in the way they both watched me, clearly taking pains not to make eye contact with one another. They were waiting; mercenary.

"It's a society which existed between the wars, also called 'the Lote-Os,'" I said.

They both frowned sceptically.

"Lote refers to the lotus fruit of the Lotophagi."

"Where did you get this information from?" Griselda said.

"I'm not sure," I said. I did not want to tell them about Hermia or my other Transfixions. And it struck me that something mentioned in Garreaux couldn't possibly be the same thing.

"Well, I think she's right you know," Hector said. "We did work out that the only root here must come from the same as lotus. There's also the rarer verb, 'loting,' meaning to conceal. But the unlikeliness of either of these led me to think it was an acronym and only an acronym. Still don't see how it can fit, but if it's a group or society I reckon she's right. Can't be anything else. Anyway, doesn't actually matter: Garreaux's hermeneutics shouldn't be rooted in that way; it was just out of curiosity we wanted to know," he was standing up. "I'm off, see you later."

But he paused and turned to face us again, shook my hand.

"Presumably it's something you've come across in your research," Griselda said as soon as he was gone. I was used to her glowering now. "Is it something you came across in *Black Modernisms*?"

No, I was not used to it, could never be used to being taken off guard like this, the experience which was generally delivered with this look.

"I noticed the book you've been carrying everywhere and I've seen you in the National Library several times, and when I first saw your room—papers everywhere—it was obvious you were researching something. Actually, it was because I was sure you were researching something that I believed you were working on a White Book Submission. Hector is right when he says it doesn't matter about the immediate meaning, but I have to admit that this is the first time I've not parsed the surface connotation of one of Garreaux's sentences after a few days effort and would like to know why he's chosen to use LOTE as his reference point here. Wouldn't you?"

"No, to be perfectly honest."

"But you would like to find out more about this society?"

"Yes."

"And is that the sort of thing that interests you then, generally speaking?"

The glower had returned.

Our new allegiance had the other Residents interested. Everyone deferred to Griselda and Hector and thus I was no longer an unknown entity, or I was—but one that was now deemed safe to befriend.

I was enjoying my *Pousse Café Royale* and salt crackers when the Cynic shouted, "Maniac!"

Not at me, I realised, but a cyclist who had gone past at considerable speed, making a sort of drably hued blur over the cobblestones which could only designate one thing: a Resident.

The Cynic went quiet. The cyclist had turned back and was now resting her bicycle against the glass and striding into the café.

"Mathilda!" she said, smiling in a way that for a Resident must have been unusual. "I saw you and thought I'd say hello."

I didn't really recognise her. I would have met her during the induction—was it Deborah perhaps? Sarah-Anne? Claire? To prevent myself mentally baptizing her "Sarah-Anne/Deborah/Claire" forever, I said I'd forgotten her name.

"Oh," she said, looking affronted. It was this affront that reminded me of the induction exercise; the person I'd asked what Soundbites were.

"Deborah?" I said. She smiled again.

"I'm just going to Eric's party. You should come?"

"I don't know him."

"Yes you do. Induction. Doesn't matter anyway. You have to come!"

I wanted to refuse, but since she had first sighted me staring absently out the window sipping a rainbow cocktail and eating crackers it was difficult to tell her I was in a rush without offending. As it happened, I really was in a rush. I was going to meet Griselda at the National Library and had missed my bus. I'd decided to sit in the café for forty-five minutes, which was pushing it. I couldn't be bothered to explain all of this to Deborah. And I had probably now missed the bus again anyway.

"Oh, don't you have a bike?" she asked, looking truly perplexed. I knew about this bike fixation amongst some of the Residents. Griselda, for example, rarely took the bus and cycled all two or three hours it must have taken to reach the city. So did many of the others. This would have been admirable, except that when they were not discussing the usual things, they liked to speak at great length about bikes, a subject which I found perhaps almost as dull as the Lesser Concepts of Garreaux.

"No."

"Oh well, I can walk with you," she said. "I suppose it would be difficult to cycle in those, and with that on your head."

"I wear these things to emphasise my newfound hatred of bikes," I said, but she had stepped out of the shop and the swinging door shut, cutting me off.

It was my first time inside the Residents' accommodation building. We took a lift to the top floor and entered the flat. I was not surprised to find that on the inside it had been gutted, with high ceilings blocked-in where there would have been fabulous moulding. Just how they liked it.

A kind of party was in motion; yellow books scattered about, but no one was reading. They were drinking Red. And some kind of music was playing. A high-pitched sonar sound and lots of feedback with an occasional muffled chime, all of which was the background to sporadic storm noises and, most prominent of all, pan-pipe music of the kind they might put on in a spa.

"Oh Mathilda," said a tall red-haired boy I didn't really remember.

"You'll remember Eric from induction. This is his flat," Deborah said triumphantly, and I realised she was quite delighted at having lured me here.

"One of our study parties," Eric said.

The place looked quite familiar—it reminded me of Christian & Tom + Eleanor's pale cocoon in miniature. There were similarly no chairs here, but some people sat on the floor.

"How've you been finding the Residency? You're friends with Griselda and Hector aren't you?" said Eric.

"I suppose."

"Difficult?"

"Eric!" Deborah said.

"We call them the Gruesome Twosome—oh, out of respect more than anything,"

"They are gruesome more than anything," I said, and everyone laughed excitedly.

"Gruesome in a good way of course," Deborah said. "We don't

have anything but respect for their dedication to the Principles and to the Project."

"How did you fall in with them?"

"Oh," I said. "I've been taking them through Garreaux. Some of the Greater Principles."

"Oh right," said Eric. "Wow." Everyone in the room's eyes changed like they had unexpectedly unearthed a deity.

"Actually I'm meeting Griselda at the library now."

I understood then what was wrong with everyone. One of the things. It was obvious: they were mentally, spiritually, emotionally trapped in 2007. *Lol*

A hammering at the door.

I thought I felt the whole room shudder. I certainly flinched. I was in a rattling blue enamel cigarette tin, a trembling lapis-panelled coach, an antique oval etui.

For a moment, in the confusion upon waking up to this banging, I mixed a little too much of my soul with the wall tiles. I partook of them too much, like greedily gulping down what you think is water before experiencing the sudden whoosh and kick of spirits. I was tile-drunk.

The hammering persisted.

She had become something of a terror already. Griselda the Tyrannical. That initial invasion—when she let herself into my room—prefigured our entire relationship. Even though I now kept the door bolted.

I would often wake to her banging away. Sometimes I would already be awake, mesmerised by the tiles or my Transfixions, or trying to invent my own improved version of the *Pousse Café Royale*, when I would hear her crashing up the staircase. I would be overcome with dread and exasperation, as was the case now.

"Mathilda? Get the fuck up!"

I finally let her in, simply to stop the banging.

"Jesus Christ," she said when I returned to my bed. "I came round this morning too you know—what's so funny about that?"

I'd realised that someone had, after all, been knocking on my door at six in the morning. The image of her standing there, so earnestly believing I might be awake and willing to go out of doors at that hour—it was just too extravagantly optimistic; I couldn't keep the laughter down.

"I've already been to the library; only came back to make sure you were up."

She stood at my window impatiently, looking down onto the gardens, then at her phone. She had scanned hundreds of pages of the Garreaux book and uploaded them.

I pretended to have a bath and went to sleep for twenty more minutes in the copper tub. I awoke then actually ran a bath and spent another period swivelling my head so that the tiles glinted against the water. The tiles were dark in the bathroom, which was windowless, and had only two bronze grilles near the ceiling which sucked away the steam.

"We're going to miss the next bus you fucking malingerer," she called through, and I almost drowned in the bath, having ducked my head under the water to laugh again—this time at her choice of word.

"The library doesn't shut until late on Thursdays; I don't see what the hurry is," I said on resurfacing. But I got ready, anxious of the fact she'd been in my room alone for such a long time. Had she just been standing there, a sentinel by the window, scowling at her phone the whole time? Or had she rifled through the reams of pictures and notes regarding my Transfixions then jumped back when she heard me getting out of the bath? *Black Modernisms* lay just near her on the window desk, Hermia's photo tucked inside.

"Were you really asleep all day?" she asked as we left.

My sleeping pattern horrified her. Corollary to this horror, I suspected, was a plan. She was trying to impose a regime on me. There was something regimental, militaristic about her own sleeping habits; a few hours per night. She thought anything more was wildly excessive and a probable affectation, at least in me, when actually it couldn't be helped. I simply basked in the immutable. I basked in the fact of the matter. (The matter being non-sleep-wake-twenty-four-hour-disorder with possible hypersomnia, and separately, Transfixion-sleeps.)

"I didn't get to sleep until morning."

"Well why didn't you just stay up?"

"Because I was exhausted."

She shook her head as if I were being facetious.

LOL "A lack of sleep leads to fascism, you know, Griselda." I decided it would be a good time to expound my theory: the sort of people who claim to require a few hours a night frequently happen to be morally bankrupt. This did not include people who couldn't get a decent number of hours' sleep because of insomnia, work or children and so on, but rather people who *claim* not to need it and thus exhibit their own productiveness. These people included various right-wing politicians, dictators and numerous CEOs, regularly dubbed "The Sleepless Elite" by business magazines. Implicit in their claim is that everyone in the world ought to relinquish sleep if they want to escape hardship. That you are being indulgent. Perhaps their own lack of sleep causes this way of seeing: they are seriously sleep-deprived without realising they are, and after this long-term deprivation, their capacity for empathy has dwindled.

I was still tile-drunk as I reeled this off and Griselda looked at me alarmed. Not quite sure if I was joking or not. I was joking *and* being serious.

She snapped:

"Don't be stupid. Luxury, which includes excessive bedrest, has only ever been the preserve of the upper-classes."

I stopped to buy myself two packets of the white floss which I was now addicted to and she watched with further amazement as I consumed it. Like too much sleep, this white floss was unthinkable, the kind of thing she would never even notice in a shop, let alone purchase.

Sometimes I observed her make an effort to conceal her disapproval. She sat through my favourite restaurants in silent horror or winced as I stopped to look at a building or veer into a courtyard or let slip an apparently baroque opinion. Generally however, her condemnation was unrestrained.

We had been going almost daily to the Library for the past week. I became aware during those early meetings that my sleep was only part of her regime, that this whole project was merely a way of getting me to read Garreaux. I could not help but feel that she was trying to steer the research towards that direction, to produce evidence that the LOTE which I was interested in was not, in fact, anything to do with the ΛOTE Garreaux mentioned, whilst at the same time keeping my attention on the yellow book.

She was trying, I suspected, to proselytise me.

At our days in the library, Griselda's main focus was why Garreaux would have been interested in an occult society like LOTE at all. The connection had of course occurred to me: Hermia Druitt had lived in Dun; the Lote-Os had been based there; and Dun was where the residency which Garreaux founded was. But I instinctively did not want to relay too much to Griselda about my Transfixions. I expected her to come across things herself. After each day of research, I waited to hear her mention the name Hermia Druitt, but she never did.

Yesterday she had made progress, however, and I consequently learnt something from her I didn't already know. Up until then there had been, for me, a discrepancy: the author of *Black Modernisms* had speculated LOTE was an artistic society dedicated to the passions of fin-de-siècle aestheticism (hence they had derived their name from the mythical lotus-eaters) and had consequently dismissed the possibility of its being esoteric. The *Compendium* I had viewed, however, listed it as just that—an occult group. It was quite possible that Helena Morgan had after all seen the *Compendium* and come to the conclusion that this was an error based on the same letter to Edith Sitwell that had mentioned Hermia as a high priestess, or some other mistaken variant.

Griselda's information resolved this ostensible contradiction: it was both. A society dedicated to the precepts of aestheticism— Beauty worship and idleness—but also fundamentally mystical in purpose. Indeed, its esotericism centred around those same aesthetic aspects. It was not merely called LOTE because the Lotus Eaters evoked fin-de-siècle culture, but because its members quite literally sought to reconstruct, to revive the supposed mystical practices of the actual people the Lotus Eater myth was based upon. Their reconstruction may well have been made up but so were the precepts of nearly every other occult group. (The Hermetic Order of the Golden Dawn, to which LOTE had been superficially compared, claimed to be derived from Ancient Egyptian Hermeticism by way of a Germanic mystical lineage authenticated by the mysterious Anna Sprengel of whom historians could find no evidence.)

Griselda was put onto this by a book of selected miscellaneous letters from the period pertaining to subcultures in the interwar years. I saw, when she brought the book to my desk that night, that the letter in question had been from Nancy Cunard to Richard

Bruce Nugent. Two of my Transfixions. I could barely breathe. Nugent had apparently mentioned the mystical content of Nancy's 1923 poem *Sublunary*. The letter was her response, which referenced their joint interest in the occult and the Lotophagi. It laid out their potential ideological underpinnings: the Lotophagi could serve as a manifesto, "but let us contemplate their ancient ceremonial practices too. The four of us." She finished the letter with some lines from the end of her *Sublunary*:

> *Then from this company of questioners*
> *That had adventured into wizardry*
> *And sat around the stealthy science of truth,*
> *Arose four friends and fled the haunted dew,*
> *Descending silent to the dawn-white valley.*

She was clearly framing Richard, Stephen, Hermia and herself as those 'four friends.' The first four members of the Lote-Os.

Griselda had managed to identify Nancy and Richard as potential members without any prompting. Possibly by now she had come across all the others. Stephen Tennant, Luisa Casati, Hermia Druitt. Surely she had come across their names in the *Compendium*. The prospect of hearing the names of any of my Transfixions on her lips left me in constant terror. It would give her power to demote them, like she had done with Amo's painting that night.

I devoured the last packet of floss on the empty bus.

As we slid out of town towards the city, she said, not for the first time,

"I just can't see why Garreaux would have cause to reference such a group." I thought I heard mockery in her voice and could only assume it was directed at me, since I was the one interested in "such a group."

"Yes," I said, "it's strange—I couldn't countenance him writing about anything interesting."

"You do realise," she said, and I could see she was annoyed now, "what is wrong with this society? A society quite literally dedicated to the worship of beauty."

"No."

"Or with making a cult out of passivity?"

"What's wrong with passivity, Griselda?"

"Don't think I'm not aware of the whole 'radical passivity is the new active' queer rhetoric, all very well but, inertia—passivity—is destroying the world. I mean maybe you're interested in this group for more critical reasons but—"

"No."

"Then I repeat: you don't see what's wrong with them?"

"No."

"Well, you of all people should."

To this I had no response.

I knew she meant one thing—that I was Black.

Black and thus I, more than so many others, more than her, should understand the problem with Beauty. With all assertions of the beautiful, but especially European ones which undermined my existence. Undermined the notion of me as beautiful. Framed art made by people that looked like me, throughout history, as something below art.

And she was right. She, unbearably, reminded me of Malachi— of an idea that had ruffled a part of me I was never quite able to smooth.

Freaks, marginal and queer, they may have been, but many of my Transfixions were of the same class and race, especially to begin with. God knows how some would have reacted had they met me.

Since I came across most of these figures in books and photographs, it was, I told myself, an inevitability that the first Transfixions I discovered would cluster around similar social and economic nodes: not everyone could afford to get photographs taken. Conversely, history had buried many other potential Transfixions. I would still pass a building, and a particular curve in the stone would send me reeling with sensations and it could only be because the anonymous mason was a Transfixion, their life otherwise entirely unrecorded.

There was also the fact that I had craved a particular kind of excess when I became conscious of my Transfixions at fourteen. My fascination with Stephen Tennant, an aristocrat, was not lost on me. But he had allowed me to embody a queer fantasy not immediately accessible. And it had taken some oaring out of, but I was starting to find Transfixions beyond the pale of recherché white queers.

One day Malachi printed out a bell hooks essay for me thinking it of interest. It was. Too much so. I understood it to say Black queer and trans people, namely those depicted in *Paris Is Burning*, worshiped at the throne of whiteness—the high fashion, the hyper-femininity: it was all about assimilating Beauty under Europatriarchy. The truth in it, unbearable in itself, seemed also to apply to my Transfixions, my relation to them, and plunged me into a depression. When I finally told him what had caused this despair, horrified at having had this effect and seeking to soothe, he argued that between the 'assimilation' and the fantasy there was another space which was not about championing the thing that speaks against you—though that can be a literally fatal trap—but instead about showing your ability to embody the fantasy regardless, in spite of, *to spite*, and in doing so extrapolate the elegance, the fantasy, Romance, or whatever it was, abstract it and show it as a universal material, to be added to the toolbox. "Look! Look: it does not belong to them. Maybe we should not want it because they have weaponised it, but it was not theirs in the first place."

"Black people consuming and creating beauty of a certain kind is still one of the most transgressive things that can happen in the West, where virtually all consumption is orchestrated through universal atrocity."

I should have let go of the fantasy, like Malachi had, and located pleasure in less troublesome, more unambiguously radical sources. But I was unable to abandon my Transfixions. Now Griselda had poked that most tender of areas.

I sat seething. Knotted and livid.

Only towards the end of our journey, too late to respond, did two of my Transfixions visit me. Two who had held attention of late. Richard Bruce Nugent, who wrote even more floridly than all those queer white Englishmen whose domain florid beauty was generally thought to be. And Hermia, of course—the consummate Beauty Worshiper, whose work, by all reports, was the most alarmingly florid of them all. These were no mere assimilators. Their love of Beauty, in that High Camp sense of the word, had not diluted their Blackness. It arose, monadically, from the same place.

It was the surest I'd felt about anything since arriving in Dun. Even still, I didn't dare argue in case Griselda dismantled me again. Something—I did not know quite what then—was at stake. It was why I had concealed my Transfixions from her in the first place.

At the library I felt better.

As much as I dreaded Griselda banging on my door, and found her condescension unbearable, by the time I was looking up my figures I felt quite glad of her. I could never have gathered the energy to make these daily study trips, was only usually capable of sporadic bursts.

And when Griselda actually turned her attentions upon LOTE she proved a phenomenal bloodhound, far better than I would ever have been, coming across books I'd never heard of and had to pretend only to have a passing interest in, noting them down with suppressed excitement in case they mentioned Hermia.

I was in half-ecstasy that night in my grey felt booth reading about Richard Bruce Nugent, hoping to see if I could find any other mention of his having visited Dun or being involved with occult societies.

I learnt that Nugent had, for a joke, gone one day to audition for a musical and got the part, subsequently travelling throughout Europe, attending a glittering round of parties. He went to a party at E. M. Forster's country house. Forster was a friend of Stephen Tennant's and it could have been there Nugent first met Tennant or Hermia. But Nancy Cunard, who'd visited Harlem and published various other Black American writers, was the most obvious link.

I read about Nugent's participation in the early ballroom scene. Hermia had been to Harlem and the prospect of her attending one of these (according to contemporary press) "perverted social affairs" a.k.a. "Ye Fairies Ball" made the room fizz black as I read. I was rubicund and faceted. I emitted a pink sunburst. I was a living bronze five-pointed star. A little tarnished though, I thought at intervals, not knowing then what was happening. It was an hour before closing time when Griselda tapped my shoulder and signalled to go. This was unusual as she always insisted on staying until the end.

"Let's go for dinner."

It was dark. I chose a restaurant I knew she would hate, partly because as soon as we were outside I remembered my resentment, and partly because I knew I could get away with it—she was distracted. That same distant look, as when I'd witnessed her coming along the street in Dun and we'd gone for a drink.

Perhaps it was just the memory of that evening, but the Old Poet had surfaced again.

"Well," she said when we were sitting down. "That was at least moderately insightful. Found very little with regards to LOTE directly, but something possibly related. I decided to look for minor belief systems, metaphysical organisations *etcetera* that have been recorded as having anything to do with the Lotus Eaters. There's actually eff all in the way of that specifically—a couple of druggy New Age websites—but I also found two references to a text called *The Book of the Luxuries*. It's a sort of treatise on philosophy and natural philosophy with some alchemical stuff thrown in, as you find with Renaissance works, you know—Agrippa and Mirandola. The whole thing's online. What was interesting is that this book mentions the Lotophagi and posits them as an ideal society. Sounds like what Nancy Cunard and—what was he called?"

"Richard Bruce Nugent."

"—were talking about in the letter. The occult stuff is mostly what you would expect—John Dee-esque—Enochian magic—angels in other words. All the typical kind of drivel occultists were interested in reviving in the late-19th and early-twentieth centuries. LOTE—if Richard and Nancy were actually part of it—was possibly a revival of this earlier thing, an attempt at reconstructing it. What's also interesting..." her eye caught something behind me, seemed to be focusing slowly on it—possibly a chandelier, or, no, I saw in the mirror that it was the mural—a motif of kelp and sea anemones that was almost (but not) too *Art Nouveau* even for me. She frowned.

"What's interesting...?" I prompted, genuinely wanting nothing more than to hear what she'd learnt, to keep her talking before she noticed our setting, which I was enjoying too much.

"...Most of these medieval Grimoires and textbooks which engage in Enochian magic are based on traditional angelic lore, even the made-up bits—they have certain commonalities. Usually there are nine ranks or 'choirs' of angel divided into three spheres—Seraphim, Cherubim, Thrones; Dominions, Virtues, Powers; Principalities, Archangels and Angels. Or ten in the earlier Judaic hierarchy. But this book entirely hinges on a classification of angels, not designated in other sources, called the Luxuries, which it claims were left out of the system—like Lilith—but were derived from pre-Abrahamic myth. It cites 'the Aethiopian scholars' a lot. Aethiopian could mean North Africa, but it could also mean anyone from Africa with dark skin. The text seems to want to justify itself by aligning its occult practices with Christianity, like much Medieval magic, but then totally fucks that up by saying angels come from earlier religions; the winged messenger deities: Iris, Hermes and 'the old Aetheopian spirits'—which is quite true, there's also the Assyrian Genius, the Persian Peri—but it's pretty heretical. Anyway, I had to make this all out myself. No one's actually properly translated the book because of the fact there are thousands of these huge manuscripts out there—alchemical and magical etc. It's written in a mixture of Greek and, unusually, Ge'ez. This was from the Manley Parker Hall collection, which has at least been digitised, otherwise I would have missed it. Oh, and it's illuminated. Lots of decorative winged figures—all Black, which I thought was unusual, but it's apparently not unheard of. Like the *Aurora Consurgens*, a more well-known alchemical treatise in the same collection which features an illumination of an angel who is unambiguously of African descent. But in this book, they are all like that. I wonder if the depiction of all Luxuries as Black was relevant to the system in any way or just a decorative thing."

I saw she was profoundly engrossed. So was I: the photo of Hermia, bewinged at a party. But also, something else snagged delectably at the far banks of my memory.

"Anyway, that's all pretty much irrelevant," she said, now more self-conscious. "What's useful for us is that LOTE is also referenced as the Enochian Order of the Luxuries and Garreaux also mentions the Luxuries twice. It's just presumed he's talking about capitalist decadence, and he most certainly is, but he's clearly also doing some kind of doubling as he always does. With multiple other meanings. He's working his knowledge of the history of the town into it. It's a kind of Markation."

And we were back to Garreaux. The spell had dissipated.

She now looked around and, I thought, made a show of distaste at our location, but her heart wasn't really in it. Perhaps it had not dissipated. I thought very strongly that despite everything—our arguments, her constant steering toward Garreaux, her condemnation of LOTE, her monkish-soldierish taste—she was actually fascinated by LOTE, in this thing which was so opposed to everything she believed in, not simply because of its connection to Garreaux, though that helped, but that she was just drawn to it. It appealed to her. She was the one being proselytised.

To prolong this mood, and baptise it, I ordered more white wine, which tasted like holy water and river stones, and we became monumentally drunk.

We spoke for the first time of our visit to the Archive.

The next day, I felt impervious, I felt benevolent. Therefore, I attended a Garreaux seminar.

Griselda did not look shocked at my voluntary presence, but I thought she must be, unless she found it impossible to accept that everyone wasn't truly like her in the end; that my interests, after all the affectation had been scraped away, would be in line with her own.

Her lightness yesterday night, her interest in LOTE, had felt like a concession, and I wanted to reward that with a concession of my own, but as I sat down and the seminar commenced I realised it was not a concession on my part because I felt none of the previous aversions; I had wanted to come and now that I was here I did not hate it.

Today Lind was talking about the multiplicity of slants in Garreaux's writing. Several of his words harboured multiple valences, including his own specialised usage of any given word. These were called pivot words, presumably because the meaning of an entire sentence hinged upon them. Thus, with his sentence, "*The Integers of parks are residential*," Garreaux's usage of 'Integers' designated something like 'people,' or 'society,' and so he was discussing the residential nature of people in parks (whatever that meant). Then 'Integers' also meant 'integers'—whole numbers as opposed to fractions. In this case he was referencing an analogy used earlier in the book about a car park with mezzanine levels; thus, the Integers in the sentence is referring to the non-mezzanine levels. Integers Inc. was also the name of a prominent accountancy firm in the '80s which was embroiled in a financial scandal. Even though "parks" was written lower-case it should be read as 'Park's,' as in, belonging to Alexander Park, the owner of Integers. Any sentence could have more than one pivot word. It also meant one should read the next sentence with all the meanings of the prior in mind and so on.

This is at least what I understood Lind to be saying.

"Pertinent to this," Griselda was saying, "is page 321. There is reason to believe that the word or acronym *LOTE* which he uses, third line down, is a pivot word as well. This is Mathilda's supposition, I have to admit, and not my own."

Lind smiled at me. Griselda glinted wickedly.

Everyone was waiting for me to speak.

"Of course, this will merit further research," Griselda said at last and everyone looked away from me. Then, just like before, Hector barged in with something completely irrelevant, at least to my ears. What had barely made sense for a few minutes, entirely ceased to make sense once more.

But I had exerted myself in a way I had not done for some time. Exercised a part of my brain, which tingled almost pleasantly. Like what I imagined the dull ache of exercise might be. I let myself slip away and watched beyond Lind's head through the slits of the blinds. The clouds had a glue-dipped countenance.

Griselda had to rush off after the seminar but we were meeting at an event later. I wandered town then went for dinner at the restaurant with the blue dome.

It was not busy, but for the first time there were quite a few other people. Some tourists most surprisingly, and a few locals. A woman in a black mantilla sat by herself in a booth forking what looked like black gnocchi. In the adjoining booth, Hector. He had not seen me. I decided not to say hello. Not even in my impervious mood could I be bothered. But also because I felt I shouldn't. That his being here in this place was suspect. It was just not his kind of place. Face weightier than usual, he was talking seriously to someone I couldn't see. They were sitting across from him but to the side, blocked from my vision. I chose a table behind a pillar and hoped they would not get up to leave before I did.

"Did you know there's a phenomenal transport museum about a two-hour drive from here," remarked a man at the nearby tourist table. But no one, apart from me had listened: his travelling companions had spoken to each other at the same time.

The waiter came.

"In a village nearby, there's this really phenomenal transport museum," I overheard the tourist say again.

When the waiter asked me what I wanted, I noticed the tourists look over, then seeing me, stared, and waited as if they had to know what *she* would get.

I ordered wildly.

I became annoyed because they continued to look after the waiter had gone. The man who had repeated himself muttered something to his travelling companions and they laughed. He wouldn't stop muttering now he finally had their ear.

"Do you know there's a really phenomenal transport museum just in a village nearby?" I called volubly across and they all looked away, terrified.

Hector leant out of his booth and saw me. I looked away just in time.

On leaving, I realised I hadn't looked up at the two faces on the ceiling. At Stephen and Hermia. Not because I'd been distracted. I'd felt them looking down the whole time. Something, even before entering the restaurant, had made me not want to look up. Had made it an unappealing prospect, so I hadn't.

*

ands House had produced an infernal brood of fox-hunting bores. All but the last. Four blockheaded brothers seemed to have been manufactured solely to set up the final act and grand finale that was Lymenick Sands, who came down one morning at the age of nine in his "mama's diadem," and announced he was going to be break-fasting instead with a Mrs. Peterson, the Doctor's wife in the village, whom he'd come to the conclusion was "a damned sight less provincial than anyone at Sands House." Unfortunately, Mr. Sands had been at the table, and little Lyme was swiftly and brutally punished. Brutal, it was said, even for a family as unfeeling and obtuse as the Sandses. This did not prevent him summarily setting out for Mrs. Peterson as soon as the family took their inevitable mid-morning nap.

Given the abundance of such early anecdotes, Lymen-ick Sands had grown not into what one might anticipate, but instead, as was regularly remarked, "the other kind—the robust strain of pansy," "not at all like that Stephen Ten-nant," who had continued donning his mama's diadems ("coronets, my dear") and didn't understand what all the fuss was about. This was supposed to make Lyme more palatable than the likes of Stephen, but for Hermia, it was precisely that same Stephenish impulse she had glimpsed in Lyme that allowed his excessive *healthiness* to be overlooked. Which rescued him from the clutches of platitude. Which spared him from the bromide life.

Lyme had invited them all to Sands House.

Presently on the train to Edinburgh—

Hermia sported a canopy-hat and veil, only throwing back the veil in the now-empty compartment as they reached the halfway mark.

"Sands House," she said. "Did we not go there at midnight uninvited—we all drove from Inverness?"

"No, we all drove from Claridge's and it was Blenheim Palace," said Flora St. Clair. "But Hamish Symes was at Sands House with Hugh last summer. Said it was so vast he got lost looking for a lavatory. Wandered and wandered polished halls and eternal corridors with endless armorials and ghastly portraits. Not even a water-closet in sight. Eventually had to urinate in a crystal decanter and fell asleep on a polar bear rug. He thought he would quite expire of dehydration and they'd discover his skeleton in fifty years. But in the morning, both he and the decanter were discovered by the parents who'd just returned, and that is why he is banned. In fact, Lyme has had to pretend to have converted—to a fox-hunting brute I mean—for almost a year in order for the parents just to be able to leave him alone in the house. He can be very convincing at that."

"Quite."

The carriage rattled.

In her room yesterday morning—

The Black Princess dropped the letter on her bed.

We know who you are, the letter said. *You shall never escape us. We won't reveal a thing if you leave at once. But you shall never escape us.*

Approaching Edinburgh—

"Who else is coming?"

"Oh, just about everybody. It's all the same, you know, since you've been away. This country, I mean, except everyone is little more worn and half the old clingers-on are now, you know, right at the heart. And there's some new blood too. But Elizabeth Ponsonby is driving up from Northumbria or wherever it is. And Brian will be there."

"Not Bryan Guinness?"

"No, Howard."

"It's almost exciting, isn't it?"

"The first *true* soirée we've had since . . . It's all been ultra-feeble you know—the party-going."

The train stopped. Hermia shivered—she had not been in Scotland for ten years.

Presently—

The train stopped

Presently—

Hermia shivered.

Presently—

Hermia had not been to Scotland in some ten years.

Lyme was not there to drive them. It was at least an hour by car. They would have to get a taxicab which they could barely afford.

"It's a pity," Flora said. "All this time and we're still not drowning in money."

"I've only lately managed to not be totally desperate, let alone *une dame riche*."

"Me too."

"Except we're both lying about not being desperate."

"Imagine if any number of dress shops knew you were back on British soil."

They both laughed voluptuously. It was an old, belaboured joke.

"Here's a cab."

On with the veil again.

"Is that entirely necessary?" Flora asked.

"Darling, is your inquiry entirely necessary?"

"Forgive," Flora said—sincerely.

Well at least Flora remembered—she who had spent enough time with Hermia walking along streets, in the countryside, in transportation, at parties, in hotels, libraries and museums to know how fatiguing the staring could become. The non-admissions. The expulsions. Some others, once they were out of it for a few minutes, entirely forgot.

("Oh, but darling," Stephen had once said, "*must* we rendezvous at that shabby little restaurant? I'm sick to death of it—let us go to..." And she had to explain that at that shabby little restaurant—which was in fact where the novelist Ada Fox dined when in London but why ought that to matter when *she*, the Black Princess dined there—was an establishment where she had every confidence of being served, where they would treat her properly, where there would be no unexpected humiliations. Indeed the maître d' had once expelled seven Americans who had objected to her presence.)

"What I mean is, you didn't used to *hide* yourself like that. If you covered your face it was to dazzle not to conceal. Not this off and on every five minutes," Flora said.

There had, in fact, always been a little hiding wrapped up in the spectacle. But Flora was correct. Not that today's blood-hued gauze wasn't spectacular.

"I do it now when I haven't the energy. Actually, stop here please driver."

"What for?" Flora protested, but on looking out of the window, there was the Balmoral Hotel.

"Oh Lord! Hermia, I daresay there will be enough of that when we arrive."

"I'd like to arrive at least blottoed in part."

"How?"

Hermia had forgotten the everlasting need of a gentleman for admittance to all such places even regardless of skin. She had become used to lawless old Dun and its cafés.

But then their old friend David Ross emerged.

"David!"

They took an arm each, forcibly, and steered him with great velocity back inside the hotel where they drank as many sidecars as it took—Hermia from beneath her veil—for them to achieve the divine state.

"Much better," the Black Princess remarked, for she felt considerably more princessly.

As the car purred then hurtled through the country arteries, Hermia began to feel even more princessly. They had persuaded David to borrow a friend's car and drive them there.

She felt a thrill of the kind she hadn't known for a time. A thrill but also the accompanying doom which used to come those summers making her way from house to house, not sure how long they wanted her there. How it might all go so awfully wrong—if they became bored of her, if an 'unsympathetic' guest were there. Spending all her money on a driver and Daimler just for a day because she was afraid no taxi would take her, as had happened once, and because she wanted to arrive properly. When people suspect one might *depend* on their hospitality, how miserly they become! Having little money, the best thing was to exhibit copious flourishes—like arriving in the Daimler—and be much in demand elsewhere. That one summer she had been much in demand and was able to turn this into a solid year of invitations, of castle and villa, pile and palazzo.

The car now rolled through the parkland of Sands House. As they approached, the horns of other cars could be heard in the distance: other guests driving from Edinburgh and elsewhere, coming in just behind them. Two cars could be seen whizzing towards them: a babble of shrieks and chattering—a sound she adored; the unmistakable timbre of the set that she had almost belonged to. Not quite her set but closer than any in this country.

("*Too too* Bright *for the Bloomsberries!*

A little too poetic for the B.Y.P.s!

Not quite Mayfair with its Sitwells, don't quite sit well with the..." An awful song made up by Lyme, about her, but it applied as much to Flora and Hugh and Lyme as well.)

In the hallway: a startlingly healthy young man on the stairs with the look of Lyme. One of the awful brothers to greet the guests.

"Lymenick is occupied—I've come to greet his friends. No service today, you know. Lyme's idea."

Lyme occupied. This was unusual. He had long ago given up pretending to rise late. She remembered his impatience those mornings before she knew he'd been up for hours, pacing his room to tire himself out. He didn't want them to think him respectable like his brothers.

She had just tossed back her veil. The brother was watching her. There was a clamour behind as the other guests entered.

"My dear girl," he said to Flora volubly. "Surely your maid should have helped you in with that case at the very least. My god, what is she got up like and *where* does she think she's going! Her lodgings will be downstairs."

In came the last of the party behind, people she didn't recognise, but yes, with the distinct chatter of her almost-set. The new blood Flora had mentioned. She was humiliated. She would turn around and leave at once. It was just what she had always dreaded. What she had always avoided in public.

"Clearly, this is not my maid. This is the Princess Hermia Drumm."

The party behind murmured.

Mr. Sands stood there dumbly. Staring and staring.

"What a funny, funny valet," said Hermia, and she passed him. The new blood, and Flora, exploded—a cacophony of laughter.

Should he stop her it would end in disaster. Better to storm out. But she had never stormed out. If she held resolute and continued up the stairs, if he stood there stunned, she would make it.

She was sure she felt something brush her elbow, felt a hand. The ruddy-coloured brother was going to bar her way up, but thank heavens, Lyme had appeared at the top of the stairs. The hand slipped away.

Some hours ago—

Hermia shivered. She had not been in Scotland for some ten years.

⋆⋆

My Transfixions deserted me. The sensations stopped.

A week after dinner at the restaurant with the blue dome, I went to another Garreaux seminar. I understood as little as usual but experienced again the pleasurable exhaustion—no headaches, no nausea, no books flashing like malevolent lighthouses.

"There's an important reception tonight. All Residents are expected to attend," Griselda said. We were sitting in the Residency Centre canteen. Griselda and Hector and the majority of Residents ate here frequently despite it not being any cheaper than eating in town. They adored it. The same sandwiches and scarlet soup. The polystyrene cups. Toast without butter. I was sure the Residency caterers had to go out of their way to find such bad bread and cheese in this country. I acquiesced and had some soup. It was almost nice after the strain of the seminar. I hadn't eaten—had been pouring over Garreaux all day hoping for a breakthrough.

"It's at the City Institute—a part of the University."

"What for?"

"Annual reception hosted by the Lyta Foundation," she said, "who fund the Residency."

"I thought Garreaux funded it?"

"In part, yes."

I went home to get dressed but fell asleep. Waking up an hour later, I mechanically did something I had managed to keep myself from doing the past week. I looked at the photograph of Hermia. I picked it up from my bedside table and peered at her face, at Stephen next to her, awaiting the reciprocal pull, the feeling of interior lightness, of elevation—like an Assumption in miniature.

Nothing happened.

I was still dazed from sleep but, knowing something was wrong, I got up and extracted a picture of Richard Bruce Nugent from between the pages of a book. Also nothing. *Worse* than nothing: a definite discomfort.

I had known this was coming. Now it was here, I was unprepared. This was no garden-variety disenchantment. I had been inoculated. For days, or possibly even since my arrival in Dun, this inverse infection had been building up. Something unbearable had crept in, accompanying the pleasure that came with my Transfixions. Scared that it would displace them altogether, I had avoided looking up at the friezes in the restaurant which would usually send me hurtling. Had kept myself from looking at the photographs all week.

In fact, the last proper occasion of my Transfixions had been at the library the night I read about Richard Bruce Nugent, before we went to the restaurant. Even then I had felt it—the tarnished star—dismissed it.

Instead of acting whilst they were still alive, I had let Griselda effect whatever psychological trick she had effected on me without resistance; let the doubt slither in unchallenged, which was what she had wanted, clearly.

I put away the photographs and looked out the window into the garden until the fountain glowed in the dying light.

I was sure it was her. Part of her scheme. Turning me away from Hermia, towards Garreaux. It had worked: the death of my Transfixions.

The phone rang.

"Good, thought you might be asleep—sorry, what was that?"

"I said, I know exactly what you've done."

Instead of denial, or confusion, came amusement,

"*Oh do you?*" followed by, "Right, listen, you better get a move on. We're meeting at the bus stop in five."

Was she confessing, or had she taken me to mean something else altogether?

"They've gone, Griselda."

"What's gone?"

"My Transfixions."

"I don't know what that is, Mathilda."

"But you do."

I heard her sighing.

"How do you know 'they've' gone?"

"The sensations, everything…"

"And what do you feel now?"

I thought about them all, Herma, Stephen, Richard, Nancy…
A hot-cheeked discomposure arose.

"Guilt. But I don't know why—"

"Guilt?"

"Yes."

"Then is it bad that 'they've' gone?"

Even getting dressed was mortifying. I felt the eye of the Residency on me. In me. I saw how their own style, though they would profess never to have one, was, whilst smuggled in, the product of a much more elaborate thought than my own. I had nothing suitable and decided at last to put on an arrangement I would usually wear, but this was now difficult. The old process of selection, my taste, it would seem, had dissipated with my Transfixions.

In the dark, at the bus stop, Residents congregated. Giuli's seaweed hair was visible beneath the lamplight first. I'd seen an early photograph of Garreaux in the '80s, with blue hair: a brief flirtation with Punk before surrendering all Taste. Giuli was talking intently with Hector as if the two had never attempted to beat each other up.

Griselda was speaking to Jenny D and Max, who both flashed their Inquisitor faces briefly at me, and then flashed again in a double-take—as if they knew a change had taken place. They smiled.

Eric, Deborah and the other people trapped in 2007 were there, rolling their eyes a lot and pretending to look glum but unable to mask their excitement. Very 2007, I thought. Imagine being jammed in the prominent social spirit of over a decade ago with all of over a decade ago's effortful sarcasm, hellish self-consciousness and flash-in-the-pan anxieties. Aspic People.

Malachi and I had been obsessed with Aspic People. An exercise, almost a parlour game, grounded in crude and totalising categories. Our favourite sort. When Woolf said that "on or about December, 1910 human character changed," she presumably meant a shift for some people in certain places. When everyone started saying 2010 was the year human character changed, again, we indulged in the idea: what caught our attention was the possibility that some people had been left behind, continuing to transmit their dead pre-2010 social realities. By which we meant sensibilities. By which we meant a collection of fickle aspects including mood, attitude and aura. The gap, to those on either side of this unbearable chasm, would naturally seem obscene. One could be emotionally, socially, or intellectually trapped in 2007, or 1982, but keep up with material trends. There were even people who'd got a part of them trapped in 1982 or '75 and still made it through the 2010 gap. It was the people specifically who had not passed the most recent change of 2010 that had us terrified. The prospect of people stuck behind in a very recent history just before the very recent transfiguration of a zeitgeist made us unaccountably queasy.

Aspic People, it should be noted, were not Arcadians. Our fear of them was bound up of course with the ostensible social shifts in groups we immediately had experience with. Malachi, for example, remembered that his brief stint studying music theory was largely untouched by polemics of the identity and that the year after he left it spread like wildfire. His year had been all about apathy and was reigned over by angsty young white men, but by the time he left their rule was over, sort of. People had said teleology, liminal and rhizomatic but not Queer or Black. A few had always said Queer or Black but that was different. It was thus partly a fear about being stuck in a place where we had no power or language to describe our powerlessness and partly a fear about inability to Escape more generally.

Malachi and I had never been able to shake our horror of Aspic People, who probably didn't exist. And now here were the most spiritually démodé people I had ever met.

I turned around and briefly threw up in a nearby bin, concealed from the group by a tree.

When I returned, the bus driver was getting on the bus and people began arranging themselves to sit next to one another, or at least not next to their inferiors. I had worked out by now something of the unspoken hierarchy that existed amongst the Residents. At the centre, Griselda and Hector constituted a group of their own, but condescended to form a kind of jigsaw alliance with Giuli, Jenny D, Max and Theo the Wisconsinite. Next were the people from 2007, led by Eric and Deborah. They were followed by a nexus of ones, twos and threes who, by virtue of their hinterland, had come together for warmth and at the same time acquired a maliciousness to make up for finding themselves so unexpectedly demoted at this stage in life. These were the ones always eating unbuttered toast, flaunting their self-taught aridity of palate, hoping to prove their Garreauxvian natures but lacking the imagination to do so in other ways. They reminded me not for the first time of Christian & Tom + Eleanor, of an entire group who had all caved, one by one, to a studied abstinence that summer.

This human tabulation was weighted by a combination of intellect and militancy.

I passed through the Toast Children.

"Garreaux is coming tonight."

"*Not* actually."

"But I was told—"

"Told *might*."

"What do you think, Felix, will he put in appearance?"

"Yes, I really do think so."

Theo the Wisconsinite, caught in their midst, broke away and began speaking to me as the bus appeared. Though, of everyone, Theo flitted from group to group, a kind of ambassadorial figure spreading necessary information and propaganda, he was also on the lowest rung of his own group and didn't want anyone getting the wrong impression.

"Felix and the rest are more vicious than usual," he whispered. "Nervy."

Even I had noticed this over the past week—since knowing the Toast Children were a distinct group.

"I can't think what it is," he said knowingly, revealing that he was still underneath it all a Wisconsinite gay who loved an underdog, and now, in his position of relative height (but little actual power), wanted me to know he loved an underdog. It was evident he suspected that it was because of me—my sudden acquaintance with Griselda and Hector—that the Toast Children were so nervy. They'd witnessed change in an order they had presumed to be fixed and believed social mobility was possible again. Were vying with one another for supremacy.

"You honestly are a dipshit Felix," I overheard one of the vicious subordinates mutter.

"And like that, Felix and the Rest become Sarah-Anne and the Rest," Theo whispered as we got on.

"I just call them the Toast Children," I said.

"Why?"

"Because they eat unbuttered toast all the time."

"But so do I. Don't you?"

We were the only passengers on the bus and our voices floated back and forth, almost ecclesiastically, a laughterless chime. Plastic bottles then passed up and down, I gulped some—straight spirit. The chime became a solemn babble.

"...which is why I'm so worried about my project," Theo was saying.

The windows were black once the bus was on the road.

"I'm very worried about my project," I overheard someone else, a few seats along, say confidentially minutes later.

"Well Jenny D said she's 'shook and gassed' about hers."

I was trying, instead, to overhear Griselda and Hector, had my ears trained on their voices—

"...had to happen eventually...took long..."

"Do you think Garreaux will put in an appearance?" Theo said to me quietly, sheepish but unable to contain himself.

"Yes," I said. "I really do think so." Actually, I had presumed Garreaux dead until ten minutes ago when I'd first heard the question posed.

Theo's eyes expanded, shock and delight.

"Me too," he said breathlessly.

The Lyta Foundation Reception was held in the large glass graduation hall that was most certainly too large for such an event. Below the glass ceiling, high up, lights were still on in some of the rooms and students in white lab coats occasionally looked out to see what was going on. Above the glass ceiling, outside, the university buildings continued upwards, towering on all sides. They were lit up in alternating green and yellow.

At one end of the hall was the stage, all the way at the other, a refreshments table. It was a gathering of some of the drabbest people in Europe. In the world. Everyone spoke in stifled tones that eddied beneath the glass ceiling.

Except I—cut loose from my Transfixions—understood now, was starting to understand: they weren't drab at all. Were part of something radical.

People tried to glance discreetly about themselves. On the lookout, I suspected, for Garreaux. Our own group diffused through this one. There must have been other Residents here from years gone by. I wondered if the person whose submission I had stolen was present. 1976.

I detached from the crowd and made for the refreshments table. People seemed to be avoiding it; were it not for four harangued-looking academics, I would have thought it off limits. They watched me as I picked up a glass.

"Thank God someone's enjoying themselves," said one of the four as I took a sip.

I caught the eye of the woman who had spoken as I was mid-sip. She then said something to me in the language.

"Sorry I don't understand."

"Oh, American?" she said, and they gently opened their circle to admit me.

"No—"

"Every year it goes untouched," she continued. "At least *they* never touch anything, the Residency lot I mean. As if it's poisoned. To them it is in a way, I'm sure—*the sheer decadence of it.*"

"Are you also from the Art History faculty, I don't think I've seen you before?"

"No," I said.

"Ah, Fine Art?"

"No, no—I'm on the Dun Residency," I said, and the woman pinkened, but also looked at her colleagues with confusion. Fascination erupted over their faces. They were not much older than me, perhaps the same age, I found it so hard to tell with professionals.

"Forgive me," she said, eyes taking in my attire, "but you seriously don't strike me as a Thought Artist and I mean that in the—"

"Dear god, look who it is," said one of them.

"The Gruesome Twosome."

And I turned around to see Griselda and Hector striding across the large vacuum of space between the crowd and the refreshment table. They both took a glass of wine and surveyed the room, whispering. I smiled in leave at the four art historians and went over.

"Oh," Hector said, as if startled. "Do you know those people?" He almost always spoke at the same volume, a little too loud (the sole exception was when colluding with Griselda), and was certainly overheard.

"No," I said, and saw the academics muttering. Felt something of a thrill as they lumped me in with Griselda and Hector.

"Oh look," Griselda said. "It's starting."

People were mounting the stage and the audience began to take their seats. The four art historians drifted across and Griselda and Hector both put their untouched wines back on the table and made their way across the hall. I followed, wondering if they had ever meant to drink.

A man who was chancellor of the City Institute got to the stage and began making an introduction. Behind him sat Lind

and Jonatan, a business woman in a business suit and beside her
an elderly man in a matching business suit whom I thought might
be Garreaux.

The chancellor was praising the Lyta Foundation for their
support.

"We're so delighted to have the senior member of the Lyta
family with us this year. As you will know, Sir Lyta was crucial in
inaugurating some of this university's many diverse programmes,
including the Lyta Business Scholarship and of course the Dun
Residency, which would not have been possible were it not for Sir
Frederick Lyta's early contributions almost fifty years ago. John
Garreaux cannot be here, but I know extends his thanks to his dear
friend. And let us take an opportunity to do so as well." The chancellor turned and beamed and clapped at the man who was not
going to speak; the audience joined in clapping.

"Also due thanks today is Sir Lyta's granddaughter, Lina Lyta—
director of the Lyta Foundation some fifteen years. Please, put
it together for Lina Lyta," he said, as if she were going to get up
and sing.

The woman got up smiling and delivered her speech: "...and
we are of course so happy to be closely involved with the University
and Institute. Our involvement with the Dun Residency in particular—which is what, after all, this reception is in honour of—goes
back generations, this being its fortieth anniversary. It has brought
so, so much to us as a foundation, keeping us in touch with the
most ground-breaking aspects of the humanities, aspects that can
become all too easy to ignore. So, we're proud to support the Residency. You see, a question my grandfather was often asked, and I
still get asked today is, why fund an artists' residency? What has
that got to do with the mission of the Lyta Foundation? A question, might I add, never asked of our Business Scholarship. But

what would good business be without lateral thinking? My own time here as a business student was often spent attending lectures I wasn't supposed to. And of course, I will never, ever, forget my many days in the student bar..."

She laughed, but no one else laughed, and for once I was in sync with the Residents, until I realised no one had laughed because there was a noise outside. Then it was inside. A woman had come into the hall followed by others. They had placards which said something about the Residency I was unable to translate. Then they were silent, pointing dramatically upwards. Beneath the glass ceiling, windows opened on all sides. People leant out and unfurled banners. I couldn't understand these either. The people with the placards then wove for a while through the crowd as Lina Lyta started up again. She repeated the line about spending time in the student bar and veritably brought the house down. It was as if the protesters were not there. There were only about five of them down here. Security had already been alerted. The protesters went running towards the other door in the hall, but it was locked. They were escorted out, shouting once more. Everyone was ignoring them, straining to hear the speech, which Lina Lyta was finishing.

She finished and the room applauded. Security could already be seen at the windows drawing up the banners.

The chancellor came back to the microphone and concluded nervously—"and please, please, help yourselves to the complimentary refreshments provided,"—people stood up but very few made their way to the wine.

Breaking rank once again, I went and took not only more wine but also cheese and biscuits.

"How is it?" Griselda asked. She was standing behind me, watching curiously.

"Oh, average."

"I think," she looked over to the table, "I'll sample some." Hector came to the table from across the hall, followed by Giuli and Theo. Before long half the room were indulging. It was one of the strangest scenes I'd ever witnessed. A drove of puritans descending, first tentatively, then wild-eyed, upon a feast.

Theo the Wisconsinite was clearly not used to alcohol.

"Well," he said, "Garreaux was a no-show, but that talk was fantastic, wasn't it?"

"Yes," I said. "Magnificent," and he smiled, which I had hoped, so I said, "But what about the protesters?"

"Protesters?"

"That came in during the speech."

He frowned in what looked like genuine confusion.

"I'm presuming it was against the Lyta Foundation," I said, "if they're funding the University..."

"Ohhhh," he said. "No, no, no it wasn't that. You mean the people that came in?"

"Yes, weren't they student protesters?"

"What? No, that was the old tutor and... You don't know? Oh, my goodness." He looked about the room, doing a full turn as if searching for someone in particular. Then he said conspiratorially, "It was about Griselda. Yes, actually, I suppose you're right in that it's a protest against the Lyta Foundation, but I didn't really think about it like that."

"A protest against Griselda?"

"It sounds ridiculous now you say it, but well, yes. As I said, I wasn't thinking about it in a wider context, reading Garreaux does that to you, doesn't it? Not a Garreauxvian protest by any means. But yes, it is a 'protest' against the Lyta Foundation. Because of Griselda. She was on an early Summer programme at the Institute.

An art programme—Thought Art in the loosest sense. One of the other students was making work to do with Garreaux. Well, she Processed his work."

"Processed? I haven't come across that term in the book."

"You haven't? I don't see how... well, never mind. It refers to the original performance, before the Residency, when Garreaux got the students to incinerate their own final projects. Griselda and this boy were arguing about some element of Garreaux. She said she didn't think his application of the theory at all genuine. Then his work went missing for days. When it came to the group crit she presented a phial. She had incinerated his work for her own project. The tutor reprimanded her heavily and argued that is not how to behave as an artist or student. Well, then she later incinerated the tutor's work too. This was apparently almost a lifetime's work—she's only thirty-something though," he laughed, and his white hair was striped green by the lights above.

"Even still, the tutor had a serious breakdown and took some time off. The University didn't do anything to Griselda. Now the tutor, who wasn't invited back to her post, is saying clearly this is because word got to the Lyta Foundation, or Garreaux, and they stepped in to make sure nothing happened to Griselda. Like she had their blessing. But the Institute have responded that nothing of the sort has gone on. That, don't forget, it was them who fired Garreaux for getting students to incinerate their work all those years ago and in spite of their relationship with him now, through the Dun Residency, would not tolerate any equivalences today, and besides, they say, neither the Foundation nor Garreaux have any influence on their procedures; there was simply no jurisdiction to reprimand Griselda in this case because of the nature of the course, and the carrying out of her project. Then, finally, they let the tutor know her not being invited back the following year was unrelated to the events at hand. It was a temporary contract with no renewal promised."

I kept up a light chatter with Theo only to hide how unnerved I was. I was thinking about how Griselda had meant to sabotage my own project—or what she'd thought was my project. I knew she was a zealot as far as Garreaux was concerned, but I had just caught a glimpse of the underside.

That she had paused such absolutism to befriend me didn't make sense. Or perhaps it was just as I had more hazily considered before, that my complete detachment from the Residency meant I did not come under her scrutiny because I could not be considered a dilettante.

Some spirit broke out that night of the kind I had never witnessed amongst the Residents and would never witness again. It was of course the fact that they were all drinking together. Their occasional and paltry bus bottles and sips of Red were quite different to this. Or perhaps the wine was interacting with the study drugs I was sure they were all on.

We began speaking quite intently to each other, barely seeing—talking blurs. Not everyone partook. Jenny D and Max didn't touch a thing. They both stood for a while and watched with a look that said, "they would not allow this nonsense in our day (the year of our Lord 1478, the great and glorious Inquisition. Or 1644, height of the blessed Witchfinder General)," and left early. Hector had a little wine but remained, as far as I could tell, entirely sober.

As we left, I expected the tutor to leap out at Griselda from the scrawny institute bushes.

We had to get taxis back to the town because we'd missed the last bus. Griselda and some other Residents suggested that it would only be a five-hour walk and a perfect opportunity for Markating the city. But when Theo was found writhing on the ground speaking in tongues, taxis won over.

"Mathilda!" Griselda was saying in the taxi.

I, drunk, wasn't listening.

We hurtled through the city, over the river. I whirled in the back of the taxi, watched strips of buildings flick past in tapes of white, then glass ribbons, then white then grey, before breaking up ... We hurtled. Over the river.

"Mathilda! We've got a meeting tomorrow afternoon. It's about the LOTE passage."

We were in Dun. We stumbled out and separated.

At home I whirled again. Whirling without magic. It was unusual—Transfixionless giddiness. It was much duller. A plain catastrophe.

PART TWO

IV

I was Hermia stroking my-her pet fox, and at the same time Stephen applying gold powder to my-his hair.

I convulsed.

I had been smoking a cigarette when my eyes caught the two paintings which hung above the pink cream hulk of the mantelpiece. One of Hermia, one of Stephen. An almighty spasm. It was as if they, the portraits, had blown the smoke back into my mouth—which was their mouths—as I blew it into theirs (mine) simultaneously.

The smoke appeared to triangulate for a moment, less than a second, making a link between the portraits and me. All that whirling regurgitated silver. Then it dispersed and I flew out of my chair with a psychic contraction; a single vigorous choke, not of the flesh. Not of the flesh, but then very much physical.

"…um…?"

"Yes, I'm fine—"

"Sit back down, you're swaying." Actually, I was convulsing. It stopped. I sat back down.

"I'm just a touch . . ." I opted for something plausible: "I haven't slept; I think I drifted off for a second and got that horrid twitch: 'Hypnic Jerk,' or whatever it is they call it."

"You fell asleep sitting up with a cigarette in your hand and your eyes wide open?" Griselda said.

"Yes."

I looked back up at the two paintings. And then the others. The room was ringed with several portraits. All of them niched in glass, mounted, with gilt frames substantially larger than they might have been considering some of them were small enamels, no bigger than playing cards. Stephen, Hermia, Nancy, Richard but also Lola Montez, Ardizzoni: *My* Transfixions. With some, the sitters were obscured by shafts of setting sun reflecting off the glass. This was for the best, I didn't think I could take any more. Below Hermia and Stephen was a large arched mantel mirror which tilted forwards. Its carved frame was in the same chiselled pink-blue stone as the mantelpiece. I could discreetly observe Griselda and Hector from this leaning mirror since they were sat a little behind me on an ottoman. The pair looked strained and jarring, almost impossible in this room.

I did not. My scalp tingled. I dropped my cigarette. A delicious floral-tasting one which had been offered to me by our host, "Like smoking a botanical garden!" I picked up the end and surreptitiously swept the ash with my hand. The rug had been singed on its floral border scheme. Right in the heart of an artichoke-ish flower. I hoped it would go unnoticed. Looking up, Griselda was watching me, expressionless, by way of the same mirror I had used to spy on her. Yes, they looked more ghoulish than ever, the both of them.

A blast issued from the nearby room.

"Something to eat?" our host had asked the three of us some minutes before.

"No thanks," Griselda took the liberty of answering for everybody.

"A wee bonbon?" they had then purred nervously.

"*No*," now Hector took the liberty. I personally would have loved a wee bonbon.

"Something else then—" and they were away, as if wanting any excuse to leave us.

"What was their name?"

"*His* name," Hector said.

He now came back into the room, a-dapple and gold, Venice incarnate. He was precariously holding a tray on which balanced an uncorked, hissing bottle and four stained-glass cordial glasses, bloom-shaped, as if he had twisted up a basilica windowpane.

The room realigned on his entry. Became even more scenic. All the golds came to the fore—harmonized; rhymed with him.

I watched as he put down the chattering tray, still processing the fact of finding myself in the home of the very same kneeling figure, glimpsed on my first daylight outing in Dun. The apparition of Hermia. His name, he was telling me, was Erskine-Lily.

If I was still processing him then I was also processing, doubly so, the portraits on his walls.

To my delight he passed me a glass of pink foam.

"None for me, thanks," said Hector and Griselda in unison.

"Just a moment—wait for this!" he said abruptly. "I think you'll all find it—well you'll *know*, I'm sure," he stood there trembling then left the room again.

From nowhere, a voice climbed the air. The voice could have belonged to a soprano or a countertenor. I thought for a moment it was Erskine-Lily until it was joined by instruments. A recording. An aria. I looked around the room for the source but couldn't see speakers anywhere.

What the room was (I had already seen Griselda dismiss it with a single ocular sweep), could be best described as baroque, in an inlaid trinket-box sort of a way, but it was more ornate than ornamental. Nothing was there to decorate the surface since the room was decorative to the core. Not necessarily Baroque either, just *baroque*.

I picked up my glass, on which I could just about discern a figure in tranquil excruciation before the pale mellow froth. The figure gave an audible hiss; the bubbles sighed. My head fizzed.

Griselda began whispering with Hector, whose lips had been kneaded in disgust since arrival. It was almost a foppish snarl. He would have hated this designation—*fop*—cropped and blanched as he was, loather of ornament that he was. He must have been in hell in this room, in the company of such an ornamental host. They both must have been in hell.

"...never..." I couldn't quite hear them.

"...fucking ba...ra..."

"Yes."

They were probably concocting a plan to leave. Erskine-Lily unsettled them. I wished they would indeed just leave, but then of course I would have to leave with them. Others were supposed to be coming. Giuli and Theo, but they had been too hungover. I wondered who'd arranged this meeting in the first place. I'd been told it was concerning the LOTE passage in the yellow book. An audience with Garreaux would have been less surprising than this, than Erskine-Lily. Had they honestly thought *this person* might be able to shed light on the passage? The light they wanted shed?

My eye caught the paintings and I almost found myself leaping up from the chair again: here I was, sitting in the living room of someone I'd never met, whose walls were adorned with my clandestine obsessions. My Transfixions.

I became panicked. It was a prank.

More panicked: it was too good to be a prank.

It was all too much. Even for me who had once expected this sort of thing to happen everyday: to walk into a stranger's room and find their walls bedecked with the faces of my self-induced fantasies. But it didn't stop there, I could tell. It was not only the figures producing sensations—because they had returned all at once, undammed, causing me to leap up, and almost doing it now—but something about the room itself, the music, Erskine-Lily, the painted ceiling.

He came back into the room and, finally, settled himself upon a loaf of brocade furniture I did not have a name for.

"I can't tell you how excited I am, forgive me if I'm..." he said and looked at the ceiling, absently tapping his copper throat where there was a small but bright reddish birthmark. He twitched a little. An elegant contortion of nerves.

Then he looked at me anxiously, confidentially, at which point my unsteadiness subsided and I ceased to think of the peculiarity of those pictures being here. Of my being here. Of him being here.

He was holding some sheets of old paper and did not look at the other two, only at me. I didn't blame him. Griselda's gaze was especially aggressive today and I now understood him to be keeping at bay an anxiety attack.

"This is what exactly?" Griselda suddenly snapped, gesturing to the air, to the aria, with a movement so violent that I inadvertently envisaged a whip following her hand with a sonic crack. The abruptness of the question startled Erskine-Lily to the point that I felt he might never speak again. He was seized, paralysed by nerves, and to make it worse Hector chimed in irritably,

"I was wondering the same thing. He suggested it was relevant to our meeting."

It must have been at this point I became overwhelmed by the desire to leap up and throw my glass of fizzing wine—utterly ambrosial whatever it was—into Hector's face. But presently Erskine-Lily recovered,

"But it has *everything* to do with our meeting," he gently murmured. His voice had shed some of the erratic nerves. "This record is potential evidence that before the society called LOTE, or the Lote-Os—based in this town in the late 1920s—before it, there were others directly influenced by the System of the Luxuries and the accompanying Book. The subject of the opera you see, is Saint Christina the Astonishing, who is entwined with the history of the Luxuries. The Luxuries being an apocryphal and blasphemous thing to believe in, Saint Christina became a public way to depict and align oneself with them. You see, she was often depicted with wings, but was a saint and not an angel. It's quite funny because Saint Christina was very much the opposite of the Luxuries. She threw herself into furnaces all the time and most likely loathed anything to do with the senses. Really quite stressful and extra. But as a winged figure, a good way to stand in for the Luxuries—one couldn't even be seen worshiping angels, you know. Not that it was worshiping exactly. And she was, of course, the Patron Saint of 'lunatics' and eccentrics. Given the Queer inclinations of almost everyone historically connected to the Lote-Os and the earlier incarnations, those terms might be looked upon more fondly as bywords. For Queer. The opera is by Ardizzoni and this recording is of an amateur staging of it."

The music was getting quite histrionic, which I loved.

"And I have managed to get a hold of this," he passed me the papers.

"Dance notations?" I asked. "For an opera?"

"Yes, it was a ballet *and* an opera, not uncommon. No, I mean the notations themselves," he looked at me, willing me, I thought, to understand. Hector was now shuffling and sniffing indignantly. But Griselda was very still.

"Instructions!" he said, at last. "They based ceremonies upon the dance notations found in Ardizonni's opera. The Lote-Os, I mean. These notations are from their own reworking of it. They were convinced that the original contained ceremonial instructions from the Order because the opera was about Saint Christina. It was their belief that the society had survived unbroken since the Renaissance—when the book was written—until the 1890s and that they were the first to revive it. I'm not saying they were correct. In my opinion, it's all relative. It may well be that Ardizzoni or the producer of the opera took an interest in *The Book of the Luxuries* and transferred aspects into their work. In this sense we might indeed think of it as a single ongoing establishment. The Lote-Os' reworking did away with Saint Christina and actually made it directly about the Luxuries. The Ardizzoni notations I cannot find, but you can be sure they used the same notations in their own production. It was not a professional performance by any means, just a bit of fun propelled by their interest in the Luxuries— who knows if it was actually staged. But if we are after all going to reconstruct, or shall we say revive, the Lote-Os in some capacity, I thought these would be useful. Do any of you know how to read dance notations? I did a little ballet once, started too late, it's a great tragedy of my life, but—"

"I think you've made a mistake, mate," Hector said.

I was sure that Erskine-Lily had winced before responding,

"Oh, but darling, I've been very thorough with my research, I—"

"What I meant was, we didn't come here to . . ." and he shook the brittle notations I had stupidly passed back to him. "What I mean is we're on the Dun Residency, and LOTE is mentioned in a book by John Garreaux. He's a theorist—"

"I know who he is, sweetness," Erskine-Lily said.

"None of us knew what the passage meant, and we heard you were interested—"

"...And *all* of you are on it? The Residency. And that's the only reason you're here?"

"Yeah, mate."

"But I thought..." he said. "Then there has been a massive mistake!" His eyes met theirs for the first time, a look of horror, mortification. I could see him visibly trembling, trying not to. His hand went to his neck again, then to a pillow tassel. He was trying not to cry.

Just as the aria was coming to an end it juddered and got caught in a loop. With those tapering, carnation-stem fingers, Erskine-Lily lifted the large obsidian ashtray from the table beside him and dropped it back down causing the floorboards to rattle. The music unjogged and came at last to its emphatic crescendo. Another song began to play.

"The Residence... I see..." he said, extremely flustered.

"Yes, so do you know what Garreaux could have meant when—"

"Absolutely not!" he seemed to flinch again at the second mention of this name. Hector persisted however, at last relieved to be able to talk about Garreaux and the Residency. I utterly glazed over.

"The Markations of any system are..."

Erskine-Lily too seemed not to be listening at all.

"The Dotage levels have more cogent implications when it comes to Markating the mark..."

It must have been at this point it occurred to me that the portraits were practically luminous, were breathing out quantities of pale vapour.

They stood out before me like a mass annunciation scene.

Each face an excavation: delirium exhumed. Blondish mist filled my vision. I tasted it in my mouth and nostrils. Enochian incense, I thought.

Yes, the sensations really had returned.

The portraits' faces were all so arch and witty that I found myself erupting into laughter that must have gone on for a minute with Griselda and Hector's, "*What*? What is it, Mathilda? What's so funny?" eventually dissolving the humour. When I didn't say anything, Hector continued speaking, as if to helpfully cover up the awkwardness but really because he wished to speak. Wished to purge the room of something so deeply, primally at odds with him.

Erskine-Lily's brow arched and I didn't know whether it was in displeasure or some secret camaraderie. With me, with the paintings.

I reached out and refilled my glass until it was brimming. The winged figure on the glass, who I was now sure was Saint Christina, whirred in saintly ecstasy. Getting up with the glass, I turned towards Hector, and caught sight of Erskine-Lily in the mirror.

A gleam.

He was gleaming, glinting, as if he'd snuck some brilliantly elaborate headdress on. Encasing Erskine-Lily's head was a thick disc of quivering gold; gold which caught the light and pulsated: rose-gold, white-gold. Protruding from it were spindly obelisks that resembled pearl. The kind of halo seen in a byzantine mosaic or illuminated manuscript—a hearty golden disc.

A living Transfixion.

For a moment, Hector's whole face became fizz as the liquid frothed up on impact. I was almost envious of him: it must feel quite splendid until it becomes flat and sticky. He stood up, as did Griselda. They were shouting at Erskine-Lily, because Erskine-Lily had done it as I was looking at him in the mirror, not me. Had thrown his drink over Hector. I was still standing, with my glass, looking at us all through the mirror. The portraits were dull and inanimate now. Hector was shouting at Erskine-Lily, Griselda was shouting at Hector, holding him back.

Glass in hand, I swooned and hit the floor. Swooned on purpose. Purposefully swooned. The carpet fizzed. I was completely conscious but rolled around as if I was just coming to. I was thinking of the fact Erskine-Lily's nails were like miniature plaques, painted the colour of smudged church gold, and what a travesty that neither cousin had seen it in their hearts to appreciate this.

I had pretended to faint because it had felt more than appropriate. Had made a convincing enough case for itself. It was something I had always wanted to try, and with the charged theatrical tenor of the room, the inviting carpet, how could I not? But more than this, I had saved Erskine-Lily from potential injury. Violence had been diverted through my antics. Without interruption, this unwanted thing, which was Hector punching Erskine-Lily, but also something attached to that, another violence, would have happened.

I was escorted home. The next day Griselda came round with a white paper bag. She'd brought me food from the city. The customary dread brought on by her early morning interventions was very much alive, but I was too curious about the previous night not to let her in.

She strode past me into the room and stood at her usual spot by the window, snapping open the curtains, then perching the bag on top of piles of books and papers.

It was really only a few hours since she'd been here to put me to bed—as soon as she'd left, I'd leapt up and spent three hours in ecstasy, unpacking and reading everything about Hermia and

Stephen and Richard and Nancy and the rest which I'd put away after the flight of my Transfixions.

I wondered if she noticed the change in the room.

"Had to add to the melodrama by fainting, didn't you?"

"Oh, I was feeling dizzy and tired all day. Don't you remember when I jumped up and you said 'sit back down, you're swaying' . . ."

"Yes Mathilda, I'm not accusing you of throwing yourself on the floor; but I'm glad—I don't know what would have happened. Hector's still fucking livid." I laughed but she looked entirely serious, hands behind her back, the old solemn, threatening face on.

"He said—I had to go back last night to get Hector's phone—he said he didn't know why he did it. The way he said it . . . I half believe him. Didn't say sorry though, except in a general way, like a society hostess apologising for the weather. No message for Hector, I mean. I told him if you hadn't collapsed when you did Hector probably would have knocked him out. Well within his rights."

"Well within his rights?"

"Yes. You don't think so?"

"It's just . . . maybe that sort of thing's okay with Giuli, but Erskine-Lily?"

"*Totally* within his right to knock him out—this boy—*man*—threw a glass of wine over him."

"It doesn't seem right," was all I could say.

"Oh, do you mean because he's effeminate?"

"Fem."

"What?"

"Fem."

"So, do you think it would be more suitable for Hector to hit me because I'm not all that effeminate or . . . *femme*?" she said the last word with a French accent as if she had never encountered it any other way. This I did not believe.

"I don't think anyone should hit anyone, Griselda."

"Don't you believe in revolution? I thought, at least, we overlapped on that."

What was she going on about?

"That's different."

"Is it? In the end?"

"Yes, it is." She was alarming me now. We were apparently having two different conversations. "...And why do you think he threw the wine?" I said.

Griselda only shrugged. She was looking out of the window now and I couldn't see her face. Nothing was said for some minutes. I almost found myself drifting off to sleep and spoke to keep awake. "I suppose Hector just irritated him—you said it yourself, he irritates people," I suggested. "From what *I* remember... before I collapsed... he was being obnoxious. I don't think we should let whatever happened rule out Erskine-Lily if he can help us learn anything more. What did you think at the time?"

She turned and looked at me again.

"What did I think?"

"About what he said? About the Lote-Os. Before it all kicked off."

"Damn idiotic," she said. "Delusional. Narcissistic too. There's nothing to learn from him. I should apologise for taking you there. Especially because that whole line of enquiry is kaput. It actually occurred to me the morning after the Lyta Reception, but I didn't have time to cancel the meeting."

"Kaput?"

"Totally. That is, the primary pivot of LOTE is obvious. It's nothing to do with that awful society. Or even the Lotus Eater myth.

It's Lyta. Yes, as in the Foundation. I realised it at the reception but needed to look a few things up afterwards. Lyta is a family name as well as a Norwegian Nynorsk verb meaning 'have to,' or 'must.' The past participle of Lyta is Lote. This can also be connected to the Old English Lutien—to conceal, lie low or hide, which later became written as the now archaic English word Lote, meaning the same thing. It's exactly the light etymologising Garreaux likes to do, very characteristic of him. He was directly referencing the Lyta Foundation and the family, but by stemming it through this other meaning of Lote—to lie low—he is highlighting, performing even, for the reader an aspect of his theory. See, he grew up with Frederick Lyta and his father knew Lyta's father. The Lyta family have been fundamental in shaping the Dun Residency. It's all part of the same auto-theory he heaps into his work elsewhere. One family name becomes a metonym for of all capitalism for him, but at the same time the family helped found the Residency. Working not just within but directly alongside capitalism is an inevitable Aspect of Thought Art."

"That all sounds extremely tenuous," I said. I was shaking a little beneath the covers.

"To you," she said. "Nevertheless, these circuitous strands are the best way of reading Garreaux."

"But in the seminar *you* suggested LOTE was a Pivot word with more than two meanings."

"I know, but that was where we went wrong. This is, rather, a Bind word, where the meaning is embedded in itself. That's the problem with Garreaux—he's always throwing up these seemingly definite allusions, which are in the end just coincidental. He based the Residency in Dun, there was also a group called LOTE in Dun for a brief period. But there was simply no connection. It happens all the time, I can give you various examples."

"What about the Luxuries?" I said. "You discovered that they were connected to LOTE and also mentioned in Garreaux."

She sighed.

"I've gone through both mentions of the Luxuries which are in a different section to the LOTE passage and tried to apply that reading to it and it just doesn't hold. He is, as originally thought, talking again about luxury—capitalist decadence. Garreaux presents a unique relation to capitalism—proximity—but one anathema to all groups and societies which exhibit a seeming proximity to radicality. The Lote-Os would have considered themselves somehow against the status quo, which is what makes them so dangerous. And then there's the fact that their engagement in the aesthetic is entirely reprehensible, further compacting the impossibility of Garreaux's mentioning them."

And, of course, why did I care? For the past couple of weeks, the significance of this society, and thus my Transfixions, had seemed to hinge on Garreaux's having referenced them. But the pursuit had swallowed my Transfixions whole.

Fortunately, I had encountered Erskine-Lily, and all had been blissfully regurgitated.

When Griselda left, I got up and looked in the paper bag, I was hungry. Inside was a Tupperware tub of green. I opened it. It looked familiar. I put a spoonful of it to my tongue. It tasted, indisputably, like apple sauce and carpet.

Hermia
English-ish Eccentrics(-ish)

VII

H ermia Druitt, coincidentally, became acquainted
with some of the Négritude women just discussed, including the Nardal sisters. But she was most
acquainted with Roberte Horth before Horth's tragically
early death in 1932. Hermia must have resonated in many
ways with the writer's prose-poem and its protagonist
Léa, a brilliant intellect who evinces "a taste for dressing" and "the eccentricities of fashion," but ultimately is
treated as a cabinet curiosity, praised by her white peers
but barred from more intimate friendships because of
her dual heritage.

In an era which produced an above-average number of eccentric dressers, including Edith Sitwell in her
Plantagenet clothes, Nancy Cunard in kohl, ivory ban-
gles and leather, the Bright Young People in their arrays

of fancy-dress (notably Hermia's fair-weather companion, Stephen Tennant, whose favourite costumes included the Queen Marie of Romania), the most outré of all had to be the Marchesa Luisa Casati, who notoriously paraded the canals outside her Venetian palazzo, naked beneath furs, walking leopards on diamond leashes. Who would have her chauffeur paint her swan feather dress in bull's blood before entering the opera house, where people would faint as she passed through the throng.

Josephine Baker

Among all the noted eccentrics, it is Luisa Casati to whom Hermia's approach to fashion bears the greatest resemblance. As with Casati, Hermia can be considered an embodiment of the quaintrelle—often equated to the "female dandy," but more specifically a woman of extreme style who did more than follow or even lead in fashion. For both, attire was a serious socio-cultural *modus operandi*, shield and sword. Perhaps most importantly, it was a kind of material poetry. This was a time of heightened "frock consciousness," as Woolf would put it.

That the two are analogous, as devotees to, and exploiters of, style, is fascinating considering in other respects they were so far removed. Namely in race, class and wealth. Although eventually amassing twenty-five million pounds of debt, spending the last of her days in a Chelsea flat, Casati forged her image through extraordinary wealth: her patronage of Picasso, Man

Ray and Augustus John, her infamous Venetian palazzo, her Capresian villa stuffed with occult instruments and antique magical textbooks, white peacocks running around indoors and live boa constrictors as necklaces, green chemical fires burning in the fireplaces and 'costumes' designed by the Ballets Russes. At one dinner party, the Marchesa remained absolutely motionless whilst a few seats along the dimly lit table sat a waxwork reconstruction of herself, so that the confused guests (victims) were quite unable to know where to look, or whom to speak to.

Whilst Hermia did not have recourse to such wealth, the equivalences were there. She could not throw enormous balls where the floors were lined with fur, but she could always *attend* such parties and outdo all and sundry. Hermia's array of outfits were hired from theatrical costume departments, created by peers, or eventually, constructed by herself (after her own costume training). Hermia wore items from the previous centuries or decades long before there was a term for such a thing. She once paraded an 18th-century gown (smuggled by a friend for the weekend from the vaults of the Victoria and Albert Museum), of the kind requiring a sideways entrance through the door, knocking over an entire champagne fountain with her voluminous pannier (the dress escaped injury). Her hair was often carefully brushed, spritzed, powdered and moulded into a rococo-style beehive, a waxed goose plume on top or decorated with a fretwork of jet and pearls (ultimately inspiring a friend to write an entire treatise positing the idea that the crimped 'Big Hair' of Versailles and other courts was ultimately inspired by the Black courtiers and servants throughout Europe at the time). Sometimes she dressed á la garçonne, especially á la 18th-century admiral, and whilst she could not afford leopards, for a period was known to go about with a sleek tame fox. Hermia's most mythical appearance came at the height of Bright Young antics. The event was the Patron Saint Party hosted in London by the newly widowed Mrs. Glenda Rope and her son Freddie—a provincial pair, recently liberated from a miserly suburban existence imposed by Commodore Rope (they famously had to sneak issues of Vogue into the house). Desperately craving glamour, the Ropes opened their doors to half of London. The party was set to bring together a range of generations and milieus: politicians and radicals, demi-monde and Beau Monde, modernists and decadents.

Hermia replied the same day to accept on the condition she could "prepare" weeks in advance. Agreeing, the Ropes found their house invaded for the next two weeks, with set designers passing in and out of various rooms installing all manner of theatrical contrivances and working mysteriously behind screens. Everything was scrapped at the last moment, and a new idea was devised. Jump ropes, much in vogue at certain ballets that season, were installed in the upper gallery that overlooked the hall.

On the night Hermia made her entrance the room went dark, causing considerable bewilderment which did not abate when a limelight scintillated on the upper gallery. There a figure—blazing wings and rippling robes—could be seen stepping off to her apparent death. But the figure appeared to hover through the air before gliding demurely from rafter to rafter and alighting in the centre of the room beside a waiter. Picking up a cocktail, she turned to query a gawping dowager about the most suitable time of year to plant lilies—"the church variety: I've a thing for them you see." Two of the guests fainted. These goings-on were described in a *Daily Express* society column where she was referred to only as "one negroid poetess."

Unlike Casati, Hermia's race brought an entirely different dimension to the matter of personal style. There were those who did not look at Hermia and see an eccentrically dressed woman, or a quaintrelle, but instead configured her unusual attire as an extension of her Blackness—wrote it off as "some wayward negro element," "part and parcel of my black blood." So Hermia interprets the prejudiced gaze of those she encounters—"All quite unaware, I'm sure, but it is a face I have come to recognise everywhere—one sees the dull, goosefat glaze of eye. The universal pallor of bigotry."

It was clearly impossible for some to look at Hermia and see anything other than her race (as they conceived it). Being confronted with a Black woman who unashamedly engaged in the realm of appearance elicited similar reactions from the supposedly more enlightened who *could* find expression for their experience: Percy Wyndham Lewis, writing about encountering a "mulatto girl" at a party, who most surely was Hermia, describes her appearance as "driven by the barbaric and primitive will to ornament," concluding that "the African blood was very much present in that one."

Perhaps Lewis had been reading Hegel, who posited adornment as an undesirable primitive urge—and a feminine property of the Other. Hegel, like so many other thinkers from Plato to Adolf Loos, sought to preserve the image of an unholy triumvirate of femininity, adornment and Otherness. To the likes of Lewis, an inheritor of such concepts, Hermia embodied the dreaded intersection so openly that she undoubtedly posed something of a challenge, a threat to the established framework. The striking and intimidating sight she presented had to be demoted through such ideological manoeuvres.

For the most part, however, Hermia found great tactical merit in her attire. For any person of colour, passing through the streets of London in the interwar years could be an ordeal. We know this from the likes of poet and BBC broadcaster Una Marson, who moved to London in 1932, living with the Moodys in Peckham where Hermia also lodged. Her poem "Nigger" was published in the League of Coloured People's quarterly, *The Keys*: "They called me 'Nigger' / Those little white urchins / They laughed and shouted / as I passed along the street [...] And though to-day he soars in every field / some shrunken souls still say / 'Look at that Nigger there' / As though they saw a green bloodhound / or a pink puppy."

An ordeal passing through the streets but also, we might imagine, in the drawing rooms of society hostesses, in restaurants and nightclubs and libraries. In stations, theatres and shops. By dressing as she did, however, Hermia found that she was able to deflect some of the attention away from her skin, to divert from the racist commentary which she often dreaded.

Not a naturally anxious or shy person, Hermia was known to remain indoors for weeks in a state of anxiety, watching passers-by from behind her blood-red lace curtains, fully dressed and ready to leave, but unable. She found herself overwhelmed by the prospect of receiving abuse in public. (Interestingly, following such dramatic entrances at parties as the one described above, Druitt is known to have hid in a bedroom for the rest of the evening with friends designated to bring her champagne.)

Her costumes had the ability to temporarily dazzle onlookers into confusion, or sometimes admiration and awe. At the very least they could shut people up, even if they went on to racialize what they saw, rather than view it as a creative trait like her outlandish peers or enshrine it as 'eccentricity.'

Even today, Western conceptions of eccentricity very rarely tend to encompass Black personas. This is because eccentricity is tethered to the idea of a rarefied and semi-fragile aristocracy. For it to work, unconventional elements require a foil of idealised social stability, hence why the history of eccentrics is even more populated by the white, privileged and wealthy than other histories. Wealth does not necessarily preclude eccentricity—the impoverished state of nobility is a commonly depicted form. Note that, however, without class, eccentricity loses prestige. Historical enumerations of working-class eccentrics, though still attached to traits like archetypal Englishness, can frequently dehumanise the subject. Such writing takes on a cabinet curiosity or 'freakshow' aspect in descriptive quality. The working-class eccentric is depicted as stupid and 'mad,' the noble eccentric is portrayed just a little left of the Artist and the Genius.

More contemporary Black figures who can be said to have occupied the sphere of the Eccentric still tend to be allowed this role in limited fashions. We might think of Grace Jones, whose performativity and engagement with style situates her within both High Camp and avant-garde visions of eccentricity, but being Black,

Jones has been presented equally as 'mad,' as behaving and dressing as she does, as creating works as she does, due to being a Mad Black Woman. The truly transgressive often dislodges the appellation of eccentricity.

Thus, on the one hand, eccentricity is *not* seen as erupting from Blackness, and on the other, the personal effects and performativity of the Black eccentric generally *are* seen as erupting from Blackness, but not as eccentricity. Instead, as eccentricity divested of the constellate qualities of creativity, nobility or genius, which is deemed something else altogether.

I conspired for a week: how to best befriend Erskine-Lily? I wasn't sure he would appreciate my just turning up at his door. I couldn't ask Griselda or Hector either, that was clear.

I hoped, by keeping their company, to alight upon something of use but they never once mentioned his name.

Recently, Hector and Griselda were in good spirits, which was foreboding. I could tell because, although they retained their baldness of manner, their vitally unromantic way of looking at the world, they had come out of their roboticness a little. They spoke more vigorously and laughed more frequently.

We were sitting in their flat.

I was extremely irritable. With the return of my Transfixions, so returned my sensitivity to all things Residency. Garreaux, the seminars, the Residency people, had all become more abrasive than ever. The sight of the Garreaux book when I walked in the door had instantly set me on edge. It was going to give me a headache again. Griselda paused to acknowledge my presence, then they recommenced speaking and I had to lie down on the sofa.

I hated them both even more than at the beginning of the Residency. All talk of LOTE, at least my LOTE, had been dropped. The Lyta foundation was worked into convoluted theories about convoluted theory.

I lay trying to read another page of *The Bostonians* as they droned on. Early on I'd hid it under the sofa so they couldn't throw it away and I would always have something to read when they went on like this.

Their words pummelled me, a constant downpour. Kept me lying there, kept me unable to think. A bright yellow hex.

Had I not been able to slip out of it before? Behind the magic glass. If they only stopped for a minute I could get up and go, could plot about how I was going to meet Erskine-Lily and talk to him about Hermia and the portraits on his wall and LOTE, but instead a noxious yellow mist drifted into the room. If it reached me I would be inoculated again. I fixed my eye on the gothic finial—the one I'd uncovered—until the mist receded.

Now that Griselda had no interest in LOTE, I couldn't remember how we had ever been able to bear each other. It was mysterious. How had this *friendship*, which seemed to me now an altogether alchemical process, happened?

"I don't know how you can just sit there staring into space. Why don't you do some studying for the next seminar?"

I sat up. Hector was gone. Griselda was standing above me.

"I am doing work," I said, because I knew this would annoy her. "Why do you consider it more productive for me to sit up clutching a textbook thinking of nothing than lying down thinking of something?"

She didn't say anything but instead dropped the Garreaux book onto my lap and went to make some coffee. I thought I would be sick. I sat very still, trying to ignore the book.

It was apparent more than ever. Our essential difference. My orchidaceous fantasies = her florid night-terrors. I was convinced she felt them, felt the extravagance of them. Hers was an eye free of all glitter. Proudly delusion-proof. She was not merely averse to fantasy, but a professional hunter and killer of chimeras. I harboured far too many chimerical impulses not to incite bloodlust. She was purposefully trying to stop my Transfixions, my Escape, me. I was certain of it. It was the great unspoken thing between us.

And something had been ignited in her after meeting Erskine-Lily. After *my* meeting Erskine-Lily. As if she knew what I was planning.

"But you're right," I said. "I'm not doing anything here," and I got up carefully, letting the yellow book slide from my lap onto the floor and half-running out before she had time to respond.

I knew that it all depended on my avoidance of them, that it was a period of mutability and therefore susceptibility. No stray thoughts. None of their tampering. I was to consecrate myself: a new Escape was at hand.

One afternoon, Griselda knocked vigorously at the door. I fell silent and eventually she stopped. But I did not hear her descend the stairs.

The telephone laid waste with its reiterative gargle. She was calling me from her mobile. I lay there paralysed by its ringing, believing that somehow the noise was conveying news of me with it through the door. It stopped and I heard my letterbox clap. Then she stamped downwards and I felt guilty.

I was afraid to see what she had posted through. Afraid to get up at all in case it was a trick and she had sneaked back upstairs to listen at the door again.

There was a ripped slip of paper with a note on it:

Couldn't wake you up. You're to meet Lind and Jonatan at Residency Centre at 2pm. G

It was almost two now. I had, as so frequently was the case, been just about to fall asleep when she started knocking.

I hoped not to see anyone from the Residency on my way. As soon as I stepped outside it started to rain in a way particular to Dun—unexpected sun, columns of fine spray interrupted by prismatic floods of light. These almost tonic rainbow flickers were an effect not just of light and light rain, but the colour of the stone, the cobbles, the proportions of the buildings.

The town was empty as usual. I passed the tower of blue granular stone which looked set to dissolve in the matching air.

Empty until,

"Mathilda!"

As I turned up the street to the Residency Centre, Griselda came marching along with Jenny D and Max, who both, of course, surveyed me suspiciously.

"Got my message? Just got back today with Hector actually."

Had they been away somewhere?

"Anyway, we're on our way to this awful event. It will still be going on after your meeting."

"Oh, I'm afraid I can't."

"Well, probably for the best. Don't know how I got roped into it. It's some kind of party hosted by the same person who threw a drink over Hector. Erskine-Lily. Hector's not coming obviously." And then I was sure I saw it—a vindictive, triumphant flash, as if she'd known I would reject her invitation before hearing what it was. Had I said yes, I was sure what followed would not have been an invitation to Erskine-Lily's.

I suppose I could have just turned up to the party. But this would be altogether humiliating, and she knew it. She was taunting me. Had she not so recently just called Erskine-Lily idiotic? Had she not deemed him delusional and narcissistic?

I went to the Centre and found the Conveyors in Jonatan's office. They fell silent at my knock and for a moment I thought they were going to pretend they weren't in, like I had done only an hour ago. But Lind opened the door for me.

"Ah Mathilda . . ." They both looked exhausted.

"Thank you for coming—we'd like you to come in later today at three o'clock if possible. It's very important so we would appreciate if you could make it."

It was typical of the Residency to ask me to meet just to arrange a meeting. Such behaviour generally means the perpetrator wants to prolong the suspense *and* to catch you off-guard in person.

I didn't get back to the Centre until quarter past three. If they were going to make me wait to hear I was being kicked off the programme, then it was honestly my prerogative to be late.

When I knocked and opened the door I was met by the back of their heads. They were both sitting with their backs to me, at the interviewees' side of the desk, and had to crane their necks to see me, revealing consoling smiles.

"Ah Mathilda, please, if you'd like to sit down."

I was surprised to see that Giuli was there. He had his face in his hands and was sitting opposite, where they should have been sitting. He didn't even look up as I sat down beside him.

"We've just been informing Giuli about an incident which has affected both of you."

"We truly don't know what to say."

A light hand—more consolation—on my shoulder. It was Giuli. The gesture took me by surprise. When I looked around, I saw he had been crying.

"It is regarding the White Book Project," Jonatan said.

How could this affect Giuli? *I* had stolen the old project from the archive. They had found out by now, presumably. Had he stolen one too?

"As we have just been informing Giuliano, two projects have gone missing during the assessment period. It's why we've taken so long with this submission to give feedback to any of the Residents. As you know, you submit your projects on the day to the administrative office. They then come to us on assessment day, when we go through each resident's submission in order. All submissions were present at this point. We conduct our assessment in a room just along the corridor. The room is locked whether we are in it or not. Not because we anticipate a theft, but to stop any accidental viewing, in other words—Audienceship—of the projects. At some point during the day, probably when we broke for lunch, the two projects disappeared, suggesting they were removed by someone who took and replaced the spare key from this office, or had previously made a copy. We have looked everywhere. We had hoped the submissions would resurface in time. Only your two have disappeared and we cannot say why, or for that matter, how. We can only apologise."

At which point Giuli's tears began again and he cupped his hands to his face. I wondered if I should do the same. Instead I comforted him, put a hand on his shoulder.

"It doesn't make any sense," Giuli said at last. "It is not ... fair."

He looked at me, wide wet eyes confidential, as if we were two Babes in the Wood weathering a storm. Hopeless orphans left for dead. I wondered if I was missing something, had not quite realised the value of what had been lost. What if, because they were unable to assess our work, we could not continue the programme? But then Lind said,

"We thought it only suitable to give you an increase of stipend for your losses. Think of it as compensation if you will."

Giuli shook his head as if to say all the money in the world wouldn't make up for this *etc etc*. He began to silently cry and again covered his face. I placed my hand on his shoulder again.

"We're so sorry, Giuli. Of course, you will not be expected to make any submissions for the White Book Project until you feel quite ready..." I couldn't help look away from Giuli to the Conveyors to see if this bit was directed at both of us. Seeing it was, I had to cup my own hands to my face, which was developing an uncontrollable smile, a smile that was turning, to my dismay, into a laugh. I couldn't stop. It was the kind which was quiet—crushed

lungs from trying to smother the sound. The kind that, thank goodness, wetted the eyes.

Eventually, with my hands still covering my face, I managed
to breathe, but the intake was such a violent gasp that it took even
me by surprise and I hoped they would interpret this as a gasp of
sheer misery.

As they began apologising again, I heard Giuli's chair scrape
back. My own display of grief had riled him up.

"*Che cazzo? Vergognoso!*" The office door slammed behind him.
Keys jangled on the key rack. Having been shocked out of my fit I
was able to see that some of the keys were missing, notably the key
to the Archive.

"Well," I said, standing up, "Thank you for informing me. I
don't quite know what to say to either of you; I'm sure this is the
first time anything like this has happened so I won't be placing any
blame for the moment."

Jonatan nodded like a scolded child, but Lind looked at me in
such a way as to say *don't fucking push it.*

Outside, Giuli stood sulking. He clearly felt a comradeship had
been established between us.

"What do you think?" He was looking at me sideways. "One
of those bastards?"

"You mean someone on the Residency?"

"Who else? Maybe they want to fuck with us, maybe they're
jealous? People like to take things into their own hands ... Mete
out justice ..."

"But who?"

"Dunno," he shrugged.

His certainty that the books had been stolen unsettled me.
There was every chance that someone had seen me steal the book,

had watched me leave the Centre that early morning. Its disappearance had the feeling of a threat. A warning. They had 'dirt' on me.

Jonatan had said they assessed submissions in order. If this was alphabetical then it meant they must have assessed mine prior to its having gone missing. But they hadn't said alphabetically. Its disappearance, therefore, could have been fortuitous, saving me from exposure. Even still, the feeling of a threat was unshakeable. Someone had the book and could give me away whenever they liked. Griselda was, of course, the one who had taken me to the Archive in the first place.

It seemed unlikely, her stealing my project, but then she had stolen and incinerated a tutor's and a student's work. Was this an equivalent, was this justice being meted out? I couldn't help but recall her face today on announcing that she was going to Erskine-Lily's.

If it was a punishment for my sudden withdrawal, my Escape, why then had Giuli's work been stolen? His trespassing in the Archives, taking a book and passing it off as his own project, was inconceivable to me. Giuli didn't have it in him. He was in this sense more devout than Griselda and Hector. Took rules more literally. It was more likely his work had been stolen to make it look less like a personal attack.

Giuli was watching me intently as he smoked. Like he had not seen me before. A look of extreme confusion. A stupid, ignorant look.

"How are you Black?" he said.

"What?"

"Why are you Black?" he said again, and when I did not reply he shrugged and traipsed off.

The next day, my phone started up again. I was being besieged. I thought about unplugging it, but eventually presentiments about the missing book made me pick up, even though I was certain it would be Griselda.

"Hello?"

"Puce."

"Hello? What was that?"

"Oh, hello is that Mathilda?"

"Yes, sorry, what was that, I didn't quite hear you?"

There was a sigh of resignation.

"Puce..." the voice said. "Solar-powered bird bath, topiary, puce and Polyfilla! There; my mouth was absolutely burning, Mathilda, I'm so sorry. The phone was ringing and ringing and I was starting to think I had the wrong number altogether, and then I got this obsessive longing to say puce, then Polyfilla, then solar-powered bird bath, then worst of all, topiary. Not especially good words even. And the longer it went on ringing the worse it got, and I thought, 'oh, my god' if poor Mathilda does answer I'm just going to have to say at least one. It wouldn't do to just say it to myself now. I was compelled. I hoped you wouldn't notice. Does this sort of thing happen to you all the time as well?"

"In other ways, I think."

"You see," he said confidentially, "I was listening to the radio; there's this advert that comes on. I was trying to think how best to translate it into English. It's about a home and garden sale. It's awful, but it came on as the phone was ringing. Anyway, are you interested at all in LOTE, beyond its relation to Garreaux?"

"They were on your wall, the members?"

"I knew it. *Please* come over at once!"

He must have procured my number from Griselda yesterday. She would not have liked that at all.

V

"Liverish."

"No, *loooong*—personality-wise."

"Beyond extra."

"Quelle dommage."

"Quelle dishwater."

"Oh, by the way, I have this book as well."

"Yes, I adore it: it's abominable!"

"But did you also know about the *cellotape*?"

"...?"

"Picturesque."

"...!"

"Another thing, do you know about these rouge landlords?"

"No?"

"It's in the English-language papers. 'Rouge landlord jailed for illegal conditions.' There's a string of them, they are getting really bad, Mathilda."

"Not rouge, *rogue*."

"I'm burning-at-the-stake, darling."

"Well I'm in an Elizabethan deathbed, wrapped in a funeral blanket."

Still laughing, Erskine-Lily got up from the couch and his limbs immediately gave way. He collapsed upon the blue swathe of carpet, then righted himself with near unbearable grace.

"But *why* was I trying to get up? Can you remember?" he fell back onto the couch—a flamingo shot down (there was pink plume on his beret).

"Oh, you got up to see about more to drink."

Our glasses were empty. We had guzzled both bottles of pink foam in the flat and by this point were so giddy and excitable that I could now hardly recall what we'd just been discussing.

Indeed, I can still only incompletely remember that first hour: a rush of chatter, too quickly drinking down each glass, puffing those botanical cigarettes. What I could always recall perfectly, however, was the flavour, the tenor that was struck up between us from the moment I entered the flat, for it later seemed that in those initial minutes we laid down the foundations for an entire friendship and settled upon the tone on which it would be conducted.

Something else I was sure about that first hour was that we did not discuss Hermia, or the paintings on Erskine-Lily's wall, but the prospect of it all was there, just levitating above us, lending an excitement, an anticipation to our meeting. It would have felt excessive, crass even, to speak of our mutual interests so quickly when it was clear we had both been waiting all our lives for a co-conspirator.

Erskine-Lily rose again, this time successfully, and went to check just in case there was after all another bottle; there wasn't. This was a shame because I'd never had a sparkling wine like it. Not even in the days when Malachi and I would regularly steal from an openly racist wine merchant in Primrose Hill.

When it hit the glass, it piled up as a foam to begin with— almost like champagne or prosecco poured too quickly, but denser, and instead of turning to liquid the foam became a sort of fine drinkable froth, more fluid, which fizzed wildly on the tongue and tasted like a light dessert wine, but not remotely cloying.

"Yes, it's an abomination isn't it? Did you know it's thirty-two percent, you wouldn't know from drinking it because it goes down so lightly."

"But what exactly is it?"

"Oh, my god," he said in a way that reminded me just how antiquated the expression was, though he was, I thought, a little younger than me. "You don't know? It's a relatively local wine. It comes from just outside Dun. They quadruple-ferment it which makes it so frothy. It's called orion, or it sounds like that," he said pointing a beringed stalk-finger to an empty bottle, "always unlabelled, so I've never seen the spelling."

Staring at the bottle, he visibly plummeted into a deep and vigorous daydream for a few minutes and then said, "Do you know if the apology money is through?"

I was rather thrown by this question, but yes, I had informed him of my meeting with Lind and Jonatan and the story of the missing books in the blur of the past hour.

"It is."

"Then would it be diabolically rude if I asked to borrow say ten to fifteen Euros?"

"Oh ... of course," I said, not unamused by this request. "I withdrew some before I came." And I pulled out some notes from my coat pocket. I was delighted at being able, for the first time, to be generous with cash. Between this and the buzz of wine I was feeling like a veritable woman of means, a formidable grande dame.

"... *Wonderful*," he sighed, and his eyes—the mystical, half-flooded eyes of a seal—swelled. He hugged me. Yes, I was practically a patroness. I felt him thin and tremulous beneath today's burgundy doublet and plum velvet robes, with a matching train.

I wondered how he'd make it down the stairs in those acres of velvet—made, in fact, from a well-preserved old theatrical curtain. But I heard him descend easily enough—and watched with delight from the window as he crossed below, train rippling behind over the cobblestones.

I was left alone for the first time in his flat. With the portraits. Clouds set the light quivering. Stray beams dived into the room only to dash themselves against silver, gold and glass things, or drown themselves in the room's dark cornered regions.

On the table lay a packet of botanical garden cigarettes, some split Adderall capsules, a copy of Nancy Mitford's *Highland Fling*.

There was a television in the room. It was one of those from the mid-noughties in which DVDs slid vertically in the side. The TV was behind glass in an old display cabinet which I opened to reach inside and press the power button. The screen went blue. I couldn't find the correct button to switch from DVD to television and turned it off again, thinking this proof of some mysterious authenticity, just like the portraits.

I was still scared of looking at these portraits. I avoided altogether the ones I did not recognise because I thought they might contain Transfixions-to-be, Hermias and Stephens to come, and that was too much.

Instead, I went to the bookshelf and removed a familiar book I had glimpsed on my first visit. *Black Modernisms*. I put it on the table we had been sitting at because I knew, on his return, it would be time to talk about Hermia and the others.

This return was announced by banging on the stairs. I didn't investigate in case it was a neighbour. Eventually Erskine-Lily came in with a wine crate tied to a kind of sledge with a long piece of frayed blue fishing rope which I had seen on the downstairs landing earlier. He explained it was primarily for the purpose of dragging crates of orion up the stairs. He hated carrying things more than anything. But if you didn't go up quickly enough the sledge would get caught.

"I need a longer length sleigh." He untied and opened the crate, went to chill some bottles, then came back through and sat on the sofa, out of breath, staring at the ceiling. On it was painted a stylised cosmos. A delphinium-blue firmament. Delicate platinum septagrams and pentagrams organised around a pointed silver sun. Or a moon in the style of a sunburst.

He sighed looking down at the sledge, still a touch short of breath.

Beneath the plumed beret, his hair was in braids which hung just below the shoulder, each end entombed in an opal pendant.

"It's always so maddening waiting for the bottle to chill, isn't it?" he said. "But I can't tell you how thankful I am for lending me the money."

I pointed to the book I had placed on the table.

"I was just wondering where . . ."

"Oh you know, I can't remember . . ." he said looking distant, and then sat up straight:

"But you don't mean to tell me you've actually *heard* of Her! The others I presumed, but . . ."

"It was through Hermia I came to LOTE in the first place. Or through the others, to her, to LOTE."

"But how, specifically, did you find out about her?"

I was unable to withhold any longer. And so I explained. I gave him the story of my Transfixions, not fully. I didn't, for example, describe the sensations. Only intimated that I had been drawn to them, was fascinated, and had thus come across Hermia by way of this interest, which was true.

"Extraordinary!" he said. "I figured out you were interested in LOTE when you came because," he said, "because, well just from looking at you, I thought, how can *she* possibly be in this very town and look like *that* and not be interested."

I wondered if he was going to mention his dousing of Hector, or my fainting feint.

"I knew it couldn't, just couldn't, be some dull reference to some dull theorist like the other two that had you interested in the Lote-Os, what were the chances? But the fact you were on the Residency threw me off entirely. I've seen them come and go for a while now. Every year. They're never not here except for the early summer and sometimes even then they have a summer programme. I actually had a few around for dinner, in the hopes that you would come."

"The invitation wasn't properly relayed to me."

"What are you doing on that awful programme?"

"The money," I said. "And it's brought me here to Dun to learn about Hermia. For free. They don't know that obviously."

"Oh, well how ingenious. But they are such desolate souls. Drab to the point of dangerous. *She* suffered at the hands of the Drab, you know," he said looking up again at the portrait of Hermia. "They couldn't stand the fact of Her."

"Where are these pictures from?"

They were almost heraldic in style.

"Oh, I can't remember," he said.

The large ornate frames made them look like jewellery.

"They're more like giant brooches than paintings."

"That's one of the loveliest things I've heard, so I'll confess that I painted them," he said, watching as if expecting me to suddenly withdraw the compliment at this knowledge.

"It's not that I like having my own pictures up. It's just I wanted real paintings of Them and this was the only way."

"But, of course, this absolutely settles it," he said. "My earlier proposal... When I was labouring under the delusion that all three of you were here because of LOTE, and not because it was mentioned in that book...Really...people should explain themselves properly."

I still couldn't fathom how he managed to get this impression from Griselda and Hector—you just had to look at them to know. I didn't say this.

"My proposal to reconstitute the Lote-Os."

"Oh, we absolutely have to. But please tell me you've come across her poem."

"*The Fainting Youth*? No. But surely it's not that all the copies are lost—it's just if they've passed through anyone's hands they've had no idea who she is. It is possible none survive but I think not. I couldn't bear that."

"Do you know where she lived, in the town—it wasn't here was it?" I asked, looking around the room.

"I don't think so."

"How did *you* come to live here? Were you born here?" I asked, and though he covered it well, I felt the slightest frosting over. Closing up. He didn't want to speak about himself, at least not in terms of biographical detail, terms I also avoided. No talk of Life Before. Before now. He had managed not to reference his history at all, even as I had ranted on about my Transfixions, about which only Malachi knew. Erskine-Lily hadn't told me, I realised, how he'd discovered Hermia. He was, I thought, an Escapist; manoeuvred conversation with the self-preserving reflex of one.

"Oh, you know..." he said, and I pretended not to notice his wish to shift the conversation. And he saw this pretence and knew I wouldn't press him.

"But I have a theory about it," he said.

"About...?"

"About where Hermia lived. You can help me with it, I hope." He went to the kitchen and came back with a chilled bottle.

"Do you know one of the things I adore about Hermia? The way she simply blotted everything extraneous out of her life. Or rather it wasn't blotting out, was it? It was simply living."

Indigo petals lingered beneath his eyes. Dark watercolour daubs that may well have been enhanced by make-up. We refilled our glasses.

"It's an out-and-out abomination, isn't it?" he said, holding his glass up to the light.

"An abomination through and through."

We drained our glasses simultaneously. Before long we became so drunk and pleased that we were lifted out of conversation and incorporated into the scheme of the room.

The sun played on the portraits.

Etiolated rays.

The stars on the ceiling gave a dull gleam.

Uproarious ornaments.

Meridian. Delphinium blue.

Rushes, ferns, precinct, recesses.

Curtains ready to blanket eyes from a turbulent day. Looking like the way the sea looks too material, too fabric.

The singed rug looked glorious.

The mantlepiece illuminous—carved pink soapstone! pink-cream soapstone!

Hermia looked down from one portrait
Stephen from another.

Hermia
Black Anxieties

XIII

Mrs. Woolf was there—Edith's rooms in Bayswater. A lecture by someone I can't recall. Afterwards we all stood about eating the infamous halfpenny buns, drinking tea black as tar. I didn't speak a word. Hope she didn't notice or she would have thought me very stupid. Quite unlike myself.

—Hermia Druitt to Stephen Tennant, December 1928

Prevalent amongst many a Black artist in modernist Europe was a symptomatic anxiety. I have already mentioned Hermia Druitt's experience with sudden bouts of intense racial selfconsciousness. By all accounts sociable, confident, a wit, the same acquired social anxiety that kept her sitting at the window, afraid to leave the house, reared its head in other ways, and in one respect made her behave in a manner she would regret for the rest of her life.

This was the avoidance of her literary idol, Virginia Woolf. Druitt, it appeared, had numerous occasions to meet the Bloomsbury luminary. Woolf, often portrayed

as a Sussex-dwelling hermit, could be equally cosmopolitan; a social animal sought after for dinner parties
on account of her personality as much as her celebrity.
Even the notoriously sharp-tongued and bitchy Sitwell brothers, presiding over such dinners, were ever
enthused by the prospect of an appearance by Woolf
(who was also the only one to put them in their place).

Hermia was once invited to a literary Sitwell dinner
the day after attending one of Edith's Bayswater salons
but, discovering Woolf would be in attendance, sent her
apologies.

Failing the Sitwells, there was still the likes of Stephen Tennant, also a friend of Woolf's, but Hermia
avoided any contact or introduction through Stephen,
who was admittedly considered frivolous by some of
Woolf's social set and therefore not necessarily the
ideal association for one already so worried about the
author's perception of her.

Still, there would be other opportunities; but here
again Hermia found her anxiety overpowering her. One
such example was Garsington. Hermia arrived at the
country residence of Ottoline Morell with a troupe of
Bright Young People. They had driven in on a fleet of
Daimlers from a party in London (the Ropes') where
Morell's daughter Julian had been. Spotting Woolf on
the moonlit lawn, Hermia proceeded straight to Julian's
bedroom, where it must have looked like she was holding an exclusive court but was actually hiding.

What any number of intellectuals, artists, radicals might think in theory, the reality of having a mixed-race woman under the same roof could take them off guard, or worse; each new encounter could prove disastrous. Hermia's anxieties were well grounded, even if at times frustratingly debilitating.

We might wonder how Woolf would have reacted if she had met Hermia in the end. Maybe it was the case that Hermia's fear was particularly well founded when it came to the novelist she so admired. No end of criticism has been written on the subject of Woolf and race, particularly due to one diary entry in which she describes the sense of "degradation" a Black man (" █████ gentleman"), "perfectly fitted out in swallow-tail & bowler & gold headed cane," must experience every time he sees the back of his hand, "black as monkey's outside." The racism is inescapable, even if not always the type of racism many white scholars have posited. We must also consider the Dreadnought Hoax, in which a young Woolf and friends posed as an Abyssinian royal entourage in a way that we would immediately recognise today as blackface. It was an attempt at negating colonial attitudes which ended up evincing those same attitudes.

Then there is Woolf's famous essay, *A Room of One's Own*, with its line, "It is one of the great advantages of being a woman that one can pass even a very fine negress without wishing to make an Englishwoman of her." The line is rather oddly placed, for many reasons.

It is above all, however inadvertently, a line which serves to exclude Black women from the "woman" of the essay. Hermia, reading this text in 1929, would have been alarmed to discover she was not, after all, a woman, by virtue of her being "a very fine negress." Surely sufficient cause to exacerbate any fear of her literary idol.

Unlike many of her modernist contemporaries, Woolf's relation to race also bears evidence of intellectual and practical resistance against complicity in the deeply racist society which shaped her. This would include her work with Leonard, laboriously researching and compiling the effects of commercial imperialism on East and North Africa.

There is also Woolf's often elided cultural interest in Black arts. Whilst cultural appreciation does not preclude bigotry, it would have been of importance to Hermia, a Black writer, to know that Woolf respected artists of colour, published a Black writer and worked with an Indian writer, at a time when many sought to divest non-white artists' work of intellectual value (more openly than they do now).

Virginia and Leonard were, unbeknownst to many today, camp followers of Paul Robeson. Both met his wife, Eslanda Robeson, the activist and actress. Woolf, famously stinting with praise, mentions Eslanda favourably in her diary as "vivacious" and (intellectually) "supple," personality traits she uses elsewhere in her journal to praise her friends Christopher Isherwood and T. S. Eliot.

Woolf was also conscious of the Harlem Renaissance and Paris-based Négritude writers, though more research into this is required. Woolf scholar Jane Goldman has identified the influence of African American writer Jean Toomer on Woolf. Toomer's *Cane*, a much-neglected modernist masterpiece, shares a particular intertextual relation with *To the Lighthouse*, Goldman having discovered the name "Toomer" noted on the margins of Woolf's manuscript of the novel.

Figures of colour were never far from the Bloomsbury Group. Any of the bisexual painter Duncan Grant's Black boyfriends and models such as Patrick Nelson or Berto Pasuka may well have crossed paths with Vanessa Bell and possibly Woolf herself. The Afro-Trinidadian Marxist and writer C. L. R. James, published by the Woolfs, also writes about his experience of meeting with Edith Sitwell. Mulk Raj Anand, an Indian English-language writer, assisted the Woolfs at the Hogarth press and describes them fondly, unlike some other figures he met or worked with, such as T. S. Eliot and Clive Bell.

It may well be that Hermia would have had a better reception with her idol compared with many of the other white artists and writers she came in contact with. In the end, there is no evidence of Hermia Druitt having ever met Virginia Woolf.

I demanded Erskine-Lily take me on a tour of Dun, something I'd never properly been given.

At night we swanned all about the town, which had become more palatial, more of a pleasure-ground than ever, amplified by Erskine-Lily's painting of it as much as my own will to envisage it as such—he seemed to be an astute historian of the place and rendered a context so thrilling I wondered if he was making it all up. This was hard to tell since it was as much a folkloric history as any other. In his company, the town, already a place of alternately consoling and faintly distressing beauty, became an extension of his flat, which was in turn an extension of his attire, physical person, persona.

We visited the square with the grey obelisk.

"This obelisk is where the two so-called angels are said to have been chastised. The town is unnamed in the story, but it says in *The Book of the Luxuries* that the citizens sealed two winged beings within a pillar. Hermia, Stephen and the other Lote-Os believed this was the very pillar and town. What certainly is true is that the book dates to around the early sixteenth-century and it's not unlikely a small number of people read and practiced its teachings, as was the case with numerous other contemporaneous mystical treatises. And, as you've gathered, Hermia and Stephen sought to re-establish this practice in their own way. There's a sort of allegory in the book—have you managed to read any of it?"

I told him I didn't even know there was a translation.

"There isn't. I managed to get some bits translated. The person doing it lost interest. Then I hired an academic but I could only afford so many pages, including a sort-of-allegory, it's extremely charming.

"It follows a section on the nature of the Luxuries: Where we consider angels to be spiritual messengers, we might well think of the Luxuries as sensory ones, communicating with the aesthetic aspects of the soul. They are described as having skin like black marble and parti-coloured wings that far outstrip any peacock. They wear immensely gaudy-sounding robes (not unappealing) and outrageous jewel-encrusted slippers (tremendously appealing).

"The book also says these same Luxuries once came to the Lotophagi—the Lotus Eaters—and revealed the lotus fruit to them, showed them how to make wines from it and how to weave and carve innumerable delicacies from its other parts. Ornaments, jewellery, marquetry and so on.

"When the Lotus Eaters beheld the Luxuries, whose mouths were something like ruby, they also stained their nails and cheeks and lips that colour with the juices of the lotus fruit and flower. (Varnish, rouge and *lipstick*, Mathilda!)

"Of course, everyone knows the Lotus Eaters from Homer. *The Book* gives another account, saying when dull Odysseus looked upon all this he was horrified. He could not distinguish man from woman. They insulted his sense of goodness, this effeminate people who loved nothing more than to dine upon the lotus and decorate endlessly. To lose themselves in the holy act of adornment, which *The Book* calls volution.

"The volute, you see, is divine: the sinuous line, the serpentine line, the corolla, the curl, the twist, the whorl, the spiral and so on, are all related in their volution, convolution, revolution. Volution is the essential and irreducible aspect of ornamentation, just as the phoneme is the smallest irreducible unit of sound in language. Locked into each coil, each curl of ornament, just like the coil and curl of your hair, and my hair, darling—Afro hair, as we call it—is the secret salvation of us all."

He had coloured said hair with a fine nacreous substance.

"We are, you know, fundamentally ornamental creatures. Especially the likes of us. And the Lotus Eaters were the arch-decorators of myth. But even the Greeks must at one point have realised the importance of ornament. They called the universe "kosmos," meaning decoration, surface, ornament: something cosmetic. Like make-up. Like *lipstick*! Like rouge. The cosmos is fundamentally blusher. But then the Greeks probably got the idea from somewhere else. They could never stick to it. Which ruined ornament for everyone. Plato was quite the basher of ornamentalists. He had it in for what he called philotheamones—sight-lovers, spectacle-lovers. Framed them as veritable trash next to his kingly philosophers who loved the true beauty of ideas, not the decorative beauty of the world. Long after the Greeks' seriously puerile demotion of the ornamental, the Romans, Kant, Winckelmann, Hegel and all the rest damned it for being cosmetic. "Inessential ornament," they called it. Quite hilarious really: if you ever need evidence of someone's brutishness, it's deeming ornament inessential!

"They humiliated our ancestors for adorning themselves in flowers and beads and gold and tattoos and braids and jewels; they're still at it. The universe as decoration, of course, comes from Black people, and the idea survives even after the ransacking and incineration of our libraries and palaces—the same very precise fractal geometry, unknown to Europeans for centuries, can be found underpinning ancient forms of adornment like millennia-old Black hairstyles, but also in the architectural organisation of whole kingdoms, most famously the medieval Benin city and palace."

"Oh but the allegory!—*The Book of the Luxuries* says that the Greeks wiped out the people they called the Lotus Eaters and tells us that Herodotus situated them in North Africa. Others West.

"The Luxuries are the primordial lotus-eater. Indeed, they were thought to have disappeared with the Lotophagi until they reappeared one day in a town in order to bequeath *The Book of the*

Luxuries. But they were mistaken for wicked spirits, for demonic tempters, and sealed inside a pillar.

"There was a woman known to visit this pillar, having observed the punishment of the Beings from her rooftop. She returned nightly, whispering to the interior spirits.

"On her rooftop one morning she noted a strange flower, growing from a crevice, something like a lily—or a lotus—but as hard as shell. She plucked this flower and took it to the pillar where she cupped it against the stone and put her ear to it and could hear a form of music inside. The music described a system. In this way, the inhabitants of the pillar dictated to her the *Book*.

"In accordance with their system she grew a secret lotus garden upon her roof and spent her days in idleness and luxury, cultivating her senses. The End!"

He was vibrating.

"I'm *quite* devout you know."

"Devout how?"

"Religious! About the Luxuries. I'm a modern day Luxurite, just as She was, some ninety years ago—Hermia."

I wanted to ask if he honestly, literally, believed in the winged beings. Did he, for example, think they were stuck inside the obelisk right now? I presumed Hermia and Stephen had possessed what amounted to an aesthetic interest in the Luxuries, that their reconstitution of the Enochian Order of the Luxuries (which may never have existed—Griselda had suggested the book was possibly a work of 19th-century charlatanism) was a matter of taste, and even of principle, but without any serious theism being involved. The great interest in all things occult that sprung up in the period had always seemed largely affected to me, except for some of the postwar talking to the dead: Stephen had grown up in an atmosphere of séances and mediums, his mother often trying to contact his father.

The glee Erskine-Lily exhibited as he related the story of the pillar persuaded me not to ask him, just in case. I would not have minded, did not mind. Whereas some individuals' credulity was entirely off-putting and terrifying, in Erskine-Lily it could never be. Would instead be a corrective to the much scarier fanaticism of the Residents.

No, what was off-putting was the way it reminded me of my own flights of grandeur, which would come when I thought about my Transfixions in the wrong way. It was clear just now that those flights had never stopped. That all this time I had been figuring out a way to augment myself, to mythicise my Transfixions and then slot myself in. And now here it was. They were all part of this, and now so was I. So was Erskine-Lily, who struck me once more as a Transfixion, a living one.

*

On the reverse of a miniature portrait in violet letters.

Erskine-Lily

(Image on frontside: portrait of Erskine-Lily in the style of an oval miniature by Nicholas Hilliard, sporting what might be a silver pinked doublet or androgynous Elizabethan bodice and hooped skirt (the portrait cuts off at the waist); a high collar with a volumi-nous, gauzy lace ruff that reaches the limits of the image; match-ing lace sleeve cuffs; emerald earrings; brimmed black sugarloaf hat with a jewelled band, cheeks glazed orchid. On the flat azurite background, a heraldic device depicting a fruit on a branch like a white-pink raspberry, faintly translucent with an opalescent lustre, leaves half green and half yellow, the branch emerges from a cloud; some gold letters below read AOTE. This fruit is simultaneously

an allegorical device and heraldic as the figure reaches to pluck the fruit whilst gazing towards the viewer.)

SPAN: ████████

MEMORABILIA: Obscure aesthete-quaintrelle and amateur painter resident in Dun. Revived LOTE, a minor society of the '20s founded there almost a century earlier, said in itself to be a revival of a Renaissance society.

SENSATION: Moonlight sighing up and down the tube of the spine, and through hollow bones.

★

he Sandses instantiated the unusual but not incompatible combination of conspicuously vast coffers, manifest in so many freshly minted families of industry (and visible in the gaudy spectacle of Sands House), with an intellectual parsimony that betokened the foxhunting people they irremediably were (vis-à-vis the present generation's addition of Lady Sands, neé Hall). Under their roof, two branches of philistinism happily entwined. It was not the first or last time they would meet but it was one of the most notable.

There was a billiard room beneath the fountain at Sands House. It was not in the original drawings. Those plans showed an underwater ballroom beneath an artificial lake, but learning this had been done in at least two other houses, the Sandses decided "it would not be *impressive*." Instead, a colossal fountain, large enough for twelve people to swim in comfortably, had been implanted in the grounds. Peering down, one could see white fish move—looking quite as if they were hewn from the same ashen stone as the fountain— and further down, when the water was clear, a glass bottom gawked straight into the scarlet precincts below.

When he was fifteen, in an animal panic, Lymenick hurled from his bedroom in the west tower the large bottle of *Smythe's Nectar* he'd persuaded his cousin to collect from Selfridge's on her way from London, and which came in a thick glass bullet vial. He retrieved the beauty unguent in the night, feeling around with his breath held underwater for any crack but found none.

The Black Princess awoke to discover a note demanding her presence in the Scarlet Room immediately or they would all just die. They had been shown the way last night by Lyme, but she couldn't help but suspect a prank; she was anxious on account of those dreary but too-energetic hearties with whom it would seem they were to share the house. She couldn't say if she was furious with Lymenick or not for this arrangement. He knew better; but then he had had to endure them longer than she—one was his brother. (But then, Lyme was neither a woman nor a negro.)

The handwriting familiar, she dressed and went down by way of the kitchens.

As she was on the point of entering the Scarlet Room, accessed from an underground passage near the wine cellar, a perfume became conspicuous. She observed that the panelled passageway to the room was strung with garlands. A mild prelude, for she threw open the door and saw the room was furiously wreathed: bowls of hyacinth everywhere, lilies in pots of crushed ice, orchid heads floating in the fountain (a miniature replica of the one above). Posies of amaranth, lavender, violet. Florets of aromatic flowering herb.

In the midst of all this, young men rolled around on rugs sniffing loose curtain tassels and writhing ecstatically. A woman—quite possibly Mrs. Peterson, the legendary Doctor's wife—sat in a high-back Mackintosh chair, reading, in paroxysms of laughter, a threatening fifty-page letter to one of their party from a Mr. Wyndham Lewis that was being passed around. Two others—Elizabeth and Edythe—lay upon the billiards table staring up at the glass ceiling where the ripple-cut-ripple of fish was visible.

"Hermia, *please* do come and talk."

"Hermia, too miraculous—you coming in now—"

Hermia acquired a cordial glass and a slim-necked bottle of Eiswein that was bobbing in the fountain. It was some time before she made it to the alcove, which designated the back of the otherwise circular Scarlet Room. There she knew Flora would be, murmuring with her brother as they always did at this stage of parties. The Mesozoic Hour, they always said, though now Hermia contemplated it she couldn't say why.

"'Lo darling," Flora said as she sat down. "*Absolument* creamy, isn't it, back together?"

"What have you accumulated this Mesozoic hour—oh, why do you call it that?"

"What?"

"Mesozoic?"

"Well," said Hugh who had just broken out of a trance, "it's when everybody becomes primordial, or is it primeval—at parties, but as to why Mesozoic specifically I can't remember, can you, Flor?"

"Oh never mind, I want to talk about what we've just been talking about."

"Oh yes," said Hugh and slipped quite suddenly into another stupor.

"Absurd," Flora said.

"What were you talking about—"

"Oh yes..."

Hermia became aware of a note beneath all the flora, like the scent of automobile or old gas lamp.

"What on earth are these?" she said, for she had also noticed, at the same time as the scent, a cut-glass bowl full of clear liquid beside her on a table. In fact, everywhere there were bowls, dishes, silver salvers, upturned cloches poised between books, brimming with this transparent essence, and strung over the lip of each receptacle were pieces of shorn tapestry, curtain tassels, strips of floral brocade, Broderie Anglaise and black Venice lace.

"The Sweet Oil of Vitriol," said Hugh, called forth by Hermia's question.

"Diethyl Ether," said Flora in her loftiest Girton College chemist voice.

"Alleluia!" Hermia said in an Italian accent, for she had always wanted to sample Ether. She was long overdue. The Marchesa Casati had been taking the stuff well over a decade ago.

"But who brought it?"

"Do you not know? Brian Howard arrived in the night."

"Brian!" said Hermia. She had not seen him in years. "Does he know I'm here?"

"He is the one who demanded we slip a note under your door on discovering the Black Princess was at Sands House. Of course, Flor told him you wouldn't be up till now. He is presently with Lyme and that show-off hearty," said Hugh who looked rather put out.

Flora sat up.

"That's what we were discussing."

At last she related the garnerings of the Mesozoic Hour as Hermia tentatively sniffed a piece of tapestry (though there was probably no need, she was sure she could already feel the effects of the Ether in the air). They had been discussing Lyme, who, it was agreed by all, was behaving strangely. Not only remote but rude.

"Almost brutish."

"As if he truly were converted."

"Which is impossible given his..."

"Appetite."

"But of course hearties can have the same appetite for buggery."

"Oh I know that, I meant the depth of his appetite not the..."

"Palate."

"I don't follow."

"Never bloody mind," Hugh said.

"Well anyhow," Flora said. "Brian is said to be 'personally investigating' the matter, I..."

Hermia wondered if it were the Ether causing an auditory hallucination, for she heard a very jarring sound.

Now Flora and Hugh seemed to hear it too. A threatening noise. In fact, everyone in the vicinity went quiet and still as a shadow rippled across the Scarlet Room.

They all looked up.

All the fish had migrated to one side of the fountain.

Then there it was again—the shadow, the noise. But now they witnessed a blur of pale. Like a much bigger fish. Like a body. Then something silver.

The noise again.

"Someone's hammering at the glass," someone laughed

with a voice that did not believe its own utterance.

But a crack was visible. No longer an inscrutable chip. Water was trickling through.

Hermia now stood up. People began making their way for the door, but they were too weak-limbed to reach it. Some managed to dive beneath the billiards table.

The silver thing must have been hefty. When it returned, all the glass cracked, shattered and fell in.

No one was killed, although a giant koi landed on the lap of Elizabeth Ponsonby in her Madame Vionnet gown on the billiards table. "Quite sore and bruise-making," but she was furious, she said, on behalf of the poor dead fish.

A war broke out between the hearties and themselves.

(*Ourselves?* The Black Princess remembered she had sworn never to use this word again.)

It transpired the hearties were genuinely bemused. ("As if they were ever anything else.")

"Must have been one of your party, bloody nasty thing to do to the fish."

Brian resurfaced.

To escape the atmosphere, he, the St. Clair siblings and the Black Princess took blankets and walked to a field and lay beneath the sky which resembled foil.

On returning to her room that evening Hermia discovered a large antique weapon, a spear from one of the suits of
Sands family armour, impaling her bed. Vertically piercing
right through the mattress. The white counterpane was pink
and red with blood. This was because, she now saw, the spear
bore right through one of the grand white fish.

She held up a lamp to examine its scales.

*

Downstairs last week—
    "... to mine the mental solarium!"
    "Enamoured Enamel!"
    Next week—
    "Nothing to do but leave the country again. You could be
arrested, darling."
    Next year in Dun—
    The letter was from England

Dear Hermia,
You shall never escape.

Presently at Sands House—
    "Enamoured enamel..." one of them had said. She could
no longer trace the meaning of this phrase, which played in

her mind almost every night before sleep, even now she was with them again. She could wake Flor this minute and ask her. But Flor was more exhausted than she after witnessing the speared fish. And now she felt herself become light . . . it was too late . . . she would sleep and forget until tomorrow.

Tomorrow in the evening, eight o'clock—

After dinner, they all gathered in the morning room, where the remaining hearties would not think to look. The Black Princess was to give 'a lecture.'

In her room (Southwark)—

The turquoise brush gleamed. Another knock at her door. She turned from the sky and came towards the figure.

Presently, the morning room, Sands House—

They gathered in the late afternoon, curtains drawn, electric chandelier off, fire dampened so not a seed of light betrayed them.

In the pitch dark, the Black Princess opened the door of an old lanterna magica, struck a match and lit the wick inside. At first, only a watery beam, barely reaching the makeshift screen. But then she adjusted the flame of the lantern and a white disc appeared on the screen like a diminutive moon.

She fed a cylinder into a sleek black object with a silver horn; like the lantern, this old phonogram was something from their parents' childhood. Strings rose up from the horn, startling those gathered, who, in the dark had not witnessed her operating the machine.

She slotted the slides into the lantern. The white circle became coloured. When she adjusted the lens, a picture came into focus: an illustration of a pale tower in a garden.

Now, over the music, a voice rose from the phonogram. Her own voice. As it spoke, the slides shifted, sometimes showing painted pictures not dissimilar to those in a fairy book, whilst others were photographs of the Black Princess and various sitters in costume. The voice said:

"And it was to be a feast day! The Free Children Utopians would feast on the tops of their towers tonight and in their gardens and in their communal palaces.

"Yes, Comrade Arke had just heard the announcement on the radiograph: 'each soul to be granted lodgings for life.'

"This, of course, was already half a century's custom, for most. Yet there had still been, until today, those in the Central Consuls who wanted the old ways back. Who would requisition whole towers and castles, for destruction, for a new project or a false repair; the people turned out, sent away to distant lodgings. Away from their gentle comrades. This was done, everyone now knew, so that the people might vote for the old regimes which those few Consultants claimed safeguarded from such horrors as requisition and relocation. 'Inheritance!' they would say, 'is

our hope. Imagine if once again the people, not we Consuls, could possess their own rooms. This true possession would be, not merely for life, but for our children, and their children!'

"But their false requisitions had been discovered.

"Then there had also been enduring Landlords, by virtue of some ancient decree, to whom the Localities gave payment for use of those last few towers and castles. Not a few, but a third of all lodgings, some said. But no longer. Now each soul was granted rooms for life, the radiograph sounded again.

"Above and below, Arke heard a cheer erupt and she found herself cheer too. She looked out the window to see others do the same. People called to those below who had not heard.

"She gave thanks for these rooms that were hers from now till death, unless she chose to move (the Exchange Bureau had offered her rooms by the sea). A poet she could be till death. No other labour need she perform unless she desired. For it had also been declared that with the defeat of the enduring Landlords and the treacherous Consultants, no more payments were requisite. Minor Duties were no longer obligatory.

"She descended the tower and passed through the Universal Gardens. In the hallowed groves and pleasure parks people ran cheering, shaking hands, on occasion stopping to talk to Arke.

"The Tyrants have been foiled, my dears!" The shining face of the Lecturess.

"Then came costumiers from the Localized Ballet, running out with streamers and banners of gold and blue. The gardeners ran out from the Botanical Gardens, half covered in earth and wearing hastily made tiaras of bluebell and white rose, handing out wreaths and bulbs. Bulbs to grow indoors, to mark the day.

"She ascended another elevator to the rooftop of a tower where Café Utopus was located. She joined the glittering proletariats. She joined her friends who leapt up at the sight of her. They sang till it was dark. And then onwards to the Café Lotus on the roof of the music hall where stray members of both the Localized Orchestra and the Universal Chamber formed a band and began playing symphonies. And Swann began singing antique jazz and what had once been called 'Negro Spirituals'..."

The lantern projections became impossible to see. The chandelier was ablaze, the doors had been thrown open. The bores came into the room.

The Black Princess' voice still issued from the phonogram.

"...and amongst them danced figures with skin like onyx, with hair coiled, gold and black, and eyes like black lamps. Everyone knew them. They came on such joyous nights. But never before had they spread their wings...never before had they brought us fruits—"

The voice was sucked out of the air. The Black Princess had leant down and stopped the device.

Erskine-Lily owned three DVDs which he watched frequently.

We dressed up in rustling gowns the colour of algae to watch one of these, a film about Ludwig II Bavaria. It was by Visconti and about four hours long, a.k.a. "sprawling."

It was a sufficiently decorative thing to have playing in the background during the day whilst chatting away and drinking, occasionally tuning in to the plot. Erskine-Lily would become rapt for several minutes in a scene before returning happily to conversation.

Today, mid-chatter, I noticed him suddenly stiffen. I thought at first one of his favourite scenes was coming up, but his face alarmed me. He had heard something.

I could hear it now. Footsteps outside. A man's voice began calling through the door.

Erskine-Lily sat there entirely still, eyes fixed a little to the side, as if by this extreme composure something might happen—the voice would go away.

I did not say anything, just waited with him, watching the film until the voice did at last go away. I'd been unable to understand anything the man was saying. Five minutes or so later, Erskine-Lily noticeably relaxed. I was going to ask him what that was all about, and turned to do so, but before even opening my mouth, noticed a small twitch of his head, as if he had anticipated my question and was begging, willing me not to ask.

I did not. I knew far too much about not wanting to be asked about the life held at bay. The Escaped from.

After the film he said,

"I'm going into town: I've some tedious chores to complete; do you think you could housesit? You don't have to stay all the time. Only please don't answer the door. Oh—don't worry, no harm will come to you." I agreed. He gave me the keys and I went home to collect a few things.

Walking back through the town that night I passed some of the locals—the woman in the mantilla made her procession, surrounded by relatives, all eating ice-cream or white floss. She nodded at me. I passed the Cynic's bar and waved and she shrugged and rolled her eyes at me through the window.

When I got to Erskine-Lily's building, I looked at the exterior for the first time and was struck by how it resembled, at least in this light, nothing so much as a greenish shell, entirely composed of moss and verdigris. Inside, on the stairwell, it was dilapidated but structurally holding together very well. You could still see the original colour of the stone. The interior of Erskine's flat was only slightly tarnished and must have been restored at some point or simply kept in good condition.

I wondered if anyone else lived in the building. In my own building, I had observed lights in other flats across the courtyard—albeit sparsely dotted. I always forgot to count, to keep track of how many lived there in total.

I was inclined to think he was not paying any rent, was simply occupying one of these many empty flats. Perhaps the man shouting outside his door had something to do with the fact that Erskine-Lily was squatting, as did his need for someone to housesit.

I had never been into or seen his room, where I was to sleep. The walls were painted, depicting an evening grove of trees bearing yellow fruits and birds with half-stretched wings. There was also, as I'd expected, an assortment of garments on racks. Some I already knew were hired from the National Opera House costume department whilst others had been designed by him and made by a local seamstress. There was also a large old poster from a museum exhibition. It showed a drawing from a manuscript, reminiscent in style of those angels in *The Book of the Luxuries* Griselda had come across. One wing was red and the other white. It wore a kind of herald's outfit, with white stockings and hose. Its face was subtly divided. One half, with wispy hair on the upper lip, was supposed to be that of a 'feminine youth' and the other, with longer hair and slightly redder cheek was that of a 'masculine lady.' It was an alchemical angel, the Hermetic Androgyne. In one hand was a mirror, reflecting trees, in the other a dusty pink egg.

I lay in the living room reading over *Black Modernisms*, occasionally standing up to look at the portraits then having to sit down again because of them. He had left out some notes for me to look through. We were planning to conduct our research into LOTE in a more serious manner. There would be things of interest for me amongst the notes, apparently.

There was a page of an old newspaper. An article stated that the Marchesa Luisa Casati was visiting the country and would be staying in the countryside, not far from Dun.

The Marchesa was a known occultist and enemy of Alastair Crowley's. I knew that some years before her first recorded meeting with him, she had planned to visit his Abbey of Thelema in Sicily. This was around the same time the paper said she visited the Dun locality. She had decided against Crowley. The prospect of being a groupie probably did not appeal to her. She already considered him a rival and envisaged their egos clashing, which they later did. LOTE was a viable alternative. Something that would have genuinely fascinated her without requiring her to become a camp follower.

After this, I found photocopies of an architectural drawing, and what looked like a kind of census. The drawing was, unquestionably, a plan for the Residency Centre. The census showed a long list of artists who had been living there in the '30s, when it functioned as live-in studios. What was curious was that, on the drawing, the name Garreaux was signed.

Then I saw a name that looked like "Hermia Druitt" circled in fine red pen on the census list.

I sat there for some time trying to make sense of what I was looking at. She had lived in the Residency Centre? When I at last turned to look through the rest of the papers there were some explanatory notes, presumably made by Erskine-Lily.

The Residency Centre had been built and designed by Garreaux's father. It was, in the '30s, a kind of artists' commune—the artists living there paid a token rent. They would write to request lodgings for year-long periods, sometimes more, and by some definitions it was the first artists' residence centre.

Hermia, Erskine-Lily believed, had lived on the top floor of the building. It had been offered to her by Garreaux Senior to live in. Apparently, he had been fixated with her. To the point that Erskine-Lily even suspected he had built and designed the commune with the intention of having her reside there. Not unlike another modernist architect, Adolf Loos, who was so fixated with Josephine Baker he drew up detailed plans of a house for her to live in. The house was never actually built, but I had always found it suspect that a man who was, like many of his contemporaries, vehemently against decorative excess (in a way that recalled historically gendered and colonial tracts on ornament), should become obsessed with housing a Black woman—one who so publicly engaged in the decorative—in a monochromatic, linear building of his own conception; she instead opted to live in a turreted, gargoyled château.

Loos' house had never been built: but *this* building had been, and Hermia had lived there.

Finally, I stood up, restless, and began pacing the flat, from kitchen to living room to bedroom and back. I was trying to reconstruct mentally the Residency Centre, trying to figure out what was now on the top floor. How much had been changed?

It was above the White Book Archive, of course, but how was it accessed? I couldn't remember any door from my previous two visits. There might well have been one somewhere behind the stacks. I wanted desperately to see it. I wanted to stand in the space Hermia had lived. Had Erskine-Lily already figured it out and been there?

Only briefly did I contemplate changing out of my gargantuan hooped skirts, put together for the express purpose of watching the Ludwig film. I didn't have anything nondescript, and Erskine-Lily probably less so. No, I would go as myself—it seemed only right for visiting the living quarters of Hermia Druitt.

Outside, I bumped into the Merman. He was just exiting the Centre, looking more feverish than ever. They were all very fond, I now knew, of taking some kind of new amphetamine when working on their projects. It allowed them to stay up for days. Deborah had even been taken to hospital because of it but was already back working on her project, elevating her in everyone's eyes.

"I've been putting in the extra effort," Giuli said. "To make up for the loss. My advice: I suggest," he continued benevolently, "you don't let them get to you. Motherfuckers. Did you keep it?"

"Keep?"

"The receptacle. They haven't told you yet?" He reached into his pocket and pulled out a small glass bottle. It had greyish powder in it. Ash. The bottle was labelled "Giuli."

"Processed?"

"Maybe the Conveyors don't want to upset you further?" And then he was off.

Passing through the studio, I tried to picture it as it might have been in Hermia's time. Would she have entered through this room or the front corridor stairway?

And then outside the upstairs offices I tried to imagine the sunlit studio-flats as they had been. It was impossible. They must have entirely gutted the place in the '70s when it became what it is today.

It wasn't until I was in the office that I remembered the key to the Archive had been removed from the key rack. I continued looking anyway, wondering if they'd kept the bottle with my name on it here, even though I didn't want to think about that now. I heard voices. People outside. Leaving or entering the computer room. I waited for silence before stepping out and making my way back to Erskine-Lily's flat.

Griselda would know where the keys were. She would probably manage to get into the Archive without a key at all.

It was about five in the evening when I woke. I found Erskine-Lily in the kitchen unpacking bags of food, clearly delighted at having made some money. He was going to prepare an elaborate feast. I didn't ask him where the money came from. I left him unpacking on the promise of returning for dinner. At home I lay watching the tiles, feeling practically wistful at having been away from them so long. These tiles could be very conducive to plotting and scheming, as well as cause inebriation with their occasionally delirious glaze. They leant a coolness of mind, a midnight blue-headedness, to me that evening.

Erskine-Lily dined chiefly on innumerable tints: a diet of ethereal broths and consommés. Every day, he swallowed Egyptian Blue Lotus extract and minute doses of gold, pearl and silver suspended in gel capsules. It was part of his System of the Luxuries. And, of course, there was his drinking of orion. Since there was no concrete System to go by—*The Book* being vague and mostly untranslated—this was all of his own devising. It was by no means an unyielding system. Tonight, for example, we dined on a main course he had just read in a novella and couldn't stop thinking about:

"*On a round table, in front of the chair, a delicious meal was spread: a large speckled brown egg, some thin golden toast, curls of fresh butter sprinkled with dewdrops and resting on ice, translucent jam made from white cherries, and a squat silver pot filled with a foaming mixture of milk and coffee.*"

This was the "preliminary course"; after this we ate another passage from the same book:

"*She brought out a little grease-proof parcel, a thermos, and a tin of shortbread from Edinburgh. She poured frothy coffee into Miss Hellier's cups and then undid the parcel and offered me a sandwich. I bit into it and found a thick layer of fawn cream dotted with black boot-button eyes. It was foie gras. The luxury seemed to crown my escape. Too delighted to speak, I looked at Clare, then at the black truffles again.*"

We became giddy from all the coffee, which neither of us usually drank, though the writer was evidently obsessed with it.

Such passages and scenes, found in novels, photographs, paintings and films, were no doubt dietary prescriptions sent by the Luxuries.

Before dessert, I informed him of my recent connivings: I knew how to get the key to the White Book Archive.

"Oh, my god."

"Yes, it was easy," I said, buoyed up by his enthusiasm. "And ingenious. I just went to Lind's office and asked for the spare key to my room, telling her I'd lost it and would get a new one cut. Both my key and Giuli's had been removed and I thought they had to be with the others. She went out the room and into the one next door, which I think is a kind of filing room, and came back with the key. I was too scared to actually tiptoe behind her to watch her take it out, but the archive key will have to be there somewhere. I would have searched the filing room earlier were it not so easily accessible; I suppose it's just not an especially serious security matter."

After our pudding of sachertorte and tokaji, we went to the Residency Centre together. We were unseen, except perhaps by locals. No one was on the streets or even in the Residency Centre. It was a Friday and the Residents would be frowning at private views and launches in the city.

In the filing room, it wasn't especially difficult to find the keys. About twenty minutes of rifling through cabinets. They were all in a drawer in little key-sized envelopes with the name of the particular room written on them. I removed the key, leaving the envelope between the others in case I forgot its place, though I doubted anyone would notice.

Erskine-Lily was silent as we made our way upstairs and finally through the large red door into the White Book Archive.

When I pulled the light cord and the room burned white, his eyelids fluttered like kingfisher wings, suggesting they had spent a lifetime averted from such lighting.

The only thing to do was to start separating the shelves one by one to look for any doorway. It was going to take hours.

Erskine-Lily was at another shelf, leafing through submissions.

"It's awful, this entire place," I heard him call. "All of it."

I remembered my near conversion. Wondered if I'd have become as fanatical as Hector and Griselda, remembered Griselda's face when she brought me here, hoping to sabotage me.

"I want to check something," I said after the tenth shelf, and Erskine-Lily looked relieved to stop. I went into the back room Griselda had taken me to.

Like the first room, it was full of red shelves blocked together which could be separated by turning the spokes on the side of each.

I went to the end row on the left, spun the wheel until it parted enough to walk through, then proceeded down to 1976. It was still there—my blank replacement book.

We decided to continue looking for the door in this room. Though there was little to distinguish it from the larger room, this part of the archive somehow felt older. Perhaps it was simply because this was where the earlier books were kept.

We were only a few rows in when I glimpsed red metal: the door. Not necessarily hidden, just concealed from view by the placement of the shelves. We took turns sliding a shelf out each until the whole door was revealed. This door had a handle and did not need a key. I pulled it open to find a small, cupboard-like room. In it was a steep staircase, practically a ladder.

We went up together. It was dark, the steps soft and dusty. A sweet smell of decaying paper.

At the top there was another door. An ordinary door which we went through, to be met by a black space. I was too scared to move in case I walked into something, but as my eyes adjusted I saw outlines. Yes, there were windows here, circling the room, which I knew from the exterior of the Residency Centre was pentagonal. It was dark outside, but I could see a light in an apartment across and then eventually the sky, which was clear and furiously starred, resembling frozen breath.

When I turned away from the window, the room became half visible, as if half of everything in it had been smeared in gold oil. Erskine-Lily had lit a candle and was lighting more. These candles, which must have been very old, released a strange smell. I found a light switch but nothing turned on.

Soon enough, however, the room was relatively well illuminated, revealing the standalone bath, the voluminous poster bed, the draped walls, the flaked ceiling. We stood looking around without breathing for some time.

"It's all the same," Erskine-Lily said. "Preserved exactly as it was."

It was Hermia Druitt's room.

He slowly made his way to a cupboard and opened it. It was full of clothes. Likewise, books were on the shelves. I ran my finger along their spines, desperately feeling the need to touch them. To touch everything. And so we worked our way around the room, lightly tracing our fingers over things, silently trying to take in as much as possible before we became too unsound to do so.

I eventually meandered to the dressing table holding a candle and looked through several jars and bottles. In the vanity mirror I saw a bureau on the other side of the room.

Inside I found papers, letters, postcards.

"Why is this all still here? It should be in a library or museum," Erskine-Lily said.

"No one knows it's here—next to no one has even heard of Hermia Druitt."

"It should be in an archive at least."

"This is an archive, just not for the public."

I picked up a book; I was too agitated now to read properly. I started tucking some of the letters away in my pockets, aware this might be the last time I would enter Her room. What had she been reading? There was a first edition of Woolf's *The Waves* on the bedside table. There was a book called *Cane* by Jean Toomer; another was *Infants of the Spring*, another was *Plum Bun*. Some newspapers dated 1975.

I went back to the bureau; more old letters in a compartment, tied up. One of the first I looked at was from Stephen Tennant. Another was from Nancy Cunard, dated 1928, and seemed to be about the publication of Hermia's book. And then a dust jacket, pale yellow with thick black letters—*The Fainting Youth*, and the Hours Press logo beneath it.

"Her book!" I turned to Erskine-Lily, giving him the dust jacket. "Look for her book."

"I have been looking," he said, after holding the dust jacket for a very long time. "I don't think it's here, not a single copy... But look..."

He had gathered a small pile of papers on the floor: handwritten, full of alchemical-looking sigils.

"Her own research for LOTE, I think," he said.

I was barely listening—I was breathing quite erratically and Erskine-Lily saw.

"What is it?"

The bed was curtained; a presentiment had come over me that Hermia's skeleton, or incorruptible corpse would be there.

The bed curtains took some time to open. We were scared of ripping them as they were snagged on something. Eventually they pulled back.

The bed was empty.

The ivory-yellow walls were draped with blanched tapestries showing faded stags, ghostly pear trees and towers. Two angels holding scrolls mid-air. Wings in various now-limp colours, jewelled slippers and robes. The skin was embroidered in brown, black and blue, hair in black, bronze and gold florets turned wheat.

Erskine-Lily sat down at the dressing table, fans of dust spread and lifted in the air around him.

This dressing table was in front of the main sash window, the other windows being diamond panes, small and round. I went to one and could see nothing through it now the room was lit, except the building across the way. It must have been three or four in the morning. If someone looked up, they would undoubtedly see the candlelight.

In front of Erskine-Lily on the table was a large, wide-toothed comb. The rounded teeth were made from mother-of-pearl and it had a silvery shell-shaped handle, inlaid with turquoise. It resembled an Afro comb. There was also a bottle of 'scent.'

We sprayed ourselves with the perfume, which smelled like sweet varnish and rust.

Finally, exhausted, we lay down on her dusty bed, side by side, and wept for a short while.

Appendix B

Hermia Druitt: The Other *Bright Young Thing*

In need of addressing is the possibility that Hermia Druitt did not exist at all. That she was nothing more than a very elaborate Modernist prank, and I have been duped, as it were, by a false paper trail. The idea was raised during the Locke Interwar History conference where I presented some of my early research for this book, and the challenge was raised by a specialist in the Modernist hoax nonetheless.

What set off his alarm bells was the admittedly indisputable fact that I have been unable to locate any birth, death or marriage papers for Hermia. The absence of such crucial pieces of historical evidence is very worrying. Yes, there is a Hestia Drummond, but she may well not be our Hermia Druitt. Without any of these documents all other evidence could be considered false—each piece possible to manufacture, from the anecdotes and letters to the paintings (Hermia has not been officially identified as a sitter in any and for the most part the artists have not been properly attributed) and even the brief census records. The fact that there is no actual copy or manuscript of *The Fainting Youth* is also worrying.

The Great Modernist Hoax (which, as it happens, is not by the aforementioned specialist) shows us that the number of public and group pranks during the interwar period was prolific. The best-known include the Bruno Hat hoax, in which various literary modernists staged an exhibition. Evelyn Waugh wrote the catalogue statement, providing us with an early parody of Artspeak, Brian Howard made the fake art and Tom Mitford attended in disguise as the artist, Bruno Hat, of German extraction. The exhibition, featuring pseudo-Abstract pictures with impromptu frames fashioned from rope and canvases from bath mats, made national news.

Then there was the earlier Dreadnought Hoax of 1910, in which Virginia Woolf and other Bloomsberries posed as Abyssinian royalty, tricking the Navy into hosting a royal visit, again making national news.

There are elements in both of these hoaxes—foreignness/otherness, puncturing of self-serious establishments (as well as betraying an ultimate proximity to them), and a cliquish humour—which could easily be transferred to a possible 'Hermia hoax.' A passing, "I saw

Hermia last week," or "the Black Princess visited," in a letter or in public amongst the initiated would make for exactly the kind of in-joke popular amongst young writers and artists of the time.

We might also recall the plot of Waugh's *Vile Bodies*, in which a hard-pressed society columnist begins giving accounts of imaginary figures and fictitious fashion trends (black suede shoes) that end up influencing reality—similar real-life hoaxes were not uncommon.

The much more recent Nat Tate hoax of 1998 also has elements that might allow us to understand how a Hermia hoax could have worked. This involved the writer William Boyd and musician David Bowie duping the art world into believing in a lost abstract expressionist artist, Nat Tate. Boyd wrote and published a biography of the fictional Tate, who had conveniently destroyed almost all his work and committed suicide at thirty-two, accounting for his obscurity. Nat Tate was soon on the lips of contemporary art dealers and critics. High society casually dropped him into conversation, saying they admired his work, saying they remembered his work, had been to one of his exhibitions in the '50s, had met him.

The invention and dissemination of Hermia Druitt, poet and anti-imperialist princess, would slot nicely into this broader hoax lineage, but it would also have been a considerably more elaborate hoax, and one lacking the stunt-like aspects of the others—both more effortful and less rewarding.

Indeed, the crafting of such a hoax would be an immense undertaking (possibly as immense an undertaking as it has been to substantiate Hermia's existence). Letters to and from Hermia would have had to have been forged but I do not recognise her hand in any of her friends and contemporaries. Other very particular features (documents fabricated, diary entries peppered with allusions) would need to have been organised, arranged and planted for someone in the future to find, with the hoaxers knowing they might not be around to see their hoax play out. More of a kind of time capsule prank. We would have to ask ourselves why someone would go to such lengths for something so unrewarding. Have to ask ourselves in the case that we believed it, at any rate. But every account, every source, confirms for me Hermia's existence.

The very fact of Druitt being more believable as an invention than a real woman who lived a life is concerning. For as much as Hermia sought to catapult herself into a life of fantasy, her reality is significant, and the inclination of society to find it difficult to *picture* people of colour in Europe prior to the *Windrush*, even fantastical individuals like Hermia, is pernicious: it is not an uncommon tendency amongst historians to find the prospect of Black lives outside of familiar narratives

implausible. The difficulties I have come across researching Hermia, as with some other figures in this book, are
more surely connected to Hermia's being a Black woman
in the early twentieth century, born outside of social
convention and living for the most part outwith conventional society.

Documentation is regularly unorthodox or harder
to come by when researching people of colour from
this period, which speaks more about how society val-
ues certain lives than the veracity of their existence. In
researching Hermia, I have come across accounts of
numerous Black Scots missing from records. The most
remarkable is an Alexander Wylie, born in Saltcoats,
Ayrshire, to a Nigerian father and Scottish mother
two years after Hermia was born. This is not remarkable because Wylie was of similar Afro-Scottish lineage
to Druitt, and living in Scotland at the same time, but
because, like Hermia, Alexander travelled to Paris to
attend an art school, after which we lose trace of him.
Wylie, it should be noted, was from a background of
considerable poverty and his journey to Paris and entry
into art school would have been difficult enough for any
of his white peers.

Finally, where the likes of Stephen Tennant and the
Marchesa Casati are marginal figures in history, Hermia
was a *marginalised* figure who also embraced outskirt
cultures through leading an equally rarefied sort of existence—pursuing Life's marginalia.

We replaced the archive key on our way out, but I still had to return my spare bedroom key to Lind.

Lind looked rather bleary. She was working on her monograph.

"Would you like a coffee, Mathilda?"

"Yes, thank you."

Lind was much esteemed intellectually by the other residents, including Griselda. Was reputed to have worked her way through more of Garreaux's yellow book theory than any other living Thought Artist.

I asked what the monograph was about. She looked at me and her eyes slightly scrunched, mouth twitched. Then she continued making coffee in silence. I spoke again,

"I was wondering, Lind, what's on the very top floor of the Residency. Is it part of the Archive?"

"Oh—you missed the initial induction days, didn't you? We informed Residents on the second induction that the White Book Archivie occupies the top two floors. Yes, the very top floor can be considered part of the Archivie—it is the very first submission, by Garreaux himself, before it took book form. Naturally, I cannot tell you any more than that."

"Archivie?"

I was unsure of whether this was rare evidence of the fact she was speaking a second language, a blip in her otherwise perfect English, or a new bit of Thought Artists' jargon.

"Yes, Archivie," she said.

Back at Erskine-Lily's, our takings were spread about the floor. We hadn't stolen much. Papers, the book that I had inserted with letters, the dust jacket, the turquoise Afro comb.

"I really wasn't expecting that," Erskine-Lily said.

"No," I said, knowing he meant that, like me, he'd expected it so much, in the way he went around expecting all kinds of things that never come to pass, that it was extremely shocking.

I told him what Lind had said and we spent the afternoon speculating about the White Book Archive and Hermia's room.

Beyond Hermia living in the building that was to later become the Residency Centre, and her knowing Garreaux Senior, we were unable to find any connection between Hermia and the current Residency, the White Book Project and the Archive. Nothing as to why her room would be preserved. The conclusion, however, was obvious to us both: that Garreaux had somehow made Hermia, her life, or at least her possessions, the first submission.

"An act of blotting out. Erasure. The whole project is committed to the 'Abnegation' and Hermia was everything Garreaux is against."

I thought again of Griselda, Processing her tutor's life's work.

"She certainly didn't submit voluntarily."

"No."

The thought plagued us both. That Hermia had undergone such an extreme conversion in her final years that she had been one of the first Thought Artists.

"The father was obsessed with her," Erskine-Lily said. "Garreaux's father. Practically building the place for her to live in. I've read through the letters and found a couple from him. They knew one another for years and he had her in mind when he designed it, as we already surmised. She originally stayed there for a token fee, but look—here's a letter asking her to pay rent, not much, but how tedious of him! I suspect if he knew she could afford to live elsewhere he wouldn't have, because he loved the idea of her living in one of his buildings. He was obsessed. The son too, I think, inherited this obsession—LOTE was mentioned in Garreaux's book, her room was preserved by him and 'archived' when he inherited the building and turned it into the Residency Centre. Garreaux Senior would have been dead, but Hermia would have still been living there."

"Of course, she could have died first, and he kept it as it was. Or he evicted her."

"She has no death record either—she apparently just vanished. No wonder these Residency people are so ghoulish. Look what's worked into the foundations of their practice, even if they don't know it, it's there. These traces never leave." He was trembling.

"I don't think they do know, not even Lind and Jonatan."

If it was a submission, they would not have been able to see it.

"Indeed, I would venture to guess that Anon, who wrote so many poems without signing them, was often a woman," Virginia Woolf said.

"And/or Black," Malachi said.

We tried not to think about Hermia's room in order to concentrate on those of her papers that pertained to the System of the Luxuries. Just four or five sheets with notes transliterated into John Dee's Enochian script. Not difficult to read once we looked up the alphabet key online.

These notes proved to be instructions for an evocation: "To Make a Luxury Appear Before You." The directions called for a period of "High Aesthesis," ten days during which one would dedicate oneself to both "sensory and intellectual Beauty, namely through material ornament and ornamental turns of thought." The eleventh day was for the actual evocation ceremony, requiring a mirror and candles amongst other things that might be expected from a ritual, including instructions for a "Black Tincture." This was made over the period of some weeks and involved unsealing a flask of substances under the cold contractive force of the moon, sealing it again and exposing the glass to the influence of Venus. On the final days it was supposed to undergo the "Peacock Stage," during which the inky contents of the flask flared iridescent. (Perhaps this was why she and Stephen were so fond of the *Pousse-café.* Its spectrum of colours symbolised the nacreous tincture which in turn symbolised, in its final peacock days, their own flight from reality into fantasy.)

Hermia had also written out an underlying theory. It referred to Kant's account of the beautiful. Kant states that the pleasing sensation caused by the beautiful issues from "purposiveness without purpose," meaning our senses perceive the beautiful object as having been designed, well-crafted, for something—but actually there is no purpose. For Kant, the ideal example is a wild tulip. ("As if!" "I know, *quelle humdrum.*") The sight of this wildflower glimpsed on a mountaintop seems so much like it has a sense of purpose, implies design, yet it has not been made for anything directly intrinsic to human pleasure or existence, and so, unlike perceiving a well-made object or even natural one, like berries which have an immediate purpose accompanying the sense of fitness (eating), the wildflower (like all purely beautiful objects) doesn't, and this sense of "finality without end" causes in us the kind of uninvolved pleasure belonging only to the Beautiful. Hermia went on to reject much of this, including the idea that only 'useless' things could be beautiful, arguing that useful objects can have the same effect because the faculty of judgement is able to separate their beauty from their use as well as comprehend their beauty as arising precisely from their use and appreciate this with aesthetic indifference.

This feeling of purposiveness without purpose is vital, however, to the System of the Luxuries because it also *does* indicate a purpose, and this is the purpose of communing with the Luxuries.

This idea of purposiveness predates Kant, surely, she wrote. *Origins in the System of the Luxuries?*

She went on to allow for a contradiction in her theory. That the sensation of the beautiful arises because something is beautiful *and* that this sensation has a functional property. If there was no beauty the sensation would not arise and one could not commune with the Luxuries—one must appreciate the beauty *in and of itself* to be able to experience *the sensation which allows one to confer with those Beings, which is indicative of their presence.*

At what time of life she wrote these notes we could not determine. It may well have been that she had dropped all interest in LOTE in her youth, like all the other members had seemingly done.

But the notes had been lying out in her room, Erskine-Lily said, not in a drawer with the other old papers.

I was reminded of the Marchesa Casati in '60s London after her bankruptcy, visited by a small but adoring coterie of queers who had heard about the chimera living alone in a rundown Chelsea flat, sifting the bins at night for fabric and feathers for her wardrobe. She had died attempting to contact spirits—the intense strain she had put herself under had triggered the stroke.

"Oh, please, let's do the ritual!"

I was burning through my stipend.

Erskine-Lily sustained himself by numerous tricks and schemes, often amounting to full-time work. Some of these tricks I knew myself, like exploiting the fact certain websites didn't charge your card until the products had been delivered, before which you simply had to order a new card and they couldn't charge you. It was prudent not to do this multiple times in one year with the same company and worked best with online food shopping, but unfortunately no such organisations delivered to Dun. He also did the simple but very effective complaints trick, if it could even be called a trick. This comprised writing to supermarkets and requesting a refund which would come in the form of a gift card or vouchers or sometimes even cash. You never actually needed the receipts in the end, though they might insist on this initially. You could simply go and photograph the barcode number without buying anything. The most I had ever managed from one complaint was £100 in vouchers, though usually less. They soon all added up, however, and meant occasional bouts of luxury when otherwise broke. Erskine-Lily was much more adept, never coming in at less than £100. But again, this couldn't be done too frequently.

Then of course there was shoplifting. The easiest and most jeopardous, the jeopardy rising exponentially in correlation to darkness of skin. Thus, if Erskine-Lily was at risk of getting caught, then I doubly so. Bearing and dress provided only inconsistent forms of deflective magic against the downright magnetism our skin held over not just security guards, but the self-appointed security guards of Life who moved amongst the customers.

I hadn't needed to shoplift since coming to Dun, but I still awoke with the stress in my stomach of having to steal and wanted to alleviate Erskine-Lily of this stress.

Erskine-Lily also had innumerable other little tricks, some I knew and some I didn't, nor did I ask. I did not get the impression these were in the same technical echelon as Malachi's more professional methods (which included bypassing payment on taxi apps and securing sometimes vast loans without having to pay them back) but still involved clever little things, amateurish and high-effort for the reward, but essential to living as Erskine-Lily lived without having any work, or family money, or any kind of welfare. Although I wondered, from his weekly trips to the city, if he didn't after all have some kind of part-time job too embarrassing—for him—to mention. On returning from these trips there was a background air of exhaustion, of fear, that was familiar. Very occasionally I glimpsed in this person of extreme charm, of gentility, an astral chill. I would observe him, in those moments of tiredness, staring up at the ceiling when his eyes, liquid brown, would become vast and celestial, and dissolve the whole room in something unquantifiable, something miserable.

Luckily Dun was cheap. Crates of orion were cheap, the cafés were cheap. Though we began dining regularly at the restaurant with the blue dome, which wasn't.

Erskine-Lily had been there once but hadn't noticed Hermia and Stephen in the friezework.

"Oh, my god," he said when I first took him. "This is it!"

He went on to tell me he was sure that this was where a performance had been staged by Hermia, Stephen and other members of LOTE one summer. The amateur reworking of the Saint Christina the Astonishing opera—the one he had played the day I met him.

"So the figures up there, and there...?"

"Quite, they had the place redecorated specifically for it. Stephen paid for it all. I can't believe it's been here all this time and I didn't know."

The waiter-owner was standing over us.

"The bill? Of course. How was your meal?"

"Oh, it was *really* abominable, not just the food—the whole darling place!"

When the bill came I briefly saw the panic of someone who has ordered more than they can afford on Erskine-Lily's face and settled the payment before there was any chance to protest.

"Let's go to the city to hire those grey cappae magnae, we'd better run though, the bus is coming now," I said to distract him.

It was our trips to the city that really left us financially depleted. We would go there for the National Library or to hire something to wear from the Opera house and also for the few hair shops. Then, whilst we were at it, to the garish restaurant with the sea anemones, then a bar above the restaurant with multitudinous frosted glass booths, by which point we'd miss the last bus back and have to take a taxi.

When we careered about the city, the sight of us both together brought out something in passers-by which when alone was not as vehement, at least for me (people, I was coming to realise, coming to love, were terrified of me). One day a group of English tourists, buffered into confidence by the language barrier, threw beer bottles as we passed. They burst around our ankles, crunching beneath Erskine-Lily's heels (which resembled green marble Corinthian columns). The timbre of aggression told me that this was more directed at Erskine-Lily than me, though I was part of it. After this we took more taxis during the day.

Whenever he had money, Erskine had clothes made. He would take them to a seamstress in Dun, the same woman in the mantilla I had seen about. He'd bring the fabrics and show her drawings of his own or a printout of a Renaissance painting and she would take them and wave him away. Sometimes it would take months and sometimes days, whilst other items were never heard of again and he didn't dare to ask or try to reclaim the money or fabrics.

"It's a miracle she does any of it," he said. "She's really a genius. She was once a couturier seamstress at one atelier or another."

I had also bought fabric, sheets of moiré, blue-black and oleaginous, with streams of truffle-brown panne velvet. I'd sketched a kind of power suit to give to Erskine-Lily who reproduced a

technical version of it and took it with him. As soon as he left I realised I'd have no more money until my next instalment, almost a
month away.

I supposed I could go to Jonatan and Lind and ask them to forward a portion of my stipend, but even if I knew they would do it,
I felt it would put them back in the power seat after the loss of my
submission. It was too much bliss not having to worry about the
White Book Project anymore.

I considered how we would eat for the next week—we couldn't
get food delivered to Dun and all of our other methods took time,
possibly weeks. The only option was shoplifting, which had to be
done outside of the town since there were no large chains here,
and even if there had been, we couldn't risk getting caught in Dun.

To avoid thinking about it I looked up at Hermia's portrait.

Sitting alone in the room, I still got caught off-guard by the
sight of my Transfixions on the walls, feeling I had practically willed
them into effect. That in abiding by our self-imposed contracts,
Malachi and I had somehow actually materialised our Escapes. We
had allowed for nothing else, provided no loopholes for the drabness to slip through. But that day the old feelings were gnawing.
I thought dizzyingly about how stupid I'd been—not in spending
all my money for the rest of the month, but in exposing myself to
the old feelings. And yes, that I was spending stupidly too, that
I should be saving every penny for after Dun—it would not last
forever. Five or so months left now.

I stood up and went to look at our papers, now mixed in with
Hermia's. It was our tendency to work lazily but consistently on
LOTE and Hermia. We were still trying to ascertain who exactly
had been part of the Lote-Os. That Erskine-Lily had come to the
same conclusion as I had, a thing that had so shocked me on walking in that evening and seeing said conclusion on his walls, had

once seemed to confirm everything. But now it was evident we shared so many common interests that it was only natural we had followed the same course. That didn't mean it was correct. People unwittingly arrived at identical and incorrect theories about historical figures all the time. We could only really be sure of Stephen and Hermia, all my other Transfixions were speculation. The Compendium mentioned Casati, Nugent and Cunard as associated figures but there was nothing material beyond the vaguely worded letter Griselda had found. It could all so easily be a mistake.

That said, we had also found a letter to Hermia from Richard Bruce Nugent, whom we knew had been to Dun on one occasion, and another from Nancy Cunard containing references that might well have been related to LOTE.

We were too scared to revisit the Archive.

The appendix in *Black Modernisms,* the one that introduced the possibility of Hermia being a hoax, had left me feeling first melancholy, then a pressurised gloom more like external weather than internal feeling. I couldn't figure out why the appendix had induced this atmosphere, because even the author had concluded that Hermia was not a hoax.

Sitting there now, leafing through our stolen papers, it became clear. The prospect of Hermia being 'made up' had awoken me to the possibility of the opposite: that not only was Hermia real, considerable efforts had been made at blanching her from history; unmaking her. By Garreaux, and perhaps others. So little of her had survived, in part because all her possessions had been hidden away in the Residency Centre. But what if other things, like birth and death records, had been destroyed alongside every copy of her poem? Even *Black Modernisms* had been missing from the British Library. The Augustus John painting had been removed from display at the National Museum.

The door burst open and Erskine-Lily poured into the room looking more delighted than I'd ever witnessed. He'd been gone a while.

"Get ready quickly, we're going into the city."

After his trip to the Couturier he had gone on a whim to the city, he told me, where he'd managed to arrange "an abominable treat."

"Pack some things—we'll be gone two nights."

He refused to say more.

Finally in the city, we turned into increasingly expensive streets, then, as we were passing a particularly imperious looking build-ing—a hotel—he linked my arm and turned into it. We were at the concierge and someone was taking our bags. We were in a carpeted lift. We were being led to the end of a similarly carpeted corridor.

"The Pink Suite," said the porter, opening some double doors.

It was accordingly pink—like shell innards. There were tasselled cuboids of plush for sitting on, lobster-shaded. There were round oak side tables and a harpsichord all painted with minute rose schemes. There were three large oils, each showing a roseate ocean, entitled *Incarnadine I, II and III*. Part of the ceiling was a grid of stained glass showing a philosophical garden with lots of very pink flowers. Pink glass portholes looked out and down into the palm court of the hotel. Warped magenta glass doors led out onto the balcony, which overlooked the city.

When the porter was gone, I grilled Erskine-Lily, but he still wouldn't give away a thing. In fact, I would never really figure out how he wrangled the suite. I later decided the most viable explana-tion was that he'd been in touch with the PR team to say he wanted to review it for a magazine, something I had never quite managed myself. Again, a less technical, more social trick, different from the way Malachi would have done it.

Around the same time the luggage arrived, a complimentary bottle of champagne (pink) was brought through. As soon as we finished it, we took the lift downstairs and asked the concierge where the nearest supermarket was and for more ice buckets to be sent up.

On returning, we sat on the balcony with our backs to the city, looking into the Pink Suite and guzzling away the two bottles of champagne we had managed to steal. Had I not been with Erskine-Lily, I would have wept at not being with Malachi.

By the second bottle, which Erskine-Lily said was no orion but good enough, we were ravenous and decided we needed to dine as luxuriously as we would sleep that night. We orchestrated, as carefully as we could, a dine and dash. First we chose our restaurant, a grand pan-European brasserie. It was neither too far from nor too close to the hotel. On the hotel's Business Centre computer, we planned our getaway, and checking we would have enough for our bus fare back to Dun in two days, booked a taxi in advance, which would hopefully be waiting for us at the arranged spot to take us back to the hotel. Then we went on to the restaurant website and planned what we would eat and drink, becoming lightheaded with hunger and excitement.

We were still drunk enough by the time we arrived at the restaurant to enjoy the meal. Usually, when planning a dine-and-dash, the black hole of anxiety in my stomach was too big to appreciate anything. We ordered expensively enough not raise eyebrows but not too much to make them suspicious or overly attentive.

After pudding, our favourite of sachertorte and tokaji, we realised we hadn't planned our actual exit from the restaurant. Everything but. How had we forgotten? As it happened, we were sat at a table by a large pillar and not too far from the door, so that some of our exit would be obscured from certain angles. But this wasn't enough. Erskine-Lily went through the obvious, suggested going for a cigarette and not coming back, but this didn't feel right.

In the end, it just happened. With glorious synchronicity we rose and walked out slowly. We caught sight of ourselves in the mirror-plated double doors—today we'd both opted for mountains of grey suede and tulle veils; two ambling church ruins on platform heels.

Outside, these heels began pounding on the flagstones; we turned right, under an archway, down some stairs and crossed the main road in a regal rush: sleeves, cape, long skirts, Erskine-Lily's court train and mantle—all fatal streamers threatening to snag, to catch on people, lampposts, traffic.

Then we were going through a large department store to the basement carpark where our taxi was waiting.

"Luxury-stained," said Erskine-Lily gravely on the bus back to Dun, "the pair of us."

"And none to start with."

"And none of it ours."

This was skirting close to personal history for the both of us. None to start with. None of it ours. An admission of having a history and not having just materialised, fully formed.

"Anyway," Erskine-Lily said in his most sibylline voice, "I'm absolutely sure it means we're bound to win the lottery if we play."

We spent the afternoon planning how we would spend our winnings but really we were dejected about leaving the hotel. Although we loved Dun, our lack of money was troubling. Erskine-Lily still had a little, but we were anxious.

When we got back, we dressed up like millionaires, as seen on TV: huge faux fur coats and sunglasses, my fake diamonds, as much costume jewellery as we could find, and went to the bar. The same bar I had been to with Griselda. The tiny square was filled with tables and chairs. It was packed. Dun was particularly busy this season, far busier than summer though I couldn't say why. It was the end of November. Some kind of early winter event in the neighbouring towns. People were mostly passing through, hardly anyone seemed to come to Dun on purpose.

A few glances, but we were largely left in peace. Possibly these costumes, which we thought hilarious, were more palatable than our own. Someone even nodded at us respectfully.

I worried that others from the Residency would be here. Namely Griselda and Hector.

Lottery tickets were bought from the proprietor. She seemed delighted to have us share in the thrill. All three of us screamed in fury when we lost, now drawing disparaging looks from the other customers. She gave us drinks to commiserate. A thimble-glass of Pink each. Erskine-Lily spoke to her, occasionally translating for me.

I made tea at my flat, which we took down to sit in the garden. It was cooler but we were still wrapped in our faux furs, papers spread out on the grass.

The problem with our research was that neither of us had it in us to properly investigate Garreaux. It left us feeling nauseous. I recall Erskine-Lily saying to me wide eyed,

"... the yellow book, it is a kind of curse. A hex; against us, and Hermia. That's what the Residency is ... to keep them chanting the curse."

It began to rain. I was feeling tired and informed Erskine-Lily that I would probably not come out for the next few days. I went up to my room to sleep.

he last occasion she had felt like this was a party in London. Before she'd left for Dun.

The most wretched party of the century, surely. Everyone had said so.

A costume party. Brimming with hearties and awful students. She'd arrived dressed as the mythical Papesse, Pope Joan, in her three-tiered mitre, sceptre in hand. This had caused a stir in itself. This and the obvious reason. People started asking if she was a jazz singer, and would she sing now? Was she Florence Mills?

She was talking to Brian Howard, complaining about how really awful the party was when she felt her scalp burn. Someone had darted by and tugged her hair which was showing beneath her papal crown. This seemed to incite a kind of game. People began running, lunging for her head, trying to take a "piece of wool," and she was very soon in danger. The papal crown clattered on the floor.

Her companions came to her defence. "A ring of England's most beautiful pansies," it was later said. Most in dresses. Teddy Thorny-Strong lay on the floor winded.

In the end it was Nancy Cunard, newly arrived, who'd poked her head through "just in case," already having viewed the crowd on the steps. Nancy who came to their, to her, rescue. She dived into the middle where Hermia stood and the next dunderhead to break through and swipe at Hermia's head was knocked in the face by Nancy's many-bangled arm. The boy fell to the floor and got up. He was enraged and went not for Nancy but for Hermia who, having a real metal sceptre, swung it at him. Then another came and Nancy knocked him. This one didn't fall, was ready to strike Nancy. Only then did any of the other men come to their defence. Siegfried Sassoon, the peace-poet, recognised by all, entered the room with Stephen Tennant, which scared the hearties away. Afterwards, Nancy asked Hermia to send along her poem.

Fortunately, she had been perusing material for a new poem when this memory swooped upon her in the library. She was reading about Atalanta and the Calydonian Boar and the warrior Queen Amina of Zazzau, now Zaria, Nigeria, amongst other such vigorous women who altogether gave her sustenance against the memory. It had been five years ago, but now she was able to think how gloriously she had acted, swiping at those boys with her solid brass sceptre.

Presently, a young man entered the library. One of the leftover hearties.

It was some days since the incident of the fish. Almost all of the hearties had moved on. Elizabeth Ponsonby had threatened to have her father bar them from a future in Parliament if they did not leave the following day. It had worked, they left the next morning: but not before, as Elizabeth demanded, they took part in a piscean funeral of her organisation.

Only two of the hearties remained. They were not so easily scared. One of them was even friendly with Lymenick and ran in one of the middling 'smart sets' which overlapped the more respectable elements of their own group (too frequently) and on the other side overlapped with such hearties as Hugh Sands. The second, seduced by Brian, would not meet anyone's eye and had evidently developed a more violent hatred for the entire pansy kind. It was the former who entered the library.

"The Black Princess!" he said, in tones that were unmistakably mocking; with that it was apparent to Hermia that he had been the one to spear the fish to her bed. She met his eye, thinking of Atalanta, of Penthesilea, of Semiramis, of Amina.

"I've rather an interesting friend coming," he said. "Anthropologist chap—been to Nigeria."

"That will be nice for you."

"I was of the opinion that it would be nice for *you*."

"I've never visited."

"Even better, you can talk about your far-off princely family. He knows a lot about the families . . . The royal families, there are—were—hundreds, did you know that? Yes, I suppose you do. Hundreds but he knows about every last one. Yoruba, Igbo, Hausa: the lot of them! I daresay he might even have met your family."

She would not tolerate this.

"I hear you've been having an awfully nice time with Lymenick."

This made the hearty pinken—carnationally so. Then the mask was off.

That face.

She saw he was the one Nancy had knocked to the ground that night. At last recovering he said,

"Funny little trick of his, Lyme I mean. My idea, his execution. Sticking that fish through your bed. Didn't think he'd do it."

She looked out of the library window, at the neighbouring hills—sculpted and half-hollowed by cold, freezing blissful winds. The light struck the remaining glass in the fountain lavender, hurled up cool javelins of light. She pined, as she often did. Fantasised about the future. The Glittering Proletariat, skin perhaps as dark as her mother's would have been.

She lies upon the black-barred galleria of her tower. Later she would ascend to Café Utopus, where there were quivering trees... a garden upon the rooftop... and the people were attending a lecture about the Past.

She became aware of his voice again, and looked up, her vision interrupted. Not the interruption but the lingering vision, brought to this world, this time, filled her with fury... She regarded the brute.

Presently—

The Black Princess regarded the brute... and she rose... and flew at the brute.

Presently—

Oh, she flew at the brute.

VI

That winter, we sorted the wheat from the chaff, binned the wheat, and made ambrosia and nectar from the chaff.

That winter, we fed on Style, having flambéed Substance with a bottle of cherry liqueur and a dramatically dropped match. We had no need of substance, we'd had our fill of it.

VII

Erskine-Lily kept life at bay by a will superior to mine and Malachi's. This only enamoured me the more. Here was a true Escape artist. There was at times something almost despotic in his desire to escape from life, to keep at bay, but that was what Life wanted one to think, to assert itself, to make itself valid. Talk about despotic. It had an unhealthy fixation with us.

Everything that was not part of Erskine-Lily's immediate curation was deemed false. The process of selection was a constant one, and possibly contributed to those bouts of glassy fatigue.

At times we spoke entirely in a language of intimations. Alongside our work on Hermia and LOTE, we had tacitly charged ourselves with the project of describing a magnificent, indescribable thing and to speak of it in ordinary language would be to mishandle and destroy it. Even now it is hard to say what *it* was, but it had something to do with our relation to Life: Black, fantasists, worshipers of Beauty. It was why perhaps Hermia was so important to us.

On a few more occasions a man came to the door, during which Erskine-Lily would sometimes go completely quiet and stare at the ceiling, or sometimes get up and hammer back, shouting fiercely in the language, meaning I never understood what it was all about. But as far as I was concerned it was Life outside the door, and if he got in, he would strangle the pair of us. I knew instinctively never to refer to it. That would be conceding too much to its existence, even though the lock was flimsy and I expected the door to burst open any day.

We both kept life a bay, armed with very little solid. With walls of froth, with tides of orion. When we could drink orion every day, we did. There was nothing doleful in this habit. It was always underwritten with a pronounced lightness. It amplified our spirits in a manner no drug could have, blasting away Erskine-Lily's anxiety, immunizing me against old feelings.

But my respect for Erskine-Lily's keeping at bay was challenged, was broken even, one afternoon.

We had managed to survive our first week after returning from the hotel on the four euros Erskine-Lily had. The problem had been knowing a compensatory gift card was on the way after having complained profusely to a luxury department food hall about an unsatisfactory lobe of foie gras we'd purchased (we'd actually stolen it weeks ago and kept the barcode). If we spent the four euros then we wouldn't have enough to go to the city and back to spend the gift card when it arrived, but we didn't have enough in our cupboards to keep us going until then. In the end, I cornered one of the Toast Children in the computer room, asking if he could do a shop for us the following week. It was Felix. He looked at me (toastfully) and said,

"I'll have to have a list. Now. If you don't mind."

I dictated the items to him which he took down on his phone. Starting with bread, to ease him in, but shocking him with butter.

"...mushrooms, garlic, berries, cream, oh, and some chocolate."

I thought he'd hyperventilate.

"What's this for?"

"My project." I couldn't be bothered to explain that I didn't have the same manufactured guilt that drove him to live on dry toast. Privilege discourse was practically impossible with people trapped in 2007.

I was now off to Erskine-Lily's to make breakfast, which Felix had dumped outside my doorstep in plastic bags. I was almost surprised he'd overcome the embarrassment it must have caused him to be seen with such food.

I stepped out of my building with the shopping and the street was unrecognisable. Stalls lined it all the way up. The town was the busiest I had ever seen it. The market square was full of stalls selling everything. These stalls also lined side streets and were to be found perched at angles on the town stairways with rubber mats on the tables to prevent the wares sliding off.

I got lost instantly. Certain superficial changes rendered my sense of direction non-existent and this was one of them.

But the prospect of finding something won out. I imagined coming across a volume of Hermia's book and running back to tell Erskine-Lily. I worked my way through a seemingly endless quagmire of batteries, soap and toothbrushes before the items became more general second-hand, then a mixture of junk, antiques and books.

I was standing at a *bric-a-brac* stall, sifting through a box of objects that I couldn't really make sense of. I was no longer taking anything in. My hands were dusty. They kept on returning to an object. Probably because it was smooth. A pleasure in running my fingers over it. I came to, took it in for the first time, even though I must have seen it a dozen times already. It was a mother-of-pearl thing. Shaped like a lily head. It had a wooden marquetry handle—a loosely spiralling stem—and my first idea was that the bulbous end of this nozzled handle was to be placed in the ear, like a Victorian ear trumpet.

Erskine-Lily had told me about the early devotees using lotus shaped objects to listen to the Luxuries inside the pillar. It was only two Euros so I bought it from the woman whose stall it was and rushed through the rest of the market, coming to St Christine's needle, where I at last found my bearings. I was tempted at this point to stop at the obelisk and use my discovery—to listen to the interior Luxuries as the writer of *The Book* had—but it was crowded. Pushing their way through the throng were Lind and Jonatan, coming towards me, apparently. I pretended not to see them.

At Erskine-Lily's I knocked impatiently, forgetting he wouldn't answer if he thought it was someone else. I was about to give the gentle rap, which though we had not mentioned it, was our signal, but the door opened.

It was not Erskine-Lily but Griselda.

"Hey," she said, and went to stand by the window, arms behind her back like a sentry. I was still standing at the door.

"Erskine-Lily has just popped out," she said. "Back soon. I'm sure you can wait."

Sure I could wait.

I came in.

She stood there looking out the window. Without turning she asked or, it felt to me, demanded to know what I had bought, so I told her it was just some old tat because I didn't want to get dragged into an argument with her about its cultural merit and the "barbarism of old objects" just as we had argued about so many things.

I set it down on the table and was on my way to the kitchen when something made me turn. She'd come away from the window.

Was picking it up and unwrapping it. I was livid. I had to stop myself from snatching it away from her. (What was she even doing here?) She knew she was going to hate it. Why bother? At that moment I would rather have flung it out the window than have to listen to her condemnation.

She had already opened it and was inspecting quietly. She said something that might have been, "Is this—?"

But I didn't hear because Erskine-Lily came in, animated, ranting on about a glorious new skirt that the seamstress had completed, and that it was starting to rain by the way, how sad for the marketeers. I was half swept up by his talk, it was difficult not to be when he was excited, but I also wanted to shake him, to warn him that Griselda the Tyrant herself was in his apartment what on earth was he doing chittering away as if there was nothing the matter?

"Oh but, Mathilda," he said at last. "More glorious news— Griselda is going to be helping us with our reconstruction of the Lote-Os."

"I don't think Griselda should help us with our reconstruction."

"Why not?"

"Because I say so," I said.

"But she's really quite wonderful—she knows heaps about the early—"

"I don't know how she's won you over, I thought you hated Residency people?"

"Oh, well she came knocking full of news about her research. She can't be as bad as them or she really wouldn't be as interested. *You* are on the Residency."

I wanted to tell him how she'd called him narcissistic. On one level he cared nothing about what people thought, on another his anxiety gave him stomach pains about the potential speculations of those he barely knew or had never met. The fishmonger's private judgements, for example. "Was he making fun of me when he said he enquired about my hat?" . . . "Was it *too* much when I asked him about gutting mackerel—did he know I never had any intention of gutting and was just being polite, trying to make conversation because I was conscious of how ridiculous I might have looked to him?" . . . "Are you sure he wasn't making fun of me? Do you think he will go home and make fun of me to his wife and children?"

This kind of anxiety was, as Erskine-Lily told me himself, irrational (a.k.a. unfounded in any intelligible material conditions that could be changed)—and consequently it didn't help him knowing this. In fact, knowing made it worse. "Could they see I was socially anxious, will it make them think I'm self-important because they could see I thought they were thinking about me?"

Informing him of what Griselda said that day would have had devastating consequences, so I entered instead into a shameless sulk. How to even begin relating that my being on the Residency was as far from Griselda's being on the Residency as conceivable? How to relate that Griselda was the Spirit of the Residency itself and that I knew on what could probably only be described as an atavistic level that she was driven by a lethal inner hatred of everything that Erskine-Lily and I stood for. That she was, unquestionably, up to something. At times I really believed this. And at times I believed it wasn't to do with any lucid repugnance. That she didn't even know, just found herself inexplicably feeling the need to interlope upon our existences because, latently, our lives threatened her in some vestigial way and made her want to put a stop to us.

I could not forget that taunting look when she informed me she was going to a party at Erskine-Lily's; when she knew I was trying to Escape her.

I left them as soon as I could, taking my package.

That night, unable to resist, I went to the obelisk. I put the lotus-shell instrument to my ear and strained to hear, and of course heard nothing. But the smell of old stone, the ritual of it, excited me.

Walking home I saw Hector coming out of Erskine-Lily's building.

"... and is due to the procession of the equinoxes, which means that, if you're an Aquarius, for example, you're technically a Sagittarius."

"Oh my god, no!"

Erskine-Lily howled and dropped a thick glass punchbowl bowl in the kitchen at this news on the radio.

"Of course, you're still a tropical Aquarius just not a sidereal one, it just depends whether you want to go by the stars or the seasons. Two definitions."

We spent half an hour foraging tiny spears of glass from the floor.

We were taking a break from our research which had gained a momentum that was surprising us both. The pleasure did not fade as we increasingly spent our days pouring through documents.

Whilst our curiosity was intense, our rigour was lacking. Because of the way we loved our subject (a strange word for something so closely bound up with our lives), it was often impossible to stay narrowly focused on any single aspect for too long.

This changed. Something propelled us as winter came to Dun. Perhaps it was the sense that we were getting closer, reaching an end point. We had good evidence that various figures, many of them my Transfixions, Erskine-Lily's portraits, had holidayed in Dun not long after Hermia moved here. They had been involved in the ballet-opera which they had staged at the restaurant with the blue dome. This was also where Hermia had given a reading from her poem. Richard Bruce Nugent and Nancy Cunard had been involved in the opera, and with what we'd found in the letters it was now definite they were members of LOTE. We already knew that the Marchesa Casati had been to Dun at the same time, and now we'd found a letter from Stephen Tennant to a friend saying he and Hermia had met the illustrious Marchesa and she had joined their "special society" in an honorary capacity.

All we'd done was trace a thread of sensibility from figure to figure. Picked up on their florid natures, deep purple dispositions, and then something within that we couldn't pin down: dress, taste, a mode of expression they were all prone to, that we were also prone to. But almost everything we'd come to of our own accords, instinctively, was true.

Dangling above all this of course was the Residency and its relation to Hermia.

Whilst looking into the production of this opera, we learnt that Hermia and Stephen had managed to lure a composer on board. His name was Edvard Lyta, related to the same Lytas of the foundation.

We had decided to invent an amethyst punch to celebrate the discovery.

Once we'd cleared up the shards, we found another bowl and sat at Erskine-Lily's window ladling lavender doses for ourselves, watching the sky give way to a weak but abundant gold, plagued by one question: Edvard Lyta and Garreaux Senior both knew Hermia. What if their descendants really were purposefully suppressing her life?

"The one thing I literally can't bear to do is read John Garreaux's book. Not even the passage mentioning LOTE, which Griselda said is related to the Lyta family: Garreaux talks about multiple things in the same sentence, and through some circuitous etymology he connected LOTE and Lyta, though of course Griselda said our LOTE has nothing to do with it, which is obviously now nonsense."

"The Garreaux book, yes I forgot: you'll hardly believe it, but Griselda has been researching just that. I said we'd meet her at some point actually; maybe I'll try now." And he got up and went into his bedroom to make a phone call. I sat there horrified. Had he been continuing to collaborate with Griselda all this time? Having heard nothing about her since the day she visited I presumed he'd come to his senses.

The ease with which he came back into the room saying we were going to meet Griselda in an hour at the lottery café disarmed me. It made me think myself remiss for not prioritising my curiosity about Hermia over my silent feud with Griselda. If she could help, it would be worth it. If she really was trying something, I only needed to tell Erskine-Lily again, more firmly, about my not wanting to work with her. If I let him know that because of her loyalty to Garreaux, and therefore also Lyta, it was in her interest to suppress and sabotage our research, he of all people would not think me ridiculous.

Erskine-Lily had got some more money somehow, enough to get a bottle of Pink. He spoke to the lottery woman, who was rather a fan of us now.

"What do you talk about?"

"The lottery," he said.

The small square was busy again when Griselda appeared.

"Let's try the Cynic's bar instead," I said. So we all wandered there.

We were greeted as usual with rolling eyes. Griselda asked if we'd like a drink and I ordered a sparkling cocktail, as did Erskine-Lily.

Griselda ignored the spectacle of the lights going off and the gushing sparks starting up. I hoped for her to make some typically

Residency-ish remark which would alert Erskine-Lily to what she was really like. Instead, as soon as the lights were flicked back on she said,

"Well, you were right, I have to apologise. Garreaux really was talking about your LOTE—the Lote-Os."

"Yes, we know," I said.

"I've managed to trace a social proximity between LOTE and not only Garreaux Senior, but a Lyta ancestor as well."

"Yes, so have we."

"What we're hoping to learn," Erskine-Lily said more politely, "is what this might add to an understanding of LOTE and the yellow book and the Residency." I wondered if he'd informed her about Hermia's room, or if she already knew what it was.

"My reading reverts back to what I thought it might have been, which Mathilda more or less knows. That for Garreaux Junior, on a social and personal level, he was writing about this Bourgeois family *and* a decadent cult, *and* he was embedding them into his other concepts."

"So nothing new then."

"No. But I have been researching beyond the book. As you know, LOTE was a society dedicated to the Luxuries, established in the '20s and situated here in Dun. LOTE was founded on the presumption that an earlier order of the Luxuries existed; their main evidence for this was *The Book of the Luxuries*. *The Book* in turn says the mythological Lotophagi were, in essence, the first initiates. Members of LOTE believed that they actually had a piece of ancient lotus bark from the original Lotus Eaters. Almost, for them, like a fragment of the true cross. Probably just a bit of old wood one of them bought abroad or something—what led me onto this was researching Garreaux and Lyta. Edvard Lyta, who was an uncle of the existing CEO of the Lyta Foundation, left a bequest to the National Museum. I was looking through the list of donations, and in it is something described as "lotus bark." I'm very sure he was not involved in LOTE beyond helping them with an amateur opera. How it came to him I don't know."

He had acquired (or stolen) it from Hermia, no doubt. Erskine-Lily must have been thinking the same because he mentioned the room above the White Archive. I pretended to go to the bathroom and seethed with anger—how could he tell her?

We walked back towards Erskine-Lily's.

In the throes of his anxiety, walking down a street full of people was a high-adrenaline, taxing experience for Erskine-Lily. Especially as he would inevitably draw attention by way of his appearance. On such days he would dive down unknown side streets on seeing a coming crowd or even a solitary pedestrian, often getting lost in the process since he had no sense of direction. When forced to proceed down the street in the peak of anxiety, his movements from a bird's-eye view must have looked comically labyrinthine. He walked in the shade where possible, feeling too prominent in the sun, would step into shops at random, sometimes stepping back out immediately if they were busy.

"But you know, I think I'd draw even more attention somehow if I went out dressed like *them*."

Which was true—I had in fact tried this before myself and hadn't fooled anybody. People could tell somehow.

On other days, especially if drunk, a warm oblivion rolled over him and he would float down the streets of the town unaware of himself, of the attention, of the gawping tourists who would fall silent or laugh as he stepped into a café to ask if they had any oysters or orion to buy. He had become something of a fixture amongst the locals, though I was not sure how long he had been here, this being one of those questions I knew not to ask. But something told me he had not always been there, despite speaking the language so fluently. (His English accent was unplaceable.)

Today he was oblivious, in a wheat-coloured wig that hung in a loose plait with a ribbon. Griselda had bought us more drinks on finding out we were waiting for my stipend to come through. We had not been this drunk for a while. Walking back from the Cynic's bar, he was delivering a very dramatic speech about his love of orion, walking very upright—looking his best, but drawing attention from some of the tourists sat outside cafés.

"I thought the whole thing dread'. Conversely, the crate of orion arrived and made everything abominable, *j'ad'* it so entirely, I must declare," he was saying as we passed a café.

Sitting outside, three men were babbling loudly. They sported all the trappings of bland Euro-wealth. *Those* sunglasses, *those* jeans etc. One of them looked very much like Giuli, and they were speaking Italian; he was surely a brother.

As we passed they fell silent, then started sniggering. One of them—Giuli's brotheralike—shouted. Although it was Italian, such braying is universal. International Cishet. Then he shouted again. It was aimed at Erskine-Lily, who turned at the third shout and, in a moment of inspiration, blew the most elegant kiss I have ever seen blown—a veritable stream of gold might well have been released with this gesture. It stunned their flapping tongues into dropping flat in their mouths. Visibly deflated their chests.

We continued walking. But eventually the two friends began laughing and elbowing their leader. About thirty seconds down the street, footsteps sounded behind us, and on turning around I saw the leader push Erskine-Lily, who hit the pavement immediately.

About to follow this up with a kick to Erskine-Lily's stomach, the leader found that he himself was on the floor. Griselda had punched him. His nose was bleeding. She clenched her fist then kicked him in the stomach. His friends were coming to his rescue, but by this point the Cynic had come out of her bar with a knife and was shouting at them; a man had appeared and the two fell back. The Cynic signalled for us to keep on going.

We helped Erskine-Lily up and continued our walk back home.

"You're both devoid," she would say when annoyed with us.

"Because it's devoid," when asked why she didn't like something.

Still, she accompanied us to all our favourite 'devoid' places without complaint. LOTE, however, she was genuinely excited by. An early Queer modernist subculture, she said.

"You didn't think so before."

"I was being devoid, Mathilda. Clouded and devoid."

I thought back to those first weeks of our friendship, when our differences had loomed large and grotesque to the point of fascinating, and loomed yet larger, to the point of repulsion.

Fascination had returned. Intense curiosity: how differently we'd been cast; a shock at tracing the psychic contours, the unexpected juttings out. But it was not purely a fascination of opposites any longer. Griselda had changed. She truly had been proselytised, and, dear god, it may have been caused by me.

Testament to this: she had renounced certain aspects of Garreaux, admitting that, smuggled into his theory and inherent to Residency, was something oppressive. It's denial of identity, Garreaux's tacit blocking of anything femme.

"'The tectonic mascness of it all; that would have you think it neutral,' as you once said."

I could barely remember telling her this. Our old arguments had been multifarious, each feeling like life or death; I had worked through so many lines of attack and defence.

"Yes, like Hector," I said. Both she and Erskine-Lily said nothing. "Well it's true. He's oppressive, carries it within him, just like the yellow book and all the other Residents."

At times I did wonder if her old self were watching us from behind those black eyes. I would try to note beneath her face, this old Griselda. The Garreauxvian. The Resident. The saboteur.

She would, after all, become noticeably restless. Generally a restless person, this was exacerbated in our company. Her productiveness was to us a rare black art and she possessed a kind of incendiary brilliance that was exciting for two idlers to be near. But I'd been worried the past two days because her restlessness was different.

It was the beginning of the final White Book Submission. Residents were allotted a month and a half to fill their books. They rushed around Dun looking drabber and more serious than usual, full of their strange new amphetamines, raw-edged and wan. A few, including Giuli, stopped talking to people altogether, ignoring them outright in the Residency Centre where they'd pitched up tents in the corners of the studio to work around the clock.

Griselda was cooking. Erskine-Lily was in the living room, futilely trying to save an especially delicate hothouse flower that he'd bought on sight.

("I can't bear to leave it in this hellish, soulless place!" he'd cried in the luxury florists we'd stepped into. "Just look at it!")

For one who ate so monastically, Griselda was a skilful chef. Several pans were on the go, reducing, emulsifying and hissing.

"Are you not going to submit your White Book Project?" I said. "We don't care—you've been working on it all year."

She poured a hot butter sauce into another pan and began stirring.

"No," she said. "That would be pointless. I've come out of it. There really is a lot there in the theory that I still admire. I don't need to submit for that though. Of course, I feel bad for Hector, but he'll manage alone. I couldn't return to it if I tried."

I had seen Hector moping around the town. In the computer room one evening I got the impression he was perpetually on the brink of striking up conversation with me. I also ran into him in the National Library looking forlorn. But it was Griselda I felt sorry for, hoping that this 'coming out of it' wasn't like the departure of my Transfixions. She was, as far as I was concerned, like any lapsed zealot, plagued with guilt in spite of herself.

Most of the time she was fine. Was the happiest I'd ever witnessed her.

I'd been anxious to see how Erskine-Lily and Griselda would get along. Joint interest in LOTE was one thing. Erskine-Lily was arguably even more diametrically opposed in construction to Griselda than I. Polar souls. To see, therefore, how quickly they found their common ground was almost a little disorienting. Erskine-Lily turned out to be deeply impressed by her encyclopaedic knowledge and they would strike up and rhapsodize about theories of volution, the correlation between Hogarth's serpentine line, fractal mathematics and Afro-poetics. But mostly, Erskine-Lily would ask, and she would answer, at length, about the feasibility of universal orion, sachertorte and other such things post-revolution.

Griselda regularly spoke about global politics and her plans for revolution. We were hooked. I'd only met one other person who spoke the way she did, and that was Malachi. The kind of Utopianism so blazing that it reached out and encased Arcadians like Erskine-Lily and me in its warmth, lit us up; rather than the more common, lazy and unimaginative kind, that scorched us, collaterally, out of the future.

That night in the middle of one of her speeches, the door knocked, and Erskine-Lily went still. It continued for some time.

"Oh for fuck's sake," Griselda said and leapt up. She opened the door, went out onto the landing, and began shouting in another language. It was then I knew the heat of her glare I'd previously witnessed had been but a gentle glow. For the second time that month, she came to Erskine-Lily's rescue. Life soon went back down the stairs, never knocked again. At least on that door.

Griselda found outlets for her zeal in other ways.

She'd been away for the weekend. Her parents were in the country, on a seaside holiday with Hector's mother. Griselda went to stay with them. I was never sure if Hector had joined her.

Whilst she was away, Erskine-Lily and I went to the city to steal as much as we could from a department store about to be boycotted for, amongst other things, illegal working conditions and a shareholder keeping migrant workers twenty to a room. One of the "*rouge* landlords" making the news which Erskine-Lily had mentioned on our first proper meeting.

We were not the only ones to make a visit. It was reported that, prior to the day of the boycott, tens of thousands of pounds worth of stock had disappeared from the shop floor; we could only have accounted for about five percent of this.

On returning from probably the most bountiful spree of our lives, we realised we'd locked ourselves out. We could have gone to mine, but Erskine-Lily seemed panicked and I understood once more that he must have been occupying the flat illegally, or at least unofficially.

"We've got to get in, Mathilda. We've absolutely got to."

The lock was weak and always getting stuck. I began kicking it and on the ninth kick it gave way, splinters flying everywhere. We would get the town locksmith to repair it when my stipend came through in a couple of days.

We were both sitting in bed watching daytime television and drinking champagne, surrounded by our spoils, when Erskine-Lily gasped and knocked a glass over. I looked up and saw Griselda had come in. We'd forgotten the door was open.

"Oh, calm down," she said. "It's only me. I thought you'd been burgled," she said, picking the glass off the floor. She refilled it and passed it to Erskine-Lily, whilst scrutinizing the bottle.

"Champagne? Really? Orion is one thing but—"

"It's for a good cause!" said Erskine-Lily.

She scoffed but looked very interested when he explained there would be a demo tomorrow outside the department store. Then she made us tell her the details again—the name of the store, the location, a description of it—before going home.

We were surprised when she wasn't at the bus stop the next day to accompany us there.

"She must be cycling."

But we couldn't find her at the demo either.

The turnout was much smaller than expected. Threatened with losing their jobs, half of the workers were back to work; those without the requested documents had been immediately sent to a detention centre. There were droves of police outside. This was presumably because one of the large shop panes had been shattered into the vast window diorama that was supposed to be half ski resort, half tropical beach. It was unclear whether the mannequins in each zone were the same friendship group holidaying at different times of the year, thus invoking the temporal logic of medieval narrative painting, which shows the same people within the same frame existing next to themselves but, in fact, at different points in time, or if it were two different friendship groups at the same time shown in different parts of the world. Either way, whatever law of chronological or geographical perspective governed the window display, both scenes had been afflicted. Half the group on the beach, reclining on imported sand, were covered in window shrapnel, whilst glass gathered on the edges of the chalet-side hot tub, on the snowboards, and lent the polystyrene snow a realistic scintillation.

It wasn't until we got back we found an article on an online news site. The damage had happened in the early morning. There was even CCTV footage of a hooded figure hurling what turned out to be cinder blocks at the window until it gave way, before fleeing the scene. I was sure it was Griselda.

"How invigorating!" said Erskine-Lily.

Hector was coming to ventilate his drabness.

"He's my cousin," Griselda said. "And actually doesn't have any friends, unless you count his chats with Giuli."

"What about Theo?" I asked.

Griselda considered this.

"Don't think they've ever exchanged more than a word."

"Who's Theo?" said Erskine-Lily.

The Cynic had a roof terrace on her bar which she liked to open at random. We had come to give her a cake as thanks for her knife wielding. She brought slices of it up for us and even sat with us briefly before descending.

The towers were visible, as were the other rooftops, delineated by the green sky, which was turning, like the surface of an ancient coin submerged in solution, to a gleaming copper. We shared a pitcher of something bright blue but very delicious and soft in the mouth. Then Griselda leaned over the terrace railing and shouted,

"Hector, up here."

And Hector could be seen looking persecuted below, then peering up and seeing Griselda, he relaxed.

"Oh god," I said.

Erskine-Lily downed a whole glass of the blue drink.

Soon enough we sat there shivering, exhausted by Hector's ministrations. Griselda, the only one able to shut him up, joined in. He was scared of her, sought her approval at every turn, but as soon as they were together she lapsed back to her puritanical self. Added to the drabness perhaps more than Hector did.

It annoyed me that Erskine-Lily sat there so meekly. At least we might have our own conversation and not have to listen to them. But he was particularly listless sitting there. Half-paralysed. I also noticed how Hector never met his eye once. It was true that Hector rarely met anyone's eye. But he had acknowledged my presence on clambering up the stairs onto the terrace. Without obviously snubbing him, he had not acknowledged Erskine-Lily.

We were weighted to our chairs by the talk. I felt sick. As sick as I'd felt that night when I'd thrown the book out the window. Griselda had spoken very little about our discovery of Hermia's room, but I'd presumed it had altered the Residency in some way for her. For one, she knew about the contents of a submission. But here she was, talking as vigorously about it all as usual.

It really was a spell, I thought. Garreaux and everything he'd created. The language, the behaviour. Erskine-Lily knew it too. Could feel it now, I saw. That flash I had seen before, when he doused Hector—a counter-spell.

"Yes, I think Garreaux extremely dull. It's fifty percent swagger and fifty percent bombast. At least with a lot of those other theorists it's the disciples who are the charlatans," I said loudly to Erskine-Lily who was energised enough to reply,

"Absolument dread'; hates all the things I adore."

Hector and Griselda had at last shut-up. They were listening.

"Me too."

"Like what?" said Hector, "What things?"

"Like...Delectable Things."

"Delectable Things?"

"Yes, he strikes me as a bitter denier of Delectable Things, on the behalf of other people."

"Delectable Things are what we dedicate our lives to."

Hector looked at me, directly.

"*He's* got to be the most bird-brained man I ever met, but you disappoint me," and then he turned to Griselda and went on talking. Griselda watched us as Hector spoke to her. She seemed unmoved, either way. We were weighted to our seats again, feeling abysmally ill. The air was now thick evening cobalt, not like winter at all except it was cooling rapidly.

("I don't mind being called birdbrained, in fact it makes me feel avian and charming—like a Luxury," Erskine-Lily said to me days later. "It's being called the other thing. *Man.* So harsh and vulgar. So...*absolute.* It always makes me feel sick. Quite disgusting," and shivered involuntarily.)

Erskine-Lily lit a cigarette. It was in a malachite cigarette holder. Everything about him now spoke of that first evening when he'd thrown a glass of orion over Hector. It hadn't been mentioned since, as if it had never happened. And now here we all were again for the first time since that day.

Who had arranged that meeting? Griselda? Hector? One of the other residents who hadn't made it?

As I was thinking about this, I noticed Erskine-Lily lift his arm, dreamily, balletically. Reached out with it towards Hector, who now sat with his back to us looking down below on the street, deep in conversation. It glowed amber-ended in the night. He extended it wand-like, onto the cover of a book, so that the ember went out. The book had been placed aside on the table. Hector's white book.

Hector turned around, saw the wisp of smoke, the black circle on the book, Erskine-Lily relighting the cigarette with a match. He looked at Erskine-Lily in a way which made me terrified. But he just sat there.

Seeing he had not done enough, Erskine-Lily stood up casually, then seized the white book and threw it off the terrace. Like a dove. It flapped. Avian and charming. White blur in the blue evening.

Hector cried out as if injured, got up, knocking over his chair, our table, the pitcher of blue drink, and ran downstairs.

My friendship with Hector began the following week.

I was alone, sitting in the restaurant with the blue dome, in a subaqueous daze. Every so often I looked up at Hermia and Stephen. I particularly liked to do this whilst tipping my head back to drink orion, its fizz sweeping through me as I took in the plaster faces, and the blue glass above. That day I almost choked on seeing a pale face cut through the shade. In a balcony directly below the frieze work, someone had just leant over. A face itself like plaster-work come to life, or barely: white, arch, stony, even as it spoke,

"Mathilda!"

He vanished and soon reappeared at my table, sitting down across from me, caught in the watery light as sun shafts rippled through the dome. But his face was not so sculptural and illuminous up close. He looked untypically frayed and was making polite eye contact which was downright bizarre, especially as he was very good at it.

"I hope I'm not interrupting you, Mathilda."

I was ready to say yes but he was already standing back up.

"Sorry, of course I am," he said and made to leave. This behaviour was fascinating/borderline cute. He was trying to manipulate me. It was the first real effort I'd seen him put into human interaction. The self-contraction, the desperation, was riveting.

"Sit down, Hector," I said.

He returned to the seat.

We both sat there not speaking.

At length he opened his mouth to say something but evidently found it too painful a labour. He shut his eyes and breathed steadily as if trying to force composure. He could not though. It showed first in his mouth—agony—then his whole face. Finally, unable to stop himself, Hector started to cry, lowering his face onto the table, into his arms. The waiter had come out and was watching us. It must have looked like we were having a very hetero domestic.

I almost didn't notice when Hector spoke at last, his voice such a high pained whisper.

"I don't know what to do . . ." he was saying.

Since the afternoon Erskine-Lily tossed his project over the railings, we hadn't seen him.

I'd gathered from what Griselda told me that the book had survived. I'd also gathered from what she hadn't told me that they'd argued. That something had changed. Their lifelong dynamic. Their common currency had become practically worthless overnight. He was alone. His life had been uprooted. But Garreaux was not important. It was only ever his shared interest with Griselda that had been important. Hence, he was here sitting with me. Contorting himself into strange new shapes in a bid for reconciliation.

My satisfaction at having read him so well was stopped short.

At length he finished crying, apologised, and began looking at the menu. He held it like something alien.

"I'm buying... please..."

When the drinks arrived, he began telling me about his life. Much the same as when Griselda divulged for the first time that late summer evening: how they'd been little brats but high achievers, how she was the real genius. How they discovered Thought Art only three years ago and he'd really taken to it like nothing else, it had consumed them both. Everything about it.

"So I was shocked, you know, finding out you were all working together on... Well even before Garreaux, I'd been squashing it all down."

"All what?"

"My interests... Suppressing them like something humiliating, squalid. Imagine smothering a fascination you think is embarrassing, burying your own impulses, thinking they are not just shameful and juvenile, but harmful, and then finding out the person you intellectually respect the most, the person you've been smothering them for, is openly immersed in that same thing. It's not just antipodal to Garreaux. It's so... different... to everything we've tasked ourselves with becoming; the image, the anti-image, in which Griselda and I have been making ourselves for at least the past ten years, Mathilda.

"Even when we were discussing the LOTE passage in the yellow book that day, I didn't know it had any connection to *The Book of the Luxuries*. It was Griselda who told me you'd both been continuing to research it. When she mentioned it was connected to an old society based on a myth of the Lotus Eaters, I couldn't believe it. I didn't even tell her about my old interest. It was me who first found out about the Dun Residency and Thought Art—only because of *The Book of the Luxuries* and its connection to this town. I'd been translating passages of it at one point. I couldn't possibly ever have told Griselda that, even when I knew she was working on the same thing herself. But I arranged the meeting with Erskine, knowing he knew all about it. Well, I was humiliated when he started raving about reviving the society and ... I thought you'd both think me insane for bringing you there. As I said, it's everything Garreaux is against."

I found my eyes drifting, as if they caught on before the rest of me, to a booth across, where I'd once seen Hector talking to someone I couldn't see. When I'd first brought Erskine-Lily here he said he'd been once before but hadn't noticed the faces of Hermia and Stephen.

"Knowing Griselda and you were working on the System of the Luxuries together ... I was in a state of disbelief. Of course, I only knew about the original instantiation: *The Book*. The whole idea was very seductive to me when I first came across it ... I was still at school ... and it never quite left me ... I still found myself returning to it over the years, in secret, but that finally stopped with the Residency, or so I thought. Isn't it the silliest thing in the world that I've been harbouring this fascination? Recently, when I was forced to think about it again—because of all of you—it still held the same appeal: Lotus Eaters living in a kind of proto-communist utopia, originally based in West Africa ... and the Luxuries! The whole thing is very enticing and radical and ... *beautiful*," he said, as if trying the word out. "I haven't said that for a very long time, Mathilda."

And he looked so ridiculous I started to laugh.

I'd long taken Hector to be socially, emotionally and not to mention sexually repressed (even if not officially in any particular closet, he had slept with Theo, and now I presumed, Erskine-Lily, and had sought to conceal both of these trysts), but a repressed aesthete-communist . . . that was something I could marvel at.

"But he won't let me in unless you tell him to. Erskine, I mean."

PART THREE

VIII

I t was a form of auto-suggestion, the System of the Luxuries. All
the ritual and incantation were part of that. Making a Luxury
appear before you was a sign of having conquered the grim imposition of reality. Of having embraced fantasy. It was like a rarefied,
and thus headier, form of the Escape Malachi and I had devised.

I still wondered if Erskine-Lily believed it was more than just
auto-suggestion. The difference was, in a way, negligible.

We had already induced a kind of glorious placebo effect from
the System so far by following Erskine-Lily's regime: microdosing
the precious and semi-precious, sipping his ethereal broths, then
feasting on meals sent through books and films. We were gearing
ourselves up, and as a consequence, a sort of beautifully manic Geist
would come upon us for days, then depart, leaving us hungover
and tinny. This Geist was like the feeling I had whenever I became
immersed in my Transfixions, but prolonged.

*

"ry the crepe gloves," Erskine-Lily said.

"Wait, here are the shoes," Hector said.

"Yes, actually that's quite good," Griselda said.

But, looking in the mirror, it was not good. A cross between an ascetic Berlin gallerist, who'd just found out about Brutalism, and an Upper East Side matriarch of the silver screen. The former was clearly Griselda and Hector's contribution, the latter Erskine-Lily's.

"But certainly an improvement on the last one," Mathilda said. There had been an array of costume changes. They had most recently put her in a t-shirt and jeans which Griselda had brought, but even Griselda had agreed that Mathilda had looked unspeakably strange in those garments, which would do more harm than good.

Erskine-Lily's attempts had been no better. None of them could really think what a historian looked like. They managed to convince themselves that spectacles and a cardigan were too on the nose. In particular, she was supposed to be a "sheet music historian," which was what Griselda had told the museum; Edvard Lyta had left a number of handwritten scores in the bequest. This detail was totally unnecessary and overdoing it but that didn't stop Erskine-Lily pulling out of an old laundry bag a matching polyester dress and blazer from the '80s with a pattern of bright green and orange treble clefs and violins.

"She would love it, this musical score historian, it's just the thing."

Fortunately, it didn't fit.

Mathilda watched their interactions, Erskine-Lily and Griselda and Hector. How well they 'gelled.' Their getting on so well continued to shock her. She didn't always know how to behave when all three were together.

She still hated Hector from time to time, from across the table, from across the room, for how easy it was for him, for men like him, to make everything *easy*. Pleasant. How they could and so often did, choose to plunge everything into turbulence, make discomfort for everyone. How she'd spent a lifetime avoiding them because of this.

But those were just moments. She would more often become swept up in the bliss. In the fact of the four of them, this unnatural, chemical friendship. It was an absurd blossoming. How well it worked.

She grew to like him. To love him, as she did Erskine-Lily and Griselda. He had fully entered into LOTE and that was all she needed.

All the curtains were thrown back. It was snowing and whiteness clung to the eyes through the windows. It was the heaviest snow in this part of the country since the 1970s, apparently, which was not very heavy, but it was strange even for Mathilda, who had only been here four months, to see Dun's squares and pavements plated white with thin polar mats all over the cobbles. If it had last snowed like this before 1975 then Hermia might have seen it.

Neither Erskine-Lily nor she were usually awake at this hour.

"I suppose it will do," Mathilda said. Like after inhaling too many perfumes, they had lost all sense of differentiation.

She was booked in for eleven in the morning at the National Museum.

The lace-brimmed white hat, which Erskine-Lily deemed "a wee bit M.O.B." (mother of the bride), would obscure her face from any cameras.

It seemed rather counterintuitive that she should do the stealing. Erskine-Lily's nerves made him unviable, as she had noticed when shoplifting with him before. It had been understood that it should be Griselda or Hector, who were already accustomed to wearing non-descript clothes, who were white, who should be more familiar with how such people behaved. Because of all this, but really because she thought them incompetent at this sort thing, Mathilda said it was too predictable, and that she would do it. She was the most likely to be noticed, but she was also the most experienced at this sort of thing. She also secretly wanted to; museumlifting was the new shoplifting.

She took with her a selection of twigs from her garden. One of these would replace the lotus bark, although they had no idea what it would look like.

A taxi took her all the way there. Pulled up outside the museum side entrance for the archive and library.

Inside, Mathilda was met by the man with whom Griselda had arranged the appointment, under a pseudonym which she now gave, "Rosemary White."

He led her down into the archive. "Of course, you won't be able to take your bag and coat in with you . . ." The man's eyes fell on her hat. He was wondering, she knew, whether he ought to tell her to take this off, and purely because it was not a typical hat, he did.

"I'm sorry," she said, looking through the glass door into the large hall, "but there's a man over there in some kind of a beanie with rabbit ears, and a woman over there in a cap. There was nothing about having to take off my hat in the user guidelines and I was here a few years ago and didn't have to then. Well, I'll have to go and fix my hair. Unless you would like me to take my weave out as well?" She was, as it happened, sporting a weave of pure white ponies' hair which Erskine-Lily had expertly sewn in last week.

"Oh . . . My apologies. Please retain your hat then."

The archivist led her first through a room with numerous cabinets, some with tiny compartments like apothecary chests, others humongous drawers which would have to be drawn out by at least four people. He stopped at one very normal sized cabinet and pulled a whole drawer out. Inside it, on a fitted cushion, were arranged various objects with tags. She followed him as he ceremoniously carried this drawer to the viewing hall, where it was placed on a desk. There was a small blue bulb on one corner of the desk and a red on the other. He pressed a button on the side and the blue lit up.

"Just press the button again when you're finished."

It was a lofty space, considerably larger in scale than the Portrait archives, with other users sparsely dotted about, professional historians. Mathilda looked down at the various artefacts. The first thing she noticed was a black leather tube. She took the lid off, but it only contained rolled-up sheet music. Then she turned her attention to an impressively carved box. This had a tag tied to one of its metal legs. She opened the lid and there, like a relic on velvet lining, like the fingerbone of a saint, was the bark. It was a polished oval of wood, very unlike any of the twigs she had brought. It looked more like resin than bark. She became flustered and had to put it down, wondering if there were cameras above her, if she were being watched now, but there was nobody about, apart from the few other users. Still, she pretended to interest herself in other items. Doing so, she noticed, on the inside of the drawer, on the panel closest to her, a sleeve compartment. There were folders in it. Notes about the bequest explaining the provenance of each item. Using the code on the tag she found the entry for the lotus bark.

"Lotus Bark." Provenance unknown, prob Victorian. Possb religious.

Beyond this, clearly, no research had been done. The rest was about the box, which had evidently been of more interest.

Maybe it was a piece of Victorian tourist tat or maybe it was an ancient piece of bark from a real plant or tree that corresponded to the mythological lotus tree.

Putting the folder back, she produced a twig from inside her sleeve, switching it for the lotus bark and closing the lid. She pressed the button. The blue bulb went off and the red bulb on the other corner went on. After what felt like twenty minutes, the archivist came in and picked up the drawer, which he returned to its hall whilst Mathilda waited in the corridor. He led her back up to the ground floor. As she was ascending, one of the other twigs slipped out of her sleeve, clattered on the stone staircase.

The archivist turned and watched as she picked it up. "Woops!" he said. He smiled and continued leading her out, and Mathilda knew he had presumed it was just one of the many accoutrements of a Maniacal Black Historian visiting a museum.

A car was already waiting to take her back to Dun. Hector and Erskine-Lily were in the back; Griselda, whose idea it had been to hire it, was at the wheel. All three were delighted by Mathilda's success. She'd never seen Griselda so enthusiastic. It was clear, just as they'd predicted, that the missing bark would never be noticed, that everyone would probably be dead before the museum got around to re-cataloguing it.

*

Shavings of the bark were to be boiled for several hours whilst some more were to be soaked in spirits—alcohol—in a dark bottle for twenty-eight days. Each procedure was supposed to extract a different property from the lotus.

"What if it's poisonous?"

"It certainly doesn't look like it's for eating."

"I'll try first," Erskine-Lily said.

The bark was very hard but Griselda finally managed to take some shavings with a pocket knife. Then she decided she didn't want to be the one to give it to Erskine-Lily if it was poisonous. So, once we had boiled it until the water went yellow, she and Hector sipped some with a teaspoon. We waited. Nothing happened. We would therefore be able to take our tiny drops of it on the day without ill effect.

We were sitting tonight in the Blue Dome, which was empty but for the four of us and the host. We wanted Griselda to see the frieze. She looked up for a very long time then looked down and said,

"We've got to go to London."

"What for?"

"Research."

The prospect terrified me, but things had been pointing that way for some time. I wanted to speak to Agnes. Elizabeth/Joan too. Helen St. Clair had mentioned diaries of her great aunt. Florence St. Clair had been a lover of Hermia's, I thought from the early letters. She had also been to Dun and had probably participated in LOTE. If there was a diary, there would be something in it about Hermia.

As it happened, I had recently emailed Elizabeth/Joan and got no reply until,

Please stop emailing my gallery, consider this a CEASE AND DESIST, Mathilda Adamarola, I have already passed your information onto the police.

Helen St. Clair
Gallery Director

It was from Elizabeth/Joan's work address.

"How's this week?" Griselda said.

"Good," Hector said.

"I don't think I can make it," said Erskine-Lily. He looked terrified.

"Next week then?"

His head shook imperceptibly—something I knew by now to mean, please do not ask.

"Why the fuck not? I'm paying for the tickets."

"I've got too much to do here."

Griselda made to say something but noticed my face and dropped the matter.

"Why isn't Hector coming?"

"I told him to stay. It's not good for Erskine-Lily to be left alone, you know," she said on the plane.

I'd seen it in him, a certain strain of loneliness—the kind which, once introduced to the system, never leaves, is only abated, is always on the horizon. In a way, a sibling of the drabness which haunted Malachi and me.

Going through customs, this drabness made itself known. I began to fear my debt, or who knows what else, would bring my name up on the system; I would be stopped and taken aside. Then, once we were in London, it came to me that I would never leave. I would be sucked straight back to life as it was before. This time I wouldn't have Malachi to claw my way out with.

This city made Dun seem altogether unreal. A fantasy. I had to remember I was here with Griselda, whom I'd met in Dun. Had to think about Dun and Erskine-Lily and Hector and even Lind and Jonatan.

Griselda's parents had a flat in Clerkenwell but lived in Sussex. We had three days. I was to go and see Agnes. Griselda was not very forthcoming about her own research here.

Agnes made me a coffee liqueur and complained I hadn't warned her. She'd have made something to eat.

We sat happily for a while, watching television and saying nothing until she told me about Elizabeth/Joan.

"Oh yes, she's here all the bloody time. Quit her job at that gallery, good for her, not such a dunderhead after all."

"Oh, at Helen St. Clair's?"

"Yes. Got a job at the BBC, quit that too. Got another one now. Can't remember where."

I was happy to hear she was still visiting Agnes, but annoyed at the news she'd left Helen St. Clair; I wanted access to those diaries.

Agnes got up and went to the telephone, flicked through her address book and insisted on dialling Elizabeth/Joan there and then, but no answer. She wrote the new number down for me.

The drinks cabinet was still half full and she poured me some of the same brandy she'd given me the day I'd found the Hermia photograph.

"I've been researching her—do you remember the woman in the photo?"

"Yes, of course. Hermia Druitt."

"Unsurprising," she said when I told her about my discovery of Hermia's room in the Residency Centre. She waved at her cabinets, "Over there are dozens of artists, writers who no one has ever heard of but me, all of them Black."

I fell silent.

"If you want to say something, then say it," Agnes said.

"You make it sound like there's a shadowy cabal specifically suppressing Black art in Europe."

"Mathilda, there doesn't need to be," she said. "There is enough in place to keep it out. But yes, there really are active racists who happen to work in galleries and museums, of course there are. I know *you're* not a dunderhead so don't be obtuse. I've met some of them, *worked* with some of them—if anything like your Hermia passed by them they would happily make sure it got lost, destroyed. Where do you think all this comes from?" she waved at the cabinet. "Salvaged!

"And some of these racists know each other, of course they do. It's not a conspiracy theory, Mathilda, if that's what you're asking.

"There was even, in the '70s, a club at Oxford, I forget the name, Society for the Conservation of Culture... something like that, and they would correspond very regularly with the museum I worked at. They believed that European culture was at risk of collapse. The society had been around for at least fifty years and who knows if it's still going but there you go. There was a time I believed in something much more like a conspiracy—a network of people actively suppressing information about Black European culture, because I couldn't explain why certain paintings were just sitting in archives, or going missing, but now I really don't know. Something in between."

We were both standing up looking at the cabinets. I'd been paying so much attention to their contents I was forgetting to look at the painting I'd been too high to properly take in before. The one with the plaque fitted to the frame saying, "The Statue." The beautiful figure in black marble or onyx.

"But it's not a statue," I said. That much was obvious. The eyes; the lips. The coloured luxurious robes that clearly weren't made of stone. And likewise the skin, though radiant, though comparable to fabulous stone, was obviously flesh. Black-brown flesh. Ornate curls.

"Yes," Agnes said. "A prime example. Obviously not a statue but a portrait of someone of Black descent. Did someone deliberately choose 'The Statue,' as a title and fabricate the accompanying information that the statue was *probably of a (white) Venetian merchant and done in black marble because that was what the merchant dealt in,* because they couldn't stand the idea it depicts a wealthy Black person in Venice at this period? Or did they just look at it and perceive a statue in Black material of a white person because that was more believable to their subconscious than a portrait of a statuesque Black person in Renaissance Italy?"

"It's got wings," I said. They were half folded but peeping out from behind. Multi-coloured wings. Like an angel. Or a Luxury.

"But surely that is another peacock just landing on or taking away from the ledge behind. Oh never mind that, I've just remembered."

She disappeared and returned with a 1993 edition of a periodical called *Black Arts Journal.* She opened it to a page and handed it to me. It was an article, by Agnes Pantal. It was about *The Statue.*

The painting had once been in the Hermitage Museum archives and later turned up in the Rijksmuseum along with several other paintings of little consequence the Hermitage didn't want. Agnes had been working at the Rijks in the '80s as a catalogue assistant. The painting had caught her attention for many reasons and she'd planned to do further work on it in the future, independently. She went to Edinburgh for another job for four years and then finally returned to research the painting and discovered it was missing. Nothing illegal, the article said, but rather something that happened frequently in museums and galleries across the world. New masterpieces were found this way, in cold storage, undisturbed for over a century. Usually it wasn't even negligence, just institutes getting overwhelmed by the sheer amount of donations and acquisitions. Albeit not helped by the unnecessary privileging of a very narrow selection of the objects they were supposed to be the custodians of, it went on.

That this one, however, was a painting with a Black sitter from the 1500s, by a lost Afro-Florentine master who'd possibly trained under Artemisia Gentileschi, herself largely unrecognised until recent feminist reappraisal—all this meant that it had the odds particularly stacked against it.

There was a book written in the 1930s called *Negro Art* which referred to a "Blackamoor from Florence known as Alessandro il Nero," and stated that Alain Locke had come close to acquiring it for his collection of African Art at some time in the '20s. The painting became something of a myth amongst those interested in Black European arts at that time. A niche area then, a niche in 1993 when Agnes' article was published, and still, by and large, a 'niche' interest today.

As I stood reading, the doorbell went. In came a woman with a silver beehive called Genevieve, out came the crème de menthe, out came the brandy again, out came the "delectables" (a range of chocolates, biscuits and cheese).

They told me they had met in their mid-20s in the '70s when they had worked as assistants in the British Museum. They told me stories about London, about living in Notting Hill in a mansion squat, and I began to feel impervious like they must have felt, began to rather like the city as I had in those early days of Escape with Malachi.

I got a message from Griselda asking my address—she wanted me to meet her and would order a taxi now.

Then the doorbell went again and it was Elizabeth/Joan.

She ignored me entirely for the first five minutes. I was surprised. From everything I knew about Elizabeth/Joan, this meant she was ecstatic to see me.

Finally, when Agnes and Genevieve were smoking outside, she reported in tenderest, matter of fact terms that she had missed me.

"So has Agnes. Now you're here—"

"Oh, but I've just got to go," I said. "The taxi's on it's way already."

"Cancel it."

I ignored this and asked her about the possibility of getting the diaries off Helen St. Clair.

"No fucking chance," Elizabeth/Joan said. "I left without warning. Almost sunk her gallery apparently."

The car took me not back to Griselda's flat, but south, further out to a place that was neither London nor Kent but both, through an anomaly of postcode versus transport zone that bored me to death. Snow whirled past the windows but never seemed to touch the glass.

It was an hour before the taxi turned up a slush-layered suburban street. Massive detached Tudor-style villas with yawning front gardens or gravel drives. Near the end of the street, instead of such a house, was a tall block, glass meshed with concrete. Reminiscent of the Wreath. It had the same long gravel drive as the rest, as if one of the villas had been lifted away for it. Unlike the others, the gravel was Garreaux-yellow. The taxi stopped here.

Griselda was already waiting outside, smoking in the sleet, unshivering. A few other people came out of the building to smoke. Some kind of party seemed to be going on. The people I recognised instantly as Thought Artists.

"Garreaux lives here, we're going to speak to him," she said.

We gave our names to the porter, who told us to take the lift to the top floor. The lift opened directly onto the living room.

There was something familiar in the way everyone was standing about. Then I realised there were no chairs.

It was a reading or conference. A woman began addressing the room, randomly it seemed. People she had just been chatting to had to step back and others turned around to form a circle around her. She spoke about Markation. "New Markation," she was saying, "is a fucking myth."

It went on for some time. My ankles ached. I wanted to sit on the floor.

Looking about the room, I wondered if Garreaux was here now. Why couldn't we have just met him after this awful talk?

The woman stopped talking and re-joined the crowd.

Then I saw him. A lithe silvery man in acid green activewear and tinted glasses. He moved to the centre of the room.

John Garreaux recited what he called an essay. It was a composite of many buzzwords. He did some kind of respiratory dance, shouted certain words as if involuntarily, with lots of wincing, fake eye twitches, just as I had seen certain fashionable poets and their acolytes do, and I realised this might be where they got it from, just like the 'no chairs' had trickled down to Tom & Christian + Eleanor.

"Lackadaisical standpoints syn the Integers. Syn *the* Integers. Siphon Dotage networks dotage—GIRT!—dotage-tuber: 9l56.Prw." An affected accent, a little cockney, a little American; he was not very good at either.

The room underwent a rapture. People twisting at the words, itching themselves, clicking knuckles. I was too scared to look at Griselda, I could feel her concentration.

It made me feel quite ill. I had to go to the bathroom where I threw up crème de menthe and coffee liqueurs and other delectables. As I was vomiting, I felt chastened, recalled Griselda once telling me that art should never be anaesthetic. Work which produced such reactions as this was vital. Knowing about Hermia's room concealed in the Residency Centre, however, knowing about the attendant drabness that had pursued me forever, which *felt* the same as the words coming out of Garreaux's mouth . . .

I found a kitchen and drank from the tap. There were no glasses.

Restrained applause came from the room.

People dispersed about the flat talking.

"Sally, I can't eat like this anymore."

"I'm sorry but New Markation ain't a fucking myth."

"Pramulation."

Griselda came to find me.

Inside a rooftop solarium, glass ceiling pattered by grey-pink sleet, I'd half-expected to find encased—moulting wine-coloured wings—a Luxury with Hermia's face. Instead the lithe silvery man poured us sparkling water and told us, after our interrogation, we all had such steamrolled ideologies these days.

"Flatness."

He was, of course, like many deniers of beauty, and also many cult leaders, handsome.

"We found her room."

"Did you go inside? Actually look at it?"

"Yes. Why has it been Archived?"

"Don't you recognise a fellow child of the Luxuries, Mathilda?" and he laughed, "—well a former one—oh I loved all that—quite obsessed with it for a while. Not to begin with. Allergic initially. But later. It's the launching point for all this—for everything."

I was reminded of Hector's admission, but Garreaux didn't seem remotely conflicted.

He removed his tinted glasses and looked at us for a while, quite confrontationally, blue eyes angry, then returned his spectacles and stared up at the glass ceiling.

"Sorry, you must be patient with me, mourning is, after all, requisite—half a century's collective resistance has been put to an end by you and your steamrolled ways. But it is also a time of excitement, the next phase of the Residency can begin. The Ineluctable Fissure has occurred."

"But Hermia," Griselda said, impatient. "You obviously sought to suppress her. Buried her life by archiving it, but how did you manage to preserve her room as it was?"

"Paid her to leave," he said. "She was not paying much rent but had no real income, to be sure. I said, if you leave now and leave everything as it is, I will pay you, and she did. I wanted her out. My father had died, I was very young. She moved into a flat in Dun and died within the year, that's about it. I wished to start my residency centre, she was the only artist living there. The room became a submission. The first White Book Project. A symbol of all that the Principals are against, therefore, underwrites the Principles. I forced myself to take this thing opposite to me into me... this thing believed in by this elderly woman who'd known my father... this decadent cult she was a part of which repulsed me... offended on some level my virility—I was young. But that is exactly why I immersed myself in it, forced myself to love it, and then archived it as the first submission. It's all there in the yellow book as well. Do you see now, how it is exactly what we need? It is the ultimate synthesis—a resolution to The Fissure which operates on us as we speak. Take that which alienates you—a foreign body—take it into you, then

1. embed it,

2. seal it,

3. synthesise it,

and then

4. watch the resolutions unfold."

"That would all be fine if you hadn't buried her existence in the process," Griselda said.

"What is this burial and suppression you keep going on about? It's most annoying. What was there to suppress?"

"Her life," I said.

"Her work." Griselda said at the same time.

"But it all became part of the synthesis. Not a suppression. It was not my intention to embed Hermia Druitt specifically in the project, but more generally LOTE and everything it stood for. She still lives through the yellow book, through the project. Lives gloriously—by pure antithesis! You still don't see that you can hold two entirely opposing modes of being inside you and remain a purist? That should be evident to you at least," he said to Griselda. "But it isn't. It is the whole point of the Residency, of the yellow book. And even if that doesn't do it for you, do you think her personal effects would have survived had they not been, as you say, preserved."

"Her book," I said, at a loss. "Was there any copy of her published work, a manuscript, or anything? Did you hear anything about it from your father?"

"Sorry, dunno," Garreaux said, and shrugged.

*

Dun had faded on return, wisped to translucency. As if being in London had drained away something of its reality by contrast.

I wandered the town for some time—it had been snowing again—then went back to my room and let the tiles do their work. Became caught in their points of compression—indigo-black schist pools.

On waking, Dun was back in focus. It was really I who had been unfocused, drained and wisped to translucency.

The phone rang.

"We've got to go to the hospital. Erskine-Lily."

Almost as soon as Griselda hung up, the phone started ringing again.

"Please, if you can, bring a bottle of chilled orion. They should have them in the café downstairs from mine. I asked Griselda but of course she won't. She shouldn't have disturbed you in the first place. I don't know how she found out herself."

I decided I would smuggle it in for him with some crystal goblets and use my own judgement when I got there.

Griselda was already waiting outside the hospital for me, looking very serious. She'd come straight from the library. Scared—the first and last time I would see her so.

It had happened only a couple of nights ago. Erskine-Lily had gone out some time after midnight with the lotus device to listen at the pillar, had sat there for several hours, extremely intoxicated. He had been found unconscious with a light dusting of snow over him.

She had clearly come to the decision that it was a suicide attempt. I was not sure and decided either way I would give him his orion.

"Where's Hector?"

"I think that's the problem," she said and went in.

He lay there, every bit the sickly Victorian child. But convalescing, I thought. He had already acquired a nightgown and old breakfast tray somehow. The doctor told us he had pneumonia and I was surprised to hear her advice: take him somewhere hot, if you can. Because it was Erskine-Lily, it sounded like an antique cure for a Romantic, ethereal illness. I had to remember that Erskine-Lily really was ill, and this was perhaps his best and worst quality: to make the serious seem charming, to twist catastrophe into something delicious for us all to consume.

"I think I did hear them," he said. "The Luxuries. A good omen for our evocation."

His cheeks, neck, upper lip were flushed to an irritated rash colour. I wondered what it could be.

"I imagine it was quite beautiful, when they found me," he said, breathlessly. "I was wearing five metres of lapis lazuli chiffon and caramel crepe de chine. It was snowing again."

We covertly sipped orion from the goblets—Griselda didn't have any but said nothing—and spoke about the Residency. Speculated about what would happen to it now; Garreaux's new phase. Nothing had changed yet. Not visibly.

Afterwards, I thought she was going to tell me it had all gone too far, our interest in LOTE—that this was the reason Erskine-Lily was ill. Instead, she seemed more determined than ever to complete our "reconstruction" of the ritual. I wondered if she was a born zealot and understood extremes best—appreciated Erskine-Lily's act as an attempt at greater knowledge now her anxiety had dulled. Either way, we planned a trip to the sea, for Erskine-Lily, but also to continue our work—to complete our evocation of the Luxury. It seemed only natural we should make a pilgrimage for it.

Hector would not be coming, she told me. He had, in our absence, returned to the Residency. Would be completing his White Book Project.

"I don't know quite what happened," she said, outside the hospital room. "Some kind of dispute."

I found out a couple of hours later.

Hector was waiting. I had gone to tidy up for Erskine-Lily's return, Griselda remaining at the hospital.

He'd folded himself in the stairwell. I gently shook him awake. His dishwater eyes had a red tracery over them whilst his perma-blood mouth was pale.

"Hector, what's going on?"

"You have to make them stop," was the first thing he said to me, almost jumping to his feet.

"Stop what?"

"LOTE."

"But Hector—"

"It's killing them."

"But Hector, you yourself—"

"You've all gone over the top." There was a life in his voice I had never heard.

"Over the top of what?"

"The Allowance."

"What allowance?" I dropped my things and opened the door. "Hector, come in and have a coffee."

"I'd rather not go in," he said. I turned around, already half-way through the door, and inspected him for signs of drunkenness. I found none. Highly adrenalised, certainly, but not under the influence of any substance. This made his attitude all the more worrying.

"The Allowance," he said again. "Okay to indulge, to purge oneself of cravings on rare occasions, but that's all it should be. Look what's happened. Erskine is in hospital."

"In other words, it's all my fault?"

"Exacerbated by you."

"Same thing."

"Oh no, I joined in too. I didn't mean for it to go on this long. It's very seductive, like I said. These lapses are an inevitable part of Thought Art though. When you've constrained yourself into a mode of being so concentrated, all the guilty pleasures will come back up; once or twice perhaps. It's different for everyone. But it's all part of it. Indeed, it's an important part of it. Hence the Allowance. Griselda, being so like me, has inevitably been pulled in by the same thing. I had already encountered it, but she's never come across anything ideologically similar and has contracted it all the worse."

When Griselda had mentioned a dispute, Hector returning to work on his White Book Project, I hadn't considered for a moment he'd somehow totally reverted to this person who, as far as I was concerned, was a totally different entity: it was palpable just standing in front of him that the other Hector, with us just days ago, had been permanently stolen away.

"And so," I said, "now you've seen the light . . . or finished your Allowance . . . all the rest of us have got to do what? Dedicate ourselves to studying Garreaux with you forever and lead equally repressed lives? Why do you care so much?"

"Don't be silly, Mathilda," he said. "I really just came to tell you not to go on holiday with them after what's happened to Erskine. Call it off. Let Griselda get back to her project—she does want to, actually. Denying her that would be an act of cruelty. She'll snap out of it eventually. If it happens after the Submission, she'll never forgive you. And then there's Erskine. He's clearly not well—if you go away with them then you *will* be to blame . . . are you listening?"

"Was Erskine-Lily part of your Allowance?"

"What do you mean?"

"Hector, it's obvious you're making him keep it secret. Whatever there is between you. I suppose all that identity-renouncing in Garreaux might have made you a bit retrograde but that's no excuse. Look at the effect *you've* had on Erskine-Lily. You know you've done something wrong, and now you're blaming it all on LOTE, and me."

He was by this point bright red—carnational.

"But I'm not the one that's been keeping it secret. It's him, Erskine."

"Erskine-Lily," I said.

"He's the one who's ashamed."

"Of what?"

"You'd be surprised," he said. "*I'm* not ashamed of being with a man, as you seem to think. That's the point. No, he's ashamed. Of the crassness of it all. It lacks correspondence to his own delusional notions of beauty that you've been encouraging.

"We briefly went to the same school. All boys' school you know; he wasn't ashamed then. Before he was like this."

"What's school got to do with anything?"

"I'm saying, if you don't stop enabling this—"

"Enabling what? Hector, I don't know what you're talking about anymore."

"All of it. If you don't stop enabling it, then I'll make sure they have nothing to do with you. I'm Griselda's cousin and I've known Erskine for years. And you probably want the last of your stipend. I'll make sure you get it if you leave them alone. Just for a bit."

"We spoke to him in London—Garreaux."

"What?"

"To try and find out why he was covering up Hermia's existence. He didn't see it that way . . . it was all about Ineluctable Fissures and taking foreign bodies into yourself. Not unlike your bouts of guilty pleasure. Except for you it's not just LOTE that represents this foreign body, it's Erskine-Lily as well, isn't it?"

That may have been true, but as I spoke it seemed absurd that even Hector could feel this deeply about our interests, about LOTE, just because it was at odds with his principles. He didn't know it was at the root of the project after all. There must have been something else. I searched his face for it—the flash beneath the lid I'd seen once with Griselda—the uncovered, juddering, hissing pipework, the scintillating underside exposing something else at stake, but there was nothing. He only said,

"Ineluctable Fissures and foreign bodies operate in an entirely different manner to The Allowance." Then he looked at me in disbelief. "You've met Garreaux?" he said. "Bullshit—Griselda would have told me."

On entering Erskine-Lily's room to tidy for his return, I found the poster of the Hermetic Androgyne had been torn. Half of it curled off the wall, hanging by a sliver.

I found the source of the rash in the bathroom: depilatory cream, a razor and various bottles, an at-home laser.

Erskine-Lily's skin was thin—a copper-brown membrane—beneath which two things always showed up—the blanched violets beneath his eyes, which he loved, and the malingering shadows above his lip and neck which he loathed.

We had recently managed to steal from a department store an at-home electronic hair removal device, but either it hadn't worked or was taking too long because he had gone back to other methods in extremity. Had burned his face. Unwillingly carnation-stained.

Hector was lying—Erskine-Lily was not ashamed of being with him. Or any man. The problem was that Hector denied

Erskine-Lily's not being one. That was what he meant, "before he was like this." That was what he thought I was enabling. Had construed it somehow with LOTE, and the Luxuries, and his own entire repressed state.

he but not *He*.

Erskine-Lily came home in a few days. Aloe vera and various unguents would have to be applied for over a week before the red faded.

"Why not 'she'?"

"Hmm."

"They?"

"I don't know."

These terms flagged up too much, Erskine-Lily said, and made it unbearable. 'he' had been mentally ironed down to a film and meant nothing as long as it was said without meaning. A kind of self-legerdemain.

In all the terms, in all the identities, there was nothing "to correspond." Nothing that fulfilled a sense of it like the Alchemical Angel poster did. There wasn't a name for it. Not now anyway. There had been a name for it in the past. Maybe there would be one in the future.

"And I can hardly go around calling myself an Alchemical Angel. Speaking of which, the tincture—"

We'd forgotten to check on it. I went to the cabinet where it had been resting, supposedly undergoing the final stage. Withdrawing the phial from a box, we saw that it had turned a radiant black. It was also rainbow-flecked.

"The Peacock Stage."

We hadn't really expected it to visibly change. Had taken the stages to be entirely metaphorical, metaphysical.

"Griselda will presumably say it's the oils, or something."

"How unbelievably Queer!" Erskine-Lily said, holding it up.

Iridescence, he went on, is inherently Queer and always has been, well before rainbow flags. "Stephen's unpublished manuscript was supposed to be published in volumes of multicoloured ink. Nugent was separately writing his manuscripts in multicoloured inks. And then, my god, peacock feathers! The excess of the rainbow has just been too irresistible: I'll take *everything* in the spectrum thank you, and have it all at once!"

But this tincture was Black *and* iridescent, which could not be skimmed over. In traditional alchemy, the coloured stages undergone by a tincture were highly symbolic. The peacock stage was sometimes also known as Venus' stage ("obviously a very Queer Goddess, mother to a whole retinue of Queer winged beings of love and erotic love and androgyny as well as being Queen of art, music and culture . . . and peacocks!") as depicted in various alchemical textbooks. Traditionally, *before* turning iridescent, the tincture was black. One of the four fundamental colour stages of alchemy was nigredo, blackness, sometimes depicted more favourably as primordial and mystic, but more often depicted allegorically as something foul and putrefied. Eventually the solution transcends to a pure white, represented by a fiery white queen. But the final transcendent stage of Hermia's tincture was not white but simultaneously iridescent and black.

Erskine-Lily said,

"But anyway, 'he' has become unbearable too."

*

rows rose from the depths of the ocean where they had been floating. Eyes had also been there, fixed at the depth, and gradually they drifted up with the brows. Slightly, the eyes shifted, and the brows shifted; and upon each face appeared a sudden mottled light.

For in that sea where all three of their thoughts had been pointed, things had accumulated in them. A freakish immersion, in that sea.

Blue light swayed and glanced through the window. They thought unsqueamishly about the feasibility of uniting with a view. That was the ultimate goal surely. That was apotheosis.

Perhaps they already had, thought Mathilda, as the whole carriage flooded blue. Perhaps they had passed through the tiles in her room.

They watched the interrupted surface creasing and melting with the light. A multitude of points incessantly rising, threading themselves with flurries of gold. Innumerable rippling and bobbing. *That* could be them.

The sea gave out a fierce éclat.

"My god!" Erskine-Lily said loudly, so the other passengers turned and gawped. "Poseidon has gone O.T.T. with the glitter-gun today, hasn't he!"

And then the blue flashed green. The train skirted away from the water, thrusting this trio betwixt trees, hurtling them past moor, past weed, past flower. Glimpses into woods, where ponds glanced, tree-fringed and flickering.

"I . . ." Griselda said, looking amiss. Clouding. Burning up from beneath. Her eyes flashed for a moment out of the window where the tiniest triangular eye of blue projected through the foliage from the increasingly distant sea, and catching her by surprise, vaporized, laser-like, that sense of unease that had been trying so desperately to creep over her, that Mathilda had detected before her.

Then the train went under a tunnel, pulled back towards the coast.

Once again they were transfixed in the blue.

And Mathilda saw a rakish figure at the table where Griselda had been. A Romantic from Arcadia had finally come to join Erskine-Lily and her at last. The one who she knew had been loitering there all along.

**

Months passed.

Mathilda wondered where and when she was with little zeal and only because the thought passed by chance through her mind. It was a tinselly sort of thinking.

She floated down the milk vein of a river, in a boat, feeling askew and delicious.

The sky swelled and was slightly violet. A dissimulation of nightingales bowled through it. The river blazed pearl.

Griselda gazed for a moment at Mathilda who lay tranced by the purplish firmaments.

Then Mathilda's concern was elsewhere—she pointed

ahead, past the currents to the place their vessel rocked and slid. "There."

Erskine-Lily cut a charming figure with zephyrs undulating their garments, and until they were almost moored, face invisible, cloistered beneath that great gold aureole, a hat.

They saw them standing, an anxious ornament, bordered by marble and pillars.

They saw them, enveloped in that floating casket and heard the multitudinous plashing radiate from their skin.

The two moored and glided off the boat; they air kissed ceremoniously, the two bowed and the other curtsied. It was part of their ceremony. (The Priestxss receives the Knight & Herald.)

✳✳✳

Though the bluebell clouds melted into rain, the nightingales did not cease their curving and swooping. Erskine-Lily turned from the window and laughed at the room. That room was fringed with Ornament's ornaments.

"Purposiveness without purpose," said Griselda.

"Trust you to fixate on that bit," Mathilda said.

✳✳

"Esplanade?"

"Colonnade?"

"Portico?"

"Pavilion?"

Whatever it was, they went for a long walk along it. Endless pillars of stone through which the sea burnt.

Finally, they sat in the porte-cochère of the hotel where tables were set up, watching the continued glare of sea through the arches. They drank and ate delectables until it was time to go up. (It was part of their ceremony: The Priestxss, the Herald and the Knight [all non-monarchical, of course] dine.)

∗

The choreography was worked out from dance notations towards the climax of the opera. A simple procession clockwise, then anti-clockwise, with some graceful gesticulations involved.

They imbibed the peacock tincture. Tiny drops on the tongue, then also dabbed on one another's eyelids. Large streaks of it on the mirror made a kind of sigil. They sat in front of the mirror as the sun set. They could see the colonnade and sea through the open windows by way of the dressing mirror.

They spoke their lines of the incantation, voices interlacing.

The idea was that it was no different to seeing a face in the pattern of a curtain or a bird in a grain of wood. They focused and unfocused their visions, now looking at the reflected sea, now looking at themselves reflected, now looking at the glass itself, now looking at the in-between of the mirror, now at the mirror backing. Now looking at the transparent streaks of cordial on the surface. The traces were drying to a dusty yellow, like pollen.

Would it be in one's mind's eye or outside? It was an evocation, so surely outside?

Mathilda didn't know where to focus now, kept on becoming distracted by the sea and remembered to return to the mirror, to let her eyes relax, but then blue water stole her attention again. She remembered purposiveness without purpose; the sensation of the beautiful.

It was on one of these shifts of gaze that she noticed something. A kind of translucency or warp in the glass which she took to be the liquid streaks on the mirror, but it was not *on* the mirror. It was inside the glass. Only when she focused— or unfocused—her eyes the right way. Somewhere between the glass surface and the mirror backing, as if a large acetate sheet had been slipped in. A giant photographic negative.

And now she saw it properly. A Luxury in the mirror. She refocused her eyes slightly to look at Erskine-Lily and Griselda. Erskine-Lily's eyes were wide. They could see it too. Wings like quartz schist, and pearl veins. Blue-black, luminous indigo, the shell and milk hue of cloud—as if the dense network of feathers contained two arches of sky in their hollow interiors. She dared to look at its face: skin like semilucent black marble, or onyx perhaps. Pink smudges on the cheeks like make-up. Lips red, like lipstick. The hair, curled, kinked, coiled bronze and black. Incarnation of luxury. Primordial lotus-eater.

It had worked. They had auto-suggested.

They had Escaped.

She felt herself pass backwards through the melting sea—met in the middle.

*

I woke up feeling gutted, disembowelled.

The whole room was lit up blue and I was convinced for some moments I was in my own bedroom in Dun, which was connected to various other rooms by a labyrinth of sea chambers by way of the tiles.

I was in need of some orion for breakfast. Erskine-Lily was already opening a bottle when I came into the morning room. They were wearing the lapis lazuli tulle they had almost died in. "My near-death tulle," they called it. "And my ambulance crêpe de Chine."

After a couple of glasses we both felt less bereft and pretty triumphant—we had projected ourselves last night into Transfixionland. *We* were now Transfixions, though as far as I was concerned, Erskine-Lily had already been one.

We did not discuss our vision, as if speaking it were sacrilegious. I didn't know if I would have been able to discuss it—I couldn't remember it. Knew it had happened but the more I tried to recall, the more it faded, like all dreams, and it was, after all, a kind of waking dream. Eventually it was unclear whether I was just transplanting false imagery onto my memory. Only when I did not think of it, it seeped in sideways. I remembered quite clearly the sensation: the feeling all my Transfixions gave me, intensified. As if each figure had consecutively led me to this.

Griselda was up long before us so we went down for breakfast without her, then went for a walk, thinking we might spot her.

On returning to the hotel we were told that we needed to check out in an hour. We had at least another week planned. Griselda had arranged and was funding the whole trip. She'd briefly entertained the idea of leaving the hotel to stay in a nearby fishing town but decided against it. Perhaps she'd changed her mind.

Upstairs we saw that the few things she had brought were gone. She had left us.

IX

"It's the White Book submission day," Erskine-Lily said as the bus pulled in. "She's gone to submit."

They had been withdrawn all day.

They were right—Griselda had returned to submit her project, had reverted; tugged back by guilt. But I was unwilling to believe that, like with Hector, it had been some brief sojourn from life proper, that she had not been entirely with us in every way.

Just to be sure I telephoned her but no answer. I patrolled the town then went to Residency Centre.

"Mathilda."

Lind and Jonatan were standing in the central studio when I came in.

"A real pity you were unable to make it to submission. We are aware there were extenuating circumstances but we noticed Giuliano managed to attend. As it is, we're not sure the direction of your work was anywhere near what we expect: if you'll wait here."

Jonatan left the studio.

"Did Griselda manage to submit today?"

"Of course," Lind said. "Everyone did."

Jonatan came back. He handed me a book.

"Quite alarming stuff."

"We don't know what to say: perhaps you should be glad it disappeared."

It was a white book—the stolen one I presumed had been Processed with Giuli's. It still had the administrative slip attached to it from when I submitted to the office.

Strange that a legitimate submission should elicit such a response. Perhaps I was not the first false Resident. But then, this was one of the very first submissions. One of the very first Residents.

"Don't ask us," Lind said without my asking. "It just reappeared."

"As you know, accommodation keys are to be returned at the beginning of next week, Mathilda."

And they walked away. I began to follow them, thinking to go up to the computer room to see if Griselda was there. They didn't seem to be aware I was just behind them.

"Yes, but Garreaux requested. The application came from the old site. It was emailed automatically to him."

"But, how did he know the other business?"

"Search traffic. He was able to see the specific search query that led to the site in the first place. That was enough, apparently."

X

Elizabeth/Joan had her epiphany markedly earlier than expected. I liked to think it was I who catalysed it, that I had set her off, in the way some psychic remnant of pagan Italy dislodges itself and unravels the stiff and stifled English psyche in E. M. Forster stories—but it was Agnes, of course.

On returning to London, I went to visit Agnes again. Elizabeth/Joan was there and insisted I stay at her parents', who were away for the month.

"Didn't you get any of my emails?" she asked.

"No?"

Agnes had been arrested again after my last visit. She had been volunteering at another gallery archive and was caught trying to remove a painting from their vaults.

Elizabeth/Joan's mother managed to get them to drop the charges very quickly. Something about the arrest had put the fire through Elizabeth/Joan, who begged her mother to take this major gallery to court. Tobydog was delighted at seeing this passion in her daughter, and, in fact, there was enough evidence to trigger some kind of public inquiry. Agnes' decades of documentation. She had worked at the gallery some forty years ago as an archive assistant.

Although the nominal purpose of the inquiry was investigating the negligence of historical artworks, two directors were suspended after Agnes was able to highlight, incidentally, their basically racist behaviour, and also flag up numerous works in archives that were of cultural merit, such as one by a 'lost' Black painter that had never once been out of the archives and was seriously disintegrating. It was hailed by an art critic in the papers as a "forgotten Black Correggio." Various galleries and museums were called in.

They were still feeling victorious about all of this when I arrived.

It transpired that the painting on Agnes' wall, the one titled *The Statue*, the one she'd written about, was a preparatory sketch for a much larger work still held by another public gallery and also incorrectly labelled *The Statue*. They were in the midst of haranguing the gallery to change the title, since it was not of a statue. Elizabeth/Joan's evangelical vigour was something to behold.

I began helping them occasionally. Was excited by their progress but scared to fully immerse myself in London life in case Dun and Erskine-Lily would fade irretrievably.

I was here to find Griselda, to speak to her. Erskine-Lily refused to come, but said I was welcome to stay for as long as I liked.

Whilst they had been affected by Hector's behaviour to the point of ending up in hospital, they had quickly recovered. Since Griselda's disappearance they had not been the same. Everyone was leaving them, they thought. I felt awful going away, but spending time with Erskine-Lily in such a state, knowing how it had been before, was unbearable.

One day, I left Elizabeth/Joan's parents' house to go to the nearby supermarket. I was standing at the wine fridge waiting for the right moment to swipe a bottle of something when I noticed a particular wine which had a label clipped to the shelf saying it was new to the supermarket.

It was called *Eria*.

I read the back of the bottle.

This continental sparkling wine gives a high-density mousse quite unlike any other. Pairs well with chocolate and summer fruits.

I stole a bottle and drank it back at the house.

It was unmistakably orion. Not quite as good as the Dun version. I wanted desperately to call up Erskine-Lily and tell them but the prospect of anything less than their normal enthusiasm was not something I could handle.

I would have to find Griselda soon. I'd already tried her parents' flat.

I managed to find a Thought Art forum online. Although they used contemporary social media, they liked to operate through old fan forums and message boards—things they might have used as teenagers—under particular threads. It was in such places dates of events were given.

I went to the soonest one. It was a couple of floors beneath Garreaux's apartment. A flat that operated as the Garreaux Centre. The event was a study party.

The door was open. Various Thought Artists were inside, standing about.

"Mathilda!"

It was Hector.

He came over, smiling, his jaw shaking.

"Woah, what are you doing here? Thank you, by the way, for letting Griselda submit in the end. Is Erskine with you?"

"Their name is Erskine-Lily."

"But is he here?"

"No, they're in Dun. Is Griselda here?"

"No, Mathilda," he said. "But she sends her apologies."

"What for?"

"Well, for fucking with you." I watched him. His grey eyes were now looking at me intently. Like he was trying to see into me. His clenched and quivering jaw fell still for a while. "Christ, they haven't told you anything, have they?"

"The Conveyors?"

"Griselda and Erskine. Haven't told you anything. The book— you got it back presumably, your stolen submission?"

"You stole it."

"Oh no," he laughed and his jaw started up again. "That was G. She didn't want you kicked off. Took Giuli's book as well to make it less obvious; well, she was going to Process his work anyway."

"Then why didn't she say anything?"

"Because she was fucking with you, Mathilda. Erskine as well. They were both at it before, you know. Just the previous summer. With this auto-suggestion stuff. Manipulation—you heard, pre-sumably, about the student and tutor whose work they destroyed. This was something new, but similar. I thought she was better— Griselda. And Erskine. Well as you know, we had our own shit going on, but he's worse than Griselda."

His eyes were wide. Fanatical. I had seen such eyes before. A very long time ago. Before the first Escape. Certain danger if they see you do not believe them. He was ready to die, I saw, for Gar-reaux. To keep himself valid.

"Thank you for telling me, Hector," I said, letting the stress come to my voice, hoping he would take it as the emotion of one who has discovered betrayal.

And then he said a name. He was smiling again.

"Sorry?"

Dead-name "His actual name. ███████ Not even Erskine, never mind 'Erskine-fucking-Lily.' He knew I was going to tell you everything, they both did. That's why they've gone quiet on you."

On the way out,

"Sadie!" Tom & Christian + Eleanor and Grace. "Where the hell have you been? You know Hector?—this is so funny. So funny."

On my second way out, over the yellow gravel, I turned and looked up at the building. There, high up was a face. A pale sentry at the window. Where Garreaux's quarters were.

I waved.

She smiled, and, it seemed, laughed.

That night I sat up and found yellow powdery spots on the sheets.

I got up and called Erskine-Lily. I asked if there was any truth in Hector's story.

Erskine-Lily, who had loved Hermia as much as I and also had Transfixions. Had probably come to Dun because of Hermia, just as I. Who was an Escapist, just as I.

"No," Erskine-Lily said. "At least not on my part. But I don't think on Griselda's either." Griselda, they told me, was simply split, genuinely interested in both sides and everything they represented. Had expressed an interest after they had all met briefly through Hector. Hector whom Erskine-Lily had indeed known at school. Who had shared mutual fascination in *The Book of the Luxuries*. Who had always treated it and Erskine-Lily like a guilty youthful pleasure. Things to be indulged in from time to time.

"Every summer, he comes to me. Returns to the Luxuries. Three years ago he found me in Dun. Then he found the Residency and didn't speak to me for three years until that first meeting. He visited a month or so after I threw a drink at him. Then more frequently."

Whilst this knowledge had dispelled the doubt that Hector had sown, it had been purchased with something much worse than doubt: I now knew the real reason Erskine-Lily had gone quiet these past weeks—their fear that Hector would reveal their old name. Would show me Old Erskine-Lily, the one they sought to Escape. Now I was part of this Old World, and they could not help that.

Simply because I knew this old name, even if I didn't believe in its authority, its precedence, I would reflect it back, through time, from life before. I was helplessly treacherous. This image of old self was death. All who contained it were deadly.

They told me they were going to be leaving Dun.

Erskine-Lily was going to Escape. As I had; as I hadn't.

XI

Bolts, twinges—the body's, the mind's, involuntary thrumming—pining for Arcadia.

Elizabeth/Joan arranged for me to lodge at her parents'. I joined in, helping her with Agnes' work. I should have loved it. I adored them both and they were very good at trying to get me interested in things. They even asked about Hermia.

"We could publish something. We could expose that Residency—for hoarding significant biographical information about her."

They set me small clear projects to work on. Contacting various academics to raise interest in Hermia, trying to get *Black Modernisms* reprinted, compiling a dossier on Garreaux.

But it was unpleasant at times looking into Hermia and not being in Dun with Erskine-Lily and Griselda or even Hector, at least as he had been for that brief period. It was the perpetual danger of Arcadias—they turned the perfectly good pale and ersatz. The dull ache I had always felt had become an unprecedented agony.

It was whilst digging though my suitcase for any papers I'd missed on Hermia, the stolen ones, that I decided to look at the white book. The work Jonatan and Lind had found alarming. I ripped off the admin slip and opened it. I was surprised to see printed text. It was a poem. I flicked to the front page.

The Fainting Youth
by
Hermia Druitt
Printed by the Hours Press 1928

That whole first row of the Archive—1976, was the second part of Garreaux's submission, after her room. It contained, I suspected, every surviving copy of the small print run of Hermia's poem.

*

Agnes and Elizabeth/Joan were coming to Dun, but not for a couple of weeks. They were now seriously interested in Hermia after my discovery of the book and hearing my suspicions that there were others. We were already in conversation with a publisher about reprinting them.

I was staying in a flat in town, paid for by Elizabeth/Joan. I'd been there for a week and was trying to figure a way into the Archive without getting caught. Trying also to figure out what had changed. The new phase of the residency that Garreaux had announced.

I walked around town the first few days. Everything was shut during early summer. It was almost worse being here than not. Elizabeth/Joan texted, telling me to watch the news. People were seizing buildings all over Europe. Occupying them. It could be the end of property, she said. I looked to see if Griselda would appear in any of the footage.

Protesters occupying a castle in Sussex. Museums being stormed. A skyscraper had almost been taken.

I decided, at last, to go to Erskine-Lily's flat. The door was locked. I knocked our knock, just in case.

("Will you go back?" they'd asked me on the phone.)

A few days later, I came back with a locksmith who remembered me from when we'd had to repair the door after kicking it in.

I could have gone in as he was changing the locks but went out again to wander then met him back at the locksmiths to pay and he gave me the key.

Inside, some things had gone. But the portraits were still up on the wall.

A new influx of Residents. Just as drab and interchangeable as the old.

One day as I was leaving the flat, my new flat, I heard a voice from the side street. English, but it did not sound like the voice of any Resident—

"There is a café here you know, Thomasz, that does the most heavenly drink," said someone to their paramour who had just stepped into a shop. The person remained outside, and as they turned around I thought, just for a moment, just like the year before, that I was looking at Hermia's apparition.

"What a glorious suit you're wearing," the figure said, catching sight of me. "We're looking for somewhere to drink a drink called orion which they sell in certain cafés here."

"Oh yes, I have it all the time."

"Are you busy? Can you show us where? We're also looking for something to eat."

I invited them to mine. Up to the flat where I would introduce them to Elizabeth/Joan and Agnes and Sirhan and Malachi.

"Thomasz! Where is he? Thomasz, wouldn't that be marvellous? This fantastical woman has invited us to drink orion and eat delectables."

"I'm Thomasz."

"I'm Hermia," I said.

"Thomasz, did you hear? So similar to my name. Isn't that abominable?"

Acknowledgements

This book is indebted to the scholarship, research, theory, thought and work of: every Black writer in Britain before me, Gemma Romain, Caroline Bressey, Jane Goldman, Anna Girling, Sandeep Parmar, Hermia Drumm, Stephen Bourne, Rosalind Galt, Philip Hoare, Thomas H. Wirth, Emma Dabiri and so many others.

The *dessert eagle f*or gifting me with a jar of maraschino cherries.

Thank you also to:

My agent Monica Odom, Elizabeth Ault, Aimee Harrison and the Duke team.

Alasdair MacKinnon and Adam Benmakhlouf for helping me pitch this nacreous cover.

Margaret Rose Reynolds, Shola Akinmurele.

Very early draft reader Rosie Šnajdr and vital final draft readers Alasdair MacKinnon and Emily McCarthy.

Amy Drumm for her surname and support and the gown. Camara Taylor, who first told me of the King James wedding deaths and for sharing many a Transfixion. And other friends like Georgie Carr, Sarra Wild, Susu Laroche, Jess Mai Walker and Lily Barson. Ed Leeson, Charly Flyte, Angel Rose Denman, Alice Davies,

Dom Polin, Jason Patterson and others who have given me a place to sleep when I desperately needed—some without knowing.

Thanks to Colin Herd, Zoe Strachan, Naomi Booth and Pamela Thurschwell, who all helped secure funding without which I would still be writing this.

This book only made it into print in the United States after being found and then championed by readers I've never met like Morgan Page, Torrey Peters and Mackenzie Wark.

Grazie mille, darlings, see you in Dun!

Author's Note

The bulk of *LOTE* was written between 2015 and 2018, which already feels like another world. It was first published in early 2020 in the UK by Jacaranda Books. It feels strange, even unsettling, that it will now in 2022 be received like it was written yesterday, to the extent that I had to put this odd little note in.

References

The bell hooks essay referred to on page 161 is *Is Paris Burning?*

On page 243 Erskine-Lily's idea of an "irreducible unit" of ornament is developed from Berel Lang's search for an irreducible unit of style in *Looking for the Styleme*.

On page 265, Mathilda and Erskine-Lily's dietary prescriptions are taken from Denton Welch's *A Voice Through a Cloud*.

The format for Mathilda's Transfixion cards is adopted from Richard Bruce Nugent's *Geisha Man*.

About the Author

Shola von Reinhold was born in Glasgow and grew up in Scotland and London. *LOTE* is Shola's first novel and won the James Tait Black Prize for fiction as well as the Republic of Consciousness Prize.